THE OLD RIDER
BY
J.S. STROUD

CHAPTER ONE

No one paid much attention to the rider on the stallion; he was nobody, just another drifter and if they looked at all the only thing they would have noticed was that wasn't wearing spurs. This was cattle country where men lived by the gun, the rope and the spur. It was strange to see a man without a pair of the star shaped tools attached to his boots; even the faded black hat that had turned brown with age brought him no attention.

There was a dark brown sweat stain along the wide brim of the hat that shaded the rider's eyes from the heat of the midday sun. From his head to his toes he spoke of being a worn out tired old drifter. He didn't wear the bright colored bandana like the younger cowboys, in fact there was nothing around his neck, even the brace of twin colts looked old and used.

Few looked up into the weather beaten face of the man but all eyes were on the stallion beneath him. This was an animal they had seen only in their dreams. Its eyes were like black coals of fire, the air from its nostrils seemed to form a haze that brought those eyes to life and every step it took spoke of power and strength.

This animal had never run with the wild herds, it had led them!

The scars on its chest and legs spoke of the battles it had been in to earn him the right to lead. Men and children alike stood stone still on the wooden side walk to watch them go by. Many of them had never seen an animal like this and few ever thought they would see one again. Tamer horses tied to the hitching rail shied away from the savage beast as they approached. The tracks in the soft dirt of the street showed that this was one horse that had never been shod. It carried no brand and was mastered by none.

It was as savage at heart as it was in spirit.

The Indians called it the black ghost or midnight phantom. It had been in their villages many times, always at night and always to steal. The black stallion with the white chest and mane was well known in the villages, it came in like a ghost and the white mane and chest would flash in the night air as it attacked the stallions trying to guard their own herds.
One or a dozen it made no difference, the battles were always the same, young strong horses went down under its hooves busted and bruised, it earned the name of Sudden Death because of these raids. Young warriors had grown up on the stories told about the daring raids of the magnificent horse.

It became a legend in its own time both feared and loved. Every child in the village dreamed of being the one to catch, ride and own the greatest horse alive and this was it!

The rider turned off the dirt street and rode into the stable, he noticed that the first two stalls were filled as he rode by but he was looking for the last stall, the one furthest from the rest of the horses. The cowboy's body leaned forward as his boot came over the saddle and his left hand held onto the saddle horn for balance as he slid to the ground below. The right hand hovered over the butt of the pistol at his side; something about the rider said he was more than he appeared to be. After removing the saddle, blanket and bridle he found a brush and begun to curry the animal, wiping the light froth from its mouth and body. He then poured some grain into the troth and closed the gate; this would do until his return.

Pulling the brim of his hat down, he hid his face from the heat of the sun before leaving the stables.

Men, women and children had gathered on the sidewalk hoping to get another glimpse of the horse that had just mesmerized everyone who looked at it, was this really the horse, there couldn't be another one like him on the face of the earth! No one ever noticed the rider as he walked by; but this was the way of his life!

There was a slight thumping sound beneath his boots as he walked to the Crooked Horn restaurant and bar.

The rider had never been there before but it looked like a hundred other saloons with two painted windows in front and bat wing doors. It would be dark inside and most of the cowboys would step through those doors and stop, letting their eyes adjust to the cave like setting but not him, he leaned against the wall between the doors and the window briefly closing his eyes to let them adjust to the darkness before stepping through the swinging doors.

The room was long and narrow, thirty feet wide and sixty feet long and more than a dozen tables were scattered about in a sloppy manner. A blond haired, blue eyed gorilla looking fellow with a scar running down his face stood polishing a shot glass behind the bar.

Don't freeze up cowboy we don't bite,

The voice came from one of the waitresses standing at a potbellied stove sipping coffee. He walked to the nearest table and sat down.

The young waitress spoke again, he's all yours mom.

The older waitress looked annoyed and came back with "I told you not to call me that!" Why is it that every cowboy in the country call's me mom?

Well, Marilyn, Sheila answered, it could be because you've been twenty nine longer than most of us can count! Marilyn picked the tally book up off the corner of the bar and headed for the table. What will it be Ace, a grin of mischief was on her face.

What's edible and what's any good the man asked, as a second thought after catching a whiff the aroma coming from the kitchen.

It depends on the cook, whether she is reading, sleeping or eating. If you want to order the biscuits they're gonna be burned, if you order the beans they're gonna be burned and if you order the gravy it's gonna be lumpy and burned, Marilyn laughed, trying to get a smile out of the man setting before her. The cook will have one of her children kill a chicken if you like.

The younger waitress spoke up again, yeah, and you better grab the chicken when it hits the table cause its tough enough to fly off ten minutes after its cooked!

Marilyn gave the younger waitress a look of disdain, shut up Sheila, you couldn't boil water in a volcano and you know it. Turning back to the man Marilyn asked again, "what will it be Ace?" I guess its biscuits and beans, he said. Marilyn smiled at the man she called Ace and said "it's your funeral" and with that she turned and walked away

. Joe leaned back in his chair and watched her leave. Maybe this town was not so bad after all.

Marilyn looked over at the bartender and said "hey, Paul, you better bring this gent a cup of that black crap you call coffee, he's gonna need it to choke down one of Eloise's biscuits."

Paul picked up a cup and began to pour the piping hot beverage,

"Ain't nothing gonna help them biscuits, he muttered under his breath as he set it on the table in front of Joe.

Joe picked up the cup of coffee with a grimace, in his opinion it needed three things, sugar, cream and a burial. It was probably the worst coffee he had ever tasted. After a few sips he put the cup down and looked around the room, there was not much to it; a couple of broken down cowboys stood at the bar with their boots hooked over the rail and their spurs dragging over the floor boards.

At one table half a dozen men sat playing poker and over in a corner sipping coffee was a dark skinned man wearing black clothing with a tied down revolver.

Marilyn came back with a large bowl of beans with several hard tack biscuits piled on top. "Ace if I was you, I would soak them biscuits in the beans before I tried eating them she stated with that she sat down in the chair across the table from him. He could not take it anymore, "alright lady my name is",

"My name is Marilyn," she cut in.

"Alright Marilyn, why do you keep calling me Ace?" the rider asked

"Why that's simple, Marilyn answered, your eyes are too narrow, your smile never reaches your eyes and no matter what you're doing, one of your hands never strays far from the pistols at you side. It just makes me think you're the better half of the dead man's hand!"

Joe began to smile, it was more of a lopsided grin, his hand still hung at his side close to the worn out 44 revolver. He was paying too much attention to Marilyn when the bat wing doors flew open banging both side of the wall as a young cowboy came into the room. He wasn't walking and he wasn't running, he was stumbling. Two other cowboys came in behind him laughing and joking.

"Hey Mike, can't you stand up", laughed the largest of the three.

Mike turned towards the speaker, "not with you pushing me", he yelled doubling up his fists and starting towards the speaker.

"Now Mike, you know what happened the last time you tangled with Roy." "Bobby you stay out of it or you will be the next one I slug!"

Bobby began to laugh; "Now Mike, you know what happened the last time you tried that too." Mike slowly began to settle down. And Joe started to relax, without thinking he had slumped back in the chair the revolver in the cross draw holster was pulled half way out and his thumb was starting to pull the hammer as he realized they were just a couple of drunken cowboys out for some fun.

Marilyn sat across the table white faced and in shock but within seconds she found her voice, "Ace" she said, "I like them boys and if you kill any one of them you better shoot me too because if you don't I'm gonna put a hole in your back the sheriff will be able to ride a horse through!" With that she stood up and left.

The cowboy called Roy, slapped Bobby in the back of the head and Bobby grabbed Roy's arm and slung him in a half circle smacking him face first into the wall next to the bat wing doors. Roy was half stunned as Mike and Bobby both grabbed his boots and flipped him to the floor together they started to drag him towards the bar, seeing Marilyn the combat stopped as Bobby and Mike both came out with "hi mom" at the same time.
   Roy struggled to get into a sitting position before the words, "hi mom" came out of the giant grin on his face.
   Marilyn was not impressed and she cut loose with both barrels, "don't call me mom!" If I was your mother I'd have drowned all three of you!" Mike began to laugh; "now mom, you know we all can swim!" Bobby piped up with a cheerful "you betcha!" Marilyn started to fume, "I meant at birth" she said. It was Roy's turn to laugh,
   "Heck" he said, when do you think we learned to swim?" Marilyn knew she couldn't win a battle of wits with the smart-alecky kids so walking to the bar she drew out a twelve inch iron skillet.
   Mike, Roy and Bobby all drew back in mock fear, "Oh no!" Bobby cried, she is going to hit me with a skillet! All three of them laughed at the threat, "Carful that thing is loaded" one of them cried "it's full of Eloise's beans!" all three were howling with laughter. Eloise was fifty-four years old, tough and grizzled, the truth was Eloise was actually a good cook but for the last two weeks she had been training her daughter Terry.
   Terry could rope, shoot and ride with the best of them, but when it came to cooking most people said she would butcher a cow thinking it was a hog.
   Eloise was part owner and Marilyn felt she had to be loyal to her partner. She could pester and pick at the cook but she did not want anyone else to.

Besides bad mouthing the food was not going to help the business. Mike may have been the youngest but he had the quickest eye and he saw one more chance to pester Marilyn, "hey mister," he said turning his attention to the man sitting at the table, "soaking them cast iron plow disks in beans ain't gonna help none.

Last week I tried nailing one to a fence post and all I did was bend some good nails." Bobby began to laugh, "Shucks" he said, "that ain't nothing, why only this morning I threw one in the air for target practice and when I shot the darn thing, the ricochet nearly took my head off!" Roy could see the banter was making Marilyn upset and moved to the bar.

"Hey, unck set up two whiskies for me and Bobby and give the boy here a cup of coffee," pointing in the direction of Mike.

"I ain't your uncle," Paul said, with a snarl, "you keep calling me that and one day I'm gonna hit you so hard your momma's gonna cry." "Go ahead, hit him, Mike challenged, see if I care, besides, he's so ugly his momma moved to Ireland just to get away from him." Roy turned red and started towards the younger man with his fists doubled.

"You keep popping off and I'm the one who is going to be doing the slugging!" A smarter man might have shut up but Mike didn't bother, he liked antagonizing the bigger man. "Oh, I'm sorry," he said "after all it's your daddy that's so ugly, his twin is the back side of a mule."

Mike never saw the fist as it hit him! He went backwards, tripping over a chair and landing flat on his back. His head was still ringing as Roy approached, "maybe I pushed it to far this time," he thought as Roy grabbed his shirt and jerked him to his feet.

Mike shook his head trying to clear the cobwebs and realized another blow was coming,
it found its mark on the left side of his head. Lights flashed and the roar of a waterfall exploded as the blow landed.

Through a hazy fog Mike saw the left fist coming, the blow was meant to take his head off but this time he was ready and jerked back,
 The knuckles of Roy's hand sliced through the air spinning his body around. Roy was off balance as Mike threw a right of his own; it was a lucky punch and landed hard behind Roy's left ear. Now mike was the one moving forward, his left hand swung in a circle trying to force the fight. Roy leaned forward lifted his right foot and drove it backwards with all the strength he could muster.
 The heel of the western riding boot sank deep into the flesh below Mike's rib cage stopping him in his tracks. For a second Mike thought he was going to be sick, the air was forced from his lungs doubling him over as pain shot through his entire body.
 Mike stumbled back trying to catch his breath. He had been hit before but nothing like this, the fight was forgotten and all he wanted to do was get one lousy breath of air.
 Roy was turning to pursue the fight as the roar of small cannon echoed against the walls of the room and both men looked towards the bar. Paul stood with a double barreled shot gun in his hands. Both men knew that Paul had fired a paper wad into the ceiling. One barrel of the weapon was still smoking, the other remained loaded. "Alright, that's enough! You two yahoos ain't gonna tear this place apart again!" he said.
    Eloise and Marilyn came running from the kitchen at the sound of the blast. "Paul put that down" she screamed. "But mom," Paul stated "I was just trying to break them up." "I don't care what you were trying to do, she yelled, "you don't need a shotgun to do it!"

Joe sat at the table watching the family feud, a crooked smile on his face. Marilyn turned on the boys, "you three pack it up and get out of here!" Bobby spoke up, "it wasn't me!" Marilyn's eyes went fire red, "Go home and sleep it off before I have the sheriff in here!" "Like heck, I am," Mike said, "I'm going to Nita's." "Hey unck, give me a bottle of tequila will ya." Paul slid the bottle across the bar ignoring the familiar remark of the younger man.

As Bobby, Roy and Mike started for the door; Marilyn walked across the room and set down across the table from Joe.

"They're just wild kids," she said making excuses for their behavior. Joe looked into her soft brown eyes, "dang" he thought, "why am I still setting here, I should be a hundred miles down the road!" Marilyn looked back into the hard cold eyes of the man in front of her. She had missed the brief look of softness that had flash across his face before he managed to hide it. A shiver went through her very soul, here set a man as cold and vicious as any she had ever met, yet she felt drawn to him, there was something about him...

As the boys exited the bar one of the card players stood up. "If they come back in here again I'm gonna put a bullet in them." The man speaking was a tall man wearing the dress of a gambler, with a tied down short barreled revolver at his side. He may have been a gambler but the quick draw gun rig left no doubt he knew how to use it.

Marilyn stood up, "you'll leave them alone," she said with venom in her voice. The gambler spoke again, "you woman, forget that I am part owner in this place and I'll blow the hell out of them!"

Joe couldn't believe what he was doing, before he knew it he was sliding out of the chair, his right hand hung over the handle of the pistol on his left side, just inches from the cross draw holster. "Mister, you got three seconds to draw or die." Joe couldn't care less about the boys, he was thinking of the soft brown eyes of the waitress. Marilyn began to yell for William to sit down. She only called him William when he was upset; "sure," he said reaching for the chair behind him with both hands.

Then with the sped of a snake he drew.

His thumb cocked the hammer of the revolver as it came up, the left hand came forward ready to fan the pistol after the first shot. William knew he was fast and accurate and that the little trick gave him an added advantage and he was sure no man alive could match his speed. As the pistol in his hand began to raise Williams face took on a look of terror.

Joe's right hand flashed, the pistol was cocked and flames erupted out of the barrel even before William's pistol had a chance to clear leather.

The slam of the bullet told him that he had been struck in the chest. The barrel of the pistol spit fire twice more, both times he felt the impact of the pieces of lead as they drove deep into his flesh.

Staggering back he set in the very chair he had been reaching for. William looked down, it was strange, his pistol was back in its holster and three holes had been blown through the front of his shirt. William managed a weak smile and said "I think I'm gonna take a nap,"

With that he slumped face first to the hard wood floor below.

Joe stood in the gun fighter's stance facing the men at the table. If they so much as flinched he was gonna blow their heads off. Marilyn started to step between Joe and the men at the table; she had seen enough of the killing. Joe turned facing her; the look of a cold blooded killer stopped her in her tracks. She had seen men killed before but nothing like this.

Joe glanced back at the table, but no one moved. William may have been their friend but none of them wanted to die for a dead man. Joe's eyes began to soften; the hard lines of his face took on the look of a nobody. Marilyn began to shiver, she knew she stood before a chameleon, a man capable of changing his looks at will and the most dangerous man she had ever met.

Joe saw the fear in her eyes and slid the pistol back into the holster; he hadn't meant to terrify the woman. With the most charming smile he could muster Joe said,

"Well you've got one less partner."

Marilyn thought she was going to be sick. Joe sat back down at the table and took a drink of the strong coffee. "Might as well wait for the marshal," he said, one hand still resting over the butt of his pistol.

Johnny Vasquez walked up to the body; he was the man in the black suit who had been setting in the corner. He didn't want people to know who he was or why he was here but this was something he had to see.

Looking down he counted a dozen holes in the back of William's shirt!

This was something he had heard of but had never seen before! He knew what had happened, the nobody gunman, the one the waitress called 'Ace', carried two pistols, one loaded with solid shells, the other carried shells with deep X's cut into the end of the bullets. The deep cuts in these shells would split apart on impact, going off in different parts of the body. William was proof of the damage they could do; his back looked like someone had used a shotgun up close. Johnny Vasquez was a professional gunman. He carried nine notches on his guns and he had been paid five hundred dollars to add three more.

Vasquez looked at 'Ace' and decided then and there he was not getting paid enough! Johnny Vasquez turned and headed for the door as the marshal and two of his deputies pushed the bat wing doors open, their pistols were already drawn and the hammers cocked. Vasquez stood still, the slightest move and he had no doubt he would be the next to die. Three forty-four caliber pistols were pointed at his guts. Slowly he began to raise his hands. After they were shoulder high he spoke for the first time. "Wasn't me that did the shooting," he said. Sweat was beginning to appear on his upper lip and his hands were shaking slightly. This had never happened to him before and he didn't like this feeling at all!

Vasquez was thinking of the five hundred dollars in his pocket, the bottle of tequila in his saddle bags and the woman in Sonora. If he lived to make it to the door he was heading south. "Who was it then?" the larger of the three star packers asked. "The gunman," he stated quietly and slowly started for the door. Vasquez hadn't made two steps before he felt the barrel of a pistol being shoved into his back. "What gunman?" Vasquez turned to see Roger, the youngest of the deputies holding a cocked revolver.

"Marshal, tell your deputy to put that thing away before he shoots the wrong man!" "Vasquez, you tell us what gunman or I'll have him shoot you myself!" The thought that the marshal and the deputy's knew who he was upset him. Somebody must have warned them about him coming into town. Vasquez had noticed 'Ace' when he came into the saloon and thought like most people that he was a nobody, then watched as he transformed into a deadly gunman and then just as quickly turned back into the role of an invisible drifter!

"He's the only one wearing two guns." The marshal was tired of the short answers and the fast guns attitude. "You better pack up and leave before I find something to jail you for!" As the marshal walked past him into the saloon Vasquez turned cold, he knew he could beat the marshal in a gun fight but he had a hunch he better kill him with the first bullet or he was gonna catch lead himself. "Marshal, you could not pay me enough to stay in this town!" He walk out the door, swung his leg up over his horse and headed south, back to Sonora, the senoritas and the tequila, glad to be alive! After one glance at the gambler called 'Wild Bill', Jim and the two deputies turned to the lone man setting at the table.

He didn't look like much and not the kind of man that could have taken Bill in a gunfight, still they weren't taking any chances, and all three held their weapons pointed at the man's chest. Joe leaned back in the chair and the cold hard look of molten steel came into his eyes. The marshal began to tighten his grip on the trigger, as he noticed the intense look coming from the stranger sitting before him,

Then just as quickly the man's eyes began to soften and his body relaxed. Joe stood up and with both hands in the air and then slowly lowered one hand and began to unbuckle the gun belt from around his waist.

Schon, the second deputy who had entered with the Marshal and Rog, reached over and took the belt with his left hand while his right hand still held the pistol pointed at the man's chest, he was taking no chances. The two deputies walked Joe to the jail as the Marshal stayed behind to question the witnesses. It looked like a clear case of self-defense; William had been the one to draw first. The deputies were drinking day old coffee as Jim entered the office. He walked to his desk and set down.

Joe's pistols were hanging on the rack behind him. Schon walked over took the guns from their holster and handed them to the Marshal. Johnny Vasquez had been right, the first weapon was a standard forty-four with a six inch barrel and solid lead bullets but the second pistol had been altered , the six inch barrel was cut down to five. The three remaining shells had deep X's cut in them, even the trigger was wired back.

Everything about this set-up spoke of up close killing. Jim looked at the man behind the bars. He had never seen a man who could look as innocent and be so deadly at the same time. Jim emptied the gun cylinders and locked the weapons in his desk then he shoved the discarded shells into the empty loops of the gunman's belt. There was a rumor around town that the Rocking 'R' was hiring gunmen. If it was true this man could be one of the best. There was no since worrying about it tonight, his wife, Sherlene, was waiting for him and supper would be ready when he got home.

Jim pulled his slicker off the rack, pitched the cell keys to Schon and said "you boys are in charge, I'm going home." "What are we gonna do about him?" Schon asked, looking at the man lying on the bunk in his cell. "Get some sleep, the circuit Judge will be here in a few days and he can figure out what to do with him. Between now and then don't get too close to the bars!"

CHAPTER TWO

It had been a long day. Joe laid back and went right to sleep, he was dreaming of the brown eyed waitress. "Wake up cowboy," Joe's eyes flew open at the sound. His right hand sprang for the pistol at his left side grabbing only air.

Marilyn was entering the cell with a tray in one hand and a cup in the other.

The smell of biscuits and gravy filled the room. Joe sat up as she handed him the tray, Marilyn took a sip of the strong black coffee from the cup and sat on the bunk next to Joe. "Why did you do it?" Joe looked kind of puzzled, "do what?" he asked. "Bill could have killed you," she said. Joe took on a sheepish grin, "Bill couldn't beat me in my sleep!" For a split second Marilyn was taken aback by the statement, and then she remembered the speed of his hand reaching for the missing revolver as he awoke. She decided then and there that Bill had been a dead man the second he had reached for the chair! Joe took the cup from Marilyn's hand and started to drink the hot beverage, "what about my horse?" he asked. "Otis will take care of him, I'll see to that." "If you can manage it I would rather take care of him myself." Marilyn nodded, "I'll see what I can do." "While you're at it can you find out what they're holding me for?" Joe asked "I already know that," she stated, "The Marshal rode out to the Rocking 'R' to see if they hired you. "What's the Rocking 'R' and why would they hire me?" Joe asked. "The Rocking 'R' is the biggest ranch in the country and growing." "To make sure nobody stops that growth, their bringing in gunmen from down south." Joe's eyes became hard and cold again, "and he went to see if I was for hire, right?" Marilyn didn't know what to say, she had seen what he could do with a pistol, what did she think he was a saint or a store keeper? Marilyn picked up the tray and asked if he wanted more coffee, after a curt no she signaled the deputy to unlock the door.

"Rog is there any chance you can let him out long enough to tend his horse," she asked. The young deputy shook his head, "Marshal will be back after a while, and we'll let him decide." Marilyn couldn't make up her own mind, she was doing things she had never done before. Sure the deputies ate at the restaurant but she had never delivered a meal before, not even for the three young cowboys and she would never have gone into a cell with a gunman but 'Ace' different, he had a soft side, almost loveable, she thought. Marilyn shook her head, what was she thinking, how could anyone love a hired gun? Joe watched the brown eyed waitress exit the cell. Life is strange he thought, six months ago he had sold his ranch and a hundred head of cattle, he was headed for the California gold fields. At that time he wanted nothing more than to strike it rich. He was tired of Oklahoma and the rock infested ground, in his opinion it was good for nothing but scrub brush, cattle and ticks. After buying a second pistol, a pack horse and a pick he had saddled up and headed west. Every night he dreamed of the saddle bags of gold he was going to find, the large ranch and fancy home he was going to buy with the gold. He dreamed of ocean voyages, great adventures and beautiful women. Then purely by accident he stumbled across a herd of wild horses. At the front of the herd was the black. Dreams of gold, big ranches and ocean voyages were forgotten. He had never wanted anything in his life more than he wanted the massive horse that lead the pack. Joe leaned back in his cell. All of his life he had been a loner, needing or wanting no one, a man alone. Joe continued to watch Marilyn as she left the office, the life of a lonely man came crashing down around him, the memories of a thousand campfires seemed to pull at him like chains, even the thought of the black could not break the feeling of despair. At that moment Joe wanted nothing more than to feel the warm arms of the brown eyed waitress around him, to look into her eyes and see the kind of love he had never known. The kind of love he had never dreamed possible.

Rog was locking the cell as a tall lanky cowboy came walking in. The Marshal was right behind him with the barrel of his pistol held to the man's back. "Open the cell door," the Marshal commanded. As the deputy started to open the cell he had just locked the Marshal said, "the other cell, there's no use putting these two together."

The Marshal had called the kid, KC; the prisoner was probably around twenty-one or two. He was what the ladies would call a good looking man. "What's going on Marshal?" Rog asked. It was hard to believe that they had two prisoners at one time and it wasn't even Saturday! "Rustler," was the reply and Roger seemed shocked by the news. "Him?" he said not trying to cover the surprise in his voice. "Him," said the Marshal in a cold flat voice, "Been stealing cattle over at the Malloy place." K.C. cut in with, "I ain't been stealing nothing!" "Seems he's been courting the old man's daughter and every time he comes around the old man ends up with better than half a dozen of his prim cattle missing, he is under the impression the young un is behind the thefts."

"That's better, K.C. said, but like I said I ain't stole nothing!" Rog locked the door behind him as K.C. headed for the bunk. "Hey, when am I getting out of here," he yelled, looking as if he had the world at his fingertips. Joe rolled over to get a better look at the cattle thief. The kid wore a pair of high topped hand tooled western riding boots, a flashy red shirt with silver buttons. The pistol on the Marshals desk had come out of a quick draw holster with a large silver star attached. Everything the kid wore spoke of money. K.C. looked annoyed as Joe rolled back over.

"What are you looking at?" K.C. spat at him. Joe pulled his hat over his face and said "a hanged man!" The young thief went into a rage and threw the metal drinking cup at the bars of the cell. "When am I getting out of here?" he screamed.

"That's up to the judge," the Marshal said as he was hanging the kid's gun belt on the rack, "Now settle down." "Well when is that?" he demanded. "In a week maybe two, depends on when he gets here," the Marshal answered.

Joe sat up, "I can't leave my horse in a stall for the next two weeks." "Rog will feed him and put him in the corral until the hearing." "That black will kick his head in if he goes in that stall," Joe warned him.

Rog looked at the Marshal, "Jim, he said, I've seen that monster and he's right, I ain't going in that stall!" Jim couldn't believe a horse had put fear into his deputy, "fine put a gun in his back and let him out of the cell. He can take care of his own dang horse!" Jim said as he left the office. Joe set up in his cell as Rog pitched him the keys that was all he wanted in the first place; Joe walked out of the Marshal's office with the pistol in his back. "You try anything and it will be the last thing you ever do," Rog warned him.

The sound of the men's boots resounded on the wooden sidewalk as they headed for the town stable. "What are you gonna do with that?"

The voice came from behind the deputy as they passed the Crooked Horn restaurant. Rog fought back the urge to run; he had never fought a woman before and didn't know if he could, especially this woman. Marilyn stood ready to attack. Fists doubled and eyes aflame. "Marshal's orders," he yelled trying to bring the woman to her senses. She screamed back, "you need a gun in his back to walk down the street?" the brown eyes had turned red with fury; every fiber in her was ready to explode. Rog didn't know what to do, he had never been in this position before, "Jim said to keep a gun on him he explained." "It was self-defense," she screamed, "What you think he is going to do kill you and run off. What good would that do? Every lawman in the country would be hunting him. He would become a wanted criminal for nothing." Rog slid the weapon into the holster, "fine," he said, "If he escapes you can tell that to your brother!"

Marilyn stomped off still in a rage, "you can bet I'll take this up with my brother!" she said slinging the bat wing doors open so hard they banged into both walls.

Joe look hard at the young deputy almost in shock, "she's the marshal's sister?" he asked. "Not really," the young man answered.

"Jim is married to her sister Sherlene but they act like their blood kin. "Now let's go take care of that horse of yours before someone else decides to take my head off."

The blacks ears picked up as Joe and the deputy walked into the barn. Rog stood back as Joe patted the blacks shoulder and neck. Joe talked softly to it trying to calm the animal as he slipped a short rope over the horses head and opened the stall gate. Instantly the animal pulled back almost dragging him over the top rail as the gate was opened.

It was a battle of wills and strength as the horse tried to break free. The animal pulled again and Joe was pulled over the railing still hanging onto the rope even as he was slammed to the ground. The black reared up and the action pulled Joe to his feet. Rog was beginning to think he was going to have to shoot the animal to save the man's life. As Rog reached for the pistol at his side, Joe ran to one side and grabbed hold of the white mane and kicked one leg over the horses back and latched on. The animal was rearing up again as Joe wrapped both arms around its neck. The horse half hopped and landed on its front feet slamming Joe's face into its neck. Joe lifted his leg as the horse spun and rammed its side into the nearest stall trying to drive the rider off. Joe muttered through gritted teeth, "open the gate." Rog swung the gate open and stepped out of the way as horse and rider bolted through. Joe slid to the ground and lay flat as the black spun his hind quarters and kicked out at the rider, the hoof missing his head by inches. Joe sat in the dirt with blood running from his mouth and nose, watching the horse run as Rog came over to help him up. "I don't think he liked the stall," Joe said as he got to his feet.

"Neither do I," said the young deputy, "We'll stop by the Crooked Horn and get you cleaned up, providing you don't put the blame on me for you bleeding!" "Agreed," Joe said as he walked to the stall and picked up his saddle bag. Do you mind my rifle is in the corner, it was the safest place I could think of when I came into town?" Rog picked up the rifle and they started for the Crooked Horn. Joe could not help but see the smile on the deputy's face. "What's so funny," he asked. "Oh, nothing, I was just thinking, one more ride like that and the judge won't have to hang you, that horse will kill you for him."

The Marshal, Marilyn, Deputy Schon and a beautiful, brown haired woman with piercing hazel eyes sat at a table drinking coffee as Joe and Rog entered the restaurant. "Why ain't you got a gun on him," Jim asked. "Since you don't know what you're doing," Marilyn snapped. Jim looked at her, "Who put you in charge of the prisoners?" His annoyance was starting to show, as a red flush crept up his neck and the vein in his temple began to pulsate. "I did," she answered, "the minute you became an idiot!" Jim settled back in his chair with a puzzled look on his face, she's interested in this man, he thought. Marilyn walked over to the potbellied stove took a pan down from the hook and filled it half full of water, "Sit down Ace" she said. Joe walked over pulled out a chair and sat down. "How did this happen" she asked dipping a cloth into the warming pot of water. "Deputy here did it!" he answered half laughing to himself. Marilyn spun on the deputy and Rog threw both hands in the air, "he's lying," he said as Marilyn took a step towards him. This time Joe broke out in laughter. This was a new sensation to him. He couldn't remember the last time he had laughed and it felt good. He hadn't had much to laugh about in his life. Even now he was a prisoner in this town and yet he felt comfortable with these people. "Maybe I'm just getting soft in my old age," he thought to himself, "Yeah, soft in the head."

Jim looked over at the dark hair woman, "Honey I think

someone is in love!" It seemed Jim had a funny side to him or was he just trying to get even with Marilyn for telling him how to do his job? These thoughts were running through Joe's head when Sherlene, Jim wife, said, "that could never happen to my sister, she's the level headed one, she could never fall in love, just ask momma." Schon couldn't help it, the deputy busted out laughing. Then both Jim and Sherlene joined in. Marilyn could hardly contain her anger; she threw the wet rag at the deputy and stormed out of the room.

Rog saw that it was safe and joined the others at the table. "Come on cowboy, let's get you back to your cell," he said as the laughter died down. Rog locked the cell door behind Joe, sat down at the Marshal's desk, spun the chair around and put his boots through the bars of the cell. "You sure like living on the edge cowboy," Roger stated. "How do you figure," Joe asked. "Well, you ride into town on a horse that's liable to kill you, get into a gun fight with one of the meanest men in town, and then you pick the marshal's sister for a girlfriend, I'd say you like living dangerously!"

Joe leaned back in his cell, he never thought of having a girlfriend before. Early the next morning as the other men in the jail slept Joe got up stretched his arms and legs for a few minutes, did some pull ups from the bars of his cell and then went into the gun fighters crouch and practiced his draw, first one hand then the other, grabbing imaginary weapons. He lived by the speed of his hands and the power of his arms, being interested in a woman wasn't going to stop a life time of habits. Joe forced his hands to remain by his side as he heard the cell door open. The smell of strong coffee filled the room as Marilyn entered the office. She carried a tray filled with pancakes smothered in butter and covered with homemade syrup; the smell of the food woke the man in the other cell.

"Hey, where's mine," K.C. asked as he came to his feet. "I'll get yours later," Schon answered. "I want mine delivered by a pretty girl," K.C. complained. "I've been up with drunks all night," Schon growled, "You keep complaining and you won't get any!" "I liked the other guard better!" K.C. said as he went back to his bunk.

Joe dug into the food, as Marilyn set down beside him she picked up his cup of coffee and began to take a sip, "what are your plans when you get out of here," she asked.

"Don't really know," Joe answered. "I was headed to the California gold fields." Marilyn look puzzled, "what changed you mind," she asked.

Joe didn't know what to say; he wasn't used to being around women and didn't know how to act around this particular woman. "I guess you could say the black did," he answered afraid to show what he was feeling. Marilyn picked up the tray feeling a little hurt, not sure if he felt the same way about her as she felt about him. After the hearing would he ride off never to be seen again? Would she always remember the sad haunted eyes of the man in the cell? Could she ever forget the way he looked at her? Yes she had only met him three days ago but she couldn't get him out of her mind! It was as if she had suddenly become possessed and there was nothing she could do about it, she had no free will of her own! Marilyn fought back the tears as she made her way to the Crooked Horn.

 Schon looked up from the Marshal's desk to see a young woman enter the office. She was around seventeen with a beautiful smile. "Can I help you?" he asked. "I'm here to see K.C.," she answered. "Sorry, you'll have to wait for the Marshal," Schon told her. Nicole turned on the charm, "I can't, pa's coming and there's gonna be trouble," she explained. "Please just let me talk to K.C." She was a lovely young lady with long brown hair, big blue eyes and a smile that would soften a heart made of stone and Schon fell for that charm.

"Fine but only for a few minutes, if the Marshal finds out it will be my hide!" he exclaimed, not really afraid of Jim. Nicole flashed him a big smile and headed for the cell. "Can we have some privacy," she asked. Schon was a little perturbed but he stepped out of the office and onto the wooden sidewalk, "great you're going to get me fired," he complained taking the keys with him. K.C. jumped up from the rod iron bed and met Nicole at the bars of the cell.

"Honey," he whispered "I've got half a hundred head of prim cattle hidden in a corral on the north side of your old man's ranch. They are down in a draw with a small creek in it and I want you to ride up there and let them go. They will drift back to the old man's place and they will have to let me go!" "Why don't we just keep the cattle," she said. K.C. began to worry, "because your old man will have me hung," he explained. Nicole turned on the charm again, "no he won't," she said "I told him I was pregnant." K.C.'s jaw looked like it was going to hit the floor. "That ain't possible," he nearly shouted. Nicole's smile turned bitter sweet, "tell daddy that and he will hang you himself!" Nicole had the upper hand on both men and she knew it! Schon opened the front door and stood there, "sorry kids, Marshal's on the way, you better go." Nicole was all honey and smiles swinging her hips as she turned and walked out of the room.

That afternoon Don Malloy and half a dozen of his men rode into town. Swinging down from their mounts they flipped the reins over the hitching post and walked into the bar section of the Crooked Horn, "my little girl's getting married," he said as the men lined up for the free drinks "and if she don't get married?" one of the men asked, "then we're gonna have us a hanging!" was the replay from the speaker. Every man there knew he was speaking the truth. Don Malloy may have been a lot of things but he was as good as his word and K.C. Jones was in big trouble! Don Malloy started out of the room, "you two follow me, and the rest of you stay here and get drunk." No one was going to argue about the free drinks and they lined up at the bar that and none of them were about to argue with the man who believed his daughter had been violated. Schon jumped to his feet as the men entered the office, every fiber of his being knew something was about to explode. Don Malloy stood glaring at the deputy. "I want to see that no good cattle rustler!" he said. By the look of pent up rage on the weather beaten face, Schon knew this was not about cattle and things were about to get out of hand. The deputy hated to draw on another man but he had no choice, the pistol leapt into his hand and was pointed at the stomach of the older man. "Mr. Malloy, I don't want to have to kill you, he said, so please drop your weapon." Malloy was tempted to force the deputy's hand but the better part of common sense stilled his hand. "Fine," he said as he unbuckled the gun belt and threw it on top of the Marshal's desk. "I still want to see the cattle thief!"

Schon shook his head, "not with two of your men standing behind me you're not!" Malloy didn't like the play but he turned to his men, "you boys head back to the Crooked Horn, I'll meet you there after I'm done here." He was not a patient man, "alright their gone, he said; now I want to see this thief face to face." "Fine, Schon said, just keep your hands outside of the bars."

K.C. lay back on the bunk of his cell and watched the big man approach. K.C. broke the silence, "I didn't steal nothin," he stated flatly. Don Malloy exploded, "we ain't talking about cattle and you know it! You got two words to say, 'I do' or you can die. Cause if you don't I'll see you hanged!" "You can't hang a man for nothing, K.C. complained. The eyes of the older man burned with a fury K.C. had never seen before.

"I found twenty head of my cattle carrying a K.C. brand in my south pasture." Malloy stated. K.C. could not believe what he was hearing, "that's impossible," he said starting to feel nervous for the first time. "You planted them!" "Prove it!" the old man ordered lowering his voice to a whisper.

"Like I said, you are gonna set in this cell until the justice of the peace gets here and then you're gonna say I do or you're gonna hang."

With that Malloy left the jail and headed for the Crooked Horn. After the soon to be father-in-law departed Joe turned to look at the rustler. "Crap, I thought I had problems," he said as he rolled over, pulled his hat over his head and went to sleep. There was nothing to do in the small confines of a jail cell and Joe was getting used to the short cat naps. Schon rattled the cage door and Joe awoke. "Hey, you play checkers?" he asked. "Sure do," Joe answered. Schon unstrapped his gun belt laid it on the desk, pitched the cell keys on top and slid a card table against the bars of the cell. "What about me?" K.C. whined. "Three can't play at the same time." Schon opened one of the drawers on the marshal's desk, "here," he said pitching a pack of cards into the cell with the rustler. The Marshal took them from a drummer last month, their marked so try not to cheat yourself!"

K.C. began to spread the cards out in a pyramid fashion for a game of solitaire as Joe set up the checker board. "Where you from?" Schon asked as Joe jumped two of his men. Joe stopped and studied the face of the deputy to see if he really wanted to know or to see if he was just doing his job, trying to figure the man out. After a few seconds he decided the deputy really wanted to know.

"Oklahoma," he said "the land of rocks snakes and weeds." "That's what I've heard," Schon said, "but is it really that bad?" "You can bet your saddle on it! My place had more rocks than cattle and more snakes than weeds and there were plenty of both, heck, how do you think I got so good with a pistol? I spent half of my day popping the heads off them bug old velvet tailed rattlers." "Well what about the sawed off pistol with no sights and the knife cut shells?" he asked. Joe shook his head, "it's plain to see you've never been to Oklahoma!" "No," Schon answered, "Why?" "You ain't never seen a razor back hog, then have you?' "Not that I can recall." "If you did you wouldn't forget it. They are a long skinny animal with a hump back and razor like tusks. They run in packs and can take a man's horse out from under him in about three seconds.

Fellow, you don't want to be on the ground with a pack of them around cause they will kill you in a heartbeat and what they kill they eat, be it man, horse or dog!" "That still don't explain the sawed off pistol or the X cut shells!" Schon stated. "Sure it does, those things come out of the brush nearly at your feet and they come at a run, you gotta get your gun out quick. You don't want to have a pistol stick in the holster or hang up on a sight. As far as the cut shells, I found one bullet won't always stop the darn things but a shell ripping apart on impact will stop a hog in its tracks." " But at thirty feet those shells are almost worthless," the deputy said, "you couldn't hit the broad side of a barn with them, besides that they could spread out in the barrel and blow your hand off if not your head!"

"Yep," Joe admitted, "that could happen but I spent a lot of time and practice perfecting that cut. Anymore and it could blow up in the barrel and any less and it won't spread." "You can keep those shells," Schon said, "I ain't about to fire them." "To each his own," Joe stated. "Hey, I can't find no marks on these cards," K.C. complained. Mind if I take a look at them?" Joe asked. "Be my guest," K.C. flipped the deck of cards to the speaker. Joe shuffled the deck and passed out one hand to each player. They went through a dozen hands before Joe finely said, "there is the mark." "Where?" K.C. asked looking at the back of his cards, "I don't see nothin." "There is a small dot built into the cards and you can only see it when the light is right. If you don't know what you're looking for it will slip past without ever being seen." "Well, you're good with cards, checkers and guns," the deputy said, "what else are you any good at?" "Well I can ride a horse," Joe said with a smile." "I guess we all know that," Schon said. "It's getting late and I've got to make rounds," Schon said picking up the cards and placing them in the marshal's desk, "we'll finish the checkers later," he told Joe as he left the office. K.C. lay down but he was not sleeping.

"How am I gonna get out of this?" kept running through his head but he couldn't think his way out of the mess he was in. "If I could only get word to my brother and cousins maybe they could figure me a way out of this mess," K.C. thought as his eyes finely closed in a fitful sleep.
Late that night Joe woke up and began to stretch, he didn't want to lose his edge. After the pull ups he got into the gunfighters stance again, it had become so routine to him that he did it without conscious thought, and began to practice his draw. As his hands reached for the imaginary weapons he heard a tapping on the wall of the cell.

"K.C." a voice whispered. K.C. woke up, "Who is it?" he whispered back. "It's me, Nicole," she answered. "What are you doing?" he asks. "I'm breaking you out!" "How," he asked. "I'm blowing the window," she replied. "You can't use dynamite, you don't know what you're doing, and you'll blow the jail to pieces and everyone in it!" "That's why I brought Eric; he's an expert with the stuff." Eric's head popped up in the window, "Hi brother," he said as he began to place the explosives in the window. "Why are you doing this? You told your old man you were pregnant. I thought you wanted to marry me?" "I do," she said, but on my terms not his, besides if I hadn't told him that I was pregnant and thrown such a fit, you would already be dead.

He was gonna hang you from the cottonwood tree at the front gate as a warning to the other rustlers roaming the valley." At the ripe old age of twenty the thought of his neck stretching from the limb of the cottonwood didn't sound too appealing. "Where is the deputy," K.C. asked Nicole. "He's at the bar, some of the Rocking 'R' riders came in liquored up and ready for trouble, he's down there trying to keep a lid on things." "Get me my gun, it's in the top drawer of the Marshal's desk and my gun belt is hanging on a hook in the office." "No," she replied, "The front door is locked and if we try busting it down everyone in town will hear." "How about my horse, did you bring him?" "Sure did along with a rifle, a canteen and enough grub to last a week." "What about the cattle, are we gonna leave them or do you want to try to sneak them off the old man's place?"

"Neither," she said, "Colton and Parker left with the herd you gathered two days ago, by now they are half way to Mexico and they even took the twenty head pa put your brand on!" Eric popped in "you two gonna jaw all night or are we gonna blow this here wall?" Eric cut a two foot section of blasting cord and shoved it into the end of a stick of dynamite. "You best get back!" he said as he struck a match and lit the end of the cord.

Eric and Nicole ran around the corner as the cord began to sizzle and pop. K.C. hid in the far corner of the cell trying to protect himself from the blast. "Hey kid, like this," Joe said taking the mattress from his bunk and doubling it then he rolled himself into a ball in the farthest corner of the cell pulling the mattress over his entire body and covered his ears with his hands to protect them from the shattering blast that was about to come.

  K.C. pulled the mattress off his bunk and followed suit. Moments later the roar of the dynamite rocked the room. Pieces of flying brick hammered at the bars of the cell as dust filled the room and drifted to the floor. Eric ran from the corner of the jail and began kicking loose bricks from the jail house wall making the hole even larger. "Come on K.C., we gotta move!" Half stunned from the blast, K.C. managed to get up. "What happened," he asked as Eric climbed through the opening and started to drag him towards the wall. 'Nothing," he screamed, "now let's get going before the whole town gets here."

Eric was half lifting and half shoving him into the hole. Nicole grabbed him by the head and began to pull. "Hey, your old man ain't gonna have to hang me," he complained, "you two are gonna do it for him!"

"Shut up!" Eric screamed and shoved even harder. Joe threw the mattress off his body with a grimace, every bone in his body felt as if they had been hit by the flying pieces of brick. "The next time you idiots decide to make a jail break, leave me out of it will you!"

K.C. still looked groggy, "heck," he said, "next time I hope they leave me out of it!" Eric pushed him the rest of the way through the opening and then dived through the opening himself. "Where are the horses?" Eric shouted. Joe heard the voice of the young woman near hysteria. "The dynamite scared them and they ran off!" she cried, "I couldn't hold them!" "Which way did they go?" Eric asked. She must have pointed because Joe heard her say that way and then came the sound of running boots.

Joe threw the mattress on the bunk and lay back down, heck anything is possible but he had a better chance of becoming a dirt clod farmer than those three did of making it to Mexico. Joe's head had barley hit the pillow before the jail door was thrown open. Schon, Rog and half a dozen armed men charged into the room, "What happened," he asked. "What does it look like," Joe answered, "you had a jailbreak!" "Which way did they go?" Rog demanded glaring at the older man. Joe didn't like the hostile attitude of the young deputy and swung to his feet. "How would I know, it's dark outside, I'm locked in a cell and besides that I almost got my head blown off by the blast and a buck board load of bricks!" In two steps Joe was at the bars of the cell, the fire of pent up rage was evident in the hard drawn lines of his face.

Schon stepped between the two men, "Alright cool down," he said, "we've got enough trouble already. Rog backed away from the bars, "fine, "he said, "let's just get after the flipping cattle thief."

Rog was taking the jailbreak personally and wanted revenge on any and all responsible. "Not tonight," the voice came from the Marshal standing in the door. "Why not," Rog demanded, "Because all you're going to do at night is stumble around in the dark and mess up any tracks they might have left!" "Then what will we do?" Schon asked, "We just can't stand here!" "Your right, Jim said, go home and go to bed, you'll need some rest for tomorrow." All of the men left the jail talking about the daring escape by the outlaws.

CHAPTER THREE

Early the next morning Joe watched as close to a dozen riders assembled themselves in the Marshal's office, these were unscrupulous men, most of them came from two of the larger cattle outfits and they were the scum of the men who worked there. Most ranchers wouldn't hire them on a bet; all of them carried high powered rifles and pistols that rode in tied down holsters. Some had new rope ready to hang the young outlaws as soon as they caught up with them. Schon and Rog were in the office also and both men held rifles cradled in their arms as they leaned against opposite walls waiting for the Marshal to come in.

Jim listened to the roar of excited men as they swarmed him, impatient to get on with the hunt. The Marshal withdrew a set of pistols from the desk and strapped them on then he took a rifle from the rack, checked the loads and turned around to have a look at the posse. Two of the men were store keepers, the other worked at the stables, "you go home," he said. As the rejected members of the posse left Jim dropped the barrel of the rifle to point directly into the face of one of the men with the rope, "the rest of you can head back to your spread as well, we don't need you."

"Hey, we were paid to ride along and were gonna!" one of the men in the posse growled. Jim swung the rifle towards the speaker, "my thumb slips and you will be riding in a pine box!" It was easy to see Jim was in no mood to argue, the white of his knuckles showed that the trigger had already been pulled and that his thumb held back the deadly hammer of the rifle. Sweat began to appear on the lip of the speaker, "we just wanted to help," he began but Jim cut him off, "like heck you did!" he glared back at them, "you're nothing but a lynch mob and if I catch any of you following me I'll put a bullet in you myself!"

"Now get out!" Several of the riders complained under their breath but none of them wanted to start a war with the lawman or his deputy's.

As the posse broke up and headed back to the ranches that had hired them, Jim began to build a war bag. "When are we leaving?" Schon asked. "You ain't!" Jim replied. "The Rocking 'R' has been pushing cattle into the Malloy place, there's gonna be a blow up pretty soon and I'll need you here to keep a lid on it." "You ain't crazy enough to go after that bunch alone are you?" Rog asked. Jim picked up the keys to the cells, "I guess it's up to him!" Jim was pointing at Joe. "Well you think that black of yours needs to stretch its legs?" Joe sat startled for a moment unable to believe his ear's, "I ain't killen no kid!" Joe shot back at the Marshal. "I ain't asking you to kill anybody, just wanted to know if that back needed to stretch its legs, that's all."

Joe shook his head, "I ain't hunting them for you either!" "You can help me find them kids before that lynch mob does or you can let them hang them, it's up to you." Jim just stared at him. Joe began to cuss, "what about the hearing?" Joe asked. The Marshal was getting aggravated, "fine," he said as he started to close the cell door.

"I'll go after them myself but if that bunch bushwhacks me or hangs them kids, it will be partly you're fault because you could have helped but wouldn't!"

Joe began to cuss again, "alright I'll go!" he said through gritted teeth. Joe hated to admit it but he was kind of fond of the wild eyed cattle thief! Jim threw Joe his gun belt and dug the pistols out of the drawer and handed them to the gunman, "don't shoot yourself with them," he said with a sideways grin. "That's gonna be hard to do seeing their empty!" Joe wasn't sure if he liked the Marshal or not but he was sure he didn't like the sarcasm!

"Well maybe you better load them then," Jim said as he walked out of the office. Joe strapped on the gun belt and began to follow. "What makes you think I won't shoot you in the back and ride off?" Jim stopped and turned around, "I sent telegraphs to every sheriff and marshal in the country, you're a small time rancher from Oklahoma as far as anyone can tell and I don't guess anybody alive has ever seen you pull a gun and those that have ain't around to tell about it! Either way you're clean, plugging me in the back would be kind of stupid if nothing else.

 and I don't think you're stupid! Jim turned into the Crooked Horn with Joe following.

Sherlene and Marilyn were sitting at one of the tables sipping coffee, "hi honey," Jim said and kissed his wife gently on the lips. "Do you think we could get something to go?" Marilyn looked at Joe, "are you leaving?" she asked "Just for a few days," he answered, "I'm riding with the marshal." "You're not hunting those kids are you?" Joe shook his head, "I ain't hunting anyone just taking the black out to stretch his legs." "Good," she said, "I like those kids." "Sis," Jim said, "I think you like just about everybody." "We'll fix you a bag," she said with a giggle in her voice as the two women got up and headed for the kitchen.

 Joe watched her leave thinking, "I have feelings for a woman that thinks of me as a gunman, a hired killer, and the lowest of the low." Jim shoved a cup of coffee in front of him, "best drink up, the stuff I make will keep you awake for days!"

Joe picked up the cup, "how long do you think we'll be gone?" he asked. "Maybe a week, why, don't tell me you are missing her already?" "What are you talking about?" Joe asked. "Marilyn of course, a blind man can see how you feel about her." Joe mumbled under his breath, "What would she want with a broken down ex cattle rancher." "What did you say?" Jim asked, knowing full well what he heard. "I didn't say anything," Joe answered. The women came back from the kitchen, Sherlene put the bag down in front of him, "honey will you have time to join us before you go?"

"Not really, I figure the Malloy outfit will have men out looking for them and I don't want them to catch that wild bunch of kids before we do."

"Why, what do you think will happen," Sherlene asked guardedly, knowing Jim could be risking his life. "I think they will hang them!" Marilyn looked shocked. "Surely they would not hang the girl," she said. "I think they will hang them all." Jim stated flatly. Joe couldn't believe what he was hearing, "nobody would kill their own daughter over a few head of cattle!"

"She's not his daughter." Jim said. "Ten or twelve years ago Nicole's real parents had a pretty good spread. A couple thousand head of cattle on five or six thousand acres of prime grazing land, not counting fifty to a hundred head of horses. The plague was going around at the time and they caught it. Nicole was sick for a long time and by the time she came out of it both of her parents were gone. She stayed with a neighbor until her uncle showed up and took over. He has run the place like it was his ever since. He even had the girl call him dad! I guess he was hoping people would forget the ranch rightfully belonged to Nicole. In a few months she will be old enough to take control of the ranch and with the help of that gunslinger of hers she could take control of the ranch even sooner by running him off."

"If he's all that good how did he get caught in the first place?" Joe asked.

Jim could not help but smile, "got caught with his pants down, literally." The kid went to the ranch to visit Nicole and while he was there he had to make a trip to the outhouse. Old man Malloy had some of his men staked out watching the place. When the kid sat down one of the hired guns slid a pistol through a knot hole and into the kids back. Told him if he moved he would gut shoot him. The kid had no choice but to set there as the rest of the men took his guns and put a noose around his neck.

The only thing that stopped them was Nicole, told them she would turn them in for murder if they went ahead with their plans." "Any way, that was the story I got when I was summoned to the ranch and arrested K.C." "What about the rest of it?" Joe asked. "She even told the old man she was pregnant and the old man really acted upset over that!"

"Sure he acted mad," Jim said, "that was just what it was acting. He may have some feelings for the girl but he loves the ranch a lot more and as long as she is alive he can never rightfully own the place. I'll bet he even put the K.C. brand on his own cattle, hoping to frame the kid. The way I see it the quicker she is dead the better he will like it!" Marilyn looked at Joe with a new kind of fear in her eyes. "You won't let that happen will you?" she asked. Joe didn't know what to say, but all of a sudden he knew he would die for this woman! "Not as long as I'm alive," he said quietly.

Sherlene spoke up there's a tin of lard in there, a couple hands full of coffee, some beef jerky and a couple slices of bacon. I threw in two slices of blackberry pie and some salt for the both of you." Sherlene sat down beside her husband, "you're not going to bring those kids back are you?" she ask. "It's my job, he stated, but I'll do everything I can to see they get a fair trial." "Yes and if Malloy has his way he will have every cowhand he's got on the jury. He might even manage to get the girl hung for stealing her own cattle," Marilyn said with a cold hot anger flaring in her eyes.

"I won't let it go that far," Jim said. Joe's eyes had taken on a darkness of their own. He may not have been a hired gun but the look of a man who knew how to kill was on his face. "Neither will I," Joe said. Jim finished the last of his coffee, "if we don't want that to happen we better get going," he said. Both ladies watched as the men in their lives walked out the door. Sherlene turned to Marilyn, "sis has a boyfriend, sis has a boyfriend." Marilyn turned red and threw a wet wash cloth at Sherlene, "shut up," she said in mock anger as she headed back into the kitchen.

    Jim threw a blanket and saddle on a mule headed roan and backed the animal out of the stall. "Hey, you coming?" he said as Joe threw a rope over the neck of the black. "I'll be there in a minute," Joe answered as he fought the black. "Want me to shoot him for you; it will make him easier to ride!" Joe turned on the Marshal, "you shoot him and you better keep firing because I'll be coming for you!" Jim began to laugh, "Man you been alone too long!" Joe was steaming, "What is that supposed to mean?" Jim shook his head, "nothing, it's just that you don't know a joke when you hear one." Joe realized the marshal was teasing and settled down, "I'll be ready as soon as I get a saddle on this thing," he said. Jim watched as Joe put a saddle on the horse and stepped into the stirrup; the black lowered its head, hunched its back and kicked straight back, and then spun to the left trying to throw the rider. It spun one more time and jumped into the air and landed on its front hooves. Joe's left hand held the reins as his right hand gripped the saddle horn. The force of the impact slammed Joe's head forward as the blacks came back at the same time ramming into Joe's face and the blood began to poor.

Joe pulled the reins hard to the left forcing the horse to turn then kicked it hard in the ribs with the heel of his boots letting the animal have its lead. The black took off at a hard run as large clods of dirt flew into the air torn from under the hoofs of the animal. Both horse and rider circled the huge corral before the animal was brought under control. Joe sat wiping the blood off his face as Jim rode up, "You sure you don't want me to shoot that thing," he asked.

Joe spit blood from his mouth "one more ride like that and I might shoot him myself!" Jim reached down from the back of the roan and swung the gate open, "we'll stop by the office and get you a badge, I want to make this legal." Joe shrugged, "legal or not I guess I'll ride with you at least until we find the kids." Joe was thinking of the waitress and the soft brown eyes and the thought of having her arms around him, "I made a promise and I plan on keeping it," he said.

The Marshal and the ex-prisoner stepped down in front of the Marshal's office, wrapped the reins of the horses around the hitching post and went in. Schon sat at the desk with his feet propped up on the bars and Rog leaned against the cell bars sipping a cup of coffee, "Don't you two have anything to do?" "Not at the moment," Schon answered, "You know it never gets busy until after dark," Jim looked frustrated, "you ain't gonna hold many prisoners in the condition this place is in. How about putting some bricks back on that wall?" Schon got up and headed for the stove, "we'll get it done before you get back," he said as he took a cup and began to pour himself a cup of day old coffee. "Besides, one cell will work for now cause we ain't ever had that many prisoners." "We're fixing to," Jim said, "so get ready."

Rog pushed off the cell bars with a shrug, "I think there is some mortar mix behind the stable, I'll go get it and I'll see if I can find some bricks while I'm at it." Jim opened the desk drawer and took out a silver plated star, "here I guess I need to swear you in," as he handed the badge to Joe. "Do you Joe, what's your last name, I forgot?" "Stroud," he replied. "Do you Joe Stroud, swear to up hold the law to the best of your abilities?" "I do," Joe said as he pinned the badge to his shirt. Joe laid three shells on the marshal's desk, got a straight razor from the shaving kit setting by the potbellied stove and began cutting deep X's in the top of the soft lead, "Do you really think you're going to need that?" asked Schon.

"You never can tell!" Joe replied as he replaced the spent shells of the sawed off forty-four. Jim and the new deputy headed south out of town. Nita and two of her girls were standing out on the balcony as they passed. The two girls were wearing tight silken blouses with some of the buttons open and they were bending over the rail and began yelling at the marshal, "hey, who's the new deputy?" they cried. The Marshal brought the horse to a stop, "Nita, get them girls buttoned up or get them inside before I close the place!" Nita giggled and told the girls to button up and both girls began to laugh, "We can't never have no fun," they complained as they headed inside. "Sorry about that," Nita said, "you know how girls are." "No," Jim said, "I don't, so keep them inside or keep them decent!" "I've got enough trouble at the moment!" Nita turned and went inside.

Neither of the lawmen paid any attention to the man standing in the doorway. It was clear he was no cowboy. Dressed in a dark suit and string tie he looked more like a Sunday go to meeting preacher than a gunman. "So that's the man I'm supposed to kill, not much to look at," thought Larry Cheatham, as he went back into the cathouse. Johnny Vasquez had told him about the job, said it paid five hundred dollars to kill a cowboy or two and run the rest out of town, Vasquez was not the kind to turn down a job so something wasn't right but Cheatham wanted to see a woman he knew who had moved to Lone Oak. He cared a lot for her and the money was right so he had headed for the small border town.

When he had first arrived he had talked to the owner of the Rocking 'R' ranch, the ranch was owned by a man named Skip MacCland. Skip was broad shouldered and narrow hipped with hair red enough to show a blood line of the Irish and if looks meant anything a temper to match! He looked mean enough to take care of his own problems. Larry had no idea why he would hire a gun out of Mexico and didn't care but Skip had changed his mind, he was no longer interested in the cowboys, he wanted a broken down old cowboy riding a jailhouse bunk killed. It didn't make any difference to Larry, besides, it looked like easy money. Pulling a cork from a bottle of fine bourbon whisky Larry headed up the stairs.

The one person on earth who knew him and what he did for a living was waiting for him. Trish didn't care about his job she loved him. She had moved here a couple of months ago to help her aunt run this place but she was his and no one else's. This he could depend on.

Around noon the Marshal and Joe picked up the trail of the escaped outlaws and by the deep cut marks from the hooves of the horses in the hard ground it was easy to tell they were riding fast. "They're gonna kill them mounts," Joe said. "Probably, admitted Jim, we'll just poke along and see what happens." "You ain't in no hurry to catch those kids are you?" "Nope," said the Marshal. "What if the Malloy bunch catches them?" Joe asked. Jim pulled his horse to a stop, "that's why I brought you." Joe shook his head, "I told you I ain't no gunman!" "Well you better be or we could both wind up being dead, because I ain't one either!" Joe looked the Marshal over real good, "if you ain't a gunman how come you're a Marshal?" "I'm a clod hopping farmer that got voted into the job.

I ain't never killed a man in my life and I'm hoping I never have to!" "For a man that's never killed anyone you pulled a pretty good bluff back at the jail. "Joe stated "Yes and I was sweating bullets when I did it! The marshal answered. If one of them boys would have pulled leather I'd have shot him alright probably ten times just to make sure he was dead!" Joe shook his head "how did I get into this mess, chasing a bunch of kids to the Mexican border with a Marshal that might not know one end of a gun from the other and a lynch mob out to kill everybody. If I had half a brain I'd ride out of here!" Then Joe remembered the promise to the brown eyed waitress, "Crap," he said to himself, and slapped the black with the reins. Jim choked in the dust as horse and rider took off.

"Ain't no way we're gonna catch them old boy," Jim said softly as he leaned forward and patted the roan on the back of the neck, "guess we'll just have to outlast them," and with that he spurred the horse and took off following the dust trail of the black.

CHAPTER FOUR

"You sure we're on the right trail?" Nicole whined.

"You bet," was the reply from the young man riding at her side. "Eric and me have brought ten to fifteen herds down this way." "What about water, we're just about out and my canteens dry!" Nicole continued to whine.

"Quit crying, will you there's a spring fed pond below that mountain and we will be there in a few minutes. You can even go swimming if you want." "That ain't much of a mountain, "she stated. "Woman you bellyache about everything. We're half way to Mexico and we've got a decent herd of cattle in front of us and food in our bellies, what more do you want?"

I want my ranch," she said, "my mother and father are buried there; they built that place from scratch and now I'm running off and leaving it, I feel like I'm deserting them!"

"Fine," K.C. said, "we'll sell the cattle in Mexico, set on the cash for a few months till you're of legal age and then hire some gun's and take the place back by force and if we have to we'll bury your uncle by his brother!"

Eric rode up, "it's all clear." "What do you mean all clear?" Nicole wanted to know. "Remember we have the law chasing us because of that little jailbreak, besides that you don't think your uncle is gonna let you ride off do you?" K.C. said. "He probably has a dozen men hunting us. After all you're the legal heir to the ranch." "My uncle would never harm me!" Nicole said, "He raised me like I was his own daughter." "Sure," K.C. said. "I have no doubt he loves you to a point but he loves that ranch more and now you're old enough to become a threat to him and the ranch. Face the facts honey, this month he can put my brand on one cow and have me hung as a rustler and next month you can give me a thousand head of cattle and there is nothing he can do about it!"

"He does not want you to have control of the ranch and he doesn't want you to have that kind of power!" Nicole rode in silence to the edge of the pond, "did they really think he would go that far?" Nicole pulled the high topped leather riding boots off and hung them from the horn of her saddle using the string from the wide brimmed western hat she wore, would my uncle have me killed? She wondered as she jumped from a rock and dived into the warm waters of a southwestern Texas pond.

  Larry Cheatham got up from the warm bed still half-drunk he wasn't hung over because some of the Bourbon still surged through his veins. His temper was starting to flare, "don't let anybody touch that," he said as he pointed at the bottle on the dresser. "Sure," Trish said as she wiped the sleep from her eyes and smiled up at him, "Whatever you say honey," and lay back on the pillow watching him. Larry was meticulous in his dress tucking the shirt in making sure the draw string tie was in line with the shirt buttons. Everything had to be perfect for the man who had come from Louisiana, not even the bulge from the short barreled hide out gun under his left shoulder was apparent. Laying two five dollar gold pieces on the dresser next to the wash basin Larry said, "I'll be back later" and shut the door as he left.

Trish turned over and tried to go back to sleep she wondered if she would see him again she was angered that he thought she was for sale! He was the only man she had ever loved and the only one she had ever married. She didn't know why she had never told anyone about the marriage but Larry had said it was best to keep it quiet for now and one day they would settle down but for now his work kept him on the back of a horse most of the time and she saw him maybe a dozen times a year! But she didn't mind she loved him.

Ashley Fry was sweeping off the wooden sidewalk in front of the general store as Larry walked by and something about him caught her attention. Laying the broom aside she watched as he crossed the street in the direction of the Crooked Horn restaurant and saloon, she was certain she knew the man. As he walked through the doors of the restaurant Ashley started across the street to the Marshal's office realizing why she knew him!

"Where is the Marshal," she asked almost screaming as she entered. Schon sat in the Marshal's chair with his feet kicked through the bars of one of the cells, "Him and the gunslinger is out on the trail. His name is Joe and he ain't no gunslinger." Rog cut in as he was placing the last of the bricks in the hole he was repairing from the blast, "He's a rancher from Oklahoma." Rog stepped back and admired his handiwork, "Maybe that will hold until we get a real brick layer in here," he said. Ashley was in a hurry, she had to talk to someone and the deputies were the only ones there,

"Listen, she said, there's a gunman in town, a real gunman, not some broken down cowboy who got lucky!" "I know the man, his name is Larry Cheatham and I've seen him kill men before!"

Rog stopped admiring his work and looked over at Ashley, "how do you know it's him and how do you know he's in town?"

"I just saw him walk out of Nita's place and it's easy to know it's him. " Ashley looked down embarrassed to admit where she had once worked, "I used to work on the water front," she admitted, "the place was shady, always in trouble with the law, Larry worked there as a bouncer. The tables were rigged but sometimes a river captain or a crew member would get lucky and win big, well you can guess that didn't sit well with the owner and he would send Larry and a guy named Johnny Vasquez after the lucky winner, only they weren't that lucky any more. Larry and this Vasquez would pistol whip them, drag them into an alley and leave them there.

The law got tired of the complaints and began to watch the place, one night there a big winner and after he left, Larry and Vasquez followed him. They weren't happy to just pistol whip him they beat the man to death and left him in the alley. The law found the body and came looking for both of them. I was serving drinks at one of the tables when the officers came to arrest them. Larry said he would go quietly then he grabs that little sneak pistol under his jacket and shoots one man in the face the other officer didn't have a chance, he was facing Vasquez when Larry shot him twice in the back. I heard both Vasquez and Larry headed to Mexico trying to hide from the law.

I left Louisiana and came her trying to outrun my past.

I didn't want anyone to know what I had been or where I had come from. I bought the store and changed my name, hoping no one would ever find out but I knew the second I saw Larry that I had to tell someone, he is a murderer and he is here to kill someone! With a price on his head he would never take a chance on coming here and getting caught if he were not being paid."

Ashley was near hysteria, Schon could feel her body shaking as he put his arm around her shoulders.

"I'll walk you home he said and then I want you to take the day off and stay out of sight.

If you know him he'll know you, Rog and I will handle Larry Cheatham, and if we can find a warrant on him we'll arrest him if not we'll keep a watch on him and if he blinks we'll know it." "Just don't let know him know that you told us anything, I don't want him to know we are keeping a watch on him and I don't want him to up and vanish."Rog started going through the old warrants in the Marshal's desk trying to find the picture of a man that fit Larry's description as Schon walked Ashley to her home. "Dang," Rog muttered to himself, "nobody leaves warrants laying around for five or ten years, why couldn't they have come two or three years ago? I can't find anything on Vasquez and I doubt if I'll find anything on this Cheatham fellow either. Schon entered the room and caught the last of Rog's complaint, Fine send a telegraph to a judge or marshal in Louisiana and see if one of them can come up with an Expectation Warrant. If they can we will arrest the man before the Marshal even gets back, if not we'll wait and see what he wants to do."
Joe pulled back the reins on the black, riding into a small draw as the Marshal and the roan caught up with him. "Slow down fellow, my old horse ain't used to that kind of running." Joe shrugged, "that ain't running, for the black that was a Sunday stroll and why are you riding a broken down nag on a man hunt anyway?" "He ain't that broke down, besides I like him!" Jim stated, "He's sure footed and wakes up every morning in a good mood unlike some people I know." Joe rode the black out on the east side of the draw and turned to the Marshal, "which way?" he asked. Jim pointed along the shadows, "keep heading east, I figure we'll pick up another set of tracks pretty soon." Joe drew back and slapped the black with the reins again and in a few seconds they were gone throwing a trail of dust and dirt behind them. Joe turned the black heading into another draw and out of sight, "Crap, I might as well be riding alone," Jim thought as he laid the heels of his boots to the roan. Half an hour later he caught up to Joe and the black, this time it wasn't hard to do, Joe sat in the

saddle studying a fresh set of tracks but these weren't the tracks of three riders, they were the tracks of five. "We might as well follow these," the Marshal said, pulling the reins and turning the horse to the south following the new trail. The sun was already dropping below the horizon as the Marshal dismounted, "might as well make camp here," he said, "my old nag has about had it, besides it's as good as a camp spot as we will find in this area. Joe swung down from the black and began to remove the saddle and blanket, "think we'll catch those kids before they make Mexico?" He asked.

The Marshal pulled the saddle and blanket off his own mount, "yep, the way I see it Eric and Nicole broke K.C. out of jail that left his two cousins out of the play." "They are a tight knit bunch and where you see one or two you'll see the others also. The only way they wouldn't have been there helping was if they were busy someplace else." "So where do you think they were?" Joe asked. "Well I think they are taking a herd of cattle across the border. They probably started off before the jail break; it's got to be a small herd if it's just the two of them driving it. K.C. and the rest will try to catch up with them on this side of the border, if not they will meet them on the other side, not a big deal either way." "What about the trail we're following, Joe asked, where do you figure they fit into the deal?"

"Men from the MacCland outfit or the Malloy ranch, maybe both riding together, as neither one wants the girl to take over the ranch," Jim said. "One thing's for sure, it will be the scum of the outfits, men that will kill a woman as easy as a man. They will try to catch them on the Mexican side of the border and bushwhack them then drive off the cattle making it look like a simple rustling job gone bad. They might even bury the bodies hoping no one will ever find out what they've done." Jim took out the makings and began to role a cigarette as Joe gathered some dry limbs from under a mesquite tree to build a fire. After placing a match in the brush pile Joe reached over and picked up the tobacco,

"I always heard a lawman's not allowed to cross the border, some kind of agreement between the U.S. and Mexico, but you're planning on us crossing over anyway ain't you?"

Jim shrugged his shoulders, "unless you got some of objection!" Joe thought about it shrugged his shoulders and said "I ain't the one who's gonna lose my job." After placing some rocks around the fire Jim picked up a large cast iron skillet and placed it over the fire, filled it half full of water and added a hand full of coffee grounds, "Besides the gambler, you ever killed anyone before?" Jim asked. Joe had a haunted look as he stared into the campfire, "I was in the war," he said. Joe never said which side he fought for or how many battles he had been in or how many he had killed, he seem as if he was suddenly somewhere else.

Jim studied the clothes of the man trying to figure out which side he had fought for, an emblem, a rank, or anything that connected him to the service but he finally gave up, he couldn't find anything on Joe that showed if he had fought for the north or the south or if he was an officer or foot soldier. Placing his handkerchief over a tin cup worked as a filter to keep the grounds out as Joe poured a cup of coffee.

No one had to tell him it was going to be bitter, he had never tasted a decent cup of coffee that had been boiled over a campfire. Pouring the last of the liquid on the ground he laid some bacon in the skillet and placed it back on the fire, "if you don't think they will try anything until after they cross the border why don't we ride ahead and wait for them to come to us?" "That's kind of what I was thinking, Jim admitted, I just wanted to hang back long enough to find out how many we were going to have to deal with."

Joe shoved the stirrup under the saddle and spread his bed role and then took a biscuit out of the bag Marilyn had packed. Joe tore it open and placed some of the bacon between the slices and began to eat hungrily. "See you in the morning," he said as he pulled his hat down over his eyes and chewed on the biscuit. "Great, he runs off and leaves me all day with no one to talk to but my horse and now he falls asleep like I don't exist!" Jim spread his bed role and lay back staring at the stars, "I would rather be home with my wife," he thought as his eyes closed and he fell asleep. That night as Jim slept Joe got up from the homemade bed and snuck out of camp. He was bare footed but felt it was better to step on a snake than to awaken the Marshal. Fifty to a hundred yards from camp he stopped and began the nightly ritual, first he began to draw with one hand then the other, turning his left hand palms out drawing from the cross draw position, getting faster and faster with each draw. It felt good to be working with the pistols again and not grabbing empty air. "Can you hit like that?" even before the words were finished Joe had spun around dropped into the gunfighters stance crouching low with the knees bent as the right hand hovered over the hammer ready to fan in a moment's notice, the pistol in Joe's left hand was pointed at the center of the Marshal's chest, the hammer was drawn back and ready to fire. Jim swallowed hard, even in the cool night air Jim knew he was beginning to sweat; he had never been this close to death. "Don't let that hammer slip," he said looking into the barrel of the forty-four, knowing the only thing standing between life and death was the weight of the thumb holding the hammer back. The barrel of the revolver lifted as the hammer lowered. "That's a good way to get your head blown off!" Joe said as he placed the gun back into the holster. "I thought you weren't a gunfighter," Jim said trying to shake the feeling of doom that had settled on him after staring into the barrel of the forty-four. Joe held a look of rage and said, "And I didn't think you were an idiot!"Joe growled. Part of the anger was from the fact he had almost killed an innocent man and partly because he had let another man sneak up behind him. Both men glared at each other in the dark of the night.

CHAPTER FIVE

Paul stood behind the bar polishing a beer glass as Larry Cheatham walked in. Paul was thinking, "If I could save enough money I could buy the women out and if I was the owner I could rip out the kitchen and maybe bring in a couple of Nita's girls. I could really make some money then!" Lost in the day dream, Paul paid no attention to his new customer.

Larry was growing impatient even as he walked to the table. The whisky he had consumed the night before still gnawed at his belly. "Hey you wake up," as he sat at a table. "Bring me a beer and a waitress," Larry ordered hoping the alcohol and food would settle the queasy feeling he had in the pit of his stomach. Paul brought the beer and set it in front of the customer, "A waitress will be here in a second," he said as he went back to his day dream. Sheila came bouncing up like a school girl, giddy at the thought of a large tip, after all the man was dressed in a fine suit and showed the makings of a gentleman. "What will it be?" she asked with a big smile on her face thinking maybe this was the man who was going to take her away from the life of a waitress. She was tired of standing on her feet all day listening to the drunken cowboys whooping it up at the bar and she was tired of cleaning the dung off the floor as they made their way to the restaurant. One day she planned to marry but she wanted a man that had never punched cattle or dug in the ground to plant a crop. She wanted a man of style one who knew what an opera was and not a man who's idea of a night on the town consisted of listening to a half dressed woman sing buffalo gal won't you come out tonight or shooting cow chips from a fence post by the light of the moon! She was hoping and praying this was that man. "Give me some fried potatoes, eggs and a cup of coffee," Larry said finishing the last of the beer. Sheila turned quick flinging her skirt as she did showing a flash of leg and the smile she wore left no doubt this had been done on purpose.

Paul brought the coffee and placed it on the table in front of the man in the suit, "Heck if I had a suit like that maybe Sheila would be flirting with me," Paul thought as he went back to the bar. "One day I'm gonna buy me one and find out." Paul had absolutely no hope; he was big and ugly with a scar running down his face, a bartender's mentality and a bad temper. None of the waitress wanted anything to do with him.

They dreamed of the day when Marilyn could buy his share of the restaurant and close the bar and drive the drunks out of the place and be rid of the bad tempered bartender for good. Sheila brought the meal Larry had ordered to his table and set them down and pulled a chair up for herself, "Where do you hail from?" she asked as she set across from him. Larry studied the young waitress, she would never know if he lied. "Chicago, Illinois," he said but this was no lie, Larry had been born in Chicago and lived most of his life in the streets and back alleys of the Great Lakes water fronts. He killed his first man there, it hadn't been a fair fight, the man staggered out of one of the local taverns too drunk to walk, and Larry walked up behind him and slid a knife in his back. He would have gotten away with it too if he was a lucky man but he wasn't. One of the man's friends had come out of the bar looking for him and saw Larry with the knife in his hand and the man started to yell. People came out of the bar with clubs and knives ready to avenge their fallen comrade! He managed to out run the lynch mob that night so the next day he moved to Louisiana trying to escape the law and the mob hoping no one would find out about his past.

But back alleys and water fronts were in Larry's blood and it didn't take long before he was back in the alleys and saloons waiting for another victim. Larry knew he was good with a knife or a gun and killing a man or a woman meant no more to him than dealing from the bottom of the deck or using loaded dice! Sheila set at the table watching as he sopped up the last of the eggs with a biscuit, "I would take a little more coffee," he said as he wiped at the plate.

Sheila got up and swung her skirt again trying to show even more of the young slender legs she was so proud of. She went to the pot belly stove and picked up the hot pot of coffee eager to serve the man she wanted so desperately to know. As she was returning to the table Mike and Roy came through the swinging doors and both men looked as if they had just been stomped on by a charging bull!

Roy walked up to the bar and removed two cups, "we'll have some of that," he said as they sat at the table nearest the kitchen. Sheila poured both men a cup of the mud and carried the pot to Larry's table. After pouring him a cup she sat back down eyes shining at the thought of being with a real gentleman. Roy knocked on the kitchen door, "Mom!" he said his voice barely above a whisper. There was no answer so he knocked again even louder, Mike held his head as the knocking continued, "Not so loud!" he complained, "my head is killing me!" Roy tried to smile through blood shot eyes, "that will teach you to mix bad whisky with day old beer!" he said winching through the pain in his own head.

Marilyn came to the door, "What do you two want?" she said irritated at the behavior of the two men. Mike laid his head on the table, "Please not so loud!" he whispered, "My head is going to explode."

Marilyn slapped the table with the palm of her hand and the room echoed from the force of the blow. Mike sat up as if he had been shot, winching in pain. "What will you have!" she repeated even louder laughing inwardly at the misery the boys had brought on themselves. Roy answered, "biscuits and gravy and tell Terry please no lumps in the gravy, my stomach couldn't handle them this morning!" Marilyn left the boys to their misery as she went back into the kitchen.

Marilyn screamed at the top of her lungs, "biscuits and gravy and please hold the lumps, their poor little old bellies can't take them this morning," she was laughing at the thought of the men cringing from the sound of her voice. She wore a big smile as she winked at Eloise and began to bang pots and pans knowing the pain she was inflecting in the young cowboys. Later Marilyn came out of the kitchen to find the men had taken their cups and moved to the far corner of the restaurant away from the banging and clatter of the kitchen. Marilyn walked up and slammed the metal plates on the table, "where's your other partner," she asked more to torment and annoy the young men than out of any real curiosity she might have had. "He went out hunting last night and we ain't seen him since," Roy answered. It was Marilyn's turn to be upset, "are you two nuts!" she screamed, "you let a drunken man go hunting in the middle of the night by himself!"
Roy and Mike both began to laugh even through their pain, "heck," Mike said, "He went hunting that new girl that went to work at Nita's place last night and besides even if we found him I don't think he was gonna let us drag him home!"

"Yeah, Roy put in, he has eyes for that little skirt! "I think her name is Michelle." Marilyn turned and walked away from the table red faced and angry, "one of these days I am gonna learn not to talk to this trio of rowdy cowboys." Even in their hung over state they had gotten the better of her!"

"Who are the jokesters?" Larry asked, the blond haired waitress sitting across from him. Sheila wanted to please the man in front of her and this was her chance, the older one is Roy, the other is called Mike.

One of their partners is missing his name is Bobby. They like to come in here and give Marilyn a hard time whenever they get a chance."

"Why?" Larry asked. "Don't rightly know, I think those boys all secretly like her but they don't want the other to know, and as far as Marilyn is concerned I think they wish she was their mother.

They know how far they can go before she smacks them. "Sheila laughed,

Larry leaned back in his chair, "so these were the men he had come up from Mexico to gun down or run off," They were young and reckless , they carried tied down pistols but like most cowboys it was more for show than anything else. They might take a shot at a snake or lizard once a month then they would probably miss! Larry doubted if they ever practiced with them and even if they did, it wouldn't be more than a few minutes a week. Like most cowboys they were more at home with a rope or a whip.

"Heck, it would be easy money, maybe later he might still be able to pick up a few extra dollars after he took care of the saddle tramp!"

Sheila almost squealed in delight as Larry laid a five dollar gold piece on the table, "keep the change," he said as he got up and walked towards a group of men playing cards. Sheila was all smiles as she picked up the gold piece and slid it into her pocket.

It took Nita's girls all week working day and night to earn that much money and she had made it in a few minutes! Roy and Mike finished their breakfast and they were getting up to leave as Larry was sitting down at the card table, "Deal me in," he said watching for any reaction from the men playing. "After this hand," the voice was that of the dealer. Four cards already lay in front of the men playing, "Sure," Larry answered , knowing full well he couldn't start in the middle of a hand. They were playing five card draw and Larry studied every hand as they played. He was not watching the cards but looking at the hands of the players. They were the hard calloused hands of a working man. The hands of men who tore rocks out of the ground and carried them across the fields, who fought the handles of plows and held tight the leather reins of the plow horses that fell timber for a living. They used doubled bladed axes and played tug of war at the end of a strong rope with half wild cattle and horses.

These men dug fence post holes with a long handled shovels and strung barbed wire down the fence line with the barbs digging deep into the leather gloves they wore, tearing away at the flesh and muscle beneath. These were men of strength and character; they were not the soft nimble hands of a gambler.

Larry studied the faces of the men playing as well looking for any sign of a professional gambler but found none. They were tanned with a rough leather like texture to the skin. "These men wouldn't know a marked deck if I used a pick axe to mark them with," Larry thought as the dealer began to shuffle the deck. Only after studying the men, did Larry look at the deck of cards; they were exactly what he thought they would be, marked, not on purpose but by time. Some of them had faded while others had small nicks or cuts. These cards looked as if they had ridden in a saddle bag at one time or another.

Some cowboy had spent a lot of lonely nights playing solitaire with them and it showed. Larry had grown up in water front saloons and in twenty minutes he would know every little nick in the pack and which nick went to which card. Maybe he would throw a few hands making the suckers think they had a patsy. After thirty minutes of playing and Larry had won his second hand Bobby walked into the room like a young man with the world at his fingertips. He sat at the table nearest the kitchen and banged on the wall with his fist, yelling, "hey mom!" at the top of his lungs. Marilyn came into the room like her dress was on fire,

"What do you want!" she said clearly angry at the young man. Bobby answered, "Biscuits and gravy please," with a heartwarming smile.

"I guess you want me to hold the lumps right?" she spat at him. "Now why would I want you to do that?" Bobby said, "If you did that I wouldn't get any gravy!" Marilyn went into the kitchen and threw a pot against the wall,

"Sometimes those boys make me want to bang my head into the wall or better yet their heads!" she grumbled at Eloise. She then picked up the order and walked back to the table, "here!" she hissed placing food in front of Bobby.

'Why aren't you hung over like your buddies?" she asked. "Because that little old girl wouldn't let me drink whisky in bed!" he complained. "Poor Bobby," Marilyn said trying to get the better of the lone cowboy, "I bet she even made you take off your spurs!" "Yes!" Bobby said, "But I didn't mind, she was a right pretty girl!" Marilyn's face turned beet red as she turned and walked back into the kitchen. Eloise watched as Marilyn began to slam her head into the wall," when will I learn?" She said over and over.

Jim woke up to the sounds and smell of bacon frying in the pan, "Dang that smells good," he said as Joe handed him a cup of hot coffee, "You believe in sleeping late, don't you?" Joe asked as he began rolling up his bed.

Jim took a sip of the coffee and pulled some of the bacon from the pan then slid it between two halves of a day old biscuit,

"I thought these things were hard yesterday," he complained taking a large bite out of the bread.

"Quit complaining and let's go, I'm in a hurry to get to the border." Joe placed the saddle on the back of the black and began to tighten the cinch,

"What's the hurry?" Jim asked, chewing on a tough piece of the bacon.

"I want to get to the border before the rest of them do, Joe stated, I'd like to be able to scout the area before they arrive and figure out the best place for an ambush to take place. Maybe even find a place where we can pull an ambush of our own without getting our heads shot off!" Jim threw the last of biscuit in the fire and began kicking sand into the flames,

"Great, the first thing I wanted to do this morning was jump out of bed and make a mad dash for the border, why can't people get up at a descent time anyway,"

Jim complained mockingly as he put the saddle on the Roan. Joe sat in the saddle watching as Jim tightened the cinch,

"Your right," he said "that horse does get up in a better mood than some people I know." Jim threw his leg over the saddle,

"Oh shut up and let's go," he said digging the spurs on his boots into the side of the animal.

Joe drew back the reins of the black and gave him a slap and within second Jim was left behind, "I hate that horse," Jim said as he once again found himself riding in the dust trail of the black.

Rick Yarlboro hated his life, he hated camping and he hated the men he was with, in fact he hated everything and everyone. "Get up you bunch of idiots, we ain't got all day!" he growled, kicking at the feet of the man next to him.

The Mexican called Frankie sat up in a bad mood of his own, "back off! He warned "We ain't planning nothing until we reach the border and I ain't had any coffee yet!" Rick may have hated every man he was with but he knew better than to cross the Mexican. The so called posse consisted of the scum of both outfits, three of men were from the Rocking 'R' and two from the Malloy ranch. They all had one order from the boss; they were to follow the young outlaws into the Mexican desert and bushwhack the small group and then bury the bodies.

Rick knew that Skip MacCland hated Don Malloy with a passion it only made sense that a common bond had brought the men together. Maybe when this was over he would find out what that bond was and who knows, maybe he could use it to his advantage. Until then he had to put up with men like Frankie. One thing he knew Frankie would never face him with a gun, Frankie was a knife fighter and a sneak, and he would just as well cut a man's throat in his sleep as face him! One day he might blow the back of Frankie's head off but until then he had to sleep with one eye open.

"Maybe I ought to kill the Mexican now," Rick was thinking as he watched the back of the man sipping coffee. Frankie turned and looked back, "did you sleep good amigo?" he asked. It was as if he could read the thoughts of the man behind him. Looking into the face of the Mexican made him nervous. Rick knew the answer before he asked but he had to do or say something to shake the queasy feeling growing in his stomach, "Did you ever kill a man?" Rick asked. The Mexican began to take on a lost look, it was as if he was enjoying the memories, "Si, amigo, many times!" he replied. "Did you ever kill a woman?" Rick persisted. This time the Mexican pulled the heavy Bowie knife from the scabbard on his belt and began to slide his thumb along the blade. Rick had seen this look before; it reminded him of a snake just before it strikes,

"Si, amigo, with the knife!" he said staring at the blade. "It doesn't bother you to kill a woman?" Rick asked. "Man, woman it makes no difference, sometimes the woman, she screams a little more," Frankie said still playing with the edge of the blade.

Rick put a saddle on the bronco he was riding. Once he had been a top hand and a real cowboy but by now he had been busted up too many times. He was old and tired and he couldn't wrestle the young strong calves anymore or spend days in the saddle. Now he knew why the owner of the Rocking 'R' had kept him around, he was considered one of the scum, a man to send on the trash missions, a man that would do whatever he was told. "If I was younger I'd ride out of here," he thought as he mounted the horse and rode south towards the Mexican desert. Frankie slid the Bowie knife back into the scabbard, "Let us ride amigo," he said rising as he spoke. "We have a busy day today, yes?"

Larry woke up early that morning he had a busy day planed. "Get off me!" he said slapping the leg of the girl sleeping next to him, both were still half groggy from the whisky they had consumed the night before. "Leave me alone!" Trish said rolling over to get away from the abuse. Larry stood in front of the mirror admiring his reflection, "Today is going to be a great day," he thought as he combed his hair. He was down a couple of hundred dollars at the poker tables but that didn't matter, he had his sucker cowboys lining up to set at his table hoping to get their hands on some of the free money. Today it was his turn, he was going to take them for every nickel they had. Larry slid the hide out pistol in place and pulled the jacket over it making sure the bulge from the handle didn't show.

CHAPTER SIX

Paul pulled a glass from under the bar and filled it from the tap, "here's your breakfast," he said setting the cold beer in front of the gambler. Picking up the glass, Larry studied the room; men were already at the card tables but they were the small time players, men who played for nickels and dimes, he wanted the real players, men who would bet their lives on the flip of a card.

Sheila brought a cup of coffee and set it in front of him, "What can I get you?" she asked, still remembering the five dollar tip. Larry took his eyes off the game long enough to smile at the waitress, "I'll have steak and eggs with fried potatoes." Sheila turned and tried to flip her skirt even more than last time, it never hurt to advertise and she could use another five dollar gold piece.

Larry watched the game as he waited for breakfast, it would be easy to pick up a few dollars but it was not worth the risk. Sheila brought the meal and a cup of coffee for herself then sat down at the table across from him.

Larry was too deep in thought to pay the waitress any attention, "Are you gonna be here long?" she asked trying to draw the man's attention back to her. "No, not long," he said as he slid another five dollar gold piece across the table and got to leave. Sheila wanted to know more about the man but he was in no mood to talk, Larry had seen a sucker come through the doors and he wanted to be the one to fleece him.

Taking a deck of cards from his jacket pocket, Larry began to set up a game of solitaire at one of the card tables, "let the suckers come to you," he thought as he began to flip the cards over. It wasn't long before the table filled with men looking for a quick buck a chance to meet lady luck.

Skip MacCland placed two cards on the table and Don Malloy followed suit. The store keeper and the banker had already dropped out of the hand. Larry knew Skip held two pair kings and sixes. Don was bluffing with a pair of nines; this was the kind of game Larry lived for. Larry dealt two cards to Skip and watching the reflection on the table Larry knew the ace and the four would do him no good. Malloy received a queen and a three, no help for the pair of nines. Skip raised a hundred dollars and Malloy matched the bet and raised another hundred, Larry fumbled with his cards not sure if he should match the bet or fold.

There was a lot of money on the table three deuces was not a strong hand but it would beat any the others held. Larry matched the bet and called, Skip took the loss with grace, folded the money in front of him and stood up, "that finished me!" he said as Larry pulled in the pot and started to fold the bills. "Where are you going?" Malloy asked fuming at the thought that Larry was leaving too and with his money.

"No use staying," Larry said, "MacCland is out of the game and the money is gone!" Malloy pulled a wad of bills from his shirt pocket and threw them on the table, "sit down!" he instructed, "I want a chance to win my money back.

This is what Larry wanted, what he had hoped someone stupid enough and mad enough to bet everything he owned on the flip of a card! When it was Larry's turn to deal Malloy was going to lose everything he owned! The banker and the store keeper had already stepped out of the game and Skip was out as well, this was going to be a game of one on one. In his enraged state Malloy had lost all sense of reason and played the game like an amateur, betting high on a single pair trying to bluff his way through and Larry knew the man was bluffing and bet even higher building the pot. Spectators circled the table watching the amateur lose hand after hand to the professional. Skip MacCland was no coward and no idiot, he knew Larry was a gunman and he had found out the hard way that he was a card shark.

Skip was good with a gun but he didn't think he could beat Larry in a fair fight so bowing out of the game seemed like the smartest thing to do.

Malloy was not that smart, he was throwing good money after bad in an attempt to win what he had lost. With every hand Malloy became more and more reckless. Like the rest of the spectators Skip watched as the pile of money in front of Malloy dwindled to nothing.

With a scream, Malloy jumped up from the table, the movement was so fast the chair behind him flipped over and crashed to the floor.

The long barrel of Malloy's revolver was starting to clear the holster as Larry's right hand went for the hide out pistol under his left shoulder.

The shots almost sounded like one as fire erupted out of the short barrel of Larry's pistol moments before the flame and lead flew from the longer barrel of the revolver.

Malloy may have had nothing more than a mild concussion as the heavy lead from the short gun struck him a glancing blow along the forehead sending blood, flesh and hair flying as the shell dug a shallow trench along his skull.

Malloy's head slammed to the right as his own bullet tunneled its way into the thick wooden card table in front of him.

Larry's hand fanned the hammer of the short barreled revolver and two more flashes of flame erupted from the barrel as lead slammed into Don Malloy's chest, shattering the bone and gristle as they made their way into his heart.

No one knows if Malloy felt the sledge hammer like blows to the chest as the bullets passed through his body or if he was even awake as he lay on his back staring at the ceiling above.

Larry ejected the spent shells from the pistol and started to replace them when he felt the cold steel of the gun being pressed into his back! He could even feel the sight on the barrel that dug into his flesh, "you even breathe and you're dead!" Rog said.

The cocking of the hammer sounded like the beating of a drum to Larry's ears. Schon ran through the door with his own pistol in his hand.

"Nobody moves!" he shouted. Covering the room, under different circumstances Rog would have laughed at the older man but he knew there was a cold blooded killer in his sights and was glad for any help he could get. "Cover him," Rog said as he reached around Larry and took the revolver from his hand. "Let's go!" Rog said shoving him towards the swinging doors. "What about my money?" Larry said starting to turn towards the table.

"You touch it you die!" The cold tone in the young deputy's voice told Larry all he needed to know. The young man was walking on egg shells with the slightest move the gambler knew he was going to die.

"Paul, gather up the money and bring it to the jail!" Schon instructed,

"The rest of you men drag the body down to the undertakers." "Marilyn has got enough problems around here without him bleeding all over the floor!"

Men were lifting the body even as the two deputies escorted the gunman out of the room. Schon locked the cell door as Larry stretched out on the bunk, "you can't hold me and you know it!" "There was a whole room full of witnesses including the deputy," he said as he turned over to wait.

Skip MacCland had never been so angry in his life. True he hated Don Malloy, he even dreamed of the day when he could put a bullet in the man but he didn't want it to be today. Skip watched as the men carried Malloy's body out of the Crooked Horn. "Maybe it won't be so bad," he thought, remembering the men he and Malloy had sent out to kill the girl and her companions.

With Malloy dead and the girl out of the picture the Malloy ranch would go up for sale or be auctioned off by the county, either way he could pick the ranch and the cattle up cheap! No one in the area had the funds to bid against him and even if they did have the money his men would see to it they didn't make a bid! The only thing that stood between him and owning all the grazing land in the valley was the three young cowboys!

Skip MacCland sat behind the desk in his office, "Those stupid deputies wouldn't let Larry out of jail for love or money."

He had tried bail but they would have none of it, they were going to hold the prisoner until a higher authority showed up and they didn't care if it was the Marshal or the judge as long as they didn't have to take any of the responsibility.

There was no way the Marshal would let him out of jail without a court order, so it was up to Skip to make sure Larry was released. Skip didn't care if Larry had killed two men in some other state, he didn't care if he had killed Don Malloy in the middle of the Crooked Horn restaurant and he didn't care if he had killed a hundred men, in fact the more the merrier, it just meant he was good at his job and right now Skip wanted Larry out of jail it didn't matter if it was for a day, and hour or a minute, as long as he had time to kill the man that had ridden the black into town!

Skip called to four of the men standing outside his office. They were a sorry looking lot for cowboys; they looked more like the kind of me who would hang around the bars at night rolling drunks and wino's for the change in their pockets. Skip had plans to take over the valley but with men like these on the payroll it wasn't going to be easy to do. As the ranch grew he would have to replace them with better men but for now they would have to do.

The judge will be coming within the next day or so and I want you men to watch the roads for him and stop him then bring him here to me. The man who brings him to me will get a hundred dollar bonus. Skip watched the men leave, they were scum but they were the kind of scum he needed. For a hundred dollars they would bring him their own mothers!
  Skip knew the judge would be standing before him within the next few days.
Marilyn was tired of the killing, tired of the drunks and tired of dealing with men like Paul and she was going to get rid of them all!
  "How much do you want for your share of the restaurant?" she asked the blond haired giant. Until that moment Paul had never thought of selling his share of the restaurant, he had his own dreams. With a thousand dollars he could build his own bar with one of those fancy mirrors brought out from back east and faro tables, heck he could even build a couple of extra rooms for some of the girls he would hire, he might even compete with Nita's business.
  "I want a thousand dollars," he said, "and the mirror over the bar." It was high, more than twice what his share was worth but Marilyn just turned and said, "I'll be back later," as she went out the door on her way to the bank. She hated to borrow money but it would be worth it to be rid of the killing.
  Just as Skip thought, it didn't take long for his men to bring Judge Hicks to him. "How much does it pay?" he asked looking at the man behind the desk. Judge hicks had heard the men talking on the way back to the ranch, if Skip MacCland was willing to pay one hundred dollars to this kind of scum to bring him to the ranch then surely he was worth a lot more.
Skip counted out a thousand dollars in hundred dollar bills and laid it on the desk, counting the bribes and kickbacks, that was more money than the judge would make in a year.
"What do you want done?" Hicks asked as he picked up the money.

"Not much," Skip began, "All you have to do is let Larry Cheatham out of jail." "A thousand dollars was a lot of money as far as the judge was concerned and it was more than enough, "When do you want him out?" "As soon as possible! Skip said, He has a lot of work to do." Skip wanted the gunman on the black horse killed and the three cowboys killed or driven out of town, all his plans hung on the gunman in the cell. As Judge Hicks left his office Skip leaned back in his chair, he was the only man in the country that knew who the rider on the black horse was.

True they had only met for an instant but that instant had been long enough to burn the man's image into his memory forever!

Years ago, Skip had looked through a pair of field glasses to see a small insignificant man wearing Captain's bars leading a troop of Calvary soldiers and the solid blue colors of the uniform made the man look even smaller. Some of the men were already wounded, wearing blood red bandages. It would be an easy victory for the confederate soldiers under his command.

His men were scattered out in the woods waiting for the cavalry to pass by then they would take the Captain and his men from the rear cutting them to pieces before they knew what happened. It was a perfect plan and it had been calculated with a precision that comes only with the experience of men who had done this kind of thing before. Hiding behind trees and brush his men cut loose with the rifles dropping the union soldiers from their saddles with the very first volley as their shells found their marks. Everything was going fine until the Captain rode back, he had looked like a man possessed as he drew the rifle out of the scabbard.

Skips men had begun to flee even before the fire power of the captain's rifle was emptied! Man after man fell trying to escape the deadly shells as they found their marks. Skip had never feared man or beast until that moment.

The Captain slid the rifle back into its scabbard and pulled the pistols from holsters around his hip, fire and flame erupted as he sighted on the men now too terrified to lift their heads. Skip lay on his belly watching as his men were cut down, he knew on day the wild man with the flaming pistols would take his life.
  The Captain stopped at the rear of the column he looked like a protecting angel or a rampaging demon straight from the pits of hell; the pistols in his hands were protecting the remains of his fallen men. The thought of the battle put a fear into Skip that he had not known since the war. For the second time in his life he knew real fear. The judge didn't know it but Skip would have paid ten times that much to see Larry Cheatham freed!

CHAPTER SEVEN

Frankie kicked dirt at the campfire as the rest of the men saddled their horses; Frankie felt at home with these men, they were men like him, cruel and vicious, all except Rick. Frankie couldn't stand the sight of the man. Rick was a decent enough kind of man that had hit on hard times. He was not a cold hearted murderer and didn't belong with the kind of men Frankie liked to ride with.

"One day he might slit his throat as he slept," Frankie thought as he threw his leg over the mount. Rick couldn't help but shutter at the thought of the Mexican behind his back. He may not be able to use a pistol but anyone could use a rifle. Rick pulled his mount over to wait for the rest of the men, "Mi amigo," Frankie said as he rode up, "you decided to wait for us that is good, si?" "One day I'm going to have to kill this guy!" Rick decided, "Before he kills me!"

"Si mi amigo," he said, "I decided to wait for my friend," Rick, pulled his horse up next to Frankie's. Together they rode a circle around the herd of cattle and the men they had been following.

Joe sat on the black staring across the river, "What do you think?" Jim asked watching the man in front of him. "I think they will want to be ten miles on the other side of the border before they try anything," Joe answered.

"They won't want a border patrol from either side to hear the battle or to come across the bodies. That will mean pushing the cattle two more days." "What will we do between now and then?" Jim asked. Joe looked at the Marshal, "you really were a clod hopping farmer weren't you!"

"Well I said I was didn't I?" Jim said "What did you expect?" "We scout the area and find the best place for an ambush and then we find the best place to ambush the ones pulling the ambush."

"That won't take two days, will it?" Jim asked.

"No," Joe replied, "we have two days, the kids bringing the cattle in will be here by then and they have been here before or they wouldn't be bringing them into a desert like this.

They know where the water is and they will know every nook and draw within a fifty mile radius. They will hide the herd in those draws as they move them deeper into Mexico.

Some of the men following them will know the area just as well as they do and some may have even been born here.

We have two days to learn as much as we can about the terrain, where the watering holes are and the best way to drive a herd of stolen cattle."

"We need to find out where they are likely to pull an ambush without the Federalies or the Rangers finding the bodies or hearing the gunfire."

"So let's get moving," Joe said, "we have two days to find out what most men couldn't find out in a month!"

With that Joe slapped the black with the reins and started across the river, soon they would be in Mexico. Jim watched the back of the rider in front of him and wondered again who he really was. He was certainly a leader of men as he has shown here. Jim was curious and was willing to let Joe lead. He had a feeling there was a lot more to this man than he wanted anyone to know! Jim spurred his horse and thoughtfully followed the black.

The sun was setting below the horizon as Joe swung down from the black, "We'll camp here," he said as he was un-cinching the saddle and letting it slide to the ground. "There is better grass on the north side of the hill," Jim said still sitting on his own mount.

"You want a cold camp?" Joe asked as he gathered small pieces of wood to build a fire. "What do you mean?" Jim asked swinging down from the roan. "I mean the hill will hide the light of the fire. If we camp on the other side we have a cold camp or the flames will be seen for miles so it's here or a cold camp, the choice is yours." Jim liked the idea of hot food in his belly, "I guess we'll camp here," he said, pulling the cooking pot from the war bag behind his saddle.
Frankie had the same idea only they were on the north side of the river following the herd of cattle.
 Sipping from the hot metal cup he watched Rick as he stripped the saddle from his horse, "Coffee, mi amigo?" he said as Rick walked up to the fire, "Maybe tonight I kill him?" Frankie thought as he handed the pot over to the man in front of him. Rick hated the men he rode with and especially the Mexican named Frankie! When this is over he was going to keep on riding and California was sounding good, maybe he would try his luck in the goldfields. Rick leaned his saddle against the butt of a dead stump, maybe no one would notice the alarm system he was building as he kicked the dried out limbs in a circle around the area where he was going to make his bed. Rick pulled the pistol from his belt and held it in his hand as he threw the blanket over his body. But somebody did notice! The Mexican watched with the eyes of a man seeing his plans destroyed. It was as if Rick was reading his mind. Tonight Rick would sleep with one eye open, there was no reason for anyone to walk near the sleeping man and if a twig so much as snapped Rick would come up firing. Frankie would have to come up with a different plan if he wanted to get rid of him! Joe sat across from the fire and watched as Jim chewed on a hard tack biscuit, he admitted he was no gunman; heck he could barely read signs and didn't know how to set up camp. "Why would a man like this become a marshal?" he wondered. Finely his curiosity got the better of him, "Why did you become a Marshal?" he asked.

"Didn't have any choice," Jim stated, "I had a good crop in the ground and everything was going great for the first time in my life. I was going to be able to pay everything off and be out of debt. I planned on marrying Sherlene and expanding, maybe buy a larger piece of land and get out of farming!" he said. "Maybe buy a few head of cattle and go into ranching. I had my life all planned out but a fire came through and burned me out, the house the barn everything. If I was going to stay in the valley I had to find a job.

I'm no cowboy and I'm no banker, for me this was the only job open!" "What's so important about staying in the valley?" Joe asked, even in the darkness Joe could see the crimson color come to the Marshal's face. "Sherlene didn't want to leave her family and there was no way I was going to leave her, the Marshal's job was open and I took it." "What about you?" Jim asked. "Nothing much to tell to tell, I was a rancher in Oklahoma." "That is not what I meant! What I am trying to find out is how you came to have that monster under you?" Jim said pointing at the black.

"Not much to it," Joe said, "I just through a rope around his neck!" "Even I ain't stupid enough to believe that!" Jim said. Joe shrugged, "To tell the truth I sold the ranch and what cattle I had and was on my way to the gold fields in California when I came across the black, he was leading a herd of wild horses. The minute I saw him I knew the gold fields would have to wait. That old horse of mine would never have caught up to the black and even if it did that monster would have killed him so I started to follow the wild herd.

Chris-crossing in front of them and letting them catch my scent, letting them get used to the idea that I was around. I would ride up wind anything to let them know I was there. The one thing I had plenty of was time so day after day I circled the herd getting closer every day. When they spooked and ran I just followed the tracks until I caught up. After a while they got used to me and let me get close enough to reach out and touch some of the horses but I never could get close enough to the black to throw a rope and even if I did he would have kicked my horse out from under me so I bided my time cause I knew one day he would make a mistake and I would be there."

"What kind of mistake did he make?" Jim asked. "He went swimming!" Joe said, "That's all it took!" "One day he started across a river and when he was about half way there I rode up and pitched my rope as quick as I could and I tied that rope to a good sized sapling, then I threw another rope around his neck, he couldn't make the other bank with two ropes around his neck and treading water so he turned around and headed back. I kept pulling him down river with my old horse until I had both ropes snugged up then I tied the second rope to another tree. Those trees had enough give to keep him from choking himself but still managed to keep the ropes tight. I built a make shift corral right there around the black and there was nothing he could do about it! After I put a saddle on him we went at it, right there in the middle of that corral!" Jim shook his head, "That is a lot of work for one horse!" "Yes," Joe said looking deep in thought remembering how many times the black had thrown him, how many times he had tried to stomp him and how many times he had to force himself to climb back into the saddle knowing that one hard jump, one twist or kick could snap his back like a twig! "I knew I could be thrown and stomped and I would have spent my last few days suffering and alone, my only company the animal that had killed me but he was worth it!" he said with admiration at the black.

Jim couldn't believe anyone would risk his life for a horse, any horse but to risk your life for the stick of dynamite Joe rode was beyond belief or reason!

Jim pulled the rifle from his scabbard and laid it beside his saddle, "see you in the morning," he said as he spread his bed role.

Joe walked over and gave the black a pat on the neck, "Some people just don't understand!" he said as he rubbed the top of the horses head.

The black stepped forward shoving Joe with its shoulder and Joe pushed back with his hands shoving against the horse as hard as he could, the black stopped and swung its head slugging Joe like a battering ram, "Their going to kill each other!" Jim thought as he watched the combatants at play. Joe slapped the black on the neck, "I'll see you in the morning old friend," he said as he turned and walked in the dark towards his own bed.

Jim lay with his head on the saddle, "No wonder other horses shied away from the black, the thing was more wild than tame. Its spirit had never been broken and no man had ever ridden the black until it had given in to Joe." Laying there in the dark of the night Jim realized the black had let the man ride him. Somewhere in the mists of the battles they had become friends. It had let Joe ride him because they were two of a kind, kindred spirits, both made of flint and iron and fire. Jim felt a shutter go through his body, he would hate to be the one these two were hunting! As Jim watched, Joe kicked a shallow layer of sand over the fire, filled the skillet full of water and placed it over the pile of sand.

K.C. walked around camp kicking the feet of the sleeping men, "Get up," he was saying, "We got a long ways to go!" Colton and Parker both pulled the cover over their heads, they were tired and worn out, "We've been pushing these cattle for a week!" they complained, "While you been lying around in a jail cell so leave us alone!"

Nicole turned on her charms and her smile, "Come on boys!" she began, "We have to make the border today." She had finely come to the realization that her uncle would have men coming for them and that their lives could be in real danger even her own!

"Please!" she begged, "Get up and help us move the herd!" her voice had cracked and tears were in her eyes. She knew in the back of her mind her uncle was planning to have her killed. Colton and Parker hated to leave the warmth of the blankets but they finally managed to drag themselves up
. Shoving the blankets aside they headed for the fire, a cup of coffee sounded good before starting the daily drive. Parker didn't wait for the hot beverage he threw his saddle over the back of his mount, "Let's get going if we're going to!" he said as he cracked the whip and started the cattle down the draw.

Parker knew it wouldn't be long before the others caught up with him Eric was already pulling the cattle into something that resembled a herd.

If you have never been stabbed it's hard to explain the feel of the knife as the tip of it cuts through the soft layers of skin covering the body, the feeling of the cold metal as it slices through muscle and veins, even the feel of the blade is hard to explain as it grinds like a hacksaw against bone and gristle.

It may be hard to believe but you can even hear the sound of steel striking bone as it passes through the flesh
. It may be hard to explain but Rick knew how it felt because he had been stabbed before! Maybe that was the reason he loathed the Mexican so much!

Frankie liked the knife and the knife brought a fear to Rick that he could not explain. Rick picked up the saddle and joined the rest of the men at the fire. He sat on the saddle as he reached for the coffee pot.

Rick took his eyes off Frankie for only a second but that was all it took, Frankie was tired of waiting, he would have slit Rick's throat last night if it had not been for the stupid sticks around his bed role.

He knew he could not have snuck up on him with the homemade alarm and he would have gotten shot for his trouble if he had; this was the last morning he would have to put up with the man he hated so much!

Frankie sat at the fire on Rick's left side, he held the knife in his right hand hidden behind the left arm, within seconds Rick would be dead! Rick had no third sense and no premonition of danger. As he sat on the saddle, it twisted and he fell to the right,

Frankie swung the knife backhand towards Rick's throat as his butt touched the saddle.

That little twist of the saddle may have saved Rick's life.

It may be hard to explain how the bite of a knife feels but Rick knew and he felt it again as the knife in Frankie hand sliced through the flesh of his shoulder, separating flesh and muscle. He heard the sound of steel striking bone and felt the grinding of the blade.

Rick was falling and he kept falling even as the blade missed it mark.

Frankie was on his feet coming towards the man as Rick landed.

There was no time to draw the pistol at his side so Rick did the only thing he could do he cocked the pistol and lifted his leg and fired through the holster!

The bottom of the holster exploded as the shell flew out of the end. The bullet traveled along Rick's leg and struck Frankie in the center of the stomach, just inches above the belly.

The Mexican looked like a rag doll as the bullet struck the back bone shattering the nerves and transforming him into a cripple.

Frankie lay on the ground looking up as Rick stood over him. Never in his wildest dreams did Frankie think this could happen to him!

Frankie watched as Rick held the weapon in his hand and pointed at the men by the fire. "I will kill anyone that moves!" he screamed as blood ran down his arm and chest.

Rick backed towards the horses keeping his eyes on the men. They were men like Frankie and they were his friends, to turn his back to these men was sure death.

Rick's horse wasn't saddled so he took the first one he came to with a saddle.

It was a paint that looked like it could run and as soon as Rick was in the saddle he put the spurs to the animal trying to put as much distance between him and the men he hated as he possibly could. The wound was deep and blood flowed as he rode Rick knew if he didn't get help soon he would bleed to death.

The only help he could think of was the very men he and the others had come to kill!

One of the men at the fire walked over to Frankie, he even bent down and looked at the wound, "Mi amigo," he said, "You're in a bad way!"

Frankie never saw the man remove the revolver but he heard the clicking of the hammer as it was cocked, and that was the last thing he would ever hear, he never heard the sound of the shot as the shell passed through his skull!

Yes these men were like Frankie and this is what he would have done.

CHAPTER EIGHT

K.C. poured the last of his coffee into the fire and began to kick dirt over the coals when he saw the rider coming across the flats; he was riding straight for the herd.

No one was supposed to know they were there and this upset K.C. The man was not riding fast and hard like a man who was about to attack, in fact he was riding slow and leaning over his saddle like something was wrong.

K.C. drew the rifle from the scabbard and waited as the rider came closer.

K C was not stupid he knew this could be a trick to draw him out into the open and he knew he was hidden by the depth of the draw and he planned on having the first shot. As K C set the sight of the rifle on the man's chest and began to squeeze the trigger he saw the blood on the man's shirt.

This was no trick, even from that distance he could see the open gash and the flow of blood running down the man's arm falling to the ground below his horse.

Rick knew he was close to the rustler's camp, if he could find it he had a chance of survival. They were not the kind of men he had been riding with, these cowboys might be quick with a trigger but they were not murderers.

They were young and reckless but they had courage and strength.

They would face a man straight on, man to man or gun to gun; he knew they wouldn't send someone else to do their dirty work; they were not the kind to stab a man in the back. If he could find their camp he would get help. At one time Rick had been a strong independent person needing nothing and no one but that had been when he was young and strong himself but now he felt like a tired broken down old man.

It was to his shame he found himself seeking help from the very people he had been sent to kill!

As he drew nearer and lifted his head K.C. realized he knew the man, the rider was one of the men that had held a gun on him as Mr. Malloy placed the rope around his neck.

The thought of the rope around his neck sent a cold rage through him.

If ever a man was tempted to shoot a helpless human being it was then, even as his finger tightened on the trigger he could feel the ruff cords of the rope as it was being twisted around his throat!

"You know that would be murder." He knew the voice that came from behind him and he knew it was the truth.

Lowering the rifle K.C. turned to look at Parker,

"I know," he said, "But it was tempting." Parker shook his head, "Well, are you going to call him in or are you going to kill him?"

K.C. lowered the rifle, "Hey Rick, this way!" he yelled. Rick figured he had nothing to lose as he rode the paint towards the speaker, the worst they could do was kill him and without help he would die anyway!

"Climb down and let's have a look at that," Parker said pointing at the cut along Rick's chest and arm.

As Rick leaned forward and swung his leg over the saddle horn a wave of nausea hit and he had to hang on as he slid off the horse.

His legs felt like rubber and they tried to buckle under his weight.

Rick mustered up all the strength he had to stand straight, if he was going to die he wanted to die as the man he had once been.

For a few seconds he managed to stand straight and tall then his legs went out from under him. K.C. and Parker watched as he fell.

"What are we going to do about him?" Parker wanted to know.

K.C. held his hands to his neck remembering the feel of the rope. "We're going to try to patch him up!" "Go through his saddle bags and see if he has anything to drink, he's going to need it when we put the stitches in him."

Parker kicked the sand and dirt off the campfire and added a few branches. Digging a needle out of his saddle bag he laid it in the fire and after it turned crimson red he took a stick placed it on the center of the needle and pushed down bending the needle in a 'C' shape, "This will have to do," Parker said as he raked it from the fire.

They found a bottle of whisky in the stolen saddle bags and held Rick up long enough to pour some of the liquid down his throat, it was a cheap band of whisky and it nearly gagged him as the rot gut hit his stomach.

Rick managed to focus his eyes as the taste of the bottled fire pulled him back to consciousness while K.C. poured the alcohol into the open wound.

Rick set up and began to scream, "What are you trying to do kill me?" he yelled as he felt the burn of the alcohol in the wound. This man had tried to hang him and now he was complaining about the treatment he was receiving!

K.C. shoved him back onto the ground, "This won't hurt near as much as the stitches," he said shoving the needle into the wound. Rick passed out from the lack of blood and the pain of the needle being shoved into his body.

"What are we going to do with him now?" Parker wanted to know as they looked down at the now unconscious man.

"Mary and a couple of her friends, Stephanie and Connie are supposed to meet us this side of the border with some grub, and if they are there they will be riding a buck board so send Colton to find them and the rest of you keep pushing the cattle south, I'll stay with him until they get here.

They can take him back to town with them, maybe a doctor there can do a better job than I did. I'll catch up with the herd after we get him loaded." Parker took off to find Colton and the herd as the others stayed behind.

"Hey, are you going to have breakfast or are you going to sleep all day?" Joe asked as he kicked the Marshal's foot.

Jim sat up to the smell of the beans. Sometime during the night Joe had put a hand full of beans into the pot of water he had put on that night, probably after he snuck out to practice with the pistols Jim deduced.

Joe put half the beans on a on a metal plate and handed the pot to the Marshal. Pushing the sand from over the smoldering ashes Joe brought out two potatoes, "You got the most beans," he said, "so you get the smallest potato!" with that Joe handed him the rest of breakfast.

Jim broke up the potato and put it in with the beans, added some of the salt Sherlene had packed and began it eat, it was a lot better than the fried bacon and the hard tack biscuits they had been eating!

"When you're finished with the pot we'll put on some coffee," Joe said as he dug into his plate of the cowboy breakfast. "Where do you think they will make their play?" Jim asked still digging into the plate of beans.

"On the other side of the hill is a draw that widens out, K.C. and his bunch will be forced into the open if they stick with the route their taking that is the way I think they will come. The men following them will set up on the side of the draw and ambush them as they come into the open."

"What are we going to do about it?" Jim asked, "We'll wait upon the top of the hill and when they start to cut loose on the kids and the herd we'll get them. From the top of the hill to the bottom of the draw must be four hundred yards," Jim said, "I don't think I can hit a horse at that distance much less a man, besides we have to give them a chance to give up it's the law!"

"You're not the law in Mexico!" Joe stated, "as far as their concerned their nothing but a lynch mob and you know it!"
"We can't shoot them in cold blood, it's not right!" Jim was beginning to wonder if he had brought the right man after all!
"Their planning on murdering four men and a girl, and if we don't stop them here they will do it someplace else when we're not around, do you want that on your conscience?" Joe barked back
. "Besides, you're the one who said you couldn't hit the broadside of a barn if you were standing in it! Chances are you won't hit anything or anyone! All you have to do is make noise and leave the shooting to me!"
Rick was surprised to still be alive as K.C. and the women loaded him into the buckboard. "I thought I would have bled to death by now!" Rick said as he was laid in the bottom of the wagon.
"Hardly, K.C. said, these three ladies will get some steak and beans in you and you'll be as good as new in a few weeks!"
Rick owed his life to these people,"listen," he said, "the Rocking 'R' men have been trailing you, they know you're traveling the draws. Ten miles on the other side of the border they plan on jumping you and driving the cattle off.
They want it to look like Mexican banditos had killed you all off and that way no one could put the blame on them."
"Who is behind it?" Mary asked. "Both ranches, the Rocking 'R' and the Malloy outfit want to see all of you dead!"
"Why?" Connie asked, "We've done nothing to them?"
"Skip MacCland made plans to buy the Malloy ranch from Nicole's uncle.
Her uncle has been losing a lot of money at the gambling tables and it's the only way he could pay back the debt he owed.
As far as Skip was concerned, he was going to get the ranch dirt cheap since most of the debt was to him and he wants to be the only rancher in the valley.

He brought Cheatham in to get rid of the three cowboys holding on to the northeast corner of the valley, only his plans changed when he saw the cowboy ride in on that black stallion and all of a sudden he decided to have him killed first!"

"You mean the broken down drifter riding the bunk next to me in the jail?" K.C. said, "What's so important about him?"

Rick shook his head, "don't know, the boss is scared to death of him for some reason!"

"That doesn't sound like MacCland!" Stephanie put in. "No it don't, Rick said, but it's the truth!"

"Mary, you Stephanie, and Connie get him out of here and try to find him a doctor,"

K.C. instructed the women, "I've got to get to the herd and get them out of the draw and warn Eric and the rest that their riding into a trap!"

"Colton and Parker should have caught up with the herd by now, they know about Rick so maybe they've got everybody on their guard!"

Judge Hicks left the Rocking 'R' a thousand dollars richer and like Skip MacCland, he didn't care if the man in the jail cell had killed one man or a hundred as long as he was getting paid!

It made no difference to him, he was tired of being a servant to the people and wanted more out of life than the position of judge and with this kind of money he could run for an office of some kind, maybe become Mayor of one of the many towns he passed through.

With some backing he might even run for Governor! Anything was better than riding around the country in a buckboard dealing with the kind of derelicts he had to put up with every day.

If he did this favor for the owner of the Rocking 'R' ranch maybe he would be the one to back him in the future. It was with these thoughts Judge Hicks checked into the hotel across the street from the Crooked Horn.

He was going to take a bath and shave before going to the Marshal's office to free the prisoner, he wanted to look respectable!

Judge Hicks couldn't believe it, those stupid deputy's had tried to give him a hard time, they didn't want to release the prisoner, said they "wanted to wait for an answer to a telegraph they had sent before they released him."

Well he showed them, told them the shooting was a clear case of self-defense and they had no right to hold him any longer and if they did not do as the court instructed he would have them jailed for contempt!

They didn't even want to give the man his gun back.

Judge Hicks planned to have a talk with the Marshal when he got back! If he couldn't find men who would obey a court order he would have them all replaced!

Larry walked out of the jail a free man and even if the telegraph came back showing he was a wanted man the Judge had told him he would resend the order and if he had to he was willing to write him a full pardon! He didn't know if it was legal or not but neither would anyone else and he would still be free to kill the drifter, pick up his money and head back to Mexico.

After that life was a gamble and he was a pretty good gambler. Larry went to the hotel and up to his room. His bed role was still lying in the corner if MacCland was willing to pay off a judge to get him out of jail that meant the drifter was good with a gun maybe too good. Skip didn't look like the kind of man that had to have someone else do his killing. Larry untied the bed role and spread it out. Here was the weapon he was good with it was not the little hide out gun strapped to his shoulder.

This was a full scale forty-four in a quick draw holster!

After ejecting the shells into his hand Larry began taking the pistol apart, he was going to check and oil every piece. It was not his nature to go unprepared into a gunfight. He wanted to make sure the pistol did not jam or misfire when he needed it most!

Larry oiled the holster and slid the pistol gently into the pre-molded leather. Strapping the gun belt on he began to practice his draw, a split second meant the difference between life and death to a gunfighter. From this point on there would be no more booze and no more Trish. He had to hone his senses to a razors edge and she was a huge distraction to him, he might even say he loved her but he had never been in love before so he didn't know what love felt like, he just knew he thought of her often when he was away and when he thought of a woman hers was the face he saw!

CHAPTER NINE

As long as the cattle were in the draw, K.C. knew the live of his brother and cousins were in danger so he pushed his horse to the limit, trying to catch up them!

Rick had told him how the fight with Frankie Vasquez had started and how many men were left.

Without their leader they might have changed their plans, they could even now be attacking his family!

He caught up to the herd and the rest of the men as they crossed the border and for the first time since he broke jail he knew for certain that men followed him and his crew with the intent to murder each and every one of them!

Now was the time to decide if they wanted to scatter the herd or try to make it to the cattle buyers further into the Mexican territory. They needed the money to fight for the ranch. Nicole would soon be old enough to legally take control of the ranch but was it worth risking their lives?

Nicole and the men sat watching the herd as it moved slowly south, within hours they were going to know if the risk was worth it as they had decided to keep the herd. They were going to be coming out of the draws into the open and if the men of the Rocking 'R' and Malloy ranch knew where they were it made no sense trying to hide now!

K.C. and his men were going to change direction and head into the valley, at least that way they might be able to see the men coming before they spotted them. Colton would ride scout circling the herd on the lookout for Mexican bandits or the ambush that was sure to come and with any luck they would survive the next few days! The rest of the men would drive the cattle with their rifles at the ready, watching every movement. K.C. and the rest of his outfit had pushed the cattle most of the night, seeing mostly by the light of the moon, trying desperately to outrun the men behind them. They had broken camp early, eating biscuits and bacon and now they were trying to get as far ahead of the gunmen as they could and with any luck they might even lose them with the change in directions and starting to move the cattle even before the sun was up.

Joe was already gone when Jim woke up, walking to the fire he poured himself a cup of coffee wondering where the temporary deputy had went. It never occurred to him that Joe had gone hunting five armed men by himself!

All that day Joe and the Marshal sat on top of the hill waiting for the ambush that was never going to come not knowing that the cattle and the men had turned further west avoiding the draws altogether. As night fell Joe built a fire behind the cover of the mountain, something was wrong, he could feel it in his bones, the cattle and the men should have been there by now! In the morning he planned on taking a ride across the border and see if he could find them. Somewhere there was going to be a massacre and he planned on being there to stop it! As the sun began to rise, Joe was up and finishing a cup of coffee. After saddling the black he headed north looking for the trail of the cattle.

Joe found the trail where a small herd of cattle crossed the border. The tracks were fresh and the center of the dung was still warm. This had to be the men he wanted to catch. Joe swung the reins of the black and headed southwest in the direction the herd had taken with any luck he would catch them within the hour!

Eric heard the bullet whiz past his face and then the sound of the rifle shot.

The men firing lay in a ditch two hundred yards to the east where smoke from the barrels of the rifles gave their position away. The first volley of shots that had been fired in had missed the mark by inches. It was the young rustlers turn to open fire but it was a hard shot with the lynch mob hiding in the ditch.

The young cowboys had been lucky during the first part of the attack; their luck might not hold if they tried to get to their horses now! To charge was to run into the face of the enemy and the hail of lead that would be heading their way.

K.C. and his men lay flat in the dirt unable to move as the enemy sought the flesh of their bodies with the lead of their bullets.

The Marshal may have been a heavy sleeper but even he could hear the sounds of gun fire echoing across the valley! This was not the spot Joe had picked for the ambush to take place. Jim threw his saddle on the roan, it was going to take a while for him to get there and with any luck maybe some of the young rustler's might still be alive!

Joe topped the rise as he heard the sound of gun fire erupt.

The loud bark of the rifles drowned out the sound of the pistols as the Malloy outfit fired time and time again at the men lying helpless on the ground.

At one time this was the kind of battles Joe had lived for turning the black into the ditch Joe dug his heels into the horse's sides, when they came around the bend they would be face to face with the men in the ditch. The rifle would have too long a barrel for the close quarter fighting and it would take too long to cock after each shot. Joe left the rifle in the scabbard and drew the pistols at his side.

Jim raced to the site of the battle trying to get there before every one of those fool hardy kids was killed. If he got there in time maybe he could stop the slaughter! Jim topped the ridge in time to see the last of the battle.

He sat on the back of his horse and watched as Joe and the black charged down the ditch.

Joe held a pistol in both hands and even from that distance Jim could see the look of an avenging angel or the look of a demon straight from the pits of hell on Joe's face!

This was the look on the man's face that had put a fear into Skip MacCland and this was the look that had haunted him to this day. This was the reason Skip had hired a gunman instead of facing the man himself.

The men of the Rocking 'R' heard the sounds of the blacks hooves coming at them and turned to fire but it was too late, the pistols in Joe's hands began to spit fire. These men had come to ambush and kill they never thought that a wild man was going to becoming at them with guns blazing! They tried to face the man and meet him head on but as they fired it was in haste and the shells were missing man and beast alike!

Joe's pistols spoke loud and clear and the shells went true, the three men went down in a hail of lead. Joe sat in the saddle of the black, pistols cocked with a wild look in his eyes searching for the other two men.

"That's enough!" K.C. yelled to the man who had stayed in the cell next to him and waving his arms trying to calm the man down. Jim put the spurs to the roan and started down the hill, there had been enough killing, and maybe he could stop the madness! "That's all of them!" K.C. yelled. "Frankie stabbed Rick back at their camp, he showed up here yesterday and we sent him back to town on a buckboard with some people we know.

Rick wound up gut shooting Vasquez and if he ain't with them then I guess he is back at these Joe lowered the pistols and looked at the small group of rustlers, "Dang boys, you almost got yourselves killed!" he said as he turned the black to face the Marshal,

"Where you been?" Joe had transformed himself back into the worn out looking saddle tramp and no one would have guessed that he had just killed three men!

"Marshal, you're out of your jurisdiction, you got no authority down here!" K.C. said watching to see if the Marshal was going to try to arrest them for stealing the cattle and breaking out of jail.

"Besides Nicole is going to own the place in a month and she said I could take the cattle." "Let me guess," Jim said, "you're going to sell the cattle, hire some gunmen and take the ranch back, is that about right?" "That was the plan," K.C. admitted.

"In that case you're going to need this," Jim said digging into the saddle bags on the back of his horse.

K.C. watched as the Marshal pulled a fancy quick draw gun belt with a silver star from the bag and a pearl handled pistol from the other and handed it to the young cowboy, it was K.C.'s pride and joy and he couldn't believe the marshal was giving it back to him!

"Don't shoot yourself with it!" Jim said as he handed him the bullets. "You mean you didn't come down here to arrest us?" Eric asked in amazement.

"Never planned on it, Jim said, just wanted to make sure you made it alright. If I was going to arrest you I would have done it on the other side of the border!" "Will you do me favor boys?" the Marshal asked. "Sure," one of the young men answered, "what can we do for you," he wanted to know? "Bury these guys and bury them deep. I don't want the dogs to dig them up or the Federalies to find them.

It wouldn't look good for the States if Mexico found out that we were having our own private wars on their lands!"

"Don't worry," Eric said, "We'll bury them half way to China," and then laughed at his own joke.

Jim rode over and picked up the horses that had been used by the dead men. Two of the horses carried the Rocking 'R' brand and the other was from the Malloy ranch. "Now if you will excuse me, my friend and I have a long ways to go."

Jim turned his horse and headed north following the tracks of the horses back to dead men's camp.

Somewhere back there was a gut shot man maybe they could find him before he died! Joe looked at the young men, "you boys be careful in Mexico, this place can be rough!" he said as he turned the black and followed the Marshal north back to the States and the brown eyed woman he found himself dreaming of.

For the first time in years Joe had something on his mind other than the speed of his hands or the battles of a war long past.

Finding the camp wasn't hard; the men didn't think anybody was going to be following them and had not bothered to cover their tracks. The two men were greeted by the smell of dead, rotting flesh as they neared the camp.

"Darn, they didn't even bother burying the man!" Joe said as they looked down at the body. Frankie had been gut shot alright but the hole through his head told the rest of the story. "I guess they didn't want to waste time on a corpse." Jim said disgustedly as he swung down from the horse, "hope you've got a shovel because we're going to have to bury him!"

Joe shook his head, "No, but I figure there is shovel on one of their horses, after all they planned on burying the bodies of the others!" Jim dug through the saddle bags and came up with two small shovels and handing one to Joe he began to look for a place to bury the body. "We'll camp someplace else tonight!" he said as he tamped the last of the dirt on the grave. "That's alright with me!" Joe said, "I've seen and smelled enough dead bodies lately that I don't plan on sleeping with it!" The sun was beginning to set as they saddled up and left the camp of the dead!

Jim rode the roan up to large west Texas pond three or four miles north of the Mexican border and dismounted, "Did you ever think of being a peace officer Joe, the pays pretty good and the hours are short."

Jim was in a talking mood as he searched for a fishhook and some line. "Now that the battle was over he planned to relax and kicking at the cow pies nearby he found some marble bugs and placed them on a hook.

The Marshal pulled his boots off and waded into the water. The perch weren't big but they would cover the pan. Joe started the fire as Jim waded around in the pond, both men needed to relax and this was their way of doing it. Joe placed some bacon in a pan and placed it on the red coals. Jim cleaned the fish, rolled them in flower and placed them in the bacon grease and soon the aroma of fried fish and bacon filled the air.

If a man was going to camp this was the way to do it, without a care in the world, Jim thought as he unrolled his bedroll, laid down and fell asleep.

He awoke to the sounds of movement and the smell of coffee. Joe was already up and saddling the black, "What's the hurry?" he asked. Joe shrugged his shoulders, "Just want to get back to town, I guess I'm tired of living in the desert!" Jim had the feeling it was not town he was thinking of, maybe Joe was missing Marilyn.

The waitress had taken quite a liking to the quiet drifter and maybe the feeling was mutual after all. Jim packed up the rest of the camp supplies and saddled his horse in thoughtful silence. First he had to take the horses back to the Rocking 'R' ranch, that meant facing Skip MacCland and the rest of the men at the ranch. Then he had to tell Malloy two of his men were dead and that he didn't know where his horses were and he had to tell both of them that their plans had failed and the rustlers were still alive and in Mexico.

The Marshal didn't know Don Malloy was already dead or that Skip MacCland had quit worrying about the rustlers, the cattle or the Malloy ranch.

He didn't care if his men came back from Mexico dead or alive, it made no difference to him at all, all he wanted was to see the rider on the black horse dead! Years earlier lying on his belly watching as his men were being cut down, Skip had a premonition of the duel between him and the gunman and ever since the man had ridden into town, the feeling had followed him like a ghost haunting him, even in his sleep!

At night Skip dreamed of the battle fought long ago only this time he didn't lie on his belly in fear this time he dreamed of standing and facing the man with his guns blazing but the dream was always the same, even as he fired he saw the bullet coming at him in slow motion seeking his heart!

Skip would wake up just as the bullet penetrated the flesh. He would awake grabbing at his chest fearing the death that was about to come! The quiet man had to die so Skip could live!

CHAPTER TEN

Joe and the Marshal topped the hill overlooking the town. The red roof of Nita's cat house was the first thing he noticed with its wrap around veranda and balcony facing the main street. "One day I'm going to have to do something about that," he thought.

The rest of the town looked like a lot of other western towns with a barn and stable and the blacksmith shop all of which were owned and run by a man named Garry. The town had a two story hotel own by a very nice couple named Damon and Mary Cook and a general store that Ashley Fry owned and of course there was the Crooked Horn Restaurant and bar along with the jail, a school house whose teacher was Connie and it also served as a church on Sundays, the bank and a telegraph office.

There were several houses scattered out around town, they belonged to the people that mostly worked in town. From the hill top Jim could even see the smoke coming from the chimney of the Lazy Bar ranch.

It belonged to the three hellions, Roy, Bobby and Mike. Just the thought of the three young men made him smile.

He didn't want anyone to know but he liked the men. He knew had known them for several years now. He knew all three of men had hired on as drovers for a large cattle company a few years earlier and had driven several thousand head of cattle had over the Chisholm Trail. Unlike the rest of the drovers, when the men got to Kansas instead of drinking up their wages or losing them at the card tables they headed to Texas looking for a ranch of their own.

Why they had settled here in a quiet little town was beyond Jim's reasoning, they were wild and rowdy with a little bit of funny thrown in and it made no sense that they would pick this town as their home.

Jim was lost in his thoughts and was jarred back to reality as Joe spoke.

"If I was you," Joe said "I'd let them horses go, they can find their own way home and it would save you a lot of riding and It might keep you from getting your head blown off by some friend of theirs looking for revenge!" Jim didn't think these men had been the kind of men to have friends but it would save him a lot of riding! Letting the horses go he fired a shot at their hooves, spooking them into a run, "They will be home pretty quick," he said as they started off the hill.

Sherlene and Marilyn watched as the two men started towards town and at the sight of them they both became excited, "You put on some coffee," Marilyn said as she headed for the mirror.

Still standing behind the bar she began taking the pins from her hair and letting it fall to her shoulders, "For once I'm glad Paul is a slow mover," she said pulling a brush through her hair, "I would hate to do this from a reflection on a skillet!" "Especially Eloise's skillet" Sherlene put in as both women began to giggle at the remark.

Marilyn went into the kitchen and dabbed some vanilla on her wrists and at the nape of her neck, "he won't get that close!" Sherlene said as she watched her apply the homemade perfume. "You never can tell!" Marilyn commented smiling at the thought of the man being that close to her.

Like Skip MacCland she had dreamed of the man since the day he had ridden into town but her dreams weren't of battles and wars, her dreams were of a family and a home and one day she planned on having both of them and this was the man she had been waiting for!

Sherlene and Marilyn watched as Joe and the Marshal brought their horses to a stop in front of the marshal's office and climbed off the mounts.

Both men looked tired and worn out and they were stiff from the long ride and stretched their bodies as their feet hit the ground. The black still looked half wild but had gotten used to the roan and let the animal stand close to him.

Joe and the Marshal tied the horses to the wooden rail and went inside. Both men wanted to clean up before heading to the Crooked Horn to see the women they were in love with. Jim stoked the coals in the stove and got a fire going as Joe placed a pan of water over the burners. Schon watched as the two tried to make themselves presentable, "Had a little excitement around here while you were gone." He informed the two men as they took out the straight razors and began to shave.

"How is that?" Jim asked between strokes of the blade. "Fellow named Larry Cheatham killed Don Malloy at the Crooked Horn!" Jim stopped shaving, "Anyone else hurt?" he asked. Jim was worried about the women. "No just Malloy, he was killed over a card game, said the other guy cheated and went for his gun and got shot for the trouble."

"I didn't think Malloy would try a gun!" Jim said "the man was a worse shot than I am!" "Maybe he wouldn't have, Schon answered, but he thought the other fellow was unarmed, but the gambler pulled a sneak gun from under his shoulder and blew a hole clear through him." "Where is the gambler now?" the Marshal wanted to know. "Well, me and Rog had him locked up and we tried to hold him until you returned. Ashley had told us he was wanted in Louisiana for murder. I sent some telegraphs but never got an answer but like I said, we tried to keep him in jail until we found out if he was still wanted or not but the judge told us if we didn't let him go he would take our badges and hold us in contempt of court!"

"Not sure if that is legal or not but I'm not going to worry about it right now, Jim answered, but I'm pretty sure Sherlene and Marilyn are waiting for us at the Crooked Horn. I'm tired and hungry, we've been eating out of a pot and drinking hobo coffee for days and I can't wait to see Sherlene and give her a big hug and wrap my teeth around a good meal and I'm pretty sure Joe would like to do the same thing only with a different woman," Jim emphasized the remark. "You think Joe wants to see his girlfriend?" Rog asked. Schon still thought of Joe as another drifter and laughed at the thought of Joe and the waitress being together, "You're kidding, right?" Schon asked.

"No, I think Marilyn and Joe are kind of sweet on each other!" Jim teased as he headed out the door. "Last one to the Crooked Horn buys!" he said as he slammed the door behind him, he had discovered you had to take every advantage you can when dealing with Joe!

Jim was right; both women had watched the men go into the Marshal's office and were waiting for them as they emerged.

Marilyn was primping with her hair trying to make it perfect, she wanted to make more than a good impression, she wanted to be beautiful. "How do I look?" she asked her sister. "Well let me think, you look just like the cat that's about to jump on a mouse and he ain't got a chance!" "That's how I wanted to look!" Marilyn said, "I don't intend to give him a chance!" The smell of vanilla filled the room, "Alright," Jim said walking into the room,

"Somebody's cooking a cake." Sherlene gave her husband a hug, "Shut up!" she whispered as she pulled him up close. "You mean you ain't cooking a cake, I'm disappointed after all you saw me a coming!" "Shut up!" she whispered again.

Jim had been married long enough to know women used the vanilla as perfume and Marilyn was trying to entice Joe. Jim was going to have fun teasing her but Sherlene put a stop to his fun with a few quietly whispered words, "Keep it up and you will be sleeping alone!" She may or may not have meant it but Jim was taking no chances!

"Yes, dear!" was all he had to say and those were the exact words Sherlene wanted to hear! All four of them sat down to a quiet meal as Paul carried boxes of booze out the front doors. "Where is he going?" Jim asked surprised that Paul would be leaving. "I bought him out!" Marilyn said with a sound of pride in her voice, "I now own three fourths of the restaurant! "Heck," Jim teased, "Get Eloise to eat some of her own cooking and you'll own the whole thing!"

Eloise heard the remark and came out of the kitchen carrying a skillet, "One more crack," she said "and I'll slap you upside the head with this thing!" Marilyn remembered the remarks made by Bobby and Roy, she drew back in mock fear, "oh no not the beans!" she cried. Everyone at the table began to laugh at the expression on Eloise's face, "you keep it up and you'll be eating you own cooking!" she said as she headed back into the kitchen.

"You call that a threat?" Jim wanted to know, "it sounds more like a blessing to me!" he said. After hearing that remark, Eloise turned and threw the skillet from halfway across the room, missing the Marshal by six feet, "you throw even worse than you cook!" Eloise had heard all of the comments she wanted and headed for the kitchen, "I meant to miss!" she said, "I wouldn't want to get arrested for assault to an idiot!"

The crew of the Lazy 'B' ranch came into the restaurant, well at least Roy and Mike came in, "We want a well smoked right hind quarter of a hog and two bags shoved full of hard tack biscuits and make sure it's the right hind quarter!" Mike ordered, "Were gonna be branding cattle on the south forty and we don't want to be stumbling around lopsided!" both men laughed at the homemade humor.

"If you boys are gonna be branding won't you be needing Bobby?" Marilyn asked. "We sure will!" Mike put in "but ever since the new girl went to work at Nita's we've been having a hard time keeping him at the ranch! He runs off every five minutes!

Talk about love sick, he's named six caves and a puppy Michelle!" "That wouldn't be so bad except, the puppy was a male and two of the calves were bulls!" Roy and Mike sat down and had coffee while they waited for their order.

These two loved to upset Marilyn and continued with their banter, "Talk about bad, the water that was used in this coffee must have come from the Mississippi River because it tastes like mud!" Mike laughed. "To heck with the mud," Roy said holding back a smile, "It smells like a catfish is hiding behind the coffee grounds in this cup!" "I'll get you a shovel!" Mike said, "We'll have that puppy for dinner!" "Alright, knock it off! "Marilyn ordered "Why does everyone give Eloise a hard time?" "Besides she's not the one who made the coffee!" "We know, Roy said, her's ain't nearly this bad!" "What did you do, they asked; try your hand at cookin Bobby asked? I'll bet Marilyn has never teased Eloise about her cookin, have you?" Mike wanted to know.

The question floored her, how could she say anything when just minutes before she had been doing the same thing! Marilyn gave the boys her best imitation look of anger, "Keep it up and I'll have you both thrown out of here for good!" she warned knowing she would never do that!
Jim stretched out his arm, "I'll be taking the badge now!" Joe took the badge from his shirt and handed it to the Marshal, "What now?" he asked. "I guess you'll be spending the night in the jail!" Joe stiffened, "I thought you were going to get that taken care of?" "I will, in the morning. I'm letting the deputies have the night off, besides I've kind of grown fond of your company and the bunks at the jail are softer than the beds at the hotel!
You won't have to pay for a nights lodging either!" Joe relaxed, "I'll go but I ain't gonna like it!" he complained. "Oh well, I'll teach you how to play cards," Jim said. Both men laughed at the remark, Jim could play cards no better than he could shoot. Joe took off his gun belt and hung it on the hook behind the Marshal's desk,
"If I'm a prisoner again, Joe ordered I want Marilyn to bring me my breakfast!" Jim didn't think he was going to have a problem honoring the request. "I'll see what I can do!" he said as he hung his own gun belt up. "Get some sleep, I've gotta make rounds in a few hours."
The blast of a shotgun woke both men. Joe sat up and began to stomp his boots on as he heard the tumbling of the lock. Jim stood at the door locking him in. "Just keeping you out of trouble," he said as he ran for his own boots. Another blast of the shotgun echoed through the jail, vibrating the walls. Joe sat and watched as Jim went out the door. Joe didn't know it but he had gotten to where he liked the Marshal.
Joe sat in the dark of the night and waited for the return of the marshal and he was not surprised as the men came through the door, it was Roy and Mike. The marshal followed carrying a ten-gage shotgun.

"Alright, in the cell you two!" he said leaning the shotgun against the wall. Both men walked into the cell and Jim locked the door. "Joe I've got to make rounds and these guys woke half the town up and some of them are gonna be screaming mad, if I unlock your cell will you see if you can keep them quiet?" "For a prisoner you sure keep me working!" Joe said. "That's because you're better at it than me," Jim replied as he rushed out.

"Heck, I should be getting a paycheck!" Joe complained as he sat behind the Marshal's desk. Roy had walked over to the bunk, laid down and passed out and Joe wanted to know why Jim had brought the men in before Mike did likewise and passed out too! "Why did the Marshal bring you boys in anyway?" he asked Mike. "I thought you were going to be branding by now!" "We was gonna be brandin but as soon as we got home the dog got a hold of the hog and headed under the house and by the time we got it back weren't nothin left but bone.

We came back to town to get another, one thing led to another and next thing I knowed we were drunk and being arrested!" "Why were you shooting?" Joe wanted to know. Mike looked kind of embarrassed, "Roy bet me five dollars that he could rick-a-shay a bullet off one of those biscuits." "Well, did he manage to do it?" Joe asked. "Heck no!" Mike said, "He was so drunk, he couldn't hit the darn thing with a shotgun from ten feet!"

"Well I'll see you in the morning," Joe said letting the cowboy know it was time to pass out.

Mike walked over to a bunk, lay down and obliged the part time marshal. Joe sat in the chair with his feet kicked up on the desk, "I could get used to this," he thought as he nodded off dreaming of tomorrow and soft brown eyes.

CHAPTER ELEVEN

Skip MacCland sat on the veranda of his home on the Rocking 'R' ranch sipping from a bottle of fine whisky, the sun was just beginning to set as he saw the rider approaching, it was Tim, one of the ranch hands and saddled horses followed the rider. The horses turned and headed to the barn as the rider approached the main house. "Brought some horses in, he stated, they were already saddled when we found them!"
 Skip didn't have to be told who they had belonged to! He had seen the horses before, they belonged to the men he had sent to gun down the rustlers on their way to Mexico, "He killed them all!" Skip said quietly. He hadn't meant to speak out loud; it was more of a statement to himself! "Who killed them all?" Tim wanted to know. Skip was brought out of a stress induced trance and without thinking Skip began to explain.
"The Marshal is more farmer than lawman, he sure ain't no gunman! That bunch of young rustlers didn't know they were riding into an ambush and even if they did I doubt if they could have beaten the men we sent after them, which leaves one person, the drifter, the man on the black horse!"
 Tim shook his head, "Ain't no way one person killed all five of them!" "Don't you bet on it!" Skip said and shut up. He didn't want the rest of the men to know he had met the drifter before. "I want you to put the horses in the barn then ride to town and bring me the man that killed Don Malloy, he's staying at the hotel in room fourteen, the one facing the street and if he ain't there he will probably be at Nita's! Don't come back to the ranch without him!"

Tim went to the barn and took the saddles off two of the mounts and placed them in a stall, gave them some grain and took the saddle off his own horse and put it in a stall also. Tim mounted the third horse, "I don't think your owner is gonna mind!" he said as he Followed the road into town.
Tim heard the blasts of the shotgun as he rode into town but it was no skin off my nose if some drunks blow off steam," he thought as he swung down in front of Paul's new bar. It was really not much of a bar just a large tent with boards thrown over a couple of beer kegs. Card tables were scattered about and the chairs were pieces of firewood stood on end. The beer was going to be hot until he got an ice house dug
But Tim didn't care, like most of the cowboys, he preferred whisky. The real bar was being built next door; stakes were already in place showing the outline of the new building. "It wouldn't be long before Paul had the bar he dreamed of," Tim thought as he ordered a whisky at the make shift counter.
"Paul, have you seen the fellow that gunned down Malloy?"
Paul stopped wiping at the planks of the bar, "He moved out of the hotel, some of the drover said they been hearing a lot of gun fire four or five miles north of town. I kind of figured it's him getting ready for something."
Thanks!" Tim said, "If he comes in tell him I'm waiting for him at the hotel, Skip wants to see him as soon as possible!"
Paul finished wiping the planks as Tim left. Paul never figured himself a smart man but even he knew when Skip MacCland sent for a gunman trouble was coming. "I best warn the Marshal!" Paul thought as he took a shot of his own whisky.
Paul was waiting for him as Jim walked through the flaps of the tent that served as a door, "looks like you got trouble!" Paul placed a hot beer on the bar as he spoke. "Skip MacCland sent Tim into town looking for that Cheatham fellow. I never figured I'd live to see the day when MacCland don't want to do his own killin!

I figure he either brought the gunman here or he is planning on hiring him to do some killin for him!"

Jim was beginning to wish he really was a Marshal, not just some farmer voted into the job. Maybe then he would know what to do about men like Cheatham and MacCland. This had been a nice quiet little town when he applied for the job but now things were getting out of hand and he knew he didn't have the experience to keep a lid on things that were about to happen!

Like most cowboys Tim hated to get out of a soft bed but the boss was in a hurry so he climbed out of bed early that morning to find the gunman. After saddling his horse he rode north and had only ridden a little better than two miles when he heard the sound of gunfire. "That has got to be Cheatham," he thought as he followed the sounds of the shots.

Riding to the top of the hill he could see a man down below. There was a fence post in the ground ten feet in front of him. Tim could see the holes in the wood and as he watched the man drew and fired, fanning the pistol with his left hand. Pieces of wood flew from the post as the soft lead found their mark.

Up until that point Tim had thought Skip was the fastest man with a gun he had ever seen but the gunman was quicker he thought as he rode towards the man. Tim had no way of knowing that Skip had quit riding the range the day the drifter had shown up, he spent his days behind the main house practicing his draw. His pistol was drawn from the holster in one smooth motion, it was quick and it was the fastest it had ever been in his life. He was just as fast as Cheatham and just as accurate!

Tim didn't bother getting down from the horse, "Boss wants to see you!" he said watching the man's expression. Tim was afraid of the man and didn't want to make him mad but the gunman was not upset, he knew MacCland would be sending for him, after all he had not killed the drifter yet!

He wanted to know all he could about Skip and the drifter both but Tim was not much help. They talked along the way all to the Rocking 'R' ranch but the only thing he knew for certain was MacCland didn't want to face the drifter with a gun.

Skip sat on the veranda sipping whisky and watching the men as they rode up. Larry saw the bottle even before he dismounted from the horse. "Liquid courage!" he thought to himself, "This guy has got the jitters bad Larry decided real bad!"

Skip met Larry half way down the steps, "How have you been?" he asked his hand was stretched out to the gunman. Larry could see the fear in Skip's eyes, this job was going to pay more than the five hundred dollars he had already received, "Fine," he said knowing the real question Skip wanted answered. MacCland couldn't contain himself any longer, "When are you going to kill him!" he sneered "That depends, Larry said, on how much it pays!"

"I already paid you!" Skip hissed. Larry shook his head, "That was to kill a nobody and I don't think the drifter is a nobody or you would have killed him you're self!"

"How much to kill the drifter?" Skip asked his patients running low. "A thousand now and another thousand after the job is done!" Larry said calmly, he knew MacCland would pay whatever he asked. Skip took out another five hundred dollars
, "I've already paid you five, this will square us up for now but I still want to know when the job will be done?"

"Tomorrow," Larry said, "after lunch!" "Then you will spend the night here!" Skip demanded. "Tomorrow I'm riding into town with you!" "What's the matter, don't you trust me?" Larry said.

"No," Skip answered; before I pay you I have to see the man dead and I want to see him die with my own eyes!" Larry didn't care as long as he got paid. "Suit yourself," he said and walked past Skip into the main house as if he owned it!

"Alright you two, get up and get out!" the Marshal growled. Roy and Mike climbed from their bunks about the time Jim through a mop in the cell, "you made the mess you clean it up!" he said. Joe was already up and shaving,

"I worked last night so you're buying breakfast!" "I ain't bought a meal since I took this job," Jim stated but since it's a special occasion I guess I will!"

Joe stopped shaving, "What special occasion is that?" he asked. "Why you get to see your girlfriend of course, what else would it be?"

It was close to noon as the two men headed for the Crooked Horn, Sherlene and Marilyn had been watching for the marshal and part time deputy and as soon as they saw the men coming they set two cups of coffee at the table they had chosen to have lunch at.

Sherlene wanted to be with her husband while Marilyn was nervous about being with the man she dreamed of.

"Do I look alright?" Marilyn asked as she played with her hair. "You look fine!" Sherlene answered playing with her own hair. Sherlene pulled out a chair as she saw the men come through the door, "We're over here!" she said signaling the men to join them at their table. She was smiling as she sat Joe next to Marilyn.

Jim knew why his wife was smiling, she enjoyed playing matchmaker! "This should be fun to watch!" he thought with a smile on his face.

Skip and the gunman left the Rocking 'R' ranch late in the morning. They wanted to be at the Crooked Horn by noon, and that would give them all afternoon to find and get rid of his nightmare but little did they know, Joe and the Marshal were just finishing their meal as they walked in and wouldn't be hard to find.

Marilyn saw them come through the doors and whispered to Joe, "That's Skip MacCland and his hired gun. I guess we'll know pretty soon who he wants killed!" Joe turned and looked at the men, as far as he knew he had never seen either man before. Larry didn't believe in wasting time, he had things to do and a woman to see.

He stood in front of the doors as he stared at Joe. "Stand up!" he ordered, "You killed a friend of mine and now you're gonna die!" Now everyone at the table knew who he had been hired to kill because men like Larry had no friends!

Joe slid back from the table and looked around the room and then back to Skip, "You're the one who hired him and you're the first one I'm gonna kill!" Joe said confidently. Skip felt a sinking feeling in his stomach and his hands were beginning to shake at the words coming from the man's mouth, he wanted to see the man die, he never planned on this being the outcome!

Jim sat at the table watching as the men faced each other; "This wasn't right!" he decided and stood up facing Skip, "I've got this one!" he said squaring up to the man.

Jim was no gunman and hopefully neither was MacCland! Jim watched as Skip's hands flashed towards the pistol, Skip was fast, real fast the pistol was half way out of the holster before Jim's hand touched the butt of his own weapon!

Jim knew within a split second he was going to feel the impact of the lead of a forty-four caliber pistol tearing through his body and destroying his life and dreams, at the same time . For a split second he couldn't think of the reason he had ever become a lawman but Jim knew one thing for sure, he was about to die!

The pistol in Joe's left hand exploded fire and lead flew from the barrel striking Skip in the chest. The halfcocked revolver in Skips hand fell to the floor and even as Skip dropped to his knees Joe cocked the pistols again but there was no need Cheatham lay on the floor dead, he had already felt the bite of the bullet from Joe's pistol. Skip leaned back, sitting on the heels of his boots, his spurs were digging deep into his flesh, "it's just a dream!" he said as his life's blood ran from his body.

Men were dragging the bodies out as Jim sat at the table thinking of how close he had come to death!

If it hadn't been for the hand speed of the drifter he would have been the one lying dead on the floor!

Jim unpinned the badge from his shirt and sat at the table staring down at the symbol of law and order, Jim knew he was no gunman and no Marshal! He looked at Sherlene and said, "Those kids will need someone to take care of the ranch until they get back from Mexico. Maybe I'll ride out there and take care of the place for them, they will need a foreman, and I think I will apply for the job!

Joe sat the table across from him and for the first time since they had met Jim saw real fear in the man and for once in his life Jim knew what someone else was thinking.

He may have been a farmer but even he knew Joe was thinking the woman he loved thought of him as nothing more than a gunman, a killer! "I'm no gunman!" Joe said in a voice just above a whisper. Marilyn wrapped her arms around the man she loved trying to comfort him, to ease the torment in his soul, to help bear the sadness of taking a human life.

Jim knew no one was going to blame him for what he was about to do, "Your no gunman!" he said as he slid the badge across the table, "You're a Marshal!"

Jim took the hand of the woman he loved and together they walked out of the Crooked Horn Restaurant to a new hope and a new life!

CHAPTER TWELVE

It's never easy starting a new life," Jim thought as he rode towards the Malloy ranch. This was not going to be easy either! Better than half a dozen riders still rode for the Malloy brand and some of them would not take kindly to what he was about to do!

One of the men sat in a rocking chair on the front porch as he rode up; he was a big man with broad shoulders and powerful hands. Billy's face showed the scars of the bar room brawls that he had been in, he was no gunman, he was a fighter.

Bare knuckle or club to club made no difference to him he enjoyed it all. Jim knew the man and knew he was trouble, the barrel of a rifle leaned against the wall behind the rocker. The rifle was for show; Billy liked to hurt people with his hands. "Better to face the man now!" Jim thought than when he has an army behind him.

Jim swung down from the roan, "Morning Marshal," Billy said as Jim walked up to the porch. Billy outweighed the ex-Marshal by fifty pounds and he was taking no chances! Jim swung a right with everything he had.

Billy saw the blow coming and tried to dodge but the fist landed solid. A look of pain came to his face as the fist struck his jaw. Bone cracked and shattered as the side of his head exploded. One second later Billy went down without knowing he had been in a fight.

A short barreled forty-four pistol fell from his holster as he bounced off the floor boards and fell to the ground. Jim picked up the pistol and slid it into his own holster; it was a lot better weapon than the colt dragoon he carried.

Men like Billy made four times the money real cowboys earned and did nothing in return but cause trouble and bust heads. Jim was sick of the lot of them, "that's for hurting my fist!" he complained as he picked up the rifle, "and this is for making me ride all the way out here to talk you into leaving!"

Jim walked through the door of the ranch house with one thought on his mind, "I'm gonna clean this place out!" It was not going to be as hard a job as he thought, there were only two men in the room, one was already passed out and the other was on the way. "What are you doing here?" he demanded.

A split second later his head was exploding like the others. Jim may have been smaller and he may have been a farmer but years of hard work had built a strong body. Splitting fence posts with a double headed axes and hauling rocks from the field by hand had made him as hard as the rocks he carried.

The power of his arms had crumbled the cowboy as easy as it hauled the stones. The cowboy lost teeth and consciousness as the blow landed. Jim picked up the cowboys pistol and grabbing the man by his boots then began to drag him out the door. "Dang, that boy looks like I hit him!" said a voice from the porch. Jim grabbed the revolver in his holster and swung around, Paul stood on the porch admiring Jim's handy work.

"What did you hit him with, a chunk of firewood?" Paul asked as he lifted Billy and draped him over the saddle. "Well are you gonna shoot him or put that thing away?" Joe asked as he sat in the saddle atop the black.

"What are you two doing here?" Jim asked surprised that the two men had ridden all the way out to the ranch. "We figured you might have trouble!" Joe said looking at the two men on the floor of the porch, "but I guess they're the ones with the trouble!" Jim rubbed his knuckles, "If you leave the guns out of it I guess I can take care of myself!"

Joe looked at the butt of the weapon in Jim's belt, "speaking of weapons, that's a pretty good pistol you're toting, a lot better than the piece of junk you were wearing!" "Well, it was a present; Billy here gave it to me right after he decided to take a nap!"

"Do you think he will want it back after he wakes up?" Joe asked. Jim shook his head, "Well if he does we'll talk about it again and I don't think he will want it back a third time!"

"I don't think he's gonna be saying much now!" Joe stated dryly, "it looks he's gonna be eating soup for the next three weeks!"

Paul came out of the house dragging the drunk, "you must have hit this one with a feather," he said, "I can't find a mark on him any place!" "He was passed out when I got here!" Jim said, "See if you can find their horses will you, I want to get these guys off the ranch."

Paul was not the type to take orders but he had known Jim a long time and he was as close to a friend as Paul had.

Paul dropped the drunk and started for the barn. It was easy to see the ranch needed a lot of repairs, Jim shook his head and looked at Joe, "This place used to be nice," he said remembering days long gone,

"at one time it was the nicest spread in the valley. Malloy and his gang of rats have sure let it go to pot! The barn needs a new roof and some of the boards in the corral need replaced. Someone needs to drag the pond and get the moss and algae out of it!"

Joe sat on the back of the black, "Since when does a farmer know so much about ranching?" as he watched Jim's face thinking there is more to this man than a lot of people would guess! As Paul brought two more horses out of the barn Jim informed the drifter that he was not always a farmer, "at one time I was a top hand, took two drives up the Chisholm Trail which was approximately five hundred miles and the second one I was the ram-rod and the boys from the Lazy 'B' ranch rode with me!" Joe turned in the saddle to look at the ex-marshal.

"Why did you give up cowboying?" he asked.

Jim had been asked this question before, it was always the same answer, "Cowboys raise cattle, farmers raise families, it was a choice I had to make and I chose family."

"You know times are changing, it is possible to do both!" Joe stated. "That's why I decided to take over here until K.C. and Nicole comes back. It will give me a chance to get the feel of ranching again or at least get my butt toughened up for the twelve hour days in the saddle."

"What do you want me to do with these three?" Paul asked as he pitched the last of the unconscious men over their saddles.

"Take them to the edge of the ranch, wake them up and tell them to keep riding and if I catch them on the ranch they will be hung as trespassers or cattle thieves, they can take their choice!"

"Kinda harsh ain't it?" Paul asked smiling at the thought of the men dancing from the end of a rope.

"That's what they were going to do to that kid K.C., remember that?" Jim asked, "And they were the ones who helped put a noose around his neck so it's no better than they deserve!" Jim was talking like the man he had known years ago, the man who had driven a herd of half wild cattle and men from Abilene, Texas to Dodge City, Kansas, this was the man Paul remembered.

"You need us to stick around?" Joe asked.

Jim shook his head, "Not really!" he said, "The rest of the men are drovers and not the kind of men these guys are. I won't have any problems with them!"

"I'll see you later then." Joe said as he turned the black and slapped it with the reins.

Paul sat and watched as the black took off, clouds of dirt and dust rose behind the animal. "You'll get used to that!" Jim said as Paul watched in disbelief. "What am I gonna get used to?" Paul asked still not sure what Jim meant.

"Riding in the dust" Jim answered as he headed for the barn; there were a lot of repairs to do. Paul put the spurs to his horse and rode off leading the horses and the unconscious men off the Malloy ranch.

"I've got a brand new bar," Paul said talking to the men who lay over their saddle oblivious to the sound of his voice,

"She ain't much right now, just a tent and some tables but come a week from now she is gonna be something and if you boys wake up in time you can come on in and I might even buy you your first drink!

That is if you can hear me!" he said laughing at the men who wouldn't be in any condition to take him up on his offer anytime soon.

As Paul rode off Jim climbed to the roof of the barn and began tearing off the shingles that had gone bad with age. They were split and cracked and these should have been replaced years ago.

Some of them had rotted and his foot went throw in the weaker places leaving large holes where rain and hail would have come through during storms, soaking the horses and grain below.

From the roof of the barn Jim saw more of the Malloy riders coming. He was about to find out if these men rode for the brand or for the pay. If they were the kind of men he had just dealt with or real cowboys taking care of the cattle.

Jim climbed down off the roof and drew the new pistol several times trying to get used to the feel of the weapon. The barrel was shorter than the colts dragoon and it was at least two pounds lighter than the old blunder bust he had been using and he didn't think he was going to be using this one to drive staples in a fence post or to pound in nails!

Jim drew the hammer back, the rolling of the cylinder was smooth and easy, Billy may have been a barroom brawler but if nothing else he knew guns and this was as good as they get.

Jim slid the pistol back into the holster and picked up the rifle, checked the loads and then waited for the men to get there; the barrel of the rifle was pointed at the lead rider as they approached.

Five men sat staring down the barrel as they brought their horses to a stop. "What are you doing here Marshal?" The leader was a tall man wearing a bright red bandana and a black Stetson.

The string of a tobacco pouch hung from his pocket and Jim centered the barrel of the rifle on the dime sized tag on the end of it.

"I'm telling you boys to leave." The speaker for the group of men stood up straight in the saddle making the pistol at his side easier to reach,

"He ain't the Marshal no more Ray, he said he ain't wearing no badge!"

The one called Ray leaned forward, "If you ain't the Marshal you got no authority to run us off!" "No, but I have!" the voice came from behind the ex-Marshal. Startled at the sound of the voice behind him, Jim's finger began to tighten on the trigger.

The tag on the tobacco pouch was a good target and the man wearing it was about to regret it! Something clicked and Jim recognized the voice,

"I thought you had left?" Jim said without bothering to turn around. "When I was riding out I saw these boys riding in and I couldn't very well let you have all the fun so I circled back. After all you snuck up on me once and I just thought I'd return the favor!"

Ray stood up in the saddle again, "It don't matter, there's still only two of you and five of us!" "No," Jim answered, "When I pull this trigger there is only going to be four of you!"

"You're bluffing!" Ray said as he grabbed at the pistol on his side.

The roar of the rifle sounded like a small cannon echoing off the walls of the barn and a half inch hole appeared in the center of the tag hanging from the tobacco pouch.

Jim knew as the shell passed through Ray's body and when it struck bone the head of the shell would expand, and there would be a hole in the man's back large enough to drop a silver dollar through!

The power of the bullet picked Ray up and slung him to the ground behind the horse he was riding.

Lowering the rifle, the used casing dropped to the ground as a fresh one slid into the chamber and in the flick of a second Joe had filled both hands with cocked revolvers ready to take on the next man to move while Jim's rifle was pointed at the next man in line.

"Well?" Jim asked, "Do you want to make it three to two?" Now every man there knew it was no bluff and more were about to die.

The four remaining riders sat looking down at their leader, "No thanks!" one of them said as they turned their horses and headed towards the gate and off the Malloy ranch.

"You know you're going to have trouble with them later!" Joe said as he pulled a pouch of tobacco out of his own pocket.

Jim took the makings out of his pocket and began to build his own cigarette. The paper was yellow with age and Jim poured the tobacco into the folded crease and licked the paper rolling it into a cylinder and then placed it in his mouth and lit the end.

Joe was looking at the body as Jim placed the rifle against a fence post and took a hard pull on the stale tobacco,

"You know you lied to me." Joe said. "How's that?" Jim asked.

"You told me if you ever shot anyone you'd put ten holes in him to make sure he was dead and Ray here has only got one hole!"

"That makes us even, you once told me you were a broken down drifter!" Jim stated. "If you ain't heading into town right away I'll help you put him in the ice house until I can get the undertaker out here," Joe said.

"Either that or we can bury him up on the hill, don't make me much difference."

"I guess we can put him in the ice house!" Jim answered. "I got a lot of work to do and besides he might have family some place that will want to claim the body!"

Both men got a hold of an arm and began to drag the body to the ice house. The cowboys spurs rolled in the dirt kicking up little cloud puffs as he was drag through the yard and into the frigid air of the room, it was midsummer and only small amounts of ice remained.

"What are you gonna do now, Joe asked, you ain't got a hand left on the spread?"

"I'm here, Jim said, and from what I've seen that's one more hand than they had!"

"Maybe it is, Joe answered, but just in case I'm headed back to town and I'll send some men back to help, if I can find any willing to ride out here!"

Jim knew the men that had ridden the cattle trails with him would come to help if he asked but he was not about to ask!

"I can handle it, all I need is a few nails and some boards and this place will be up and running in no time!"

Joe whistled for the black, it still amazed Jim that the horse was willing to let the man ride him. "One of these days that thing is going to throw you and stomp you!" Jim said as Joe swung up on its back.

"Maybe, Joe answered, but one ride is worth the risks!"

Joe drew back the leather straps and slapped the side of the black and the animal took off like a jack rabbit, kicking up the clods of dirt Jim had grown accustomed to.

Jim had to admit maybe one ride was worth the risks with all of his complaining.

He wished he was the one on the back of the black, he would love to be the one leading the pack instead of eating the dust every time the black took off!

After Joe left Jim kicked dirt and sand over the blood trail, he didn't want the dogs or other animals lapping at the blood. Jim walked into the bunk house and stoked up the stove, some of the coals were still hot so he threw in a couple pieces of wood and placed a pot of water with some beans in it on the front of the stove hoping it wouldn't boil over after he went back on the roof of the barn.

The sky was clear and the sun was burning down as Jim climbed to the top and continued tearing the rotted shingles off the neglected building stopping only for a drink of lukewarm water from the canteen at his side. It was a lousy job but someone had to do it and he was the only one left.

CHAPTER THIRTEEN

After several hours of tearing at the shingles he saw a cloud of dust appear in the horizon, it was from a wagon. He sat on the roof as it drew nearer in the distance he could make out the shape of two women; he knew it had to be Sherlene and Marilyn.

A second cloud was coming up fast from behind and no one had to tell him it was probably Joe! Jim climbed down from the roof and awaited the arrival of the women. Sherlene looked gorgeous with the afternoon sun dancing off her hair.

The new dress she wore showed the curves he loved to admire. Her hazel eyes were shining with the love she held for her husband and Jim knew he was a lucky man to be married to her! Marilyn sat beside her, this was the woman Joe was in love with and Jim couldn't blame him, she was a beautiful woman in her own right.

The two of them together could take a man's breath away! There was no mistaking they were sisters!

Jim walked to the wagon and helped the women down, he held his wife close, it had been a long time since they had been together and Jim missed being in her arms.

"Hi honey what brings you ladies out here?" he asked glad for even the few minutes they could be together.

Sherlene looked hurt, "You don't think we'd let you do this all alone do you?" She said as she took his arm in hers and headed towards the house. Stopping at the top of the steps Jim and Sherlene stood at the front door watching as Joe brought the black to a halt in front of the house.

"Saw a dust cloud from the ridge headed this way and I thought it might mean trouble so I doubled back just to make sure everything was alright."

Marilyn stood smiling up at Joe, no cowboy in his right mind rode in a wagon when it was easier to saddle a horse, besides the ride was a lot rougher in the wagon. Marilyn knew he would have seen it was a wagon from a half mile away, she also knew he would have known who was in it!

Joe came off the black in one smooth motion, "Can I help you ladies?" he asked as he walked forward to take Marilyn's arm. It was a beautiful afternoon and the women being at the ranch made it even better. Joe took Marilyn's arm and walked with her up the steps. "If Jim doesn't mind I think I'll hang around, maybe pass him up a few shingles if he is still going to be working on the barn roof!"

Sherlene knew Joe was not interested in the barn or its roof, "I'm sure Jim is still planning on working on the barn." She said. As she nudged him in the ribs Jim took the hint, "Just as soon as I check on the beans!" he replied.

"Sherlene shook her head, "You're not eating beans while we are here!" she said.

Sherlene turned to Marilyn, "I saw a chicken pen as we came up, it was near what looked like an ice house, and if you can find a chicken we can make these boys some mashed potatoes, fried chicken and gravy. If you boys want she offered we can even whip up a pan of biscuits!" Remembering Ray's body was still in the ice house, Joe spoke up,

"If you don't mind I think I'll see about the chicken while she helps you in the kitchen!" "There's no hurry and I can always throw Jim a few shingles!"

The women started cleaning the kitchen as Joe went in search of a chicken.

From the top of the barn Jim heard the cackling of the hens as Joe went into the chicken house. A few minutes later he heard the crack of the axe and the flopping of the bird. It was going to be a while before Jim got any shingles; Joe still had to pluck and gut the chicken before he gave it to the women.

It was a lot of work for one small bird but it was better than eating anything brought out of the ice house!

Jim decided he was going to clean everything out of the ice house after the undertaker left. He was sure between him and Joe they could keep the women out of the room.

"It was getting close to dusk before Joe began to pack the shingles up to the barn roof. "I hate chicken!" Joe said as he laid the first bundle down.

"Tell that to the women, Jim teased I'm sure they would not mind going into the ice house for a couple of steaks!" Jim laughed at the thought of the women walking into the dark room with nothing but a lantern and finding the body!

He knew they would come out of the room white faced and screaming!

"I'll tell them you did it and who do you think they will believe?" Joe dropped the bundles of shingles, "I should have let Skip shoot you!" he said sarcastically as he went down for another load.

"Joe, we're going to have to do something about old Ray before the women find him!" Joe put down another bindle, "Tonight we sneak him onto a horse, take him out onto the range and bury him like I wanted to in the first place!" Joe said flatly.

"I don't care as long as we get him out of the ice house and away from here, if the women stumble across him we're both cooked!"

Joe shook his head it's your funeral if we get caught!"

Marilyn came out on the porch and began to ring the dinner bell, "Dinner is ready!" she said as the men climbed down from the barn.

It was easy to tell the women had put a lot of work into the meal, a lantern sat in the middle of the table giving the room a cozy look and a romantic feel. Fine linen covered the kitchen table , china and silverware replaced the metal utensils both men were used to . Chicken, mashed potatoes and gravy circled the lantern.

Sherlene was bringing hot biscuits out of the oven as they entered. The smell of the food filled the room, "Great, I'm starving!" Jim said as he reached for a piece of fried chicken. Marilyn slapped at his hand, "This is not a beer joint or a restaurant, you'll sit down and say grace before we eat!"

Jim was forced to oblige, the women had done a lot of work and were proud of the meal they had prepared.

"I take it you men are sleeping in the bunk house tonight?" Sherlene said as she filled the plates. Jim knew this last remark was meant for him and it looked like it was going to be another night of sleeping alone.

"Yes I guess we are!" Jim answered staring into the plate set before him.

At least having Joe spend the night would make it easier to sneak off with the body!

Joe tore into the food as Jim pouted over his meal picking at it like a man lost in thought.

Joe spread a large chunk of butter on one of the hot biscuits. "It isn't that bad, after all you got me for company!" Joe said with a smirk.

"Yes and I'm sure there is an old coon dog around here some place too but I ain't interested in sleeping with it either!" Jim growled.

Joe laughed out loud at the thought of Jim in all his misery.

Sherlene and Marilyn began to blush, "alright you men, out of here, we've got to clean this place up!"

Sherlene began to pick up the dishes as Marilyn ushered the men out of the room. Jim took the makings out of his pocket as Marilyn shoved the men out of the house. "You two can stay out here and out of the way until we are done with the dishes, she said, and if you want later we'll put on a pot of coffee!"

Joe reached for his own pouch of tobacco as he leaned against the hitching rail and poured a fine string of tobacco into the crease of the paper, rolled it and lit the end.

"Do you think they will come back tonight?" Joe asked as he flicked his cigarette and looked out into the darkness of the night.

"If you're talking about the Malloy hands we ran off, I don't think so! The only reason they hung around was because of the free booze they were stealing out of the liquor cabinet, that and the fact they had no place else to go.

With old man Malloy dead and the girl gone they weren't making a pay check and what little they had in the bunk house ain't worth fighting or dying for!

My guess is they will steal a few head of cattle and head for the border!" "Kinda like the kids did!" Joe said.

"Yes, kind of like the kids, the only difference is, I figured Nicole had a right to protect her own property and these guys don't have a right to steal from anybody!" "Well, what are you going to do about it?" Joe asked. "Don't know if I can do anything, there is only one of me with thousands of head of cattle spread out over miles of open range.

The Rocking 'R' and the lazy 'B' ranch will both have cattle mixed in with the herd and even with a full crew it would take a week maybe two just to sort out the different brands and separate them from this herd.

Then it will take another week to move them closer to the main house so I can keep an eye on them and then I can't watch them night and day!"

Joe shrugged, "I could always take a few days off, Rog and Schon can take care of things around town until I get back."

"The two of us with the black might be able to bring the herd in closer to the house but we still wouldn't be able to keep a close eye them! Joe agreed. "Well, maybe we could get some help from around town?" Joe stated as the women came out of the house carrying coffee for the men.

"Keep an eye on what?" They asked at the same time.

"The cattle, Joe answered, Jim is worried about losing them!" "Why can't we help, Marilyn could take some time off from the restaurant and we are both good riders?" Sherlene asked thrilled with the idea of helping to round up cattle.

Sherlene loved adventure and this sounded like a good one. Marilyn's eyes lit up at the prospect of being around Joe, "Sure we can help, and Terry and Eloise can take care of the restaurant till we get back.

Without Paul and the drunks being there it will be easy for them to take care of it! Besides, I've been looking for an excuse to take a vacation and this sounds great!"

Sherlene and Marilyn went back into the house, making plans on how they could help with the roundup.

The rattle of a wagon and the clop, clop of the hooves of the horses could be heard in the distance as the men sat on the porch and drank the coffee.

Soon it was apparent the wagon was headed for the Malloy ranch and as it drew nearer Joe reached for the lamp hanging from a nail driven in the beams of the porch and in a few steps Joe was swallowed in the shadows. As the wagon neared, Joe lit the lamp, he was standing behind the trunk of a large oak tree and as the wagon got closer he put the lantern on the ground. This would make him impossible to see from almost anywhere.

When the wagon pulled up in front of the house Jim stepped from the corner of the house, the rifle was in his hands as he watched from the shadows.

"Hel-low in the house!" the voice; belonged to one of the young cowboys that loved to terrorize Marilyn.

"Bobby, what are you doing out here in the middle of the night?" Jim asked, hardly believing that the man would ride this far just for the fun of pestering Marilyn, "Brought you something!" he said. "Who is that in the wagon with you?" Jim asked. Bobby looked kind of sheepish. "This is Michelle, my wife!" Marilyn ran from the house, "When did you get married?" she demanded.

Under her sharp eye Bobby wilted, which was really quite funny. "Well, we're not married yet, but we're going to be as soon as we can find a Justice of the Peace!" "You get married without me being there and I'll skin your hide!" she threatened as she stormed back into the house. "And you're not getting married by any Justice of the Peace! You're getting married in a church with a preacher!" Even the thought of one of the cowboys getting married without her being there was enough to infuriate the woman!

"I've done everything but change their diapers for them over the years and if they get married without me I'll tan their hides there in the church, right in front of the preacher and the whole congregation!" She told Sherlene as she stormed around the room.

Bobby got down from the wagon and then helped his future bride from the wagon.

"Maybe you best go inside." Bobby instructed as he removed the tarp from the back of the wagon. "Here's your present boys!" Bobby beamed with pride as he revealed Rick still alive lying in the bottom of the wagon bed.

"What am I supposed to do with him?" Jim asked. "I ain't no doctor!" "Well, he rode for the Malloy brand and Malloy is the one who sent him on the ambush that got him cutup. The way I see it the Malloy ranch is responsible for him, besides he's got no kin folk that I know of and as far as I know this is the only place he's got left!"

Jim knew Bobby was right, Rick had no kin folks and in a lot of ways he was the same as Joe had been, a homeless drifter riding where ever the jobs took him.

Jim grabbed Rick by the heels of the boots and began to pull him from the wagon, "Easy, Bobby said, he still ain't in that good a shape!" Joe jumped in the wagon and picked Rick up by the shoulders and together they carried Rick from the wagon.

"Where are we going to put him?" Joe asked. "He ain't dead yet so we might as well put him in the bunkhouse."

Bobby held the door open as the men carried Rick inside. "I got some medicine for him in the wagon." Bobby said as they laid Rick on one of the bunks; Rick had not so much as flinched as he was being carried!

"What are you giving him?" Joe asked surprised that the man was still unconscious after the rough handling of the move.

"A mix of whisky and opium, called Laudanum." Bobby climbed into the wagon and retrieved the bottle of medicine. After I put this in the bunkhouse I want you to pull the wagon down to the icehouse, Jim told him.

"Why would anybody load ice in the middle of the night?" Bobby asked as the men went through the door. Joe turned around,

"Shut up, we don't want the women to know what we are doing!"

Bobby set on the wagon seat and watched as Joe and Jim loaded the body of a dead man into the wagon.

"Crap, if Michelle sees that she is gonna jump out of the wagon and walk home!" Bobby complained.

Both men spoke up at the same time, "Then keep him covered!" Jim jumped up on the back of the wagon and began to pull the tarp over the body,

"Hold on a minute!" Joe said as he climbed into the back. "If you ain't superstitious you'll need this!" Joe said as he undid the gun belt from around the dead man.

Jim looked down at his own gun belt; the fast draw holster with the bullet loops sown into the belt was a lot better than the rig he wore.

It was a pain in the butt carrying the shells for the new gun in his pocket and the powder flask, ball and caps to the old gun were a pain to get to plus the old pistol was slow to load. "Thanks!" Jim said taking the new gun; maybe it would bring him more luck than it had its predecessor!

Joe took the spurs off the dead man's boots because the grinding of the spurs was sure to give away the fact that someone was in the back of the wagon and if they wanted to sneak Ray out it had to be done!

Jim turned back to Bobby, "After you drop Michelle off take him to the undertakers, he will know what to do with him and after that see if you can get a couple of men to come out here and give us a hand,

We need to move the cattle closer to the ranch house!" "Will do!" Bobby said as he pulled the wagon away from the ice house, it wouldn't pay for the women to see where he was parked and get suspicious and the last thing in the world Bobby wanted was for Michelle to look into the back of the wagon!

The women came out of the house as Bobby pulled up. "It's getting late," Sherlene said, "Why don't you spend the night that way you can always leave in the morning?"

Bobby felt stuck and didn't know what to say, "That would be fine, Jim said but he has to get back to town, he's going to send us some men to help with the round up and we'll need them in the morning and besides I don't want him rushing cause I knowed a fellow one time rushing around in the dark that lost half his load!"

Michelle climbed into the wagon and set next to Bobby, "I don't mind riding around in the dark with Bobby!" she said snuggling up next to the man besides her. "Besides the only load we have is that dumb tarp and I don't care if we lose it or not!"

Jim took Sherlene around the waist and pulled her close, both couples stood and watched as Bobby pulled the wagon out of the yard,

"By mom!" Bobby cried as they rode out into the darkness hopping to get one more rise out of Marilyn before they vanished from sight.

Michelle snuggled up closer to Bobby, she had heard the remark Bobby had made to Marilyn about them being married and if she had her way it was going to be true,
If she had her way he was going to pop the question for real and she was going to be engaged before the night was over! It was a beautiful Texas night, the stars were shining under a full moon and she was riding with the man she loved and if there was a more romantic setting she had never seen it!

Bobby held the reins in his left hand while his right arm was around Michelle pulling her closer. He liked the feel of her body next to his and the way she smiled and even the color of her eyes! Maybe tonight he would ask her to marry him, after all what could be more romantic than a moon light buggy ride?

"I hope they make it!" Joe said as he tuned to walk away. "What is that supposed to mean?" Marilyn asked. "Nothing, Joe answered, but it's dark out there and anything could happen!" "Yes, they could even lose the tarp!" Jim said laughing at the thought of Michelle finding the body and freaking out in the dark! "Boy, Bobby was going to have his hands full if that happened," he thought to himself.

CHAPTER FOURTEEN

All three of the men riding behind Paul had managed to wake up before they reached town and they didn't have to be told they were tied to their saddles. The bindings on their feet and wrists told them all they needed to know.
 The bouncing of the horse had made the drunk sick and he was throwing up on the saddle. Vomit and booze was running down the side of the horse, "let me up!" he cried choking in his own waste!
Paul stopped the horses and walked back to the men where he began to cut them loose one at a time. The bindings had been tight and the men had lost circulation in their arms and feet. Paul had to catch them as they unloaded and then place them on the ground until they were strong enough to stand on their own.
 "What happened? One of them demanded to know.
 "You got run off the Malloy ranch!" Paul informed them.
  "Where's my gun?" the one who had been drunk was asking.
 "It's back at the ranch and if I was you I would forget it!" Paul was beginning to lose his patients. "What do you mean?" again it was the drunk with the belligerent attitude.
  "Look, three things are gonna happen if you ride back! One, Jim said he would hang any one of you caught back on the Malloy ranch! Now I don't think he is going to do that but what I do think is he is gonna bust you upside the head as hard as he can then he is gonna pound on you for a while and in that case you gonna look worse than your buddy here! Number Two, that gun slinging pal of his is gonna give you back your gun then make you use it! One way or another you still ain't gonna have that gun and you might wind up dead!" The drunk stood up and tried to clear his head,
 "I'm going back for my gun!" he stated. Paul shook his head, "it sure ain't a good day for the Malloy riders is it?"

The drunk turned around to look at Paul as he drew back his fist and let it fly. The drunks head looked as if it was attached to his shoulders with a rubber band as the massive fist landed, driving it backwards, almost to the point of breaking!

"Number Three, is for the doctor," Paul said as he loaded the man over his saddle and tied the bindings
, "Well do you two want to ride sitting up or laid over?" Neither man wanted to move but then again neither wanted to ride draped over their horse either!

"We're coming!" they grumbled as they climbed to their feet and mounted the horses. Paul stroked the horse carrying the unconscious man, "Sorry about that!" he said feeling sorry for the animal. "When we get back to town I'll make sure you get cleaned up!"

The unconscious man woke up just before they entered the town, he began to complain but this time it fell on deaf ears and he was no longer drunk and his head felt as if it had been hit with the blunt end of a pole axe.

"You're trying to kill me!" he complained.

"If you don't like the treatment keep your mouth shut!" Paul said as he pulled up to the tent that served as a bar. "If you boys want to come in I'll buy you a drink!" Two of them shook their head slowly trying not to increase the pain.

Paul cut the third man lose with the knife at his side, "you coming in?" he asked as the man put his boot in the stirrups and pulled at the reins, "Not with you!" he said as he started to pull away.

Paul reached up and grabbed the man by the arm and pulled and this time he was not gentle, the man landed flat on his back in the street,

"I told that horse I'd see to it that it would get cleaned up when we reached town and that is just what I plan to do, so you either walk him over to the trough and give him a bath or I'll do it for you!"

The side of the man's head was red and bruised and there was a large knot that took up most of his face. He was trying to catch his breath from the fall but he was still belligerent, "And if I don't give him a bath?"

Then I'll bust you harder than Jim ever could have!" Paul threatened.

As the men rode off Paul walked into the bar and saw Nita behind the make shift bar selling drinks,

"What are you doing here?" he asked as she handed him a shot glass filled with the good liquor from below the bar.

Nita put on her best smile, "It's the least I could do for my new partner!" Nita filled her own glass and tapped it against his and took a sip.

Paul was about to explode, "What do you mean, new partner?" "Well, Nita said, I heard you've been trying to hire some of my girls and if that is the case I figure we're going to be partners, either that or I'm gonna start selling booze at my place!" Nita smiled again, "It shouldn't take long for me to put you out of business!"

Paul knew she spoke the truth and he didn't have the funds to go against the woman, his dreams of being a private owner and the Lord of his own domain was over.

This woman had the money to bury him! At the very least she could put him out of business for good.

Bobby and Michelle took the buggy and wagon road back into town, it was a longer ride but Michelle didn't mind she just snuggled up closer to her future husband.

Bobby didn't mind because it w

The town was deserted as they drove up, even Paul's make shift bar was closed.

Several dogs began following the wagon and howling at the top of their lungs.

Michelle tried to shoo them away but they became more aggressive and some even tried to jump into the back of the wagon.

"What is wrong with these crazy dogs!" she screamed as they ran alongside.

Bobby took out his pistol and fired a round into the ground in front of the dogs. The pack of dogs took off running at the sound of the revolver and the smack of the bullet landing beside their paws.

Michelle watched as the dogs ran, some forward and others back.

The street lamps lit the back of the wagon and she could see that the tarp had moved during the night and the toe of one boot showed from beneath the tarp. "I thought we dropped Rick off?" she said as she pulled back the tarp to check on the man.

Ray lay face up, his dead eyes stared up into the heavens and it only took a second for Michelle to realize this was not Rick and a dead man lay in the back of the wagon.

Michelle turned on him with flailing fists, swinging at his face and arms,

"How could you?" she screamed as she swung at the man beside her. "Stop it!" Bobby yelled. Between the dogs, the gun fire and Michelle's screams the horses were acting up and he was having a hard time controlling them.

As Bobby yelled they bolted, tearing through town at break neck speeds, "You're going to get us killed!" he cried as he fought for control of the runaway team.

Bobby had fought runaway teams before but never in the middle of the night and never with a hysterical woman trying to claw his eyes out!

He was pleading with her to stop and he knew he couldn't push her away because she might fall out of the wagon and get run over.

He was doing his best to bring the team under control and his soon to be bride at the same time! He spoke again, this time in a lower voice

"Stop it honey before you kill us both!"

This time Michelle listened and stopped the beating, she even pulled herself against Bobby and held on as he fought the frightened horses,

"Stop them!" she begged as the wagon rocked from side to side. He set the break with his foot as he pulled with all his strength against the reins.

Bobby felt the horses turn to the right so he jerked the reins to the left. The wagon was up on two wheels as the horses turned then rocked and came up on the opposite two wheels,

"Hang on!" Bobby cried as the wagon launched forward and they were being bounced around on the wagon seat as it hit the ruts in the road. "We're gonna crash!"

Michelle cried as Bobby fought the team. Lights were coming on as they charged through town. Ray bounced out of the wagon and into the street. The dogs were no longer interested in Ray they were doing their best to get out of the way of the runaway wagon.

The lead horse stumbled and fell dragging the animal next to him down into the dirt.

They skidded in the dirt as the wagon tongue slid beside them. The wagon came to a stop with chains and braces locked tight but still on its wheels!

Bobby hopped down and ran to the horses; they were trying to stand even as he approached. Michelle was climbing down from the wagon,

"Quick! Bobby said, go get the doc!" "You mean the vet?" Michelle asked.

"They're the same thing!" Bobby said, "Just go get one of them!"

Michelle ran towards the stables! The horses were standing as Paul came running up, "What can I do to help?" he asked as Bobby ran his hands over the animals, checking for broken bones. "Will you go get the undertaker?" Bobby asked.

"Why, Paul wanted to know, the horses weren't dead!

Did you run somebody over?" "No, Bobby answered, he was shot!"

"Who did you kill?" Paul demanded trying to understand how Bobby could shoot someone while fighting a terrified pair of horses.

"I didn't kill anyone, Jim did!"

"Jim could not have killed anyone, Paul answered, he is out at the Malloy ranch!"

"I know he is out at the ranch, that's where he killed Ray!"

"Who is Ray?" Paul wanted to know.

Ray is the guy Jim killed!" Bobby replied.

"Well then why do you need an undertaker?" Paul persisted

"Because Ray is laying out in the street!" Bobby said.

"If Jim killed him at the ranch how come he's lying in the street?" Paul was curious. "Look, Bobby said, Jim shot him at the ranch and I brought him to town in the wagon and he got pitched out when the horses bolted and he is laying out there now!

So could you please go get the undertaker and pick him up before someone else steps on him?"

No one ever said Paul was the sharpest person on the planet, Bobby thought but he might as well have been talking to a tree stump but in the end Paul finally understood,

"Sure, he said, why didn't you say so in the first place!"

Paul took off running as Bobby continued to check on the horses.

Doc was young but well trained; he took over Bobby's place and began to check the horses. "They will be alright." He said after checking the bumps and bruises.

"What about Ray?" Bobby asked. "Paul dragged him off the street; he will be alright until I get there." "What are you going to do with him?" Bobby asked. "Put him in the ice house for tonight and tomorrow we'll bury him." The doctor answered. "Great! Bobby said, that's where I picked him up from!"

"Now, if you will excuse me, the doc. Answered I'm headed to bed! In the excitement Bobby had forgotten how late it was, "Sorry about waking you up, he said, it's just that I was afraid one of the horses might have broken a leg or something!"
"Don't worry about it, he answered, a couple of cowboys from the Malloy ranch woke me up earlier, one of the men looked like he had been kicked in the face by a bull and I had just finished wiring his jaw shut when you decided to charge through town!"
"Thanks again, doc." Bobby said as the man left heading on his way home for a much needed rest. "What are you gonna do now?" Michelle asked not sure if there was anything they could do.
"Well, the first thing to do is unhitch the horses and put them in the stable, their gonna need feed and water after the night they have had and after that I'm headed out to the Lazy 'B' ranch to get Roy and Mike up.
 I figure their gonna want to help with the round up on the Malloy ranch.
You might as well go home and get some rest because I'll be with them for the next few days trying to get the herd together
. Paul stepped out from the group of men that had gathered around the wagon, "I'll buy you two a drink before you leave, it will help settle the shakes!"
"I've got to take care of the horses first, you two go have a drink and I will join you as soon as I can." Bobby said.
 Schon came up about that time and took the horses by the reins, "Don't worry about them, I'll take care of the horses, you two go have that drink." Schon said as he started walking the horses to the stables and after wiping them down and putting salve on the cuts, Schon gave them some grain and water. It was turning out to be a long night for the deputy. He would be glad when things quieted down, all he wanted to do was go back to the office, kick his feet up and sleep for the rest of the night!

Bobby tossed the second shot of the strong tequila down as Paul poured himself a third, "That's all I can have, Bobby said, I've got a long ways to go! If I drink a third I might not be going anywhere!"

Michelle sipped at her second drink but hers was no shot glass, she drank from a large beer glass. Bobby took her hand, "Come on honey, it's time to go." He said as Michelle signaled for a third.

Michelle turned like a caged panther, her honey sweet eyes blazed with anger Bobby had never seen before, "We were engaged!" she cried as she began swinging at the man in a half drunken rage. Bobby wrapped his arms around her, this time it was not an embracement of love, it was an act of survival! She was trying to tear his eyes out with her claws and Bobby was forced to hang on for dear life! "How fast life changes," he thought, it was less than an hour ago he had stopped the wagon on top of the hill overlooking the town where he had gotten down on one knee and proposed.

It was the perfect setting, Michelle looked so innocent at the time, and the smile on her face had lit up the sky as she accepted his proposal. He had held her in his arms marveling at how lucky he was but now he was terrified that if he let go she was going to scratch out his eyes! Paul watched the fight with excitement, he loved a good fight and this was stacking up to be a good one! "Have another drink,"

Paul said pouring a third as Bobby held Michelle in his arms. Paul knew the more she drank the madder she would become and he looked forward to the fight. Bobby held Michelle in his arms until she calmed down then took a drink from the glass, this time his was not shot glass but a beer mug.

Michelle picked up her own drink and downed what was left and swung the mug at Bobby's head. Paul was right, the more she drank the madder she got. She could not believe Bobby had held her in his arms and told her how much he loved her, then got down on his knee and proposed to her all the while knowing there was a corpse in the back of the wagon!

She was crying hysterically, "The wedding is off!" she screamed. This time Bobby couldn't believe what he was hearing, Michelle ran from the bar as Bobby stood in a trance, how could she do this to him? Didn't she know how important she was to him?

Paul poured another shot of tequila and sat and watched as Bobby stood in disbelief, "She will come back, he said, after she cools down!" Bobby was not so sure, "How do you know? Bobby asked. "I know women, Paul said, and I know she loves you, she will be back!"

"Great, now I'm taking advice about love from a lonely old bar tender that looks like a large blonde haired gorilla!" Bobby decided he had never felt so desperate or alone in his life, "Could my life get any worse?" he thought as he reached for the glass in front of him. He was ready to start crying into the empty glass as Schon walked in,

"Alright close up!" he said. Bobby tried to stand, "It's alright, I'm leaving anyway!" he said as Paul started to object. Schon watched as Bobby staggered through the door, "What's wrong with him?" Schon asked seeing the look of pain on Bobby's face.

"Girl troubles!" Paul said and that was all Schon needed to know,

"Maybe I better keep an eye on him." Schon said as he started out the door. Young men with girl problems could do desperate things! Schon watched as Bobby made his way to the stables and it was apparent he was not used to the strong bite of the tequila.

Apple shied away as Bobby walked into the stall, it seemed the horse was not used to the smell of the tequila either! Bobby stroked the animal's neck trying to calm her down. Apple was a small black and white Pinto with one white stocking.

She was too small to hold a thousand pound bull tied to her saddle with a rope but she was a good cutting horse, quick and agile. During the fall Bobby collected the wild apples that grow on the Lazy 'B' ranch for the horse, they were her favorite food and she would follow the man around all day for one bite or one small apple, this was the reason Bobby called her Apple.

Schon watched as Bobby picked up the saddle and lost his balance. Stumbling backwards Bobby slammed against the boards of the stall, slid down and wound up sitting on his butt with the saddle in his lap! "How about I help you to the hotel?" Schon offered as he picked the saddle up off the man.

Bobby had never been this drunk in his life; the barn was spinning from the bite of the tequila as Schon helped him to his feet.

"Can't, Bobby said, I'm going to tell Mike and Roy that we got to help Jim and the gunfighter round up cattle tomorrow!" Schon shook his head, "even if I saddled you're horse for you, I don't think you could make it out the barn door, much less to the ranch! It's either the hotel or the jail, your choice!"

Unlike his partners Bobby was not much of a drinker and until tonight he had thought of himself as a lover but after the night he just had he was not so sure of that either. "I've never been in jail." He said as Schon led him out the stable doors. "You're not going to be locked up, Schon explained; all I want to do is get you some place where you'll be safe. I don't want you hurting yourself until after you're sobered up!"

Bobby stumbled along as Schon led him to the jail, "You ain't gonna lock it?" Bobby asked as Schon laid him on the bunk in the cell. Bobby lay on his side and pulled his knees up to his chest, "I'm gonna be sick!" he said as the room began once again to spin. This was the worse ride he had ever been on!

"I ought to bust Paul upside the head for giving you that much tequila!" Schon said as he handed Bobby a hot cup of the strong black coffee. "Sit up and have a real drink, it might make you feel better!" Schon knew it was going to take a while for the coffee to do any good but might as well get a good start!

Nita was having her own problems, as Michelle lay in her arms sobbing, "Bobby asked me to marry him and I said yes!" Nita did not understand, "Wasn't that what you wanted?" Nita was still confused, "if you didn't want to marry the cowboy why did you say yes?"

"I do want to marry him, Michelle answered, but I broke off the engagement!" "Why would you break off the engagement if you wanted to marry him?"

This was making no sense to the woman. "He was hiding a dead man in the wagon behind me all the while he was telling me how much he loved me. He didn't even tell me it was there and if it weren't for the dogs barking I might have never known. Then he took a shot at the dogs and made the horses bolt! I was on a runaway wagon that almost killed me all because of him and his stupid dead body! How could I ever trust a man like that?"

Nita stroked her hair as she sobbed in her arms, she knew they were a far cry from Bobby's arms and Michelle needed to be in his arms but this was the best she could do.

Nita knew there was going to be no sleeping tonight and it was going to be a long lonely night for both of them.

CHAPTER FIFTEEN

Joe awoke with the feeling that he had never felt so alive, every fiber of his body felt the love he felt for the woman waiting for him in the house and he almost sang as he got out of the bed. It was a gorgeous day and it was about to get better, he was going to see the woman he dreamed of.

The smell of mesquite logs being burned in the wood stove lingered in the air and found its way into the bunk house, he could even smell bacon being fried in an iron skillet. He picked up the small water bowl and filled it with water and soaped up the rag that served as a wash cloth and hanging the mirror on the handle of the stove damper Joe began to shave using the four inch piece of honed steel known as a straight razor.

Rick was sleeping in the bed next to the wood burning stove; Joe put down the razor, dried the soap off his face with the rag and walked over to his bed. The man didn't look good so Joe pulled back the bandages covering the knife wound.

It had been bad; a ten to twelve inch gash ran just below Rick's neck.
The blade had bitten deep cutting along the ribs to the bone and across the shoulder. It was a clean cut and the kids had done a good job stitching it up but Rick had lost a lot of blood.

Joe couldn't see any sign of infection so he covered the wound with the bandages, maybe later he would wash it and change the bandages and put clean ones on but for now the thing Rick needed most was rest, that and all the liquids the women could get him to drink.

Rick began to groan from the pressure of Joe's hand replacing the bandage and as Joe started to step back Rick's eyes opened. The look of both fear and shame crossed his face, "Who are you?" he asked as his eyes focused on Joe, this was a man he didn't know.

"I'm not the one who did this!" Joe said pointing at the gash in his shoulder.

"I know." Rick said as his mind went back to the night of the knifing. Even in his weakened state he remembered the look on Frankie's face as he had attacked him.

"That was Frankie!" Rick was in a talking mood "I killed a man once, he said, it was years ago in Dallas. I was young then and it was a fair fight but I could never shake the shame of taking another life and I swore it would never happen again but I guess I was wrong, I was supposed to help kill some kids but I could never have done it. I guess Frankie figured that one out and decided to shut me up and when he tried to kill me I killed him instead.

I didn't want to but he forced me into it, it was either kill or be killed!" Joe shook his head; there was no sense in letting the man torture himself, "He won't be back, the men he rode with took care of that!" "What about them, Rick asked, they will be looking for revenge!"

"No they won't, we buried them south of the border, and they won't be looking for anybody, ever!" Joe could see that Rick was tired, "Get some sleep," he said as he gently pushed the man over on his side. "I'll check on you later," he promised as he headed out the door.

The sun had risen over the horizon as Joe headed for the barn; it was turning out to be a beautiful morning. Barn swallows dove at his head as he entered the door of the barn trying to drive him away from the nests they had hidden in the rafters.

Even the sound of the desert owl could be heard in the distance. The black trotted up to the barn as he saw Joe approach, he knew it was feeding time and he looked forward to the small scuffle he would have with the man feeding him. The horse loved to shove at him with his head and the feel of the man's hands as he scratched him behind the ear. This man was not his master, he was his friend.

That morning was one of those mornings Joe was right about, some animals do wake up in a better mood than some people and this was one of those mornings. Jim woke up in a lousy mood; he pulled his shirt gently over the red blisters covering his back. He couldn't believe that he had burned that fast or that bad. After Joe and Paul left he had removed his shirt exposing the white flesh of his skin to the merciless west Texas sun as he tore the shingles from the barn. It had only been for a few hours at best and in return it had turned his skin into a bright crimson color. Small blisters covered his back and shoulders.

This was not going to be one of his better days and even the smell of the mesquite coming from the kitchen stove or bacon frying in the pan did nothing to help his disposition. All he wanted was a cup of coffee and maybe some ice to lie across his back.

Glancing at the bunks he could see that Joe had already gone as his boots, hat and pistols were missing. He was not surprised; it had been a restless night because of the burns and the fact that he had heard Joe talking to Rick.

Jim ran the razor up and down the leather strap putting a fine edge on the piece of steal before he began to shave. The last thing he wanted was a face full of cuts to go along with the blisters! Rick lay in the bed watching as Jim finished shaving, taking his right hand he felt along his own face and realized it had been more than a few days since it had felt the touch of a razor. "Do you think I could borrow that," he asked. Jim watched as the shaking hand went back to the man's side, he was in no mood to watch the man cut his own throat and he was in no mood to shave the man himself!

"Maybe tomorrow," Jim said as he laid the razor next to the bowl that served as a wash basin. He was tired, he was hungry and he wanted to see his wife! He knew Joe was already going to be in the kitchen drinking coffee and eating breakfast and he might even be laughing and going on with the women.

Maybe Jim was a little jealous, after all he was the one who was married so why was he sleeping in the bunk house with the rest of the men when he could be spending the nights in the loving arms of his wife!

It was turning out to be a miserable morning; with the blisters on his back he doubted if the day was going to be any better than the night. Joe was exiting the barn as Jim walked out of the bunk house. Joe looked in a good mood for a person that was about to spend his day chasing wild cattle out of a Texas draw or dodging the horns of the always dangerous cattle known as the long horn but of course Joe was going to be riding in the saddle on the back of the black!

For the next few days his life was not going to be easy but it was going to be an adventure! Joe was in a good mood and smiling as he slapped Jim on the back, "Are you ready for this?" he asked as he headed through the door. Jim was not ready for anything but hated to show a weakness in front of the man he considered a friend.

"As ready as I'll ever be!" he stated through clenched teeth and winching from the pain of the slap to his back.

Sherlene wore a pair of Levi's, boots and a bright red bandana was tied around her neck as the broad brim of the Stetson hung over the arm of a chair. Even in the men's attire she was beautiful, the curves beneath let everyone know this was no man! This alone brought a smile to Jim's face; maybe today was not going to be so bad after all!

Joe only had eyes for the woman standing beside her and like Sherlene; Marilyn was dressed in the same working attire. The yellow bandana tied around her neck set a golden tint to her light brown hair. It was with difficulty that Joe made his way to the table, every fiber of his being wanted to take the woman in his arms and tell her how much he loved her! Joe sat at the table watching the women work around the kitchen as the smell of bacon, eggs and pancakes filled the room. The coffee was black and strong just the way he liked it. Sherlene and Marilyn sat sipping coffee as the men attacked the hot breakfast with a ravenous appetite. Marilyn set aside her cup, "how is Rick," she asked.

Joe was the one she was looking at and for a just a second he felt a twinge of jealousy, "How would I know!" he answered and for a split second he regretted the answer. This was not what he had meant to say, this made him look cold and hard and that was not the impression he wanted to give to the woman sitting next to him!

Marilyn knew there was a softer side to the man but it had been buried deep a long time ago. "I'll go check on him," she answered. Joe felt the flair of anger and jealousy at the thought of her being in the room with the injured man. "I'll check on him later!" he answered. "Don't bother!" Marilyn said sarcastically, "I'll check on him now!" Joe couldn't help the jealousy raging in his heart, why was he acting so stupid? "Why bother, he asked, the guy ain't nothing but a bush whacker and cattle thief and they should have hung him from the first limb they came across!"

Joe couldn't believe he was saying this. Why was he trying to pick a fight with the woman he loved and planned on marrying, yet he was deliberately trying to antagonize her! "He is no bushwhacker and no murder, Marilyn snapped at him, I don't believe he ever would have killed anyone, he is just a man who grew too old and was forced to do whatever he was told!" Marilyn stomped out of the room fuming at the man she was in love with, "How could he be so cold?" she wondered as she headed for the bunk house.

Rick lay on the bed watching as Marilyn came through the door with a tray in her hands and it was easy to tell she was upset. "What's the matter?" he asked as she set the tray down and began to remove the bandages, "Nothing!" she said as she pulled at the last of them, she was on the verge of crying and Rick winched in pain as the last one came off. "Maybe I had better wait for the other fellow," Rick said as Marilyn poked and prodded at the wound.

"What makes you think they are any better at this than I am?" she said still fuming at the callus remark Joe had made. Rick let loose with a cry of pain, he was better this morning!" "Who was better this morning?" she asked astonished. "Don't know his name, never met him before but he was the fellow with the cross-draw holster." "If he checked on you why did he tell me he didn't know what condition you were in today?"

"Don't know, Rick confided, love does make a man say strange things sometimes!" Marilyn began to calm down, maybe he was not as cold and callus as he tried to appear! Marilyn went back to cleaning the wound but this time she was a lot gentler. Rick thought about asking for a shave but that might have been pushing his luck and if Joe was the jealous type he did not want to get tangled up in that mess!

Sherlene had finished washing the dishes as Marilyn came into the house, "Are you ready for this?" she asked as she put down the dish rag and placed the dark brown Stetson on her head. Marilyn was not only ready she looked forward to the adventure,

"You bet!" she said as she reached for her own hat. Hers was black with a silver band, she knew it was an expensive hat and not really the kind a person wore on a trail drive or a round up but she loved it, she had ordered it from a magazine. She remembered waiting for it with anticipation, it took six weeks for the hat to arrive and this was the first time she would be able to wear it without looking out of place.

Marilyn placed the hat on her head with just a little tilt, "Wait until Joe sees this," she thought as she admired herself in the mirror. "Come on we ain't got all day to admire ourselves!" Sherlene said thinking sure Marilyn looked good but so did she!

Both women started out the door at the sound of a wagon coming to a stop in front of the house. This was not the job they had volunteered for! Jim pulled a large chuck wagon up to the front porch, "Here you go ladies," he said as he stepped down from the wooden plank that served as a seat. The canvas tarp over the wagon looked like the sail of a ship at sea, blown tight from a strong wind. One thing for sure neither one of the women wanted to be the captain of this ship and Jim couldn't help seeing the expression of disgust on their faces, "Relax ladies Joe's saddling your horses now, and I'm the one riding the blister end of this thing.

I was hoping you would stock it for me though? I ain't the best cook on the planet and I'd probably forget half the things we would need." "There are just four of us, Sherlene said, how much do you think we will need?" "There are four of us now, Jim said, but there will be more later!" "How many more?" Sherlene asked. "Well if my guess is right Roy and Mike are going to show up plus Paul and Bobby, that makes eight of us altogether and there is a chance of a few others, granted not much of a chance but a chance. That means you will have to pack enough food for at least eight people for a week!"

"We don't mind packing it as long as we don't have to ride in that thing and we are not going to do all of the cooking either!"

If Jim had ever entertained thoughts of them volunteering to drive the wagon those thoughts were now gone! Sherlene started a list, "We'll need flour, bacon, beans, eggs, sugar and coffee." There was a lot of food to be gathered but the women knew their jobs and it was a lot better than Jim would have done, if it was left up to him everyone would be eating beans for the next week.

Joe brought three horses out of the barn as the women were loading the wagon. One of them was a light chestnut color with two white stockings, one was a beautiful black and white paint and the third was Jim's horse following behind the others. "I didn't think the women were gonna volunteer to ride on the wagon so I didn't saddle your horse." Joe informed him. "Thanks, Jim said, now I have to walk back to the barn for my saddle!" Joe didn't mind the little remark,

"That will teach you to put me in jail!" Joe joked as Jim started back to the barn. The women had finished loading the wagon as Jim came back with his saddle and bridle and after placing those in the wagon Sherlene informed him that they would need some meat for the round up. Neither man wanted to eat anything from the ice house.

"We'll kill it on the way!" Joe said as Marilyn started towards the ice house door. "What about Rick, Sherlene asked, we can't just leave him; he will starve to death before we get back, even if he doesn't get an infection." Rick was something Jim had not planned on; Mike or Roy should be here by tomorrow." He said. They can take care of him "What does he do until then, lay there and suffer, Sherlene asked, and what if they don't come, he can't get up[and make his own meals, he will starve to death in that bed, if he doesn't die of thirst first!"

"Great, why is everyone asking me these questions, Jim thought, why hadn't I stayed a farmer? This was not even his war, "What am I supposed to do, he wondered, fine, we'll put him in the wagon for now, at least I'll have some company!"

Jim growled as he looked at Sherlene. Sherlene smiled sweetly at her husband, there's no way she was going to ride in the wagon! "Can you back that thing?" Joe asked as Jim climbed aboard. "I can back it as soon as you get those horses out of the way, Jim snarled!

Jim began to back the wagon up to the door of the bunk house just as soon as Joe moved the other horses out of his way. "You're one lucky man, Jim said, you're about to spend the next week with two beautiful women!" Rick didn't know what he meant but anything was better than lying stiff and alone in the small rough bed for the next week.

"What do you mean?" he asked. "You're going on a cattle drive," Jim said. Ricks eyes lit up at the prospect, it had been almost five years since he had ridden the range like a real cowboy, even if it was in the bottom of a wagon, at least he could smell the aroma of the open fire and he would be able to watch the night sky as the stars flicker overhead and hear the cry of the lonely coyote looking for a mate.

This was the life Rick had left behind as he grew older and this was the life he missed! It didn't matter how he got there as long as he could go one more time, he would give anything to be on a real cattle drive with men he respected and in the process earn respect back again for the first time in years. He wanted to die an honest man, a man he could look at in the mirror and not be disgusted at. With Jim's help Rick managed to stand and then he began to walk, this was an adventure he did not want to miss out on.

Joe pulled Rick into the wagon and laid his head on Jim's saddle, it wasn't the best pillow in the world but Rick didn't mind one bit, he had used them before. There was a pistol belt hung beside Rick's bunk, "this is probably yours, Jim said, the pistol was probably taken when you were delirious but if you will hang on a second I'll see if I can find you a new one." Jim went into the ice house and after stumbling around in the dark for a few minutes he came out carrying out what he went in for, the revolver that had fallen out of Ray's holster.
   Rick looked at the pistol; it was pearl handled with several notches on the handle. He knew the owner of the weapon but before he could ask about it Joe cut in, "Don't worry nobody is going to come looking for it." "That was a relief, the former owner had been a hot head that Rick thought was crazy and if the man was still alive, being in possession of the revolver could have gotten him killed.
   Rick sat back admiring the weapon as Jim climbed on board. There was no need to crack the whip; the team of horses behind the harnesses was ready for whatever lay ahead. Jim had to lean back to reach the wheel brake and after jerking back hard on the long oak handle the brake was released. Soon the horses were starting forward and everyone knew the real journey was about to begin.
   It may have been an adventure to the others but for Jim it was a journey. There were still small bands of hostile Indians roaming the area plus Texas had more snakes than any place he had ever seen. Rattlesnakes, water moccasins, coral snakes, cottonmouths and copperheads all lived in Texas. He had even heard of a lizard called a Gila monster.

It was said to be short and stocky its color was supposed to be black with an orange belly and its bite was deadly as any snakes. He had never seen one and was not even sure if it really existed but it was one more thing to keep an eye out for and these were just the natural enemies. There were still the rustlers and thieves and flat out killers that roamed the deserts and hills looking for their next victim. It was a journey filled with all the dangers of a cattle drive.

A large jack rabbit bolted towards the Texas desert as the wagon rolled through the arched gate that led to the main house of the Malloy ranch. From here miles and miles of desert stretched across the landscape. This was wild country, open range and every man and animal there was as free and dangerous as the west Texas wind blowing across the prairie. From his perch on top of the wagon Jim could see dark clouds forming in the north. Lightning flashed across the sky and to the ground below. Soon the ditches and draws would be filled with the raging waters known as a flash flood, anything and anyone caught in the draws would be swept away, killing cattle, horses and riders alike. This was one of the most feared things in Texas, nature at its worst. The water would fill the ditches long before the storm reached the wagon but when it got there it would come down in sheets soaking anything in its path. Lightning would dance around the wagon like giant balls of light, killing anything it touched. The women might tie their horses to the back of the wagon and climb inside for the comfort and safety of the tarp covered wagon but he had no doubt Joe would drape a parka over his shoulders pull down the wide brim of his hat protecting his eyes as the storm struck and together he and the black would face nature's fury head on. Jim hoped the women had not ridden so far ahead that they could not get back to the wagon before the storm struck and before the draws filled and left them stranded to face the storm alone and without shelter. Jim could feel the temperature drop as the storm approached. He knew the snakes and lizards would be hiding in burrows and under rocks trying to escape the fury of the storm.

Even as the first drops fell he saw the women ride over the horizon and he knew Joe would not be far behind. Lightning flashed across the sky as the women reined in next to the wagon, it was their choice, don the ponchos and face the storm or climb into the wagon and wait it out! These were massive clouds moving at high speeds, the storm would be strong and powerful but short in its rage.

Joe rode up to the wagon and donned a poncho as the women climbed inside for the protection of the covered wagon. Small pieces of hail began to pound the ground as the storm grew nearer, the canvas of the tarp popped in the wind as it was blown from side to side, even the horses tied to the rear of the wagon tried to escape the storm pulling at their reins as lightning struck the ground in a long flash of fire and light as the pellets of ice begun to strike hitting like the sting of bees against soft unprotected flesh. Joe sat on the back of the black like a statue taking the hits as they came.

Jim might have crouched under the protection of the tarp if it had not been for Rick laying on his back, still in pain and taking up most of the room. The women laughed and carried on joking with each other as the rain and ice came down drenching the men and animals alike. The women were playing a hand of five card draw betting on which man would give up and come into the protection of the wagon first!

CHAPTER SIXTEEN

Bobby groaned as Schon shook him awake, he had never felt this bad in his life, "What did I do," he asked as his head exploded in a cascade of light. "I think you drank too much!" Schon answered. Slowly the memory of the night came back to him, "How could I have been so stupid!" he moaned holding his head in his hands. He had to do something to make things right with Michelle. He knew she would not speak to him, Bobby knew she might not even look in his direction. He wanted to tell her she was his world and without her his life would be an empty void, like a desert beast without even so much as a small wind to make their lives tolerable.
  His head throbbed from the bite of the tequila and his stomach felt as if it had been kicked by an angry bull but it was his heart that hurt the most! "Can I borrow a pencil and paper," Bobby asked quietly, he wanted to write Michelle the greatest love letter anyone had ever written but Bobby was a simple honest man and as he took the pen in hand and wrote his letter to the best of his ability.
  "I love you, I'm sorry, please forgive me," was all the paper said. Bobby gently folded the paper and handed it to Schon, "Will you see Michelle gets this?" he said. Schon was the same kind of man, "I'll see she gets it!"
  Schon said as he placed the letter in his own pocket, he knew Bobby's hopes and dreams lay in the small piece of paper and this made it important to them both! Bobby's misery reached into his very soul as he saddled his horse and headed to the Lazy 'B' ranch.

Bobby watched as dark clouds formed in the northern sky, today was going to be a day filled with grief and misery. Before he reached the safety of the ranch he was going to be facing the fury of the storm. Mike and Roy both were waiting for Bobby to get home, they were fed up because Bobby was spending all of his time chasing the girl of his dreams.

He was the third owner of the Lazy 'B' and that meant one third of the work was his to be done. There was a well to be dug, fences to mend and cattle to brand. Bobby was going to do his share of the work or they were going to give him what for!

Even as the storm struck they watched for him out of the dust covered window, this was not going to be a happy reunion.

Bobby donned his slicker and pulled his hat down facing the down pour. He felt like this was the first day in a life of misery. The rain was coming down in sheets as Bobby rode into the barn; life had kicked him down one too many times.

It was out of instinct that he stripped the saddle off the Apple and gave her a bucket of grain and it was this same instinct that led him to take a burlap sack and dry the animal before going into the house. Bobby didn't want to face the men he called partner and friend until he had a hold of his emotions he didn't want to break down in front of the men he respected.

Roy and Mike watched as Bobby walked towards the home they shared, it was hard to believe what they saw, Bobby looked like an old man, he was young and strong and vital but he walked with his shoulders pulled in, head down and back hunched staring at his feet as he walked.

This was not the Bobby they knew, this Bobby had been broken and whipped by the world around him.

The men of the Lazy 'B' worked hard they fought hard and they drank hard but they never stabbed a man in the back or kicked a man while he was down.

If they had plans to chew Bobby out they were forgotten now, they knew this man well enough to know just by his action that something was very wrong! Mike poured a cup of coffee and handed it to him as he entered the house hoping the hot liquids would help revive the man's spirits.

The rain would keep them in the house for a few more hours which gave them enough time to try to find out what was wrong. Finally Bobby explained to them what had happened between him and Michelle and that Jim was planning a round up and he needed their help. Even as they spoke, the men on the MacCland ranch were planning their own round up. With no owner on the ranch, no wages coming in and no whisky left in the cabinet there was no reason to stay but they were not planning on leaving empty handed.

Doug was sullen and quiet as he led the small group of Malloy hands up to the house of the MacCland ranch, they had discussed stealing whatever they could and rustling cattle, this would make them a band of outlaws but who would mess with them? The men at the MacCland ranch were just like them without work or wages, they would listen to them. Skip MacCland hadn't hired cowboys like the Malloy ranch he hired gunmen and thugs bent on taking over the valley, they were not loyal to the brand, they were there for the money.

Doug didn't care about any of this, his face was disfigured, and the cheap whisky he drank felt like liquid fire as it passed by the stitches in his mouth.

His jaw was wired shut and he couldn't eat or sleep he couldn't even speak without bolts of pain shooting through his head. Doug was a cruel and vicious man who cared little if at all for human life, he lived on hate and anger. He was a man the others feared and hated, this was the life he chose and enjoyed. He had never been treated like this before and the man responsible for it had to pay for the beating and in his eyes the ex-marshal had to pay with his life!

As the men rode up to the ranch Doug was already making plans of his own. Daryl sat in the veranda watching as the group of men approached, the last of a bottle of tequila sat beside him, Daryl picked up the bottle and downed the last few drops as they dismounted he didn't have to be told what they wanted. Daryl was not a stupid man he knew what they had been thinking even before they showed up because it was the same thing he was thinking! Doug had been the foreman at the Malloy ranch because of his raw strength and short temper, at five nine and two hundred pounds of muscle few would dare to oppose the man.

Daryl was just the opposite, tall and lanky with a gunfighters build. Daryl used his brains instead of his fists, he was sneaky and smart. Together with the men of both ranches under them they could make a force few if any in the valley could with stand. They wouldn't have to hunt in the brush and draws to gather cattle; they could take what they wanted because cattle out in the open is quick and easy pickings. It didn't matter if they were from the Malloy ranch, the Rocking 'R' or the Lazy 'B', with a dozen men under his control they wouldn't take a hundred head of cattle they would take a thousand!

Even with his disfigured face and busted jaw Doug was more of a match for the men that were left, Doug would be his second in command and they would be the largest and strongest gang in the area, maybe the state!

But Doug wasn't interested in the cattle or Daryl's plans; the only thing he wanted was weapons! His pistol and rifle were missing, stolen by the same man that had busted his jaw and ran him and his men off the Malloy ranch! While Daryl spoke of friendship and power, Doug searched the house looking for weapons he so desperately wanted. It was in the drawer of Skip's desk that he found the pistol, it was not as nice as the one that was taken from him but it was a forty-four and the shells in his belt were forty-fours.

He checked the chamber to make sure the pistol was loaded then slid the revolver into his holster. The fifty caliber Sharps rifle hung over the fire place mantle, he took it down and checked the loads but the rifle was empty so he tore the desk apart looking for shells. Daryl watched as the mad man ripped the place apart looking for the shells. He wasn't sure if he could trust the man or not but he needed him and now was no time cross him; he would do that later after he got what he wanted! "You'll find some fifty caliber shells in the bunk house," Daryl said, hoping to bring the man to his senses. "If you go after the marshal you will have to face the gunfighter and you won't live long when that happens!" Daryl warned.

"You think I'm scared of him, Doug snarled through his wired jaw, with the fifty in my hands I'll kill the both of them before they can get within a hundred yards of me!" Doug was going insane and Daryl was smart enough to know it. "Maybe it wouldn't be so bad with just eleven men under him and besides Doug might get lucky and kill both of them, he said to himself, and even if he died big deal it would still leave the valley wide open and he was sure to kill at least one of them before Doug himself was killed.

Daryl knew that if the ex-marshal or the gunman had to crawl, one or both of the men would put a bullet in the ex-foreman of the Malloy ranch!" Daryl threw his hands in the air, "fine, go after them, he said, but we can't help you!" The look of a man possessed was on Doug's face as he turned to face 'Daryl, "just you don't try and stop me, he said as he laid his hand on the handle of the pistol riding in the leather holster at his side.

Daryl knew he was quicker than Doug, he could put three bullets in the man before he pulled the trigger but in his enraged state of mind Doug might be able to get a shot off even with three slugs in him and Daryl didn't want to wind up gut shot with a dead man at his feet, he was not prepared to take that kind of chance! "Forget it, he said, besides there was no reason to kill the man, he was of some importance alive and worth nothing dead and just maybe he could kill the only men that might be capable of stopping them!
Doug went into the bunkhouse where he found a full box of fifty caliber shells sitting in the window sill. He picked up the box, loaded the rifle then put the rest of the shells in his shirt pocket. As he left the bunk house a new gang had formed, maybe the largest gang in the country, and they were all sitting on the front porch watching as dark clouds rolled in from the north.
   Large drops of water struck the ground kicking up small puffs of dust as Doug put his feet into the stirrups and swung up into the saddle. Daryl watched as the man rode off into the storm and he knew in his heart that this would be the last time he would ever see the man alive, he knew Doug had gone insane!
Doug was not headed for the Malloy ranch he was headed into town, this was going to be a man hunt and he needed supplies. Maybe the doctor would give him even more Laudanum for the pain in his jaw, if not then he wanted whisky or tequila, anything to relieve the pain. After that he would need food and supplies once the killing was done he was going to leave the valley for good. If he never saw this place again it would be too soon!

In his present state of mind he didn't care if the rain had turned to large chunks of ice and that it was pounding like a blacksmiths hammer at the sides and head of horse he rode on or that he rode in puddles that rose high above the horse's hooves. He didn't care that the creek was half full and rising as he pistol whipped the horse into the raging waters, not until the horse was being swept down river did he realize the danger he was in. Doug tried to free his feet from the stirrups as the horse rolled in the currents.

All of a sudden he was remembering that as a child his mother took him to church and the reverend was one of those fire and brimstone preachers who said that Jesus saved those who had taken Christ as their Savior and they would spend eternity walking on streets of gold while the cursed and dammed would spend eternity in a lake of fire to burn forever and ever.

Doug wondered if hell would be as bad as a blistering Montana winter as the horse rolled and slammed him into a rock, the weight of the animal broke his back and crushed his ribs as his lungs filled with water and went under for the last time. The weight on the end of the stirrup acted like a rudder banging at the horse's ribs and legs, spinning it in circles and catching on rocks while brush kept pulling it under, then letting go only to grab again as the horse fought for its life, kicking at the ground below desperately trying to reach one bank or another.

Then as the creek widened out the water became shallower and the horse managed to stand. Boiling water of sand and mud rushed under its belly as it started for the bank. Mercifully Doug's foot slid out of his boot and the water soaked weight dragging the horse down was released. It stood on the bank fighting for air as Doug's body was being washed downstream!

The midday sun had turned dark almost to the point of pitch blackness as the storm clouds covered the sky. Thunder roared and vibrated the ground as lightning flashed across the heavens setting fires to the trees and brush below.

Hail struck like falling bullets around the home of the Lazy 'B' ranch as Roy and the others stood on the porch watching for the sign of a tornado between the flashes of lightning. Cattle on the open range would have to find shelter for themselves and the horses were already in the barn yet nothing could protect them from the full force of a tornado but the roof of the barn could and would protect them from the chunks of hail falling from the sky above.

As lightning lit up the darkness the outline of a horse could be seen in the distance. Bobby let loose with a shrieking whistle hoping to call the horse in. Chunks of ice the size of a silver dollar pounded the sides of the house unmercifully if the chunks got any bigger the horse would be beaten to death standing in the open with no place to go!

Bobby whistled again as the horse drew nearer. Bobby made a dash for the barn and saddled his own horse and headed as fast as he could toward the lone horse as Mike and Roy followed. They surrounded the horse and Bobby reached down and grabbed the reins as hail struck like balled fists trying to knock the man unconscious as he tied the reins to his saddle horn and rode for the barn.

Bobby lit a lantern then took the saddle off the shivering animal. Long cuts ran down the sides and chest where patches of hair were torn from its hide. Even in this light Bobby suspected what had happened, someone had tried to cross a creek that had turned into a river and had sucked rider and horse alike downstream and this was the result, a horse in torment and somewhere out there was a man afoot or dead. In a storm like this the odds of survival were not good. Bobby knew the rider was most likely dead and to go out looking for the man or woman now was to put more lives at risk. Later after the storm they would go out looking for the body, but for now he would take care of the injured animal.
  Bobby placed oats in the trough in a stall then led the horse in, then taking a burlap sack he began to wipe the water from the freezing animal and then put liniment on the wounds, later after the storm one of them would go for the vet. Bobby listened to the hail pound on the roof of the barn as he waited for the chunks of ice to turn into rain before heading back to the house. The others would be waiting for him on the porch. This time they wouldn't be riding to help Jim on a round up, they would be going to find a missing rider. The body would probably be washed downstream by the raging water of a flash flood.

CHAPTER SEVENTEEN

The steel shod hooves of the horses pulling the wagon slipped on the hard wet rocks of the trail as they fought their way through the storm. The tarp snapped and popped as the wind tore through the enclosure rattling the pots and pans alike hanging from the top of the wagon by long metal hooks. Two women sat huddled in one corner seeking the safety of each other's arms as the drops of water turned to ice then hail.

Each inch of ground covered was a battle for the trail worn animals as they pulled the heavy wagon through the thick Texas mud towards a large oak tree standing like a lone sentinel in the deserted landscape. This morning wild game, deer and antelope had played on the very spot the wagon now stood but that was this morning.

now it was desolate of life as the wagon rolled forward. The only sounds were the striking of the ice and the moan of the wind as it beat upon the tarp. The crack of the whip echoed across the desert as the driver urged the animals onward. People had been smiling and laughing as they loaded the wagon and hooked up the team but not anymore, all they wanted to know was if they were going to live to see the rising of the sun tomorrow.

The winds had picked up and the chunks of ice had become larger and through the cracks of the tarp Sherlene and Marilyn could both see the funnel cloud as it stretched down to the ground. It was lifting dirt and grass and uprooting small trees and brush then raising them high into the sky only to let them loose to shatter into a million pieces below.

No place was safe in the open desert as long as the storm raged. Lightning jumped from cloud to cloud flashing across the sky in long bolts as the sounds of thunder rolled across the valley echoing from the distance. Sherlene could hear the cries of small animals being sucked from their burrows as they began their journey towards the heavens.

Soon the air would be sucked from their lungs and their struggle for life would end as the storm claimed another victim.

Jim leaned back into the safety of the wagon as pieces of ice and hail pounded at his legs and body bruising them down to the very bone, the pain was getting unbearable as the attack continued. Inside Rick lay against the hard wooden rails, a small trickle of blood ran from the wound across his chest and shoulder, a look of terror and uncertainty was upon his face. He didn't have to see the danger to know a tornado was coming. The darkening sky, the strong violent winds, the sudden cold chill in the air and the sound of a rushing train speeding through the desert was enough to let him know of the danger they were in. He could hear the drops of rain turn to ice and hail as it tried to tear through the heavy tarp striking with a rage only nature in her wildest fury could achieve.

The horses reared high into the air with their front hooves pawing and straining against the chains and halters that confined them. They were pulling at the wagon with all the strength they could muster as the wagon half slid and half rolled across the muddy ground only to come to a stop inches from where it had started.

A lone rider on a black horse rode towards the front of the wagon with a rope in his hand as ice slammed into his face and shoulders. Cuts and bruises were already beginning to show as he bent down and ran the rope around the chains and braces between the two worn out horses pulling the wagon. Then he turned the black and started forward, the rope pulled tight against the saddle horn then began to stretch as the black sank it's hooves deep into the mud and then began to pull with a strength that rivaled or surpassed the strength of the team. Chains began to pop and snap as the tug of war continued.

This was a war of wills, the strength of the black against the forces of nature. The massive muscles of the black bulged and rippled from the strain but slowly the mud filled rims of the wagon began to turn and mud and water was slung against the bottom of the wagon as it began to move with a speed it had not seen since the storm had begun. The safety of a cliff face was less than fifty yards away as the rider of the black stallion with the white mane drew back the reins and slapped the black alongside the rump. It was not a hard slap and it was not meant to hurt the animal it was a slap of desperation.

The rider wanted it to know the lives of every person there was depending on its strength and power. The black began to move as if it knew what the rider was thinking digging its hooves into the mud and dirt as if it's very life depended on every step it took. Mud and rock was flung toward the sky as the massive animal picked up speed dragging the tired team of horses and the heavy wagon behind it.

Even the fury of the storm and the winds behind it couldn't stop the power of the black as it headed for the face of the cliff. Jim's whip cracked again and the team of horses in front of the wagon began to help the black pulling with all of their strength and power towards a place of safety that had looked hopeless moments before.

Within minutes the face of the cliff loomed over them protecting them much like the hand of a mother protecting a child that she loved. Everyone knew they were safe as water and mud ran down the face of the cliff and under the belly of the wagon.

These rocks had with stood a thousand years of raging storms and would withstand a thousand more. Untying the rope from the saddle of the black, Joe gave it a throw leaving it dangling from the chains as he rode back to the wagon to check on the women inside.

The rock overhang was protecting the wagon and the people as the raging storm passed by. It was a strong summer storm ripping and destroying everything in its path but even with all of its fury it could not last long and they all knew that it would destroy itself as the funnel went back up into the clouds just as suddenly as it had reached its tail to the ground. Pulling back the soft canvas door flap he could see the women huddled together for warmth. Rick sat in one corner shivering from the dampness of the air and the weakness of his own body as Joe took his own jacket off and handed it to the women.

"Cover him up with this and I'll see if I can find some dry wood as soon as it clears up a little," he said. Marilyn moved towards the entrance, "Honey, don't go," she said moving forward and looking up into the eyes of the man holding the flap. It was the first time she had ever called him that and it sounded strange even to her ears! Joe held the flap not believing the words that had just been spoken, "I'll be back," he said as he lowered the flap and rode away.

Jim set the brakes to the wagon and tied the reins before climbing down from the hard wooden seat to face the world around him.

He knew Joe would be riding along the face of the cliff looking for small pieces of dry firewood to build a much anticipated fire.

As the storm continued to rumble around them Sherlene and Marilyn climbed from the back of the wagon to watch the storm as it passed by. Few had ever gotten to witness the true power of nature and fewer still had lived through it.

Standing beneath the rock ledge both women felt safe enough to stand and watch as the tornado destroyed everything in its path, ripping up small trees and brush pulling animals, small and large alike out of their hiding places and pitching them across the sky like a bullet from the barrel of a gun. Larger trees with the root system planted deep into the ground fared no better than the smaller ones as their limbs were twisted around in the air like the blades of a windmill before they broke loose and flew into the air to join the others high above the wagon. Sherlene and Marilyn watched as limbs as well as whole trees fell from the sky dropping like arrows from above as the storm moved on. Streaks of lightning danced from cloud to cloud as thunder rolled across the desert floor letting all that could hear it know who the master of the storm was. Rick tried to drag himself across the bed of the wagon to see just how powerful one of God's true creations could be. Joe was on his way back to camp as Sherlene returned to the wagon and began to replace the bandage that had been covering Rick's chest. Behind the black was a half rotted log being drug by a short rope.

"We'll camp here," Joe said as he climbed down from the saddle and began kicking pieces from the log. He knew the rotted wood would be easy to ignite with the aid of a single match. Taking two long metal rods from the beneath the bed of the wagon he shoved them deep into the ground then hung a third between them both. Placing small twigs between the metal stakes Joe struck the match and carefully put it to the kindling and smoke began to rise as the damper pieces of the wood began to burn sending a cloud of smoke through the camp burning the eyes and choking the lungs as it drifted up the face of the cliff.

Sherlene dipped a pot into the water barrel that was tied to the side of the wagon then added a large hand full of coffee grounds before placing it over the fire. Soon the smell of the rotted wood was going to be replaced by the smell of the coffee.

Bacon was placed into a pan and added to the fire. After it fried to a golden crisp brown the drippings would be used to make the white gravy that Jim loved. If he was lucky the women might even cook up a batch of the hard tack biscuits Elois was so famous for.

Unhitching the team and walking them out into the open Jim tied them to a twisted pine stump standing in the middle of a field of buffalo grass. There was no cover there but the rains had stopped and the day was already becoming warmer as the sun began to shine from behind the dark threatening clouds. Sherlene and Marilyn was helping Rick down from the wagon as he returned and Jim could see a look of pain with each movement and a small amount of blood that was running from beneath the bandage then dripping to the ground below.

Rick stood white faced and shaking as his knees tried to fold out from under him. The wound that ran across his chest and shoulder had taken a lot of strength from the man.

Rick sat on the log Joe had dragged up to the fire and looked down at the wound.

It had been eight maybe ten days since the half breed had used the knife on him but it was hard for him to remember. First because he had been in too much pain then later it was the mix of laudanum and whiskey that had kept his mind in a haze and that made it was hard to distinguish between reality and dreamland.

Now the memories were beginning to come back to him in the form of the nightmares he had been having.

He didn't have to tell anyone here about the nightmares they all knew. More than once he had sat up in the wagon screaming as he kept seeing the knife sinking into his chest taking his life again and again in the dark recesses of his mind while sweat and terror showed on his face as he remembered the morning of the attack.

He had known Frankie was dangerous, real dangerous, maybe one of the most dangerous men he had ever met in his life but the smell of the coffee and the promise of a warm fire had called to him that morning and just for a second he had forgotten about the half breed Mexican, but that was all it had taken, if the saddle had not twisted when he sat on it the blade of the knife would have sank deep into his body penetrating the lungs and heart with the force of the blow. As it was the impact of the blow had driven him to the ground.
  As Frankie stood and lunged at him Rick had fired from the hip blowing a hole through the bottom of his holster and striking Frankie in the guts with the soft lead of the forty-four. The lead may have been soft but the impact was hard, tearing through the flesh of the body and destroying the heavy bone in the center of the back.
  Frankie had fallen like a crippled mannequin as the bullet tore through him. Rick remembered the twisted shocked look on his face as the bullet ended the attack and completely destroyed what had once been the strong body of a human being. He remembered hearing the sound of gun fire in the distance as he had rode away.
  No one had to tell Rick that Frankie's own men had finished him off! They would have killed him with a bullet through the head to end his pain and finish what he had started. Rick could see this without being there, that was just the way it was! They would not have the time to wet nurse a cripple even if they had wanted to! They were not the kind of men who would have compassion on a fallen comrade and Frankie would have done the same thing to anyone of them but with a knife!

Rick doubted that they had even taken the time to bury the man after they had killed him. Rick sat in front of the fire shivering as Marilyn placed a blanket around him. "You had better keep him warm," Joe said as he swung down from the back of the black, "Or we will be digging another hole." Rick looked at the speaker with a look of wonder in his eyes, "We buried your partner," Joe stated as he pointed at Jim. Rick had known that but the Laudanum kept his mind in a state of limbo and it was hard for him to remember things.

Rick snuggled down into a sleeping position as the warmth of the fire relaxed the pains of his body. Sherlene had changed the bandages on his wounds and he had eaten a good warm meal and the call of sleep was too much for him and as he closed his eyes he heard Sherlene ask, "What are we going to do if he dies?" "I guess we will dig a grave if that happens, Joe stated, but until then we will do the best we can for him." For the first time in years Rick felt safe enough to sleep without fear.

The rest of the small band finally got to eat the meal the women had made. They had cooked up fried potatoes with a slab of steak that filled each plate and hot biscuits with a pot full of white gravy. Jim sat and wondered what would happen next as he drew the knife across the soft tender meat slicing through it as easy as butter.

A few days ago he had run the entire crew off the Malloy ranch at gun point but things had not went the way he had planned and he wound up killing one of them. If it had not been for the rider on the black stallion backing his play the simple orders could have turned into a blood bath! As it was only one man had died and he was an idiot, going against a cocked rifle with a revolver still in his holster! After the shooting they had put the body in the ice house and sent it back to town in the back of a buckboard.

Now they were stuck with Rick as he fought to live in a world he had learned to hate. Jim threw the last of his coffee into the fire and walked off, maybe tomorrow would be better he decided as he watched the sun set behind a lingering cloud.

He could hear Sherlene and Marilyn cleaning the dishes and putting up the things they had used during the day. Joe was unsaddling the black, it was a massive horse and it would run free for the night as the rest of them slept.

Jim had been around the horse enough to know it was as good as any watch dog and nothing would come near the camp with the black standing guard.

The women placed their bed rolls under the protection of the wagon as the men made beds near the fire using their saddles for pillows and the sweat stained pads for their mattresses as the stars shown above leaving the valley clean and pure to the human eye.

Darkness began to settle over the travelers as the animals of the night came out looking for the food they knew they would find hidden in the cracks and burrows of the desert floor.

CHAPTER EIGHTEEN

Doug had never been run off from any place in his life, he was strong, violent and a man to be feared not terrorized! His massive fists had won him the reputation of a fighter and the scars on his face and hands testified to the battles he had been in.

No one alive had ever done to him what the ex-marshal had done to him! Doug's jaw had been broken, his face was swollen and disfigured and he had lost face in front of the men who served under him.

The rest of the men who had been run off the Malloy ranch were riding behind him in one long line. Each man was lost in their own thoughts as they rode towards the MacCland ranch. Daryl would be there along with half a dozen men and Doug knew together they could destroy the valley and everyone in it.

Daryl was as smart and cunning as Doug was vicious and together they could build an army of men that could take over the valley. Daryl was sitting on the veranda drinking the last of Skip's whiskey as the men approached. Like Doug, Skip and a hired gun out of Mexico had went against the ex-marshal and the quiet spoken gunslinger that had ridden into town on the back of the black horse that everyone had been so mesmerized by.

Nobody knew who the gunman was but they all knew the horse, it was the stallion that had terrorized the inhabitants of the valley for so long and it was hard to believe anyone had captured or tamed the beast but here he was, being ridden around in broad daylight!

Doug swung down from the saddle and walked up the steps of the porch.

Daryl could see the look of pain in Doug's face as he took a drink from the mix of whiskey and Laudanum stored in the metal canteen at his side.

That was a bad mixture to be drowning your sorrows in as Laudanum was made from alcohol and opium! It was very habit forming and after a while it would mess up your mind to the point any decisions you made would be that of a drug addict and drunk and totally unreliable. Daryl made up his mind he would have to keep a close eye on Doug!

To Doug's disappointment Daryl didn't want to go after the men responsible for destroying his face and the plans him and his men had come up with to take over the valley, all Daryl wanted to do was take the valuables from the MacCland ranch, steal the cattle and run. He wanted to build a gang of men that would hit and run taking what they wanted then move on.

Doug wanted men and power; he wanted to destroy the valley and all of those responsible for the beating he had taken at the hands of the marshal. Doug knew he would need Daryl's help to take on the gunman and the marshal both. Either that or he would have to back shoot them to get the revenge he so desperately needed. Doug quit listening to Daryl as he started through the MacCland home in search of the weapons he so desperately need to kill the men he had learned to hate and despise. Hidden in Skip's pillow he found a thirty-eight fully loaded with a hand full of shells tucked along the seam.

A fifty caliber Sharps Buffalo rifle hung over the filthy mantel of the rock fire place but he couldn't find any of the high powered shells for the long range weapon as he slowly and methodically tore the room apart. Daryl stood in the doorway watching as Doug destroyed the room and the home in search of the shells.

Daryl was beginning to wonder about Doug's sanity as he watched him go from room to room acting like a raging blind man destroying everything in his path, "There in the bunkhouse," Daryl sneered as Doug headed into the kitchen then turned to face the would be leader. Without a word Doug stomped out of the house in search of the shells, stopping only twice on the way to the bunkhouse to drink from the bottle hanging from his side! Yes Daryl was clearly going to keep an eye on Doug!

A full box of fifty caliber shells sat on a window sill along with some change a plug of tobacco and a pack of cards. Picking up the shells Doug loaded the rifle and started back to the main house. Daryl stood out in the yard leaning against the hitching posts as Doug approached and pushing himself away from the post Daryl stood between Doug and the horses. "Where do you think you're going?" he asked as his hand hung over the butt of the pistol at his side trying to intimidate the larger man.

The barrel of the rifle swung around and centered on Daryl's chest as his thumb pulled back the hammer, "You got two seconds to step out of my way or die!" Doug said in a flat cold tone. The smell of whiskey filled the air around Doug and drifted to where Daryl stood his dreams of controlling the largest gang in Texas was falling apart as Daryl looked down the large barrel of the fifty caliber rifle. Shrugging his shoulders Daryl stepped aside, "If you start a blood bath you're going to have every lawman in the country down here!"

"Then I'll kill them all!" Doug said reaching for the saddle horn with his left hand while putting his boot in the stirrup. For just a second he was vulnerable as he lifted his body into the saddle and Daryl was tempted to go for the gun at his side but he was not sure how much Laudanum and whiskey Doug had drank or how many bullets it would take to stop the man in his drunken state!

Daryl wanted to build the largest gang in Texas not wind up gut shot bleeding to death in the dirt with a dead man at his feet! Doug's acts of stupidity may mess up his plans but he could make new ones and Daryl knew he was not going to die to hold on to these!

Doug swung the horse around and started out of the yard, he didn't like the idea of showing his back to the man standing behind him and gave the horse a kick in the ribs to get moving. The Laudanum and whiskey was driving the man insane Daryl decided as he watched him ride out of the yard, why else would he give up money and power for something as stupid as revenge! Daryl stood in the yard trying to decide if he should put a bullet in the man's back as he rode out of the yard! It was one thing to think about murder but it was another thing to do it.

Daryl knew he had no qualms about killing Doug but he might still be of more use alive than dead, that and who knew he might just get lucky and kill both the lawmen! Daryl knew that could and would work to his advantage.

Doug began to drink from the canteen as soon as he left sight of the yard the laudanum gave him the power and strength that he needed. He began to feel as if he was floating on a cloud. It wasn't long before large drops of rain began to fall from the sky but he was in such a drunken haze he rode onward unaware as it started to beat down violently at the man and the horse beneath him. But in his drunken condition Doug barely noticed the heavy down pour as it turn to ice and hail or the strong winds driving the pieces of ice into the sides of the horse sounding like the heavy blows of a young man's hammer.

The horse's hooves sank deep into the mud as the cold waters ran between its legs and then lifted higher towards its belly and for a few seconds the horse stayed on its feet as the waters of the flash flood rose higher and higher finally lifting the horse and sending it tumbling down stream with the speed of a runaway train. The pain in Doug's jaw was forgotten as the roar of the water fought its way through the drug induced fog that had taken over his mind!

With the last few remaining seconds of his life he saw the rocks approaching through the murky waters and even as he felt his face slam into the rocks he felt the weight of the horse and the horn of the saddle snap his back and his lungs being filled with the muddy water as he tried to cry out in pain! Doug's life was about to end but the torment was not over, his foot was stuck in the stirrups and his weight was dragging the helpless animal down.

He felt the pain every time his body became tangled in the brush or lodged in the cracks of the rocks below and he felt the pain as he was being jerked upwards by the animal as it fought desperately for its life against the deadly rushing water.

He also felt it every time a bone was broken or a muscle was pulled right up until the moment he finally mercifully died! Then like a ship with a broken rudder his body became a weapon and slammed unmercifully against the horse's side and ribs spinning it in circles and then pulling it down with the sheer weight of the water soaked body.

Hooves dug into wet muddy ground in desperation as the water washed over its back forcing it under even as it fought to survive.

The horses lungs were beginning to fill with water as its hoof found solid ground and the horse began to pull its self from the cold waters of the creek leaving Doug's body in the torrent of water as his boot finally slid out of the strap and floated down stream. The small brown horse with the dead man's saddle stood shaking as the rushing waters carried the body downstream and away from the animal he had almost killed The hot sun had already started to decompose the body and the smell was sickening. Sand and mud was packed into the mouth and nostrils of the drowned man and water rushed out of the lungs as they drug him from the creek, washing away the filth.

As the men dug the shallow grave they could not help but wonder about the man's last moments on this earth and what kind of man was he? This country was still new and wild and it took a lot of grit to tame it and a lot of lives but one day this was going to be a great place to live, a place to be proud of, a place where men could raise cattle and families alike.

CHAPTER NINETEEN

Daryl walked out of the yard and into the house as Doug rode off, one thing he was beginning to be sure of he would never see the man again! "All right, get out!" he said as he took a bottle of whiskey off the table that the men were playing cards at. "What's the matter?" Garry asked looking into the face of his boss and longtime comrade. "Nothing," Daryl said after taking a long drink of the golden liquid. A warm fire ran down his throat and into his belly as he stood looking at his old friend.

"Doug just left, he said, he went after the marshal." "After the beating he gave him I'm not surprised and between him and Paul the guys face looked like it has been put through a pepper grinder." "Paul knocked a drunk upside the head, but the beating Doug got came from Jim!" Garry shook his head in astonishment, "Doug ain't gonna quit until he's dead or the other feller is rotting in the grave!" "That's what I'm worried about, Daryl said, he is gonna start a war that is gonna get us all killed!"

"Why didn't you kill him before he rode out of here then?" Daryl was getting tired of the conversation and was beginning to get aggravated with the other man, "He has enough Laudanum and whiskey in him that a bullet from a buffalo gun wouldn't stop him and since he was the only person holding one I figured it was best to let him go!"

Garry sat at the table and scratched his head, "What are we gonna do without him?" he asked as Daryl walked back and forth in the confines of the small kitchen. Doug had been the perfect patsy for his plans, he was slow and strong, the men were willing to follow him because of the strength of his arms but he was no gun fighter and most of the time he would listen to reason but he had changed, growing reckless and insane under the effects of the drugs.

"Tomorrow I'm gonna ride to Dallas and recruit a few more men and I want you and the other to round up all the cattle on the ranch and hold them on the northeast section until I get back. Then some of us will start driving the herd towards Kansas as the others gather the rest of the cattle in the valley. With any luck we will be out of the valley before anyone knows we're gone. If not we will have a dozen gunman backing our play." Garry shook his head, "There ain't three gunmen in the whole town and you know it!

The deputies are young along with the men of the Lazy 'B' ranch and as far as it goes, Jim was not nothing but a clod hopping farmer, voted into the job.

All that leaves is the feller that helped him kill Skip and the gunman out of Mexico." "I ain't taking no chances!" Daryl growled, "That still leaves seven men who know how to shoot a gun and I'm not gonna lose a herd of cattle because of a few lousy gunmen!"

Daryl walked out of the kitchen taking the bottle of whiskey with him stopping in the doorway just long enough to tell the others to go to bed that tomorrow was going to be a busy day! Garry followed Daryl out of the room and in a quiet voice asked, "What are you gonna do about Jake? He's an honest fellow and is well liked by the others and rides for the brand. There is no way he is gonna help us steal cattle!" "Don't you worry about him, Daryl whispered, I'll take care of him tonight!"

Daryl waited until he could hear the heavy breathing of the men sleeping before rising from his own bed. After Skip's death the men of the MacCland ranch had taken over, taking what they wanted and sleeping where they wanted. He could hear loud snoring of the men as he crept around the room looking for the sleeping body of a cowboy named Jake.

Daryl went into the barn and saddled his horse and then Jake's and began to walk them quietly up to the hitching rail. He tied both horses in front of the bunkhouse before going inside in search of the man. Some of the men liked Jake but Daryl thought he was a turncoat traitor riding for the brand. Not for one second did Daryl think about sparing the man's life as he sought for him among the sleeping drovers.

Finding him in the last bunk Daryl drew the long blade of the Bowie from the scabbard and placed it over Jake's stomach just below the ribs. He could feel the rise and fall Jake's chest with each breath he took up until Daryl's hand covered his mouth.

A look of terror crossed Jake's face as he fought for air. Pulling his feet up under his legs Jake shoved up arching his back but Daryl held him fast with his right hand then shoved the wide blade of the Bowie forward the razor sharp blade of the bowie cut easily through the light material of Jake's shirt sinking to the handle as it pierced the heart.

The look of terror was replaced with a look of pain as Daryl turned the blade towards Jake's lungs cutting into the cavity opening then up so the blood from the heart could drain into the body. Slowly the look of pain was replaced by the image of death.

Leaving the knife imbedded in Jake's chest Daryl removed his hand and wrapped the body in a blanket as Jake's eyes glazed over in death. Looking around the room Daryl checked to see if anyone had heard the soft sounds of the scuffle but these men were so drunk that and earthquake couldn't wake them!

He then picked up the body and walking out. Daryl had never considered himself a weak man but it took all his strength to lift the limp body and lay it across the saddle before tying it down. Daryl was sweating and breathing hard as he led the horses out of sight and returned for Jake's belongings.

Taking his saddle bags from the barn Daryl headed back into the bunkhouse taking what few belongings the man owned. Daryl placed them in the bags and walked out; all traces of Jake had vanished as Daryl left the room. Picking up a shovel and pickaxe that was leaning against the barn Daryl laid them across his saddle as he mounted the horse and rode off into the night leading Jake's horse and behind him.

The soft mud was muffling the sound of the horse's hooves as they rode through the rod iron gates. Turning towards a short cliff on the south side of the ranch Daryl lead the horses through the deserted paths and animal trails keeping his eyes open for any riders that might see him or the dead man. It was nearing three o'clock in the morning when he made it to the area he had been looking for. There was a short cliff with an overhang where Daryl stopped and stripped Jake's body from the saddle.

Daryl placed the corpse face first near the cliff overhang along with all of his possessions, even the saddle and blanket from his horse was stripped off the animal and laid beside him. It was as if the man had never existed as Daryl used the pick and shovel to bury the man and all of his possessions. Placing a short rope around Jake's horse Daryl rode off again, this time to the east and after a few miles he stopped and removed the rope from the horse's neck and drew his pistol and shot the animal in the front legs shattering bone and cartilage.

The animal screamed out in a cry of pain only another animal could understand as it fell to the ground bleeding while a large amount of blood flowed from the open wound. Daryl ride off in silence leaving the animal to suffer knowing it would not be long before the coyotes and scavengers found the dying animal and devoured what little proof remained of Jake's life. Riding toward the ranch Daryl discarded the pick and shovel by throwing them into the brush along the way.

It was a tired pony that carried Daryl through the gates of the MacCland ranch early that morning wanting nothing more than a bucket of oats, a little water and some rest as he rode it into the empty stall. Stripping off the saddle Daryl went straight to the kitchen looking for a cup of fresh coffee only to be disappointed at the men around him.

The fire had gone out of the stove and the pot sat cold and empty. Placing a hand full of kindling on the bed of coals Daryl waited for the fire to flame before adding more wood. The men were beginning to move around as Daryl added water and coffee to the pot. Taking a shell from his gun belt and placing it tip up Daryl began to spin it like a kid with a top, a man lost in thought as he planned the day ahead.

It was going to take money, food and supplies to move a herd of cattle from Texas to Kansas, that and men. Counting the men from the Malloy ranch he controlled eleven men that is if Doug was still alive!

He was till spinning the bullet deep in thought as Garry came into the room. Garry looked around the room in search of the other men before stating the obvious,

"Jake is missing, his horse and all his gear is gone.

Most of the men think he ran off, their saying he didn't like the idea of becoming a rustler!" "What do you think happened?" Daryl asked.

"I don't think anything," Garry stated, "I just hope someone said a few words over him. I would hate to think about anybody dying without a few words being said over their grave! "Don't worry about it, Daryl said, I took care of that!" "I kind of figured you did!" Garry answered. Daryl whispered to his old friend, "Just don't let anyone else know or you will be the next to vanish!"

A shiver went through Garry's body as he looked at his friend, Daryl did not know how to joke and he was not kidding, he knew he would be the next die! Daryl pushed a hand full of bills across the table he didn't have much but it would have to do.

"Take a wagon into town and buy some grub, coffee, beans, bacon and anything else you can think of until I get back, except whiskey! I don't want to be riding the trail with a bunch of drunks and I sure don't want to go against a posse with a drunk guarding my back!" Garry was riding out of the yard in the wagon headed for town as Daryl left for Dallas and the men they would need to carry out his plans.

The men of the Lazy 'B' ranch stood on the porch watching the ice and hail turn back into soft pellets of rain as the storm began to drift pass the ranch leaving all signs of a violent summer storm behind. Now the once dried up creeks and draws over flowed tuning into massive rivers in their search for freedom.

Thunder rolled across the sky shaking the very foundation of the home as lightning flashed jumping from cloud to cloud in long glowing ribbons lighting up the evening sky. As the three men watched a lone horse topped the ridge overlooking the ranch, "Come on!" Mike yelled as he ran for the cover of the barn.

Throwing a saddle on his own horse he rode out into the coming night as the lightning flashed lighting up the darkening sky around him. Mike's horse threw sopping wet clumps of grass and mud against his legs and belly as he rode towards the rider less horse as it limped along the rocky ridge of the hill.

Roy and Bobby flanked the horse on both sides to keep it from escaping back into the face of the storm. "Hold him!" Bobby cried as Mike reached out grabbing for the loose reins dangling from the halter around its head. The horse turned and tried to bolt but gave up easy as it realized it had no place to go.

Mike turned the horse and rode towards the barn with Bobby and Roy following behind. Riding into the barn he pulled the saddle off the tired mud soaked animal and began to wipe him down using a burlap sack that had been hanging from a nail. Blood seeped out from long cuts running down its legs and chest, "What are we gonna do about the rider?" Mike asked still wiping at the blood and mud clinging to the matted hair. "That will have to wait until morning," Roy said, "It will be completely dark soon and there is nothing we can do about it.
If he is still alive he will have to fend for himself at least for one more night because there is nothing we can do about it!" Standing in the door way of the barn Roy watched as Mike took care of the wounded animal,
"it looks like he slid off an embankment; either that or he was caught in a flood." Roy looked over at the speaker, Bobby was young but he was not stupid,
"No one in their right mind would be riding a ridge in this kind of weather. Whoever was riding that horse was most likely caught in a flood," Roy replied. "Do you think he is alive?" Bobby wanted to know.

"I doubt it, Roy answered, if I thought there was much chance of that we'd be out looking for him."
Smoke was rising from the chimney long before the sun decided to show its face on the desert landscape. Roy, Bobby and Mike sat at the dining room table sipping strong black coffee as they made plans for the day.

"We'll follow the tracks as far as we can then split up. Bobby you will ride the ridges looking down into the creeks and draws, Mike and I will ride along the banks. It you spot something fire three times, that way we will know you found something." "What if we don't find anything?" It was Bobby doing the asking, the blonde haired youngster knew the answer but still had to ask.

"If we don't find a body it means there is not one to be found!" Bobby didn't like the answer but knew it was the truth;

no one had to tell him what scavengers would do to the remains of an animal and when it came right down to it people were just animals and one more piece of flesh to be consumed after they were dead. Coyotes, bobcats and buzzards all had to survive and this was how they did it by living off the bodies of the deceased.

The men of the Lazy 'B' ranch already rode in search of the body as the sun began to rise above the desert plains bringing light and a new day to the valley below. The pony's tracks had cut deep into the soft mud and sand giving the men a good trail to follow.

Each man rode in silence wondering what they would find or if they would find anything at all as the morning passed into evening leaving long shadows as the sun began to lower itself beyond the sand colored horizon.

Riding together they topped the ridge and looked down and from there they could clearly see a man's body half submerged in a pool of warm stagnating black water. Gasses had caused his belly to swell and he was floating face up staring straight up into the desert skies.

The stench of the rotting flesh was filling the air around the pool and preventing the men from riding closer as the animals tried to pull away.

Taking the lariat from his saddle Roy gave it a toss letting the loop land so that when he pulled the loop it would close over Doug's out stretched dead hand.

Tying the rope to the saddle horn he felt the muscles bulge and strain as the animal began to pull the body from the murky water.

Even as the horse was pulling it from the waters the first of the scavenger let its self be known as the head of a large water moccasin slithered out of Doug's shirt and back into the water, angry at having its future meals stolen out from under it.

The snake began coiling up on top of the water. The white of its mouth looked like balls of cotton as it drew back its angry head.

The sun was glistening off its two needle sharp fangs showing the weapons of its kind and threats of the slow death it could bring. In great gasps the moccasin drew in large amounts of air filling its long slender lungs to the point of buoyancy, its body was floating high on top of the water as it struck out over and over again, its face was filled with a look of maniacal rage.

This was a big snake by all standards and one of the largest these men had ever seen.

It must have been at least seventy inches long and looked to be every bit as heavy as a man leg. This was one of the most feared and dangerous snakes in North America.

It could be very aggressive when confronted or sometimes they would show a more cautious side and leave but not this snake!

The snake coming out from Doug's clothing all three men drew their weapons and fired at the same time as the snake began swimming towards them. Each one was firing quickly into the water in front of the snake and missing.

The impact of the bullets were sending small wakes splashing over the animal as it came ever closer the look of rage was sending a cold chill through the men as they cocked their weapons and fired again but this time one of the shells found its mark and went ripping through the snakes body turning the water blood red and sending its body slowly drifting to the bottom of the stagnating pond.

After dragging his water soaked body to the top of the hill Roy dismounted from the horse and rolled the corpse over looking for even more of the unwanted intruders.

They didn't want to be surprised by a snake that was still hidden in the folds of the clothing. After he was satisfied that there was nothing left he started to work on the grave that was eventually going to be the last holding place for Doug's broke and disfigured body.

Mike sat in the saddle and watched as Roy began to dig taking large scoops of dirt out at one time.

He knew that the heavy rain from the previous day had soaked into the ground and was making the hole easy to dig.

Untying shovels from the back of their saddles the others got down to help. It was not long before the grave was dug and a hole six foot long and four feet deep penetrated the ground and it was filling in with seeping water as the three men were placing the body in the slowly filling hole

It is said to be bad luck to keep a dead man's rope Roy stated as he pitched the loose end of the rope down into the waiting hole leaving it to rot in the ground with its companion. The sun was beginning to set and shadows had covered the valley as Mike, Roy and Bobby began to pitch dirt into the hole covering the man below. As the weight of the dirt pressed down on Doug's chest water and sand began to run from his mouth even a trail of blood showed around the edges of his lips. As the other men threw dirt into the grave Roy took off the sheep skin vest he was so proud of and dropped it down into the hole so it would be covering Doug's face, it was one more sacrifice he was willing to make for a man he had never met

. As the last of the grave was filled in Mike stopped and began to build a cross by placing two sticks together and tying them with a piece of rawhide, it was not much but it would do until something better was made and it would mark the grave if someone came looking.

The three men stood looking down at the mound of mud and dirt with their hats held in their hands not willing to leave until the right words had been said over the grave letting the Lord know one more was on their way before him and the judgment that was about to come!
   "I don't think I've ever seen him before, did either one of you know him?" Roy asked.
   Mike shook his head as Bobby answered, "I've seen him before, I think he used to hang around Nita's trying to pick up on some of her girls.
   I don't think he was very good at it through or he would not have been out here riding alone."
   "Probably not but at least you can say a few words over the grave seeing as how you knew him better than the rest of us."
   It was a simple ceremony with Bobby leading the way. "Lord we did not know him and we did not know his heart but you did so here he is waiting for your judgment!"
   Bobby finished the sentence with "Amen" as Roy through the last scoop of dirt over the pile. These loud rambunctious cowboys tried to do what was right and descent by a man they had never known but if they had known that here lay a man so full of hatred and anger that he was planning to hunt and kill another human being it might have been a different prayer said over his grave.
   The man was so disfigured by the force of the flood that they didn't even notice the broken jaw or even ask themselves how he had died they just assumed the damage to the body was caused by the rocks in the river and the weight of a lame horse !
   "We will ride out to the Malloy ranch in the morning and see if Jim needs help with the round up but until then we might as well head back to the homestead.

I doubt if we will be able to find them tonight and besides coffee and beans are beginning to sound pretty good right now and a soft bed ain't gonna hurt either!" Roy said swinging up on the horse he called Brandy and began the long ride back to the ranch with the others following close behind.

CHAPTER TWENTY

The lead bull known as buttermilk swung its massive horns from side to side as it turned to face its antagonists. A thousand pounds of raw power stood behind the seven foot span and even the grizzly would respect and fear the power of the Texas Longhorn but here yapping and barking was a small dog trying to intimidate one of the most dangerous animals alive with nothing more than a yelp

Buttermilk stood hunched back and pawing at the ground digging a hole with its lead hoof while kicking up dirt and rock as it got ready to charge.

The crack of the whip brought the bulls head around stopping the charge before it began spinning to face the new threat.

The bull was called Buttermilk because of its cold heart and bitter attitude and it started to charge again but this time the tip of the whip struck the bull's nose cutting into the flesh and causing a trickle of blood to run,

The sharp pain was enough to stop the bull in his tracks.

K.C. drew the whip back one more time but this time he let the tip fly towards the dog doing the same damage and ending a bad confrontation that would not have ended well for the dog!

K.C.'s whip caught the side of the dog bringing a large whelp as it landed, pain filled the animal as it turned to run, all thought of the bull banished as it sought to escape the bite of the whip. Vaqueros sat in their saddles laughing as the mongrel fled for its life.

The small herd of stolen cattle was not in the holding pens yet but every man there knew they would be soon.

Don Magel rode forward checking the herd, true it was a small herd but they were in good condition especially for the fast pace the young drovers had set.

For the last half hour the men had been looking over the herd and finally the rich Mexican shook his head speaking for the first time. "I can do nothing with these cattle they are stolen!" K.C. looked angry, "I would never bring you stolen cattle!" he exclaimed.

Don Magel couldn't help but laugh at the innocent look on the man's face; they had known each other for a long time. And they both knew what the other was capable of. Don Magel slapped K.C. on the back, "you bring me nothing but stolen cattle and one day the Federalies will raid my place and take everything I own.

They might even hang me for the cattle you bring!" Both men knew there was no truth in what they were saying it was a ruse to bring the price up or down depending on which man was speaking.

K.C. looked irritated again, "These ain't stolen and they ain't mine, he began, we brought them down for her!"

Don Magel looked at the senorita; even in the cowboy garb it was easy to tell she was pretty and young.

Long brown hair flowed from under the brim of the western hat she wore. She was American maybe fifteen or sixteen years old and for the first time Don Magel was serious,

"I cannot buy cattle from her, she is too young!" K.C. could see his buyer was about to back out of a deal,

"Why not!" he demanded.

Don Magel's eyes had turned hard and cold reminding K.C. of the bull, Buttermilk,

"It is one thing to buy stolen cattle it is another thing to buy stolen cattle from a child." Don Magel snapped.

It was K.C.'s turn to become angry, "She is no child, she will be eighteen in a couple of months and we are going to be married!"

"Then why are you selling her cattle?" He asked, for a second K.C. was stumped, should he tell Don Magel the truth?

If he told him they needed to sell the cattle to buy gunmen would he drop the price of the cattle knowing they were desperate.

Or would he be an honest man and give them an honest price for the cattle.

In the end honesty prevailed and K.C. decided to tell the truth.

Don Magel listened with interest as K.C. told him that Nicole was the legal owner but until she turned eighteen her uncle had control of the ranch and wanted to see her dead and the only way they could live a life without fear was to see him dead first.

They needed the money to hire gunmen of their own and as soon as she turned of age they could go home and take the ranch that was legally hers.

Every time Don Magel dealt with the young Texan or his friends there were strings attached. "Why you don't just marry her, Magel asked, and then you would not have to sneak around or hide out!" K.C. decided that for a smart man Don Magel was not too bright,

"She would have to have her uncle's permission before we could get married and I don't think he is going to give it to us!" K.C. informed him sarcastically.

K.C. had courage and skill but to the Mexican he was as dumb as a stump.

"You don't need his permission in Mexico and a marriage here is as good as one in the States.

If you marry her here and now you will have control of the ranch you both seek and you will be the rightful heir if anything was to happen to her!"

For once in his life K.C. was listening to some good advice but it was going in one ear and out the other!

"Where is a preacher?" K.C. asked looking around in mock disbelief as Nicole skirted the herd and was now riding up to where the men sat.

"What's so funny?" she asked seeing the smile on K.C.'s face. "Senor Magel says we can get married here in Mexico and it would be a binding marriage the same as a marriage in the States!" K.C. told her.

Nicole loved K.C. but even she thought at times he could be a little slow. She knew Senor Magel was speaking the truth but that was something K.C. was going to have to figure out for himself she thought as she removed the hat from her head and slapped the thick layer of trail dust from the clothing she was wearing.

Don Magel bowed slightly to the lady as Nicole held her hand out to be introduced. One day K.C. might learn the fine art of chivalry but it was something she was going to have to teach him because it was something he was never going to learn on his own.

Don Magel kissed her hand then looked up into the eyes of the lady he had just met. He had no idea why she had fallen in love with the hellion at her side but he was going to do all that he could to help the both of them.

Don Magel turned to his men ordering the vaqueros to help put the cattle in the holding pens until a deal was made and he owned the cattle legally.

Carlos swung the gates open and signaled the men to bring the cattle in. Buttermilk went through first swinging its massive head from side to side as if daring any and all to come closer as it walked to the center of the ring and turned facing the gate and the men standing behind the strong wooden barrier.

Buttermilk stood in the center of the ring with its legs spread and its head lowered swinging its massive set of horns from side to side as it defied each and every move the men made. Joe was already up and setting at the campfire sipping at a cup of piping hot coffee when Jim began to stir.

Sherlene and Marilyn were preparing a hot breakfast for the men hopping to hold them through the rigors of the upcoming day. He could make out the sounds of bacon frying in the cast iron skillet as he rolled from the warmth and comfort of the make shift bed. The light smell of biscuits filled the air calling to him as he made his way to the warmth of the fire. "Well, we made it here, now what are we gonna do?" Joe asked.

The set of twin colts were rolled up in the worn leather holsters and both were lying beside him at the fire. It seemed the deadly weapons were as much a part of the man as were his arms or legs, the man never moved without the weapons moving with him; they had become an extension of his body!

Jim poured himself a cup of the hot black coffee burned his lips as he tried to take a drink from the rim of the tin cup. They hadn't talked about what they were going to do or how they were going to do it but now the time had come to make a plan.

I want to push the cattle closer to the main house so I can keep an eye on them until K.C and the others get back from Mexico, until then I guess I'm in charge and responsible for whatever happens.

Old man Malloy didn't hire anything but thieves and gunmen, that is the reason I ran them off in the first place.

As it is I think they will try to come back and steal anything that ain't nailed down!

Jim took another drink of coffee before continuing, "I don't think K.C. and the others know Nicole's uncle is dead and I doubt they will come back to the states until they think they have enough guns and men to take the ranch from her uncle, by force if necessary." "So what do you plan to do?" Joe asked.

"I figure if we push the cattle close to the main house I'll be able to keep an eye on them from there and that way I won't have to spend the next three months stuck out in the tumbleweeds and cactus waiting for the kids to get back!"

Joe strapped the set of revolvers around his waist then picked up the saddle and headed for the black.

The stallion turned at the sound of the man's footsteps and facing the rider as he come forward.

After a hard day and a goodnight the black was ready to play shoving at the rider with his shoulder as he tried to place the saddle across his back. Joe half stumbled as the weight of the animal struck him forcing him backwards.

Joe dropped the saddle and then shoved back at the black with both hands. It was a game the black enjoyed. Joe pushed with all of his strength as the black lowered its head and swung it towards him striking the man on the left shoulder.

Joe jumped and grabbed at the black's head then hung on as the animal lifted him from the ground. "You ready to quit?" Joe asked as he dropped lightly to the ground below, this time the black stood still as Joe picked up the saddle and blanket then placed them across his back.

Tightening the cinch Joe put his foot in the strip and pulled up into the seat of the saddle. Slapping the animal with the leather reins he rode out of camp to face the early morning sun of the day ahead. Jim was in no hurry to leave the warmth of the fire or the women in camp, he and Sherlene had only been married a few months and it seemed as if they never had time to be around each other.

At first it had been her job at the restaurant then his job at the jail and now it was a herd of cattle that didn't belong to either one of them!

Jim picked up his blanket and saddle and placed them near the string of horses before going back to camp. Sherlene was putting away the dishes as he approached, at times he could still act like a little kid. Jim stood drilling the tow of his boot into the ground as he stammered, "I'll saddle that horse of yours if you want to ride along."

Sherlene broke into a smile, "I'll ride along with you if you don't mind saddling Marilyn's horse so she can ride with us." "Why would I want her to ride along with us?" Jim asked still not sure where Sherlene was going with this.
"She isn't riding with us we're riding with them." Jim was stunned, "Why would we want to ride with them?" Sherlene slapped at him with the side of her hat, sometimes he could be such a dummy and that it aggravated her,
"They will need a chaperon!" she answered. "Why?" he asked , Sherlene slapped at him again with the side of her hat catching him on the side of the arm, "Just saddle our horses!" she demanded half playing and half serious knowing her husband would do whatever she asked just because she asked it!
The black was moving fast kicking up large clods of dirt with each step it took a trail of dust followed behind testifying to the power and speed it possessed.
 The rider had given the horse its lead and the black loved to run eating up the miles in its passion for speed.
Joe felt the power and strength of the black rippling through the muscles that strained under the leather bindings of the worn saddle before he pulled the reins back bringing the massive horse to a stop at the sound of the gunfire, three shots in a row the signal that something was wrong.
 The black spun on a dime and was heading back to camp as the echo of the shots rang across the valley sending an army of small animals scurrying for their holes in their quest for safety. This time the clods of dirt were larger and flying higher as the rider urged the black on trying to get to the trouble before it was too late.
  Joe's right hand covered the butt of the pistol on his left side as he rode into camp scanning the area with his eyes looking for whatever trouble had brought him scrambling back. Jim stood by the horses saddling Sherlene's horse.

He knew the shots would bring the man running and it was a mean trick but he would be danged if he was going to saddle a horse for Joe's girlfriend much less ride chaperon for a couple of love sick, full grown adults even if she was his wife's sister!

Jim wanted to be alone with his wife for a change and he was starting to get awfully cranky!

A light froth covered the black as steam rose like a vapor from the heat of his body. Until that moment Jim had forgotten how much the horse reminded him of a demon that was being controlled by a madman on his back.

Joe's hand still hung by the pistol at his side, it was a stupid move but Jim couldn't help it, "Hey, you gonna help me saddle these horses or set up there all day?" Joe pulled at the reins spinning the horse to face the man talking; sometimes he didn't know why he considered this man his friend!

As the marshal, Jim had arrested him the first day he rode into town then drug him all over Texas and part of Mexico chasing a bunch of wild kids he was never going to arrest. Then he had managed to get him into a gunfight with the owner of the Rocking 'R' ranch!

Sometimes Joe thought the ex-marshal was nuts!

Joe slid off the black, "Why am I saddling your horse?" Joe asked walking to where Jim stood. "You ain't saddling mine, Jim stated, you're saddling Marilyn's, she is riding with you!"

Joe took on a whole new attitude, things were looking up.

"The women are gonna hold the cattle in a herd as we drive them from the brush, that way we won't spend all day chasing a bunch of cattle we've already caught more than once."

Sherlene and Marilyn came from the wagon carrying a whip and a rope both women wore pistol belts strapped low around their hips.

The walnut handles of the small thirty-six caliber pistols they carried looked new but the weapons were well oiled and ready to use. Bight brass caps covered the nipples of the black power pistols being carried in dark leather holsters.

The caliber of the pistols may have been small but everyone there knew they were deadly at a short distance. Joe saddled Marilyn's horse it was paint with a large brown patch over one eye. Jim saddled a buck skin for Sherlene both of the horses were in high spirits and ready to run as the women swung their legs over the back of the saddles.

Jim put the spurs to the roan in an attempt to keep up with the young strong horses the women rode while Joe fought the reins on the black to keep it from running off and leaving the women behind.

As they were leaving the camp Sherlene spoke up "I'm worried about leaving Rick by himself, she said, after all he was lucky to be alive!" "Rick said he felt much better, Joe answered, I talked to him before we left camp

. He said he would be alright; he even wanted a chance to look out for himself for the day. He thought it would help him to build strength if he had to do for himself.

Sherlene and Marilyn had packed their bags with lunch makings and left some out where Rick could get to it easily and not have to strain his shoulder then together they left camp and headed into the sand hills of the open desert. Cattle began to appear in the draws and ditches as the men looked for them driving them out from among the cactus stands for the women to watch after as they went back into the draws looking for more of the half wild cattle.

The day turned to night and still they hunted on, driving more and more of the cattle out into the open by the light of the starlit skies.

Not even the lone cry of the distant coyote could stop the men or the women as the hunt continued well into the night. A small fire was hidden among the juniper brush sending a thin trail of smoke towards the heavens as the morning sun began send rays of hope to the inhabitants' of the valley.

Sherlene rode circles around the herd singing to the cattle as Marilyn poured coffee and water into a shallow pan. The coffee was going to be strong and black but it would taste good and cut the dust from parched throats.

Joe and the black were bringing in a dozen more cattle pushing them into the herd as Jim rode up. The roan was not as fast as the black or as strong but it was good with cattle guiding the bulls and cows alike into the cornered herd without any problems before turning towards the fire, soon they would be heading north towards the wagon.

The larger stronger bulls were already milling around in the herd some stood facing each other, heads lowered shaking a massive set of horns trying to pull a bluff while the more aggressive ones were charging at one another, and the sound of combat could be heard around camp as the bull's butted heads.

Cattle would drop to their knees staggered and hurt and some would die as they slammed together trying to prove who the dominant male was and rightful leader of the fast growing heard.

The crack of the whip would drive the bulls apart but they would meet over and over again, each time doing battle until one of the bulls was declared the victor
. Sometimes one or both of the animals would die during the battles and when this happened a new bull would step up and take over the herd.

The four riders circled the herd then began to drive them north towards the wagon and the Malloy ranch. It was an exhausting drive but it would be well worth it if they had to defend them later.

CHAPTER TWENTY ONE

Daryl kicked the blanket off and then added some twigs and branches to the smoldering ashes. It was not long before the fire was going and water was boiling in the pot the smell of coffee filled the small camp
. After three days of riding he knew he would be in Dallas by night fall. Cinching the saddle down tight and pulling at the reins he began the last leg of his journey and finally Daryl could see the bright city lights sparkling in the distance as the sun set below the horizon.

Riding into the western town he sought out the nearest livery before looking for the men he needed.

A small man wearing dirty clothes and smoking a cob pipe sat under the lights of the barn door as Daryl approached and swinging down from the cutting horse Daryl gave him the reins. "He will need rubbed down, some grain and water.

I'll be back later to pick him up." The stable hand was not impressed with the way Daryl was giving orders.

"If you want your horse pick him up in the morning, I'm going to bed!" Daryl was tired and worn out from the long ride, his back hurt and he wanted a whisky, "What about my horse?" he asked wanting to be on his way.

The man stopped long enough to tell him "the last stall is open put him into yourself," before walking away.

Daryl stripped the saddle from the back of the animal and placed a bucket of oats in the troth before he left the barn, the sound of his boots pounding on the wooden sidewalk blended in with the sounds of the night.

The night life was just beginning as Daryl walked past the first couple of bars in search of a restaurant. Women of the night stood on the steps of the bars and brothels doing their best to show whatever they could, without the law stopping them.

They would call out to potential customers smiling and waving as they passed by trying their best to bring in at least one more customer before the excitement of night was brought to an end. Daryl skirted the women deciding he was too tired and too hungry to mess with them at the time.

He could smell the food before he saw the saloon or the food being cooked over the wood burning stove at the back of the room.

Following the smell of the food Daryl entered a large building the business in the room was mixed, one half of the room was a bar the other half was the restaurant.

Steak, eggs, biscuits and gravy was being delivered to the tables as he walked in.

The waitress was tall and slender and her clothes were stained with the food she was serving but it smelled good and the tables were clean.

Daryl sat down and turned one of the cups in the upright position letting the waitress know he wanted coffee with his meal. The waitress filled his cup from a large smoke stained pot as she took his order.

Daryl looked around the room as he waited for his meal to come.

Men played poker at some of the tables while other stood around the roulette wheel placing bets on where the ball would stop while several men threw dice at a craps table.

Two men sat eating a meal at one of the corner tables. They both wore black suites with string ties and the pistols at their sides were setting in holsters tied high on their hips. Notches were cut into the handles carved out of the hard bones from the horns of the cattle Texas was so proud of, more than a dozen notches were carved out of the handles.

Daryl studied the men as he waited his stomach rumbling from lack of food.

He decided they were nothing more than cheap imitations and would be gunmen living on the reputations of others. The only men they had ever killed had been shot in the back. These were cowards and it showed in their eyes.

The waitress placed a tray containing steak, eggs and potatoes in front of him then filled his coffee cup before moving on to another table.

She was moving from table to table carrying the stained pot with her filling the cups as the customers held them out from their table.

Daryl held his own cup out then stopped the waitress as she drew near, "Where is a good place to spend the night?" he asked admiring her as she walked up she looked tired but she was still a far cry from being ugly! Two blocks down on the right is the Texas Palace, it's the nicest place in town and the prices aren't too bad." she answered while she was filling his cup with the hot liquid.

Daryl watched her leave as the two gunmen got up and went to the bar.

The waitress watched as Daryl finished his meal and left a five dollar gold piece on the table as a tip.

"Come back again," she cried as he left the room and started down the wooden sidewalk. More and more people were moving out into the street in search of the saloons brothels and women of the night as the moon rose high above the large Texas town.

A glass chandelier hung in the entrance to the Texas Palace Hotel swinging slightly from side to side as Daryl entered the room.

It created long dark shadows that rose and fell with the motion of the lights. Thirty feet away a man stood behind a glass topped mahogany counter watching as Daryl took the pen in hand and signed his name to the hotel register,

"That will be five dollars in advance!" he told Daryl. He was tall and slender with a handle bar mustache. Daryl handed him the money and turned to leave when the man spoke again. He was pointing at the weapons on Daryl's sides, "I'll take those!" he said. Daryl placed his hands on the butt of the weapons then faced the man in the gunfighter's stance with his knees bent ready to draw. The slender man's face went pale as he looked into the eyes of the cowboy and realized death was but a short time coming. "The sign!" he said pointing up to the plank hanging above his head.

Fear showed in the man's face and movements as his hand began to quiver, "NO GUNS OR WEAPONS ALLOWED IN THE ROOMS" was burned into the lacquered piece of wood.

The clerk pointed again at the weapons, "I can put them in the safe till morning if you like." Daryl shrugged his shoulders then began to unbuckle the weapons from his side, "I'll want those back in the morning," he said as he passed them to the clerk. The man with the mustache was not smiling any longer as he looked into the eyes of the man standing before him.

Daryl looked around the lobby; the only person in the room was a fat bald headed man setting at a table playing solitary. The suite he wore was a cheap wool and cotton blend with a slight bulge under his left shoulder. The boots were black with long brown scuff marks at the ankles and the heals were worn down with age and over work.

Daryl decided he was looking at the security guard as he walked across the lobby and headed up the stairs.

If he was the security guard then he had to be related to someone important. If he was going to hold onto the job it was most likely the hotel owner or a high ranking official that was responsible for the position the guard now held.

The window facing the street was half open as Daryl entered letting the noise and the dust from the street below enter the room unhindered.

An oak table covered in a light coating of dust stood in one corner and a single dresser was standing against the far wall. A water basin and a pitcher both covered in finely painted roses was filled and sitting on the dresser along with a bar of soap and a straight razor that had been placed on a yellow stained towel.

Taking off his vest and hat Daryl hung them from the bed post then taking the thirty-two caliber derringer from the holster of his boot he slid it under the pillow and laid down for the night. He awoke to a full sun glairing through the open window.

Running the edge of the straight razor along the bottom of his boot served as a razor strap putting a fine edge on the piece of hardened steel. Removing two days of stubble with one smooth swipe as the five inch blade slid over the rough sun tanned skin of his face.

The clerk turned to face the stairs as Daryl walked down the steps the smile on the man's face looked forced as he spit out the words, "Good morning, Sir."

Daryl was in no better mood than the desk jockey, "Give me my rig!" he barked as he held out his hand for the gun belt and weapons taking them from the clerk's hands as soon as the safe was opened.

Strapping the belt around his waist Daryl took the pistols out one at a time spinning the cylinders to check the loads and placed them back in the holsters and the tie down loop was placed over the hammers before he walked out.

"I'll be back later!" Daryl said upsetting the clerk. It was the speed and ease of the way Daryl handled the weapons that scared the man and if it came to a show down the hotel security guard was going to be a dead man.

The city born clerk had never seen the kind of speed this man possessed and hoped he never would again!

The sound of metal striking wood resounded as the large wheels of the Mexican spurs spun across the planks of the sidewalk singing as Daryl entered the restaurant and found the same waitress serving breakfast, her clothes clean and her smile was genuine.

"I'll have bacon, eggs, coffee and biscuits," Daryl ordered. The waitress was writing the orders down on a tablet as fast as they were coming at her. She was teasing when she asked but her advice sounded good,

"Would you like a half a cow with that?" Daryl thought about it for a second, her southern slang for steak sounded good. "Skip the bacon and biscuits and bring me steak and eggs with plenty of coffee."

The waitress turned the cup face up and filled it from the pot that seemed to always be in her hand, "Don't worry cowboy coffee is what we've got plenty of around here," she said after noticing the man looking at the coffee pot.

With the turn of the hip she was off and waiting on another table. Daryl used the knife on the table to cut into the meat he had ordered. He had thought about drawing out the bowie knife he kept in the back of his belt to cut the steak up with but the steak was so tender he could have cut it with the edge of a fork.

"More coffee?" the waitress was in a good mood for someone who had been on their feet most of the night and already part of the morning.

Daryl nodded as she filled his cup again. "Where is a good place to have a few drinks?" he asked. The waitress stopped long enough to think about the question, "The Bull's Horn.

It's as good a place as any if you're looking for a fair drink at a descent price.

The women are a little pushy and most of them won't take no for an answer. If you wind up at the Irish pub it has the best whiskey and the dealers are honest but the bouncers are short tempered and vicious.

You better walk soft around them and a fellow named Butch. He is the leader of the bunch and he gets a kick out of beating men when their down and putting the boots to them!"

"Thanks, I'll remember that!" Daryl was beginning to like the tall waitress with the easy way about her.

Maybe after this was over he would come back and see her again. His thoughts stopped as he caught sight of his own reflection, his shoulder length hair hung below the brim of his hat and it made him look like a wild man.

"Is there a barber in town?" he asked pulling a five dollar gold piece from his pocket and handing it to the waitress. She smiled and put the tip in her pocket, "One block east then turn north.

There is a candy striped pole outside the front door, you can't miss it." She went back to work stopping only long enough to watch Daryl walk out of the room leaving the spike marks of the Mexican spurs in the wooden floor.

The red and white stripes of the pole were easy to spot it stood at the doorway drawing men and children to the barber shop. Inside men sat in chairs under the window waiting their turn as the barber worked on the people inside.

His fingers were fast and nimble and hair was falling to the floor below almost as soon as a customer could sat down on the soft leather cushions of the ancient chair. Men were making bets as the honed blade glided across Daryl's face cutting throw the short stubble in one easy stroke.

A trickle of blood appeared in the corner of the lip testifying to the closeness of the shave. One of the men sitting on a bench began to laugh then got up and held his hand out, the barber laid the razor down then dug into his pocket bringing out a fifty cent piece and placed it into the man's hand,

"Alright Jake you got your fifty cents now leave me alone until I finish the man's shave will you?" The man laughed than came out with "A.J., I got fifty cents says you cut him again!" Daryl took the towel from A.J.'s hands then wiped the blood from his lip, "fifty cents says he don't!" Daryl growled throwing the bloody towel to the floor and walking out.

Daryl hadn't wanted a shave anyway but it came with the hair cut so he figured it couldn't hurt!

Laughter from the barber shop was still following him as he entered the bar.

Butch stood at out the end of the bar scowling the waitress had been right, he looked to be around six-two or three weighing around two hundred and thirty to forty pounds. His build was massive with broad shoulders and the muscles on his arms were twisted and knotted reminding Daryl of vines wrapped around the limbs of an oak tree.

Short cropped red hair spoke of a bad temper and a touch of the Irish. Freckles the size of buckshot covered his face and hands.

In one glance Daryl knew this was the man he had come to meet. If he could get Butch to ride with him he would be his second in command.

Give me a double whisky Daryl ordered and then sat back in silence to watch the man at work. Daryl's hopes of seeing the man in action soon vanished as he realized the men in the bar were terrified by the very presence of the giant in front of them.

If he wanted to see Butch in action he was going to have to set the fight up himself! That meant putting the money up to get some cowboy drunk enough and stupid enough to take the bouncer on in a knockdown drag out bare knuckle fight.

Looking around he could see there was no one in the bar at the moment stupid enough or drunk enough to take on the giant! Placing a five dollar gold piece on the counter was enough to get the bartenders attention and a bottle of fine Irish whiskey was slid down the bar to where he waited

Picking the bottle up and heading for the first table available Daryl waited for the real reason he was here and that was to see if Butch was as tough as the reputation he held or even as tough as he looked.

Evening turned to night as Daryl sat sipping from the bottle in front of him and soon he realized his wait was not in vane as two cowboys come stumbling in. One was holding the other up as he reached out and grabbed at one of the girls working the tables. Glasses, a tray and a bottle of whiskey flew through the air as the barmaid screamed and ran

Butch was there in a second, the drunk was short and stocky and without saying a word Butch threw a left hand punch.

Leading from the floor his shoulder had dropped and his fist came up with all the power he possessed striking the man under the ribs and lifting him off his feet.

The drunks face turned white as he fell to the floor coughing and gagging. It was plain to see he was not going to be getting up for quite a while!

The second man threw a right towards the bouncers head

It was a wicked punch and struck the larger man solid.

The sound of bone striking bone filled the room as the punch landed. Most men would have staggered or fell from the impact but all Butch did was shake his head before charging. Wrapping his arms around the man's waist Butch lifted him from the floor and threw him sideways and down.

The cowboy landed on his back and was trying to get up as Butch came forward and stood over the fallen man.

Butch leaned forward and down as he threw a right of his own putting the weight of his whole body behind the punch. The sound was sickening as the fist landed hard and solid. The power of the blow was devastating as it destroyed the man's face!

Pieces of bone stuck through torn skin as the nose broke and spread across the cowboys face. Butch held the man's head to the floor by using his hair but mercifully the cowboy was unconscious as Butch threw the next punch shattering his jaw and knocking out three of the front teeth.

The roar of a small cannon filled the room as Butch drew his fist back for the third time,

"Let him go!" the voice sounded scared and unsure of its self. As Butch turned to face the speaker he could see that the bartender was holding a short barreled shot gun and wisps of thick black smoke drifted towards the ceiling as he held the menacing weapon tightly in his shaking hands.

The muscles of Butch's jaw began to bulge out as he fought down his anger.

"Let him be, the boss doesn't want any more killing!" Butch stood up facing the barman then turned and kicked the fallen cowboy in the guts.

The unconscious man groaned in pain then rolled up into a ball.

Blood was running from his face to the floor as Daryl sat and watched. Butch was walking past his table when Daryl kicked the chair out from under the table blocking his path.

Daryl's voice was cold and hard and there was no fear in his eyes as he demanded Butch to "Sit down!" Butch spit out his answer, "I'll break you in half!" as he shoved the chair aside and stepped forward.

The speed of the forty-four stopped him in his tracks as Daryl leveled the barrel between his eyes.

The sound of the spinning cylinder thundered above the beating of his own racing heart.

At six foot two and over two hundred and thirty pounds no one had given Butch a direct order since he had turned fifteen, at least not anyone who wasn't paying him!

Looking down the barrel of the gun and into the eyes of the man behind the weapon Butch began to feel small and insignificant.

He had no doubt Daryl was about to blow his head off.

Beads of sweat began to form as fear clutched his chest and heart.

Butch was cold and vicious but he was not the kind of man or murderer that sat before him now! Daryl repeated his words, "I said sit! I've got a proposition for you and before you say anything I want you to listen!" Butch didn't like taking orders but he didn't want to push his luck against the big bore of the colt or the deadly pieces of lead contained in the cylinders.

Butch pushed the chair back under the table, "What do you want?" he asked.

Daryl un-cocked the revolver and laid the weapon in his lap, "I'm running some cattle from Texas to Kansas and I need a second in command to keep the men in line!"

"Why don't you do it yourself?" Butch asked aware that Daryl still held his hand close to the deadly weapon.

In a flat cold voice Daryl answered, "I could force the men to follow my lead but I would have to kill half of them to get the job done.

I need someone who can put fear into the men without having to resort to killing them and I figure that someone is you!"

"Why me?" Butch asked. Daryl smiled, "Because your big, your mean and you can scare most men into place without having to kill them!

When you do your fighting it's with your hands and your boots most of the men will walk easy around you just for those reasons, if not you can beat always beat them back into line!" Butch was beginning to like the idea of pounding someone without the blast of a shotgun going off, "What if someone dies?" he asked.

"Then we bury them on the trail!" Daryl answered. Butch liked the idea of beating someone to death with his bare hands he dreamed of it many a night as he slept in a cold lonely bed. Butch thought he had beaten a man to death once or twice before but had always had to run before he had a chance to check his work.

He was always running from the eyes of the law or a stranger passing by never having time to see if the man was dead or alive!

He didn't know why he enjoyed this so much but he began to think of how it would feel to sit and watch as a man bled slowly to death after one of the beatings he had given him.

"What does it pay?" he wanted to know but it really didn't matter to him he was thinking of the real satisfaction he would get!

Daryl knew greed would get the man to do things fear could not, "Whatever the price of three hundred head of cattle will bring maybe more!"

The whistle that followed the number let Daryl know the payment was sufficient.

"We're going to be running three to four thousand head of cattle from Texas to Kansas.

I've already got a dozen men ready to ride for me and they're already rounding them up. When I get back we're gonna start the drive but I need at least four more men to make the drive. I was thinking you might know a few men we could use as drovers."

"They ain't drovers, Butch answered, but I know a few men, they can handle cattle ok and their pretty good with a gun, but I ain't too sure if they will ride with us not on this kind of job."

"When will you know if they will work for us?" Daryl asked.

"I'll know tonight, they usually come in before the place closes and I'll talk to them as soon as they get here,"

Butch replied thinking he was finally going to get out of this place and maybe one day be somebody because second in command could lead to bigger things in the future!

Daryl saw the glint in Butch's eyes, "The owner of the ranch we will be taking the cattle off of was killed in a gun fight and at the moment no one can legally claim the ranch or the cattle on it but it won't be long before the next of kin shows up and tries to stop us.

I want to get the cattle moving and out of Texas before that can happen!

Once we cross the border into New Mexico the cattle will belong to us and there is nothing anybody will be able to do about it!"

"I'm sure can find some men, Butch answered, if you want we can meet at the livery stable after I get off work and we can leave from there." Daryl poured himself a drink from the bottle sitting on the table, "One more thing, I'm not gonna risk my life ridding with a bunch of drunks. If they can't stay away from the bottle leave them!" Before leaving the table Butch nodded his head in agreement, "No drunks! I got it!"

Daryl took the last drink from the bottle then stood, he was two inches shorter than the other man and fifty pounds lighter the combination was not good he had absolutely no doubt he would not last two minutes in a fair fight against the larger man but if it ever came down to it he would make sure it was not a fair fight! Happy with himself for achieving his goal so quickly he headed back to the hotel.

The clerk with the handlebar mustache was standing behind the mahogany counter as he walked in.

The fat man set playing solitary at the poker table pointed towards the sign saying no weapons allowed in the rooms but Daryl ignored the man as he headed up the stairs taking the steps two at a time stopping in his room just long enough to gather what belongings he had and then walked back down to the lobby.

The fat man had put down the deck of cards and stood staring in anger as he came down the steps.

"Try for it!" Daryl challenged placing his hand over the revolver at his side and nodding his head at the bulge under the others jacket.

Daryl's smile showed his true nature, he lived by the speed of his hand and the accuracy of a bullet while the security guard made his living off of the fear of others.

His hand slowly began to drop as he realized Daryl's bullet would tear through his heart long before his hand reached the short barreled pistol beneath his vest.

He knew he was an overweight security guard hired for looks and nothing more and with a feeling of shame he turned then walked back to the table and sat down, the little infringement was not worth dying over!

Daryl handed the key to the clerk and walked out knowing that for once in his life he was going to have the riches and life he deserved!

CHAPTER TWENTY TWO

Parker rode drag bringing up the last of the cattle and pushing them into the holding pen as Don Magel and his men formed a circle at the gate keeping the cattle from bolting and charging back out into the open prairie.

One of his men closed the gate as Parker took his hat and began to beat the trail dust from his pants when a tall Mexican vaquero handed him a flask made from animal hide.

The smooth soft leather felt cool to the touch, as Parker pulled the cork the smell of a fine wine filled the air around him.

A sweet mild sensation met his lips as the wine lingered on his tongue. He had never tasted the sweetness of the wine before,

"What the heck is this?" Parker asked surprised that a liquid fire was not running down his throat and burning with a hot passion in the bottom of his guts!

"It is called burgundy!" Carlos answered taking the flask from Parkers out stretched hand.

"It is a fine wine that is made from the grapes that grow on our ranch!"

"I think I could live on that!" Parker said liking the sweet taste that lingered on his lips

. Carlos began to laugh, "It has a sweet taste but be careful it has the kick of a mule!"

Parker tuned his horse to ride away but was unsure of where to go, "Come, Carlos said, the ranch is this way." Carlos pulled at the reins of his horse and rode east as Parker followed. Away from the town and the holding pens filled with cattle.

Parker listened to their bawling fade off into the distance as they rode onward.

K.C. and Don Magel had ridden north towards the small Mexican town behind the stock yards. Don Magel was part owner if not full owner of the bank and most of the businesses in the border town with large assets in Mexico City and Monterrey.

The tall lanky cowboy with sandy colored hair and a face full of freckles rode beside the important man.

It was a strange looking pair that rode down the main street of town.

The cowboy with his faded clothes and worn out boots rode a horse the color of oak layered in streaks of sweat and dirt.

The chaps and saddle were used and showing signs of the wear and tear only a hard drive could provide. Pieces of the long sharp barbs of the Mexican desert cactus stuck out from the brightly woven wool blanket and they were buried deep into the leather of saddle.

The cowboy was no better off than his horse as dust hung in the very air around him as it was jolted from his body with every trot the horse took.

Don Magel rode on a saddle made of the finest leather with silver Conchos outlining the die stained saddle.

The leather was as black as night against the white of his horse.

Don Magel's skin was almost as dark as the saddle after years of riding in the heat of the desert sun. His eyes were dark and piercing and there was a hollow haunted look behind them that told of a misery most men would never know.

K.C. stopped at the cantina and swung down from the trail worn horse,

"If it's alright I'll wait for you in here," Don Magel nodded and rode on towards the bank.

K.C. walked in and saw that Colton and Eric were already sitting at the bar drinking tequila and sucking on some citrus fruit.

A senorita wearing a long black dress covered in lace danced to the beat of the guitar player's music.

K.C. took a drink from the bottle then bit into the lime and compared to the Texas whiskey it was strong and bitter and the worm at the bottom of the bottle seemed to come alive as he tried to fight down the urge to heave!

Licking at the salt on the back of his hand seemed to help fight down the nausea as he took another drink.

The cowboys at the bar knew just what he was going through, this was the first time either of them had ever tasted the bite of the tequila and it was having a devastating effect.

"Where's Nicole?" he asked trying to take his mind off the sinking feeling in his stomach.

Eric took a drink from the bottle, his face and neck was tuning bright red as the liquid fire came alive burning his throat and turning his tongue to flames.

Gasping for breath he tried to answer but couldn't.

"She's down at the hotel," Colton stated.

Like Eric he was having a hard time trying to drink the tequila, "Don't they have any whiskey in this place," K.C. asked tired of trying to drink the Mexican liquor.

Colton shook his head in denial, "All they have is this and hot beer!" K.C. held up his fingers signaling the bartender for three of the hot beers as the dancer came up and put her arm around Colton dragging him onto the dance floor.

Come we dance she cried showing all the flair and passion of the hot blooded Spaniard she was but Colton managed to pull away and back to the table.

K.C. was finishing his drink when Eric pulled him aside, "When do we get paid for the cattle?" "We'll get paid tomorrow after the wedding," K.C. answered. "You mean he is going to make you go through with the wedding, Eric asked, why, does he hate you that much or is he trying to get even for some of the cattle you've stolen from him?"

"Neither, K.C. answered, him and my pa were friends before ma and paw died and I guess he kind of figures he is obliged to watch over me.

I'm sure he thinks if he gets me married I'll have to settle down, you know, raise a family or something."

"Well are you going to settle down?" Eric asked.

"I don't know, K.C. answered, I've never been married before and I dang sure never raised a family before! The truth is I just don't know for sure what I'm gonna do!"

"Well you better make up your mind quick, Eric whispered, because tomorrow may just be the last day your ever gonna see as a single man!"

As K.C. and the others sat in the cool shade of the cantina Parker and Carlos rode towards the Magel hacienda.

The youngest of the small band of rustlers wanted food and a bath a lot more than whiskey and booze.

The large twisted iron gates leading to the main house spoke of a wealth few of the men had ever seen.

Vaqueros sat along the top rail of a coral watching as their fellow cowboys fought the stallion in the middle of the ring.

Parker realized that the vaqueros were placing bets, as they rode past he could see money being passed from one hand to another.

Each man was betting on how long a rider would be able to stay in the saddle or if he could ride the horse to a standstill winning the wages and respect of the men perched on the top rails.

Parker followed Carlos to the front of the Magel ranch bunkhouse.

The adobe walls were painted white reflecting the heat of the desert sun and inviting the men into the shade of its cooling walls.

Long open windows ran the length of the rooms letting in the wondrous smells and gentle breezes of the desert around them. The fragrance of the cactus flower and the wild rose filled the room as Parker entered.

A large metal tub was leaning against the back wall and towels and wash cloths were piled on a bench next to the tub.

Carlos pointed to an empty bunk, "You can sleep here tonight if you want or you can always ride back to town and sleep at the inn."

"We haven't come across a clean stream or pond in a week and I would sure like to use that tub and after that I want to sleep for a week!"

"The choices are yours, Carlos said as he smiled and pointed to the back of the bunkhouse, the pump is behind there and the water bucket is hanging from a nail by the back door."

Parker laid the tub flat on the floor and started out of the bunkhouse in search of the bucket and the bath he had ridden out to the Magel ranch in hopes of finding.

The room of the inn was not near as nice as the open spaces of the bunkhouse.

The adobe walls were cracked and dry; a lone bed was jammed in the corner along with a night stand and a vase filled with a dark brown liquid.

Nicole couldn't believe the dark liquid was what passed for water at the weather beaten inn. The pounding on the door came as a blessing as she answered it to see the bright smiles of children staring up at her.

"Come," they cried pulling at her with small eager hands.

A buckboard filled with women waited outside the door of the inn.

At the crack of a whip the horses began to trot in the direction of the Magel ranch and in the wagon the women were talking a hundred miles per hour but Nicole had no idea what they were saying.

The few words of Spanish she knew were lost in the mists of a million others!

Cactus flowers and wild roses lined the dusty path leading to the hacienda.

Mexican cowboys driving small herds of cattle waved at the women in the wagon hoping to be noticed others were calling some of the women by name then went riding off in a great hurry eager to show off their abilities 'with the mounts they rode.

Nicole smiled a knowing smile. Even if she could not speak the language it was easy to tell who liked who.

Nicole had no idea what they were saying but the women in the wagon were almost as excited as the children had been.

The fence around the hacienda was made out of desert rocks stacked together and bonded by stucco.

Twisted rod iron gates secured the area around the main house from attack while a large veranda circled the main house giving the home an inviting atmosphere.

Don Magel was setting in the shade of the veranda as the driver of the wagon brought it to a stop.

An older slender man wearing a black suit with the collar turned around sat beside him and all the women and children called him padre then climbed down from the wagon and raced towards him with their hands out stretched.

Each of them were looking for a blessing that he was quick to give greeting them all and then calling each one by name as they approached.

Nicole couldn't help but feel she was the one being railroaded as the women persuaded her to follow them into the huge living room of the main house.

Fine furniture graced the room as the reflection of oil paintings glistened off the polished floor. One wall was half filled with the opening of a massive fireplace, while a wooden mantel glowing bright from years of polish stretched from wall to wall and the portrait of a beautiful woman hung over it.

Her hair was as black as the ravens wing and her eyes as dark as night.

The brush work of the artist had been superb and the painting seemed to have a life of its own. At any moment Nicole expected the lady in the painting to step out of the canvas and back into the life she had once lived in this very room.

The dress she wore was made of white lace and beautiful red roses decorated her hair as a long white veil flowed from behind.

Don Magel stood beside Nicole admiring the painting and remembering the woman.

"She was my wife," the words were spoken in a hushed whisper that seemed to echo of a long lost tortured love.

Nicole turned to see the pain in the eyes of the man beside her.

Don Magel stood with a lonely haunted look on his face; years of separation had not erased the pain of her leaving.

Nicole knew of her death and the suffering that the fever had brought to so many loved ones even as her parents had died of the disease.

Lola had died long ago but the rich Mexican rancher could not forget the beauty of her memory.

Nicole had learned that for a short time Lola had watched over K.C. after his parents died till finally she too fell victim to the horrible sickness that had taken her from the man who loved her so dearly.

Don Magel held his arms out as if dancing with an invisible partner then began to move around the room.

He was swinging to the music of a long forgotten guitar and holding his wife in the arms that had never forgot the deep passionate love he held for her. Nicole was grateful to the women when they rushed her up the stairs and into the main bedroom. Lying across the bed was the white gown from the picture.

Fresh roses and a veil were nested against a soft pillow and a porcelain tub filled with water sat on the floor in a private bathroom next door.

The fragrances of soap and lilac drifted into the room as Nicole stood admiring the dress.

For the first time in weeks she became aware of the trail worn clothes, the calloused hands and the smell of cattle.

She hadn't realized when K.C. told her they would have to get married here in order to sell the herd that it would be so soon or so fast.

Then the realization struck her, "I'm getting married," she said more as a question than a statement. "Si, one of the women answered, Hoy!"

Nicole looked around the room at the women standing there

"What does that mean?" she asked as she felt her legs go to jelly as the answer came back, "Today!"

Nicole hung the gun belt over the handle of the door before slipping into the cool inviting waters of the tub.

K.C. came up gasping for air; water was trying to fill his lungs as he breathed in.

The vaqueros that had thrown him into the cattle pond sat on their horses laughing as he came to the surface,

"Here, one of them said throwing him a piece of homemade soap, maybe soon you will be clean enough to take a real bath!"

K.C. grabbed at the bar and then threw it back, his bloodshot eyes glairing with rage.

"Keep it!" he yelled then started towards the bank.

Manuel's horse blocked his path with it body, "Don Magel says you are to be married smelling like a man not a pig and we are to make sure you do not embarrass him at the wedding, even if we have to bath you ourselves!"

K.C. picked up the bar of soap and headed back into the deeper waters of the pond,

"One day I am going to repay this favor!" K.C. threatened as the men stood watching over him. The youngest of the vaqueros sat straight up in the saddle showing pride few of the other carried,

"Manuel does not fear you or any other man!

He has been married many years to my sister and she has taught him the true meaning of fear!"

Manuel took a light swing at the youngster as he put the spurs to his horse,

"Better luck next time," the young cowboy said riding out of the deep water and heading towards the barn.

"Where is he headed?" K.C. asked. "He is going to get your horse so after you are done here you can ride to the ranch and climb into a real tub by then you might smell better!"

"Two baths in one day!" K.C. thought he was going to be sick as he climbed from the foul muddy waters of the cattle pond.

Jose was back with K.C.'s horse and after catching one whiff of the man Jose turned away, "Maybe we should soak him in the watering trough before we let him into the tub, Manuel suggested, he smells like a mix of rotted wine and cattle urine!"

Alright I'm bathing," K.C. said as the smell of the stagnant water consumed the air around him.

Nicole sat on the edge of the bed winching with pain as Delana pulled the brush through her now short brown sun bleached hair, "easy, she cried, I don't want to be bald for my own wedding!"

Delana tried not to laugh as she laid the comb gently down, large clumps of matted hair lay at her feet while the scissors that had done the damage was sitting on the cabinet along with a comb that now contained twisted and broken teeth.

Picking up the comb Delana attacked Nicole's hair again and again twisting and pulling, as her older sister Michelle, applied lipstick and makeup to Nicole's slender sun tanned features.

Soft leather shoes were wrapped snugly around Nicole's feet and a small red rose was nestled behind her ear.

There was a knock at the door and a quiet whispered exchange and the girls turned to Nicole and pulled the silken veil over her face as the women led her from the room.

The warm soapy waters of the tub had cut the trail dust from K.C.'s body leaving his once dark tan three degrees lighter.

Bottles of cologne sat alongside his bunk ready and waiting for him to choose from.

Manuel had went to the lockers of all the vaqueros collecting clothes new or as close to new as he could find that would fit the young groom.

Pants and shirts lay on the bed next to the bath; they were the best the vaqueros owned. Wide silver thread was sewn into the seams of the coal black pants while red roses made from the finest material were sewn above the pockets and along the cuffs.

The shirts were white silk, tailored to fit the wearer and a pair of black boots sat under the bed along with a set of Mexican spurs, the silver and gold wheels glistened in the bright sunlight that was coming through glass windows of the vaquero's home.

The pants were tight showing the outline of his slender build but the boots fit perfectly. K.C. stood in front of the mirror admiring himself as Don Magel walked in,
"The vaqueros will want those back after the wedding." K.C. turned to look at the man who had just entered.

Like K.C. he was dressed for the wedding, "It is time to go, Magel said, the padre is waiting and this is one time I do not wish to be late!"

K.C. followed him slowly towards the main house, he was a man in a daze hardly noticing the tables that set out in the front yard or the children and adults that drank punch dipped from fancy bowls that set in the middle of the tables.

Men, women and children stepped aside as Don Magel led the way.

K.C. stopped in front of the fireplace and waited for his future wife, the large portrait of the Mexican dancer stood smiling down at him.

K.C. could barely remember the woman but he remembered her eyes and the soft gentle hands that had held him so long ago.

"I hope you're watching this," K.C. said as he looked up the steps and waited for Nicole.

For just a second Don Magel thought he saw his once beautiful angel floating down the steps as Nicole made her entrance.

The clothes and the slender build looked so much like Lola that he could hardly believe his eyes or contain his love as he looked up at her.

Red and yellow rose petals decorated the steps adding beauty to the dress Nicole wore.

Don Magel waited for her to hold out her hand before escorting her to the front of the room. Vaqueros and senoritas alike filled the room growing silent as the bride came forward.

Magel was the one who said, "I do," after the padre asked who gives the orphaned bride away. K.C. stood like a man in a trance too terrified to move as the ceremony came to an end.

Like Manuel the hot headed kid and the fast gun was just now beginning to realize what real fear was.

His knees went to water and blackness engulfed him as he heard the words, "I do," come from his own lips.

The words echoed through his mind a thousand times as the floor came up to meet him.

K.C. saw the vision of an angel standing over him as his eyes began to focus.

Slowly the room stopped spinning as light replaced the darkness and he sat up.

Don Magel handed him a glass of the bright red burgundy wine and a new strength started to run through him as the sweet wine touched his lips.

In the distance K.C. could hear the playing of a guitar and the laughter of children.

The party was beginning as vaqueros dressed in bright clothes helped him to his feet.

Don Magel danced across the room the beautiful young bride may have been on his arm but his eyes were closed and everyone knew he was remembering the day of his own wedding when he had held the love of his life in those arms and dreamed of the life they would have together.

Now the love was gone and only the memories remained.

A sadness blanketed Don Magel's expression as he let go of his lovely partner then bowed low and left the room.

K.C. took Nicole by the hand then began to dance slowly to the music hopping one day they might share the love with each other that Don Magel and Lola had come to know.

As the dance and the party broke up Manuel poked K.C. in the ribs with his elbow,

"Enjoy tonight because tomorrow we ride."

It was a simple statement but it came as a surprise to the young outlaw, "What do you mean," he asked.

"Don Magel's orders, we are to take control of the Malloy ranch so the new senora can claim her inheritance!"

K.C. had come hoping to sell cattle to buy the men and guns they needed he did not want the men he had grown up with risking their lives in his private war!

CHAPTER TWENTY THREE

From the back of the black Joe could see the cloud of dust rising from the desert floor. It was a long ways off but coming fast and it wouldn't be long before the men creating the dust cloud would be close to the camp he and the others shared!
 Slapping the black with the reins they rode off towards the horizon and into the desert plains. Tall thorny Cactus, brush and rocks would hide his position until he found out who the riders were.
 Pulling the rifle from its scabbard and injecting a shell Joe rode down into the draws and towards the approaching men. Jim let the cattle go that he was chasing from out of the brush and rode to intercept the riders that he had seen as he came out of one draw. Joe emerged from another brush covered draw and both men rode together rifles at the ready.
 If there was a fight to be had it was going to be short and bloody as the long range weapons took care of the would be attackers.
 Roy brought his horse to a stop as he saw the men approach, Paul and the others behind him did the same.
 The cloud of dust settled as the men sat on their horses.
 Joe rode forward not sure of the men or why they were there but as he got closer he saw they were the young cowboys Marilyn was so fond of.
 Jim had sat back on the roan he had recognized the bunch at a glance since he had known most of them their whole lives and had ridden the trail with them more than once and had watched them grow slowly into manhood.
 The boyish attitude the lopsided grins and their goofy manner was a part of their character that he liked and admired.
 It didn't surprise him even a little bit to see the bartender riding along with the men of the Lazy 'B' ranch.

He had known the bartender long enough to know when and how he had gotten the scar running the length of his face. Jim knew one day someone was going to pay for the damage that had been done to the man's face.

Mike wasn't used to getting ordered around and he was dang sure wasn't used to having a gun pointed at him but there was little he could do about it as Joe sat on the big horse with the rifle pointed at him.

Roy was the first to speak, "You can point that the other way if you don't mind we don't bite and we're not here to start a fight."

"Why are you here?" Joe asked. Roy was getting a little irritated at the man's attitude. "Thought we might as well ride out here and help Jim with his round up.

We figured he could use the help and besides four more hands can't hurt."

Marilyn almost giggled with delight when she saw the riders come into camp then quickly suppressed the growing smile before anyone could see her happiness,

"What are you three doing here?" she asked trying to make it sound as if her world had just collapsed and was taking her with it.

"We could not get a decent plate of burned beans in town and thought we might as well ride out here and see if Jim has got any!"

"What makes you think my beans are burned?" Marilyn asked trying to make her voice sound as rough as she could.

Roy smiled at her as he climbed down from the horse,

"What makes you think they aren't?" he replied trying to get the better of the woman him and the others considered more of mother than a friend.

Joe had heard all the little digs he wanted to hear and turned the black riding back out into the desert in search of more of the wild Texas cattle that had made it their home.

Taking a metal plate from his own saddle bags Roy slapped the dust off then walked towards the fire, the pot sat empty hanging from the metal rods.

"Elois could take lessons from you, he complained, you would work a man all day then starve him all night!"

All but Paul sat laughing at the expression on Marilyn's face.

The look of surprise and delight turned to anger as she faced the young man,

"You ain't worked ten minutes in your life and if you ever did you would probably fall over from a heart attack!"

"That may be, Roy retorted, but it's still better than starving to death!"

Marilyn stood with both fists on her hips as Roy mounted his horse,

"Tell you what; we'll go round up some cattle if you will rustle up some grub!"

Marilyn was still fuming as the men rode out of camp,
"Rustle up your own grub!" she yelled.

Sherlene sat on the back of her horse watching as the men rode away,

Marilyn could see the slight smile on her lips as the men left,

"It was not that funny," she said after placing a saddle on her own horse and pulling the cinch down tight.

"Sure it was, Sherlene answered, every time those boys get near you they manage to do something to get under your skin. Yet you are so happy to see them you about giggle every time they come around!"

Marilyn swung her leg over the saddle and began to ride out of camp and as Sherlene put the spurs to her own horse and then shouted at Rick, "put on a pot of bean while we are gone." Rick raised his hand letting her know he heard and understood what she said. He was healing rapidly now and could take care of himself and the camp. As Sherlene caught up Marilyn shouted, "We're gonna let them cook for themselves tonight, ain't we?"

"We sure are!" Sherlene answered knowing that Rick would take care of the evening meal; she just prayed he was a clean cook!

Dusk found the women driving thirty head of cattle towards the growing herd in front of the chuck wagon.

Sherlene had no more than beat the dust off her britches before the men attacked her and Marilyn with complaints. Rick had not put the beans on nor had he cooked anything! The fire had gone out and the ashes were gray and cold. The cooking pot sat empty while the men sat starving.

They had arrived long before the women had and hadn't offered to start a meal either they had just sat and waited for the women to return!

Sherlene was starting to fume, "Get some wood busted up and the fire going!"

Marilyn brought skillets and pots out of the wagon and tried to avoid eye contact with her. She knew her sister when she got in this mood you stayed out of her way!

Sherlene did not like it when the males of the species tried to tell her what to do!

She had a mind of her own and cowered to no one!

"I am no one's maid and the only reason I am cooking is because I am hungry too!" She spat out. Everyone began to scramble to see if there was something they could do to help. Suddenly Sherlene asked,

"Where's Rick, I told him to put beans on before I left this morning!

When I get a hold of him I'll wring his neck! He better have a good reason for not doing what I said!"

Jim sat back and smiled, he knew his wife was strong headed and that was just one of the things he loved about her, he didn't have to coddle her like a lot of women.

She could out ride, and out work any man he knew yet she could still be soft too, and beautiful, she filled his world with just a smile!

The next day saw Joe and Jim chasing cattle out of the brush and ravines and as darkness began to fall they had collected better than fifty head and turned them towards the small temporary camp.

Sherlene held the main herd in a tight circle singing to them as the new bunch of cows was added to the mingling herd as Jim rode beside her and Joe turned the black towards camp.

The wild eyed cowboys would be there and Rick with his cut-up shoulder.

But Joe had no interest in them, he was riding to see the brown eyed waitress he had come to know and love, the woman he was planning one day to marry.

Marilyn stood over the campfire with a pair of long tongs in her hand; the drifting smoke from the fire carried the smells of the meal she had prepared. Joe knew biscuits and gravy was waiting along with hot coffee and by the sound of the meat sizzling in the cast iron skillet he could guess that steak was on the menu as well.

He stripped the saddle from the black before heading to the campfire then stopped in the darkness and watched as the lights from the fire silhouetted her body.

He was hungry but it was not food that would satisfy this hunger.

A passion was beginning to build bringing a longing to his very soul that he was helpless to stop. Suddenly he understood the motivation that had moved Jim in the decisions he made in his life.

Marilyn handed Roy the tongs as Joe took her by the hand and lead her away from the prying eyes of the people in camp and out into the starlit skies of the desert night.

Mike and Bobby sat at the campfire bragging about all the women they had met in their short lives and about the ones they were going to meet.

Roy cut into the conversation, "I'm gonna find me the prettiest, smartest and richest girl in town then I'm gonna marry her!"

"Alright who do you think that is?" Mike asked. After a few seconds of thought Roy gave up, "I don't know but I'm gonna find out! I'm tired of living with you two yahoos and I want someone soft to cuddle up with on cold nights!"

"I bet I know who it is!" Bobby answered as the other men turned their eyes on him. He waited a minute to drag it out then blurted out Stephanie Milton, the bankers daughter.

"He always did have an eye for a pretty blonde." Mike said smiling. "Yeah, and it don't hurt that she is rich too!" Bobby jumped in pushing Roy on the shoulder.

"Of course he could always marry Nita! She is rich, good looking and owns half the town. She even owns half of the bank and half of Paul's saloon!"

Bobby ducked the punch that Roy threw his way over this remark.

"She doesn't have a dime in my place!" Paul shouted angrily.

Everyone's attention was now on the man whose face looked as if it were going to burst, it was so red.

"I've had enough of women and their tea trotting ways trying to tell me how to run a bar! As far as I'm concerned I'll never have another female partner!"
he said getting redder by the minute. "Who's paying the carpenters while you're out here on this cattle drive?" Bobby asked.

"I guess Nita is." Paul answered. "And who is selling drinks and paying for the boozes the drummers are bringing in?" Mike asked. Paul didn't bother to answer as he sat in silence thinking of the mistake he had made "Now who do you think is going to own half of your saloon when you get back?"

Paul looked almost sick when he answered, "Nita."

They were on a roll and trying to get a rise out of the bartender,

"Yup, it looks like you can start paying me rent, Roy stated, cause I'm gonna marry Stephanie and since her daddy owns the bank that means he will also own half of the saloon too and I can live like a king!

Between those two women it looks like you could be out on the streets."

"What makes you think Stephanie would marry an ugly old broken down cowboy like you?" Mike said trying to get the best of Roy.

"Because I'm good looking and sexy!" Roy answered. "And you're full of crap, Mike stated, her old man may have all of that but she doesn't and besides you said you were gonna marry the richest, sexiest and prettiest woman in town. And we all know that Nita is the richest and one of the prettiest plus she has girls working in the cathouse that's ten years younger than her and bringing in a lot more money.

plus some of them are built like brick outhouses and will keep bringing in the money while she is just going to keep getting richer.

So how are you gonna be happy and do all of that if you marry Stephanie?" "That's easy the day I marry her I'm gonna walk into that bank of hers and sit in the middle of all that money and with the beauty of all that money circled around me I ain't never gonna be able to look at anybody else!

Paul sat in silence staring at the fire; he knew the boys were just joking about marrying Nita and her girls.

Everyone in town knew Roy was wild about Stephanie since he had first laid eyes on her!

He was just too chicken to do anything about it!

Paul knew what they had said was true though,

Nita was rich and intelligent and she was in charge of his bar, signing his checks and paying his bills!

It had just dawned on him that by the time he got back to town he may not be the sole owner and proprietor of the new saloon!

In fact he would be lucky if he still owned half of the business because Nita really was a shrewd business woman, smart, cleaver and he had been dumb enough to trust her!

In the light of the campfire Bobby could see the worried look on Paul's face,

"You sure look bad for a guy who is about to get rich!" "How do you figure, Paul answered, I just found out I've lost my bar!"

"You ain't lost it yet and if Nita becomes your partner you will make more money than you even dreamed possible.

She will put a couple of pretty looking women in that back room of yours and after that she will probably fire your ugly mug and put a pretty girl showing a little leg behind the counter.

Then she will double maybe even triple the price of the drinks and all you will have to do is sit back and rake in the money!"

Paul went back to staring at the fire, he was not too worried about having Nita as a partner any longer he was just trying to figure out how to spend all that money!

Walking along in the desert Joe pulled Marilyn even closer as the sound of a lone coyote crying to the moon pierced the silence of the night.

The stars lit by the glow of a full moon showed them the path as they walked along in silence the beating wings of a bat could be heard as it soared high above them, even the cry of the desert owl blended in with the darkness giving the world of darkness a life of its own.

As they walked along lost in their own thoughts Jim was riding alongside the cattle humming the words to a song he could not remember as Sherlene rode beside him.

"It's a good thing you can't remember the words to that song or the cattle would stampede!" Jim knew she was teasing, she was a kind loving person with beautiful brown hair and hazel eyes and her smile could light up the skies she also knew her young husband loved her with all of his heart

But it was also the truth; he couldn't sing a lick and couldn't carry a tune in a leaky bucket while using both hands! It was a simple statement but it was the absolute truth and he knew it.

Roy and Mike came riding out to meet them at the end of the song, "We'll take the rest of the watch if you all want to ride in and maybe grab some grub or a cup of coffee before you hit the hay." They were riding towards camp as Joe and Marilyn walked out of the desert. Sherlene put the spurs to the side of the chestnut forcing the horse to run as she saw the look on her sister's face.

Something had happened and she wanted to be the first to hear the news.

The chestnut locked its legs sliding to a stop in front of the fire as Sherlene swung down from the saddle.

Hope and excitement was in her eyes and face as she took Marilyn by the arm, come on she said as she led her away from the fire and back out into the darkness of the night, "You're gonna tell me everything!" she said.

Marilyn knew it was useless to try to get away from her prying eyes. Her younger sister was a strong willed person with a strength and determination few possessed and fewer still could stand up to.

There was a power in her that only her closest friends and family knew of and Marilyn knew that power well! There under the stars she forced Marilyn to tell her everything,

Joe had proposed and they were to be wed as soon as possible but that was not enough for her sister. Sherlene held her by the hands, "Tell me everything," she demanded.

Marilyn couldn't resist so she told her how they had walked on the moonlight and how Joe had climbed to the top of a rock and helped her up only to get down on his knees and ask her to marry him.

She could have told her how Joe first told her about his life and how he thought he would never find someone he wanted to spend the rest of his life with or how he never realized how lonely his life really was.

He felt he didn't need anyone, just that horse and all the gold he could find in the gold fields. But then by pure chance he came into Lone Oak, Texas and there I was and for some strange reason he couldn't explain he couldn't get me out of his mind.

She could have told her sister this but she wanted this for her memory only. Sherlene's face lit up with excitement at the news of her sister getting married, the thought of her sister finding happiness filled her soul with a joy that made her feel giddy.

She held Marilyn tight and they cried at the thought of the happiness the wedding was about to bring.

At camp Jim could not believe his ears, Joe had told him he and Marilyn were going to be married but it was still hard to believe the gunman was about to become a part of his family. Sure he liked Joe and he knew he had feelings for his wife's sister but he never expected him to settle down or to get married.

He had always thought Joe would drift on leaving a fond memory and that was it, but now he was talking about marriage, which possibly meant a family which meant children and a home of their own, all the things Jim had planned for himself and Sherlene.

It had never occurred to him that Joe might want the same things he wanted. No matter how hard Jim tried he could not see Joe as a father!

Mike and Rick had relieved Bobby and Roy and as Bobby sat listening Jim told them about the impending ceremony then Bobby asked him one question,

"Does that mean I can call you daddy?" he asked.

Jim doubted if any man's face could get any redder as Joe tried to turn the conversation in a safer direction

, "Tomorrow we should be able to round up the rest of the cattle in the area, after that we can drive them towards the main house.

With the help of Sherlene and Rick I should be able to keep an eye on them from there and at least that way we won't be spending the nights sleeping on the ground but for now that's just what we are gonna do, let's get some sleep!"

Jim felt the power of the boot as it struck him on the foot, "For the last time get up before I throw it out!"

Sherlene stood with the metal egg turner in her hand threatening the sleeping men,

"Alright, alright we're up!" Mike growled trying hard to intimidate the small woman in front of him as he crawled out from under the blankets.

Sherlene was not impressed or intimidated, she knew these men in their quest for a good joke would walk right over her as they had done her sister and there was no way they were gonna start calling her mom,

"Just get up, she said half in jest and half in truth, before I throw the eggs in the fire and let you cook for yourselves!"

Mike held out a tin cup hoping for a cup of the coffee he could hear boiling over the top of the campfire and waited for her to fill it. Sherlene just looked at him,

"You're legs aren't broken, yet, pour it yourself," and walked away from the camp.

The men might burn themselves trying to get to the pot but she was not about to become their waitress, if that's what they wanted they could ride back to town, she was here to help round up cattle and that was what she was going to do!

The horses were waiting and she was ready to ride so throwing a saddle over the back of the buckskin she tightened the cinch and climbed into the saddle,

"If you boys ever get ready, we've got some cattle to bring in." she said as she put the spurs to the sides of the horse.

Jim put his plate down and headed for his own horse it was going to be a long day if he planned on keeping up with his wife.

Joe was already headed for the black as Jim rode out of sight. Sherlene would be riding in the draws and ravines searching out the long horn cattle in the worst imaginable places. Places filled with rattlesnakes, water moccasins and copperheads even the poison lizard known as a Gila Monster was at home in the Texas desert and Jim knew Sherlene would be in those draws by herself or with a partner and he was sure he was going to be there if she needed one.

She loved to ride and she was at home in the saddle as well as the kitchen.

Dust rose in a dark cloud around Sherlene as Jim caught up with her and the buckskin they would work together in the desert heat just like in the life they lived.

CHAPTER TWENTY FOUR

The stable hand stood waiting for the payment that was to follow as Daryl saddled his horse. Daryl could smell the aroma of whiskey that still lingered around the man with his hand held out.

It was clear Daryl owed the stable bill for grain, water and a place for his horse to spend the night and two dollars was high but it was better than leaving the horse out on the street. If Daryl had been alone he might have chosen to pay the man in a different manner the problem was he could hear people outside and decided it was better to pay the drunk than take the chance.

Daryl pulled the cinch tight before reaching into his pocket and handing the man the money. Butch and the men he had rounded up were supposed to meet him at any time.

Butch was a cruel and vicious person, strong and dangerous, but he was good at what he did and just the kind of man Daryl wanted as his second in command.

Daryl slid his rifle into the scabbard and tied the reins to the hitching rail before sitting down to wait , it wasn't long before Butch and two other men came into view. Daryl could feel his anger growing as he recognized one of the men, it was one of the would be gunslingers.

It was with disgust that he realized that Butch had been taken in by the imitation gunman. Daryl swung into the saddle and rode away without saying a word.

Butch quickly caught up to him and rode beside him in silence as the rest of the men brought up the rear.

Butch knew that his new boss was not pleased with him for some reason but rather than confront him he kept quiet
. The lights of Dallas grew dimmer and dimmer as the miles fell away, the bright lights turned to darkness as the desert skies took on a life of its own.

Daryl rode into a cottonwood stand before unsaddling his mount and preparing for the night. Small sticks were placed on a flat rock then larger sticks were laid across them and finally a match was applied and a fire began to blaze.

The fire was beginning to spread as he placed a tin cup with water and coffee in it on the flat rock. The others pulled a bottle from one of the saddle bags and began to pass it back and forth as Daryl waited for the coffee to boil.

Butch was in a talkative mood, "There is one more man coming, he is supposed to meet up with us on the road."

"So, Daryl asked, what do you want me to do about it?"

"Well, I was thinking if we hear him coming we could fire a couple shots in the air to let him know where we're at," he replied still unsure of Daryl's mood.

Daryl pulled the blanket over his head, "I don't care what you do!" Daryl said disgusted with himself for trusting someone else to hire men for him and disgusted with the men Butch had hired!

He was hoping for tough men, men who had no moral values or a conscience.

He wanted men who would do as he told them and not ask questions.

This is what he wanted but instead he got imitation gunmen and drunks!

He was still grumbling to himself when he heard the sound of the horse's hooves long before he heard the three shots.

Butch stood with a smoking revolver in his hand as the sound of the shots echoed across the valley.

If he hadn't heard the pounding of the hooves or the clicking of the hammer Daryl might have come out of the bed firing the heavy forty-four he held cradled in his hand instead he just came out of the bed angry!

The man who had ridden into camp looked no better than the rest of the men Butch had hired. He was tall and lanky with some of his front teeth missing.

His shirt was stained with what looked to be bad whiskey or rotted wine, Daryl could smell him even before he got down from the sweating horse.

   He walked up to Butch smiling, "sorry I'm late, I had to borrow a horse if you know what I mean."

   Daryl knew what he meant and didn't think it was that funny.

   His plans consisted of stealing thousands of head of cattle not one lone horse and he wasn't about to be hung for one lousy thief.

   "You can spend the night then I want you to ride out of here!"

   Daryl snarled. For a second the new man stood tall and straight, "Butch hired me and I'm staying until he fires me!"

   The new man was trying to use Butch's name and the fear others held for Butch like a weapon, trying to drive that same fear into the man in front of him but this time it wasn't working. The bluff might have worked on a lesser man but all it did was infuriate Daryl, he hadn't become a foreman on one of the biggest ranches in Texas by letting other men pull a cheap bluff and he was not about to now!

   Daryl cocked the revolver in his hand and slowly started to raise the barrel, no one had to tell the new man he was about to die as Butch stepped between the quarreling men, "he will ride in the morning!"

   Butch urged not wanting to see a friend die for nothing.

   "See that he does!" Daryl warned turning away from the men and heading back to his bed with the pistol still in his hand as he listened to the men move around camp before finally falling into a fitful slumber as the sounds of a man in pain echoed through his dreams.

   Daryl suddenly became aware of his surroundings as a man in flames stumbled around the campfire screaming in mortal pain.

   The flames ran up the sleeves of his shirt and across his stomach.

He was running towards a shallow pool of water fifteen feet from camp as the flames spread covering his face and hands as he ran.

You could hear the fire sizzle as his body hit the water sending up a cloud of pure white vapor the new man laid there crying in torment and pain as Daryl stood and watched.

"It was spilled whiskey Butch said, he caught his clothes on fire it happened when he tried to light a cigarette and the match fell onto his shirt and ignited the alcohol. It was like a torch that had been soaked in whiskey and used to light up a dark night burning bright and hot. Only this time a half drunken man had become a human torch!

The camp reeked with the smell of scorched blood and burned flesh.

The burns were deep, covering the man's hands and arms. Skin was peeled away showing the burned gristle and muscle beneath while part of his face was blackened from the smoke and soot of the burned clothes.

He had burns on top of his head where hair used to be before the flames had burned it off leaving nothing but burned flesh and blisters.

Tears ran down his face as the man sat in the dirt staring at his burned disfigured hands. "Kill him!" Daryl commanded.

It was time to find out if Butch was the kind of man he needed as a second in command.

The new man looked up in shock and disbelief seeing the look on Daryl's face the man knew that this time he was going to die!

"I can ride, he cried, I will leave right now!" "Sure you can ride," Daryl said with contempt, "you can ride long enough to get out of camp then you will stop and cry and whine until the law catches up with you riding that horse you stole. Then you will rat us out trying to save your own stinking hide!" Daryl looked over at Butch, "you hired this idiot and he's your responsibility and by now he has probably got half the lawmen in Texas following us so you either kill him or I will, then I will kill you!"

The man looked up in horror as Butch bent down and placed his hands around his throat squeezing with strength he had never felt before.

Pain ran through his burnt charred hands as he struck Butch in the face over and over again. Fear and sorrow over whelmed the pain as the larger man stood above him and slowly squeezed the life from his already burned and disfigured body.

Butch's hands were still around the man's throat as he looked at Daryl, "What do you want me to do with him now?" "Nothing," Daryl said showing no emotion at all as he walked towards the man's horse. "I'm gonna hang him,"

Daryl said as he took a rope from the saddle and then placed it around the man's neck after throwing the other end around the limb of a cottonwood tree.

Daryl used the man's horse to lift him high into the air. The men in camp listened and grumbled as the weight of the man's own body snapped his neck then swung back and forth between the tall trees of the grove
. The limber branch cracked and popped under the weight of the body but held fast as the body came to rest reminding them of a pendulum tied to a string.

"He was just another worthless drunk that was good for nothing so all of you shut up!" Daryl said as he took the pistol from the dead man's holster and fired two shots into the night skies before putting it back into its final resting place.

There was a new kind of fear in camp as Daryl walked back to the campfire, these men were finding out what Butch already knew.

The man with the easy smile was as cruel as any man alive and to cross him was certain death!

After the hanging Daryl walked back to the fire and poured a cup of hot black coffee then used his saddle as a chair while waiting for whatever was to come next.

The previous party atmosphere was as dead as the body swinging from the tree.

Butch and the others went back to the camp and guzzled whiskey in an attempt to forget what they had just seen then gathered their blankets and went to bed unwilling to face him as Daryl sat up and drank coffee from a tin cup.

He could hear the sound of the hooves striking rock as the sun began to rise, Daryl had been right!

The others were still wrapped in their blankets when the posse rode up, a dozen men in all, armed to the teeth.

The hammers of long barreled rifles were cocked and the rifles were being held steady in their hands as they rode into camp.

Daryl had never met the men but he knew a posse when he saw one and this didn't look like the kind of posse that went after petty horse thieves!

A large man almost as big as Butch was riding in the lead, he was wearing a U.S. Marshal badge while the man beside him was almost as big.

They looked enough alike to be brothers with the same build, dark hair and piercing brown eyes that and they seemed to weigh every word spoken with the same facial movements.

The action was a matter of habit with some lawmen and Daryl decided these were two of the best.

Close to a dozen men were spread out along the outskirts of the camp. One false move or one false gesture and these men would cut loose killing everyone in camp.

Daryl moved slow and easy raising his hands above his shoulders before he spoke, "Can I help you?" he asked aware the lawmen and the posse would be jumpy after riding most of the night and running into a group of men they were not expecting.
The smaller of the two lawmen held the rifle pointed at Daryl's chest as the other dismounted. He could see the marshal's name imbedded in the metal of the badge and it was a name he had heard before by the drunks and derelicts while hanging around the bars of Dallas.
 Butch's eyes had come open and he was looking around in a drunken stupor as the posse moved in closer.
 Maybe for the second time in his life Butch had enough sense to keep his mouth shut and was relying on Daryl to do the talking.
 "Like I said before, can I help you?" Daryl asked again and it was a sigh of relief he saw some of the rifles swing over to cover Butch and the rest of the men as they lay in a drunken stupor. If they woke up to the sight of the rifles might just help them keep their mouths shut! Daryl decided.
The lawman took a paper from his pocket and began to unfold the wanted poster as Daryl stood watching.
 It was a picture of the man swinging from the limb just yards away in the shadows of the grove. "You seen him?" the marshal asked.
Daryl almost smiled as he looked at the picture, "WANTED DEAD OR ALIVE FOR MURDER AND ATTEMPTED BANK ROBBERY" was written on the paper in large bold letters.
 "Yea, I've seen him, Daryl answered, he came into our camp a little while ago and tried to steal a horse and he might have gotten away with it too except he was drunk and riding in the dark.
 I guess he spilled whiskey on his clothing then got too close to the fire and burst into flames. The idiot tried to shoot me even as I was trying to put the fire out.

If it had not been for Butch jumping him I think he would have killed me even after I got the fire put out!"

"Well, what happened to him?" the marshal asked interrupting and getting tired of listening to what he believed to be a bull crap story.

Daryl pointed at the drag marks leading from camp, "follow those a few hundred feet and you will find him swinging from a tree."

"Why did you kill him?" it was the smaller of the lawmen asking.

"He tried to steal a horse and shot at us. What were we supposed to do with him?" "You could have tied him up and taken him back to Dallas!" the lawman said.

"I could have, Daryl said, but I wasn't headed that direction besides I figure he cost us enough time already!"

The lawman's anger and impatience was starting to become apparent, "How do you figure that!" he asked.

"If he had not shown up we would have already been on our way.

As it is we've had to sit around her waiting for you!

We figured you would be following him because he was in too big of a hurry and that could mean only one thing, the law was after him!"

Butch sat quietly watching as Daryl played the marshal. Some of the men from the posse had let their rifles hang down and walked into camp.

They were helping themselves to the coffee as the marshal followed the drag marks.

"You men keep an eye out while David and I look for Caldwell's body.

If he ain't swinging we're gonna have some more questions for these boys."

Daryl heard the body hit the ground after the rope was cut. Within minutes the two lawmen led the horse with the body laid across the saddle towards the camp.

"Alright everybody load up we're riding out of here,"

it was the one without the badge giving the orders. Badge or no badge Daryl knew the only person in the country that could give orders to a U.S. Marshal was perhaps a Texas Ranger!

It was with a sigh of relief that Daryl watched the lawmen and the posse ride out.

Hopefully it was the last time he would ever see either of them again.

A quarter of a mile from the camp, David pulled the reins of his horse bringing it to a stop beside the other lawman,

"Perry, you don't believe that load of crap do you?" Perry shook his head, "not for a second. Besides I took a look at his neck, it was broken alright but he was dead before the rope was ever put around his neck and by the look of the bruises my guess is he was strangled then they put a short rope around his neck as an afterthought."

"Why do you think they killed him?" David asked. "I'm not sure but I'll just bet their up to something and he was with them but he got burned bad and became a liability.

If they found out a posse was after him they might have killed him just to make sure he kept his mouth shut!"

"That is kind of what I thought, David stated, we're not gonna let them get away with it are we?"

"I was figuring on letting the posse take the body back to Dallas, Perry answered, then I was gonna trail me some outlaws and try to see just what their up to."

"If you don't mind I think I'll just ride along with you for a while." David handed the reins of the pack horse to the next man in line before turning back towards the men they were going to follow.

I'm planning on cutting across country and come up on the other side of them Perry said as soon as we are out of sight of their camp and we can sneak around without them seeing us, they parted company with the posse two miles from the outlaw camp.

Daryl stood by the fire wondering if he had fooled the lawmen or if they had fooled him.

Butch poured a cup of the strong black coffee; that had been sitting on or next to the fire most of the night.

After pouring from the pot without using a bandana to catch the grounds Butch spit the first mouthful of the grainy liquid into the flames then spit several more times trying to get the last of the coffee grounds out of his mouth,

"What do you think," he asked finally as he started picking at the bitter grounds still stuck between his teeth with the tip of his tongue.

"They might have bought our story but I'm not too sure about it." Daryl answered. "If they don't buy your story maybe we should make a run for it and try to out run them." Daryl knew better than to run, "Why, Daryl asked, all we did was hang a murder and a horse thief. Right now we're gonna ride out of here nice and slow like we own the whole world just in case they are watching.

If we start running now they will know something is up and then they will follow us for sure." Daryl placed a bandana over his cup and poured himself another cup of the strong coffee catching the grounds in the homemade filter.

"Make some fresh will you?" Daryl asked as he handed the pot to Butch then wake up the men, we want everything to look normal just in case that posse is still hanging around!

Drunk or not it ain't normal for a bunch of cowboys to sleep this late!"

David snuck through the brush on his hands and knees trying to get as close to the men as possible without being seen or heard then freezing less than fifty yards from the fire as he saw the head of the snake moving along the shadows.

Without seeing the body he knew it was a large snake and under normal circumstances the snake wouldn't have been a problem, one shot from the pistol at his side and the problem would have been over but this was not a normal circumstance.

He was lying on his belly and the snake was a copperhead and it was less than six feet in front of him.

He knew the snake could feel the heat of his body and the pounding of his heart against the soft cold ground.

If he drew his pistol and fired everyone in the camp would know he was there and they would know they were being watched.

If the snake attacked it carried enough poison in its fangs to kill a man as well as a horse.

Sure Perry might be able to save his life but it was a gamble he was not willing to take.

The snake coiled around its own body at the sound of the pistol cocking and David knew in less than a second the snake could be sinking its fangs deep into his flesh and sending its deadly poison racing through his body as it sought to take his life.

The copper scales glistened in the sunlight as the snake sucked in the desert air filling its lungs before hissing at the intruder.

David's skin felt clammy and cold to the touch of his hand. Sweat was beginning to form as he watched the forked tongue flick in and out of the snake's mouth testing the air before attacking.

A standoff had begun between man and beast as the two watched each other, the round eyes of a man sat looking into the slanted eyes of a demon lay hidden close behind the fangs filled with a slow painful death.

Time seemed to stand still for the Ranger in the brush as he heard the men break camp and ride away.

It was the sound of steel striking rock that broke the standoff as David heard Perry whisper his name as the sound of metal on stone grew nearer and with the addition of a second threat the snake uncoiled and slithered into the shadows of the rocks.

David holstered his weapon and began backing out from the brush and away from the potential danger hidden in the shadows.

David stood up slow and easy trying not to startle any more of the snakes that might still be in the area.

Others could be hiding under a rock or limb and one fast move could spook them into striking and he knew where you find one of the large poisonous snakes you will usually find more! Sometimes whole dens with hundreds of snakes in them would sleep and live together before coming out from under ground to spread out and claim their own land and their own den

. Like people some would protect it with their lives while others would slither away David knew it was the few that were aggressive that a person had to worry about, like the copperhead, it will lay and wait for a person to come back across their path, they are not satisfied with running an intruder off they want to inflict pain or kill anything they feared and they feared man and the weapons they carried. And that was why man had learned to fear them. David watched the ground around his feet for any slight movement as he walked through the brush.

Perry saw the Ranger as he stood up then walking the horses towards his partner he could see the paleness of his skin and the beads of sweat dripping from his brow.

"You look just like you ran into a dead man head first."
David shook his head and then wiped the sweat from his forehead using the back of his hand,
"I didn't run into any dead men but for the last ten minutes or so I was not sure if I was gonna become one or not, I was in a standoff with a big old copperhead and I was not sure who was going to win that one!"

"Well, at least you didn't fire off a shot and let them know we're on to them."

"Yeah, David said, I would much rather have my face bit off by a big old snake than let the bad guys know we're following them!"

It had been a long hard ride for most of the night and Larry knew that David must be as tired as he was but the U.S. Marshal couldn't help but tease his brother, "You gonna lay in the brush with them snakes all day or are we gonna follow that bunch?" he asked picking at his younger brother.

"Next time you can crawl around on your belly!" he said taking the reins from his brother. "Not me, Larry said grinning, I don't want to stain my badge!" "That's why Rangers don't carry badges, David answered then pointed his finger at the lawman's chest, that and they make too good of a target!"

"Bang," David said as he pointed at the badge pinned to his brother's chest. "You couldn't hit me with a bag of rocks," Parry said tuning his mount and riding off.

David swung into the saddle he was not sure who he was more aggravated with, the snake or his brother,

"Let's go!" he said digging his heals and putting the spurs to the animal beneath him. It aggravated Parry when his brother teased him about his badge even if he was right it made a great target!

The hard tack biscuits and beef jerky was getting old to the men following the outlaws , most of the time lawmen lived on them for days but both of these men longed to be back at home where they could have a decent meal even the outlaws ate better than the lawmen.

They at least knew how long they were going to be out of touch with civilization and how long they were going to be away from towns they could at least plan their meals and they could have the comfort of a campfire most of the time.

Lawmen had no fire, even a hot cup of strong black coffee was a luxury to them when they were on the trail of an outlaw.

The miles fell away as they followed the hoof prints of the horses neither one sure where the men were going or what they were up to, they just knew from instinct that these men were up to no good fast!

CHAPTER TWENTY FIVE

"Wake up amigo," it was Manuel standing over Parker's bed, white lights seemed to flash with every word.

Parker pulled the covers over his head trying to escape the coming dawn. As the foreman of the Magel ranch went from bunk to bunk making sure each man was up and ready to do a day's work.

Colton and Eric's feet were on the floor before Parker rose up from the bed, "Why are you waking us up, Parker complained, we don't even work for you or Don Magel?"

The tall Mexican was wearing a wide grin seeing the gringos in misery, he was a friend of the gringo that led the group of rustlers and knew the others as well but it was still fun to watch the young men in the kind of pain that too much tequila brings.

Manuel was already dressed in the working clothes of a vaquero, the fancy clothes he had worn yesterday were gone and there were no strings of silver sown into the seams of his pants or bands of coins around the wide brim of the sombrero he carried in his hand.

Manuel was a true working vaquero and not the dressed up gringo or the city born want to be. He took pride in his dress and his life and he had earned the right to lead the men of the Magel ranch through years of hard work and dedication to the brand.

The dark pants were tucked inside brown high topped leather boots and a pair of chaps was rolled up and lay at the foot of his bunk along with a pistol and a cartridge belt.

Parker could see the barrel of a rifle leaned against the wall behind the head of Manuel's bunk and some of the other vaqueros were moving around.

Parker climbed from the bunk getting ready to face the morning sun as a wave of nausea struck him the day old tequila attacked sending bolts of pain through his entire body.

As his stomach twisted into a torturous knot he doubled over and ran for the exit while the other men watched.

No one was laughing at the youngest man in the bunkhouse because every person there had been through the same thing he was now going through, they knew it was the worst kind of hangover imaginable!

Colton and Eric climbed from their bunks in better spirits than Parker, they had quit drinking early in the evening and the effect of the tequila had passed as they slept.

They started for the cook's quarters as Parker lay over the top of the hitching rail losing what little remained in his belly.

They all knew K.C. and Nicole were in Don Magel's home celebrating their wedding as the rest of the men slept in the bunkhouse.

The smell of fried tortillas lingered in the air calling to the men as they came closer. Fresh eggs and coffee sat on the dining room table along with butter, cheese and fresh onions picked from the garden and peppers and herbs filled a bowl sitting in the middle of the table.

Colton was rolling a tortilla stuffed with eggs, peppers and cheese as K.C. and Nicole entered the room.

Don Magel walked behind the couple and like the vaqueros he was dressed in the working clothes of a cattle man.

Gone was the white hat, the silver studded gun belt and the Spanish spurs with the golden spikes.

Instead he wore pants tucked into a pair of warn leather boots and the rolls of the spurs were made of a hard stainless steel.

Don Magel and Manuel looked and acted so much alike that Colton was beginning to wonder if they were father and son even their clothes were alike.

Except for the years between them they could have been brothers or twins enjoying a meal together as they watched over the riders of the range.

Colton knew just by the way both men acted this was their home and the vaqueros were a part of their adopted family.

K.C. set rolling eggs and cheese in a tortilla as Don Magel gave the men their orders for the day, some of them left the table as other enjoyed the morning meal.

Colton didn't speak Spanish but he knew K.C. did, "What's going on," he asked as most of the men left the room and headed for the stables. "They're going with us," K.C. stated, it was a simple statement but it brought up as many questions as it answered.

"Why would they want to ride with us to Juarez?" was Colton's next question.

"We ain't heading to Juarez, K.C. said, Don Magel says the men we would find and hire in Juarez aren't any better than the men Malloy hired out of Dallas or Houston.

They would cut our throats for the change in our pockets.

He says most of us would never reach the border alive! Manuel and some of his men are going to ride with us to help us take Nicole's ranch from her uncle!"

"Why would he do that," Colton asked "Not sure, K.C. answered, but I'm not about to look a gift horse in the mouth!"

Colton swallowed the last of the tortillas and got up to leave, "Just make sure he don't turn on you for your woman," he warned, or the ranch and the cattle on it!" K.C. couldn't help but wonder about the words Colton had spoken as he left. Maybe Don Magel would turn on him for the woman he had held in his arms for so short of a time.

After all he was willing to ride clean across Texas to help her take control of her ranch!

K.C. watched the man as he finished the breakfast sitting in front of him wondering if his father's old friend might turn out to be his worst enemy!

K.C. got up and followed as Don Magel finished eating and started out of the room.

Nicole came running up to K.C. as he left the room and threw her arms around him,

"Why can't I go with you?" she demanded. "I can take care of myself and you know it! I can help you, I can ride and I can shoot!"

"We talked about that, you know it will be much safer here and if for some reason I don't get your ranch back for you at least you will be alive to try again!"

K.C. hated to leave her behind but he couldn't face the thought that she might get hurt or killed and that was something he couldn't live with! She was his life and he hoped and prayed he would make a good husband and father.

He still couldn't figure out what Nicole saw in him or why she would fall in love with him of all people.

She had everything, money, beauty and she was easy to be with and he felt like he had nothing to give her but she had chosen him and he was going to do everything in his power to live up to her expectations of him!

"Stay here for a few days before starting back to Texas then you will be riding in a buggy with some of the other senoritas who will be going along to look after you.

It will be a much easier on you this way and if everything goes right we will be moving into our new home upon your arrival!" he pleaded.

K.C. knew that Don Magel and the rest of the men would be in their graves or in a federal prison for the lives they were about to take if their plan didn't work.

Nicole hugged him tight and kissed him with all the passion she could muster then stepped back and watched him leave as a tear ran down her face.

Don Magel's horse was saddled and ready to ride as the men walked form the hacienda. This was not the pure white stallion he had ridden for show; the horse standing at the hitching rail was a roan with hair almost as dark as burnt sugar.

The saddle was worn but the padding was full and the leather was soft showing the signs of being comfortable and used often.

The rifle butt in the saddle boot looked to be as used as the rest of the gear, with scratches and nicks running the length of the stock.

K.C. couldn't see the rifle barrel but he was sure its bluing was faded and the bright metal was beginning to show beneath the wood of the worn walnut stock but the weapon was going to be well oiled and in perfect working order or Don Magel would not have the rifle in the boot of his saddle!

K.C. grabbed the horn of his saddle and swung up, the fancy gun belt and pistol was the only flashy weapon to be found but it was his pride and joy and there was no way he was going to leave it in Mexico! Magel and his men headed towards Texas with K.C. and his men riding beside them.

Parker grew sicker as the miles fell away and by noon it was apparent that he needed a slight rest if he was going to make it through the rest of the day.

The vaqueros stopped beside a clear cold pond where cactus rimmed one of the banks and sharp rocks and trees lined the others. Hoof prints of wild cattle and wilder horses could be seen in the sand and mud of the waters.

Water moccasins swam along the banks hissing at the men as they hunted for food in the territory they considered their own personal domain.

Every man there knew someone or something that had be bitten by the fanged death and remembered well the scarred rotted flesh of the victims.

Whenever the snakes drew near the sound of gun fire would echo across the desert sand as bullets tore into the flesh of the snakes.

The men took sticks and flung dead snakes out of the water as far from camp as possible where other scavengers would devour the flesh of the snakes in the middle of the night or after it had rotted and the men were long gone.

Manuel took some salt pork from his saddle bags and gave a piece to the ailing rider. "Eat," he instructed Parker then handed him the animal skin flask at his side, "A little hair of the dog," Manuel stated.

Parker took a sip then fought the instinct to spit it out as the warm alcohol touched his lips. "Drink it, you will feel better in a little while,"

Manuel said after taking a drink from the flask as well.

Pushing the cork back into the opening Manuel handed Parker a piece of hard cheese, "Rest in the shade, he ordered, we will be leaving soon."

Parker leaned against a mesquite tree and watched as a large moccasin swam across the pond sending light waves of water towards the bank with its whipping tail while other snakes swam along the bank of the shallow pond in schools darkening the water as they twisted their bodies around one another!

Parker couldn't remember ever seeing this many snakes in one hole in his life and any man that stepped into the water was a dead man.

He was beginning to feel better as the wine and cheese settled the queasy feeling in his stomach.

The cooling shade of the tree felt good but it was not going to last long, K.C. and Don Magel were both in a hurry to get to Texas and the Malloy ranch.

The vaqueros jumped to their feet as Magel stood. He spoke in Spanish but Parker knew what he was saying, it was time to go.

He was climbing to his feet as the vaqueros rode past.

These men were at home in the heat of the desert sun or the freezing cold of a winter's night. Vaqueros were the pride of the Mexican cowboys and Parker knew these were some of the best.

It was with mixed feelings K.C. watched the men ride by, if the hands from the Malloy and MacCland ranches were working together he would need all the help he could get because between the two of them they would still have better than a dozen handpicked gunman and thieves working for them.

The other problem was the men Don Magel had picked were men that lived on his ranch, accepted his money and rode for his brand, men he trusted with his life and if he really wanted Nicole, if he had made plans to take her by force then these men would back any play he made! K.C. knew he was going to have to find out what Magel was up to before they rode against the ranches and before Magel made a play against him or his small band of men.

The gunmen they were going to face at the Malloy ranch were bad enough if they could not trust his back to the men they were riding with then he and the others were in real trouble! K.C. rode in silent thought beside Manuel as the miles fell away.

Riding the trail north was a lot faster going than when they had brought the herd down into Mexico. They were covering ten miles to one without having to fight the half wild crazy cattle for every foot of ground they covered.

It was easy for all the men except Parker who hung onto his saddle horn as if his life depended on it. Sweat was running down his face as a chill passed through his body.

Don Magel was the first to realize this was not a simple hangover, Parker was sick and carrying a fever. He called a halt to the men and told them to prepare for the night,

"If the young one is not better by morning one of my men will take him back to the hacienda." Manuel started a fire and was fixing a vegetable stew as Don Magel checked on Parker again. Cool wet compresses taken from the men's canteens were laid on his head when Magel said he had seen this before, Parker was sick from drinking from the stagnant water of a cattle pond. K.C. set talking to himself if Parker die's it will be my fault he said, I am the one who brought him from Texas and I am the one who had led him and the rest of the men into the poison waters of a Mexican desert!

Lines of fear and guilt ran the length of his face as Don Magel sat on the blanket beside Parker forcing him to swallow the stew Manuel had made and it seemed the more Parker complained the better he liked it.

Not until Parker became sick and lost everything in his stomach was Don Magel satisfied, "tomorrow he will feel better!" he said as he finally left the man in peace!
K.C. opened his eyes to the voice as the smell of coffee and pancakes lingered in the air giving the camp a warm pleasant feeling
, "I don't like to complain, Manuel was saying, but if you don't get out of that bed you ain't gonna eat!"
Parker sat at the fire tearing into a large stack of the soft moist cakes stopping just long enough to say "these are the best cakes I've ever had in my life!" then dug into the plate with a ravenous appetite.

He was showing almost no signs of the suffering he had gone through last night. "Thanks!" K.C. said after taking a cup of coffee from Manuel's out stretched hand.

The coffee was hot and black but it helped wash down the pancakes and he was grateful for that especially after his second plate full of the warm sweet bread.

Don Magel was giving orders again, "Saddle up, he said, we've got a long ways to go before sundown."
It had been a long night, he kept dreaming about Nicole.

He missed her already and almost wanted to go back for her but he knew the danger was too great he just couldn't risk it!
He walked instead to his horse and began to saddle her.
He loved this horse it had been a gift from his father before he died and was his only link to him and his mother.
He missed and thought of them often but when he did he would push the memories away as quickly as they emerged they were just too painful.
He was grateful he had his brother Eric and his two cousins, Colton and Parker.
He talked to the animal as if he was talking to a person as he stroked its mane.
 K.C. didn't know what the future held but one thing he knew for sure was that he would face it like a man and do what needed to be done!
He walked his horse over to where the boys were, "Are you sure you want to do this? We might not get out alive and I wouldn't blame you if you wanted to back out!"
 "What, are you nuts? I ain't gonna let you have all the fun!" Eric said. "Us either!" Colton and Parker answered at the same time.
 "We started this together and we will finish it together, as a family!" Eric stated firmly. "Then let's do this!" K.C. said.

CHAPTER TWENTY SIX

Jim sat at the campfire staring into the flames as Sherlene sat drinking from her coffee cup, the reflection of the fire sent beams of light dancing through her hair as her eyes sparkled with the reflection of the rising sun, reminding Jim of shimmering gold as he looked into her eyes.
"Joe and I are going to drive the last of the cattle from the northern draw while Bobby and Mike drive them from the eastern draw.
  I was wondering if you and the others could start the cattle moving towards the ranch house. If we can get them to the main pasture then we can watch them without having to sleep under a wagon or lay out in the open with the snakes, the bugs and the rocks."
  Sherlene was only half serious when she added you forgot the ticks, chiggers and lizards!" "I ain't forgotten them!" Jim answered.
Marilyn and Joe sat across the fire listening to the complaints, "how can anyone forget about the ticks or the chiggers!" Joe asked checking for the small blood suckers even as he spoke!
  It didn't matter if a man or woman found one or a hundred of the blood sucking little vampires attached to their skin, it was something they would never forget as they pulled at the body trying to release the head from the flesh while the bug fought to stay attached.
  After all the blood of the victim was the blood of life to the parasite.
  The sore they left would stay with a person for weeks scabbing over only to itch week after week and sometimes the white spotted vampires would bring the fever with them slowly crippling and then killing the victim months or even years after the initial bite.

"Sure we can get them moving, Sherlene answered, but Rick is going to have to handle the wagon and with this many cattle it's going to take all four of us to keep them from spreading out or stampeding.

Paul and the other men walked up to the campfire, "Today is going to be my last day, Paul said, I've got to get back to my bar before Nita winds up owning the whole thing!" "Yeah, and we gotta go too, Roy said, if we don't get to our ranch and get the branding done pretty soon we're gonna wind up losing a lot of cattle to the carpet baggers, scalawags and other types of thieves!" "There is not a lot of difference between the two, Mike said, but we prefer not to lose any to either!"

"Sure, Jim said, I appreciate what you men have already done but I figure the four of us can handle it from here."

Sherlene spoke up again, "if you count Rick there are five of us," she stated. "I don't count Rick," Jim answered, he was still aggravated with any man who he thought would hire out as a gunman.

Marilyn was quick to come to his defense, "He still counts as a man!" she said.

For the first time in days she was angry at Sherlene's husband and her brother-in-law. He was treating the injured man like a turn coat traitor.

In her eyes Rick had proven his worth since he had gotten better and thought he deserved a second chance.

Jim shrugged his shoulders and walked away, if she wanted to baby the man she could but he wasn't going to have any part of it!

He was saddling the roan as Joe came up, "The women are gonna break camp and get ready to start driving the cattle as soon as it is done.

I told them we would saddle their horses for them before we left." "Fine, Jim answered, but you can saddle Marilyn's!"

Joe was saddling her horse as Jim saddle the buckskin for Sherlene, after swinging up on their own mounts the men rode out of camp and left the women's horses tied to the wheel of the chuck wagon they were ready whenever the women were.

   Bobby and Roy were hitching the team of horses to the wagon tongue as they rode past. The black was feeling frisky after long inactive night and was kicking up large chunks of dirt as it took off.

The animal was ready for the freedom of the desert and the challenge of driving the long horn cattle from their strong holds.

  Jim knew Sherlene and the rest would already be driving the herd of cattle towards the ranch and as he rode into the first draw he could hear brush breaking in the distance as Joe and the black chased the wild cattle out into the open.

   He was going to bring his own cattle out of the draw as soon as possible but the roan was not near as fast or as strong as the black.

   Hunting the long horn cattle was wearing the older horse out that and the older horse was having a hard time climbing the banks and dodging the sharp barbs of the tall desert cactus. They searched for cattle that had learned not only to survive in a hostile barren land but had also learned to dominate that land with the courage and strength they possessed.

   Few animals would ever be able to flourish in the land as the long horn had, standing strong and fierce in the face of any enemy and the men riding on the back of the horses were their enemies.

The roan was tired and lagging, sweat ran from under the saddle in wide streams,

"You've had enough, Jim said feeling sorry for the animal beneath him, you have given it all you've got and I can't ask you to give any more.

We're gonna hold Joes herd until he is ready to call it a day then we're gonna drive them into the main herd." "We got them, Jim said as he rode up to Joe, if you want to search the last of the draws we can call it a day."

"I've got one more draw left, Joe said, and then I'll be ready to head in."

Jim sat watching the herd as Joe and the black rode off. "Let's bring em out," Joe said to the black pulling the reins and slapping him lightly with the loose ends of the reins. He knew better than a dozen cows and calves hid in the far end of the draw.

As Joe rode into the draw searching so did the black he was quick to charge into the brush hunting them while twisting and turning to the will of the rider as Joe worked the whip sending the tip flying through the air with the speed and accuracy of a true cowboy driving the cattle from their hiding place with the sting of the whip and the force of their wills. The black heard the pounding of the hooves and the breaking of the brush a split second before the rider and as the man turned so did the black.

The bull was large and coming fast, a thousand pounds of bone and muscle with a set of horns seven feet across as big at the base as a large man's arms and as sharp at the tip as a knight's lance.

The bull was attacking from the rear, brush and cactus fell away as the hooves trampled them to the ground.

Joe's hand was reaching for the weapon at his side but he knew he would never make it the bull was too close and coming to fast!

Even with all his speed he couldn't make the draw in time.

The black spun and kicked out with his back legs almost throwing him from the saddle.

With the speed of the move Joe felt a ripple of power pass through the black as the hooves made contact with the head striking it with all the power it possessed.

The black was shoved forward from the force of the blow almost stumbling as it fought to stay erect as Joe flew from the saddle.

Joe had jumped from the saddle and ran to the back lifting the hooves and checking for any signs of injury but none were found, the black stood there with his head held high knowing he was the victor.

The bull lay behind the black the wide width of its horns was lodged in the crevice of a rock holding its head erect and for a second it looked as if the bull was going to get up and start the fight all over again even though a stream of blood was running from the top if its head down its face and into its eyes.

"I'm not taking any chances!" Joe said as he drew the short barreled forty-four from the holster on his left side. Walking up to the downed animal Joe placed the weapon to its head and pulled the trigger.

Jim heard the sound of the shot echo across the valley and then silence as Joe drew the bowie knife from its sheath, "No use in wasting the meat," Joe decided as he sank the blade deep into the flesh.

Even before the first section was cut he could hear the pounding of the roan as it ran across the desert in search of the man, the black and the spot where the shot had come from.

Jim brought his horse to a stop overlooking the draw and watched as Joe used the knife cutting through hide and into the muscle then cutting one joint of bone loose from another as he took the prime cuts of meat from the animal.

Jim sat and watched as Joe cut the hind quarter from the dead animal, "If I was you I wouldn't take that piece of meat back to camp, it's gonna be as tough as boot leather!"

Joe shook his head, "I know but I wouldn't feel right about letting it lay and rot and besides the women can use it in a stew or something!"

"Well, if you're gonna get that to the chuck wagon before it rots we better get going!" Taking the whip from around the saddle horn Jim gave it a crack and it was not long before the cattle were moving towards the camp and then on to the home pastures of the Malloy ranch.

It would be good to get some order back into their lives and maybe he and Sherlene could get started on that family they had talked about.

Jim wondered if he would make a good father, if he would give the right answers to their questions as they got older.

Would his moral characters rub off on them, would they be the kind of people who would do all they could for other people? Or would they turn out like the bunch that he ran off from the Malloy ranch?

These things ran through his mind as he guided the herd toward the ranch.

Joe was thinking also, lost in his own little world. He wondered how he got so lucky. He remembered the days in the Army and the rigorous details that he had fought during that time. That life seemed like a thousand lifetimes ago yet he could recall each of them as if they happened yesterday.

Some were fond memories others still gave him nightmares.

He never in his wildest dreams thought he would marry and settle down but he is, that is if he survives whatever is lying in wait for him in the next few days.

It seems strange to him that the older you get the more self-reflective you become.

He never use to dwell on things before he just worked with what came his way but now he has someone else to think about, someone who means more to him than his life and that could get him killed or give him the incentive to survive no matter what!

Joe leaned over and patted the black, "I never did thank you for saving my life back there, thanks. If it hadn't been for you that bull would have knocked me off your back and stomped me to death!" The black nodded his head as if he understood what Joe had said and seemed to walk with his head held a little taller!

CHAPTER TWENTY SEVEN

"We'll stop here." Daryl said calling a halt to the pathetic group of men behind him.

Foam was building on the animals while streams of sweat run down their chests and legs. The heat of the midday sun was taking its toll on the animals as they carried the heavy loads but the men cared nothing about the heat or the animals.

They had one goal in mind and that was money and lots of it! Taking a drink from the canteen by his side Daryl turned to look back, something about the lawmen in camp that morning had bothered him more than he liked to admit.

Maybe they weren't as stupid as he thought and maybe they were playing him for an idiot he couldn't decide who had fooled who.

He thought they had bought his story but that was this morning now he was not so sure they could be following him and his men at this very moment!

He could order one of his men to wait here and stay out of sight and if someone came by shoot them in the back. If it's more than one person they could put the spurs to their mount and high tail it back where we are and then we could figure out what to do.

In the end he decided to leave a man behind to watch but who could he trust, who would be able to outwit the lawmen if they were being followed? In the end he sent one of the first men Butch had come up with, his name was John Carpenter.

He had a quieter manner about him than the rest of the men and normally he didn't trust quiet men, they were schemers but Daryl got the impression that this particular man was a loner and would do whatever he was told!

Perry put the field glasses back in his saddle bags.

The high brush and cactus hid his position, "you were right, he said turning to look at his brother, they left a man behind, and he's hiding in that draw."

"It figures, David said, we might as well settle down and chew on a piece of jerky, there's no way we can ride across that open valley without being seen!" Perry took a cleaning kit from the saddle bags, "You can have some of that stinking jerky, I'm getting ready for a gun fight!" David said pulling a piece of the meat from his saddle bag, "you can get ready for a gun fight but after I finish this piece of jerky I'm gonna find me a nice shady spot and take a nap!"

"Just make sure there aren't any snakes in it!" Perry warned then pulled the pistol from the holster and ejected the shells into the palm of his hand.

After dropping those into his shirt pocket he proceeded to swab the barrel using a metal rod and a piece of cloth torn from an old shirt.

Lard would have to do for oil as he applied it to the cylinders and barrel.

A light coat of the lard was rubbed into the leather of the holster as well.

No lawman wanted a pistol to stick in the holster when he needed it the most! He spun the cylinder bringing it to rest as the hammer fell into the groves, "you gonna play with that thing all day," David asked as he listened to the smooth sound of the gears tuning.

Perry spun the cylinder one more time then placed the weapon in the holster.

There was time for him to practice his draw before they moved on and that was what he was doing. Time after time the weapon was pulled and cocked as his hand speed improved with every draw.

David sat up and watched as the other one practiced, "You may be as strong as a bull but you're never going to make it as a gunfighter, David said, you got too many muscles and they keep getting in the way!"

"What do you know," Perry asked as he placed his hand on the pistol and started to draw again?

David's hand was up in a flash the weapon seemed to jump out of the holster as the hammer was cocked and leveled.

Perry had forgotten how fast his little brother was, "I may not be as big as you but I got the speed," David said smiling at the look of wonder on his brother's face then he spun the pistol around the palm of his hand and placed the weapon back in his holster.

Perry knew he could never match the speed but that didn't mean he was going to give up trying! "It looks like its getting dark enough so we might be able to ride without being seen, what do you think?" David took his horse by the reins, "might as well, I doubt if that sentry stuck around for more than an hour anyway."

The two lawmen saddled up and rode out of their hiding place together.

The rifles from their scabbards were lying across their laps as they crossed the open part of the valley and then rode towards the hill were they had watched the outlaw hide.

If there was a fight to be had the long range of the rifles was a lot better weapon at the moment than the short barreled hand guns that the lawmen trusted with their lives.

They could make out a smooth spot in the ground when they rode up that showed where the man had lain.

Several cigarette butts were burnt to the nub and a place where a horse had stood tethered for a short time was evident. By the amount of tracks left in the area and steam rising from the pile of horse dung told them that the man had left just minutes before their arrival.

A wisp of smoke was rising into the air and a red glow was burning from the tip of one of the cigarettes.

"We better follow his tracks as far as we can. If he saw us there is going to be trouble." Neither man bothered to dismount, it was going to be slow riding and they were going to have to watch their backs that is if they didn't want to catch a bullet in it! In the moonlight it was easy to imagine an enemy hiding in the shadows of a draw or behind a bush with the barrel of a rifle pointed at their chest just waiting for them to get close enough to pull the trigger. Both men rode with their fingers on the trigger of the rifles knowing at any second that their lives might depend on how fast they could fire back at an unseen attacker.

The lawmen rode slow watching the shadows and listening to the sounds of the night. As long as the birds were chirping and the bugs were singing they knew it was safe, it was when the desert was silent that a person had to worry!

A slight glow warned the lawmen that the outlaws had made camp for the night and the smell of coffee and bacon drifted to the men hidden in the darkness of the night. "It looks like we're sleeping cold camp," David said as he dismounted his voice was held to almost a whisper he knew the words would carry a long ways in the dry desert air and now was not the time to make a mistake .

"Here," Perry said whispering himself as he dug into his saddle bag to bring out more of the tough stringy jerky and the bag of biscuits. "I'm getting mighty tired of this diet," David complained.

"So am I, Perry admitted, I'm almost as tired of them as I am of sleeping on the ground and drinking water in the morning!"

"Yeah, David said, there are times when I think I would shoot someone just for a cup of hot coffee!" "Well you ain't gonna have it in the morning neither!" "Yea, I know," David said aware of the fact that a cold camp meant no fire and no coffee! The lawmen could hear the sounds of men breaking camp as the desert sun rose above the light green cactus plants in the horizon.

Their shadows were casting long dark figures in the sand looking a lot like the knights of war more than a thousand years ago.

The smell of coffee and food called to the men as they sat on their saddles in the dirt eating hard biscuits and drinking warm water from the canteens at their sides.

"I'm tempted to shoot the four of them, David whispered, for one lousy cup of coffee!" Larry grumbled something between the mouths full of cold tough jerky but David couldn't figure out what it was but one thing he knew his brother was tired of the cold camp as well!

"After their gone we can use their fire to boil us some coffee, Perry said, maybe even cook us up some bacon.

I've got some in the pack and we can always catch up with them later." For once Perry was beginning to make sense to the other lawman.

David shook the sand from the saddle blanket then checked for any of the long pointed barbs from the cactus that might have imbedded itself in the material before laying it across the back of his mount.

He had made the mistake of placing a saddle over one of the barbs before and the horse had nearly kicked his head off trying to get away from the pain that the needles inflicted. Later he spent hours digging the sharp points out of the horse's tough hide.

The sound of men riding across the desert slowly faded away as the distance increased between the two parties.

Perry had saddled his horse and was riding towards the other camp as David mounted.

The smell of breakfast lingered in the camp as the two brothers rode in.

A small fire still burned in the circle of rocks and pieces of bark and limbs were piled near the ambers.

"Larry, throw some of that wood into the fire to get it blazing," David said as he pulled the coffee pot form his saddle bags.

"This morning the warm water and cold biscuits are going to be replaced with hot coffee and crisp bacon.

"You know I don't like to be called Larry, I prefer Perry, at least then I don't have to explain why may name rhymes and I don't have to shoot someone for poking fun!"

The two men who rode together were brothers and they even looked a lot alike but that is where the resemblance ended, David was younger a lot more slender and faster, he loved the excitement of being a peace officer, the Friday night fist fights and the occasional gun fight was a way of life for the Ranger. He liked chasing bad guys across Texas it was the kind of life he enjoyed.

While Perry was bigger and had a massive chest and arms but his great strength cost him in speed he was no gunman and he knew it.

When it came to a show down with handguns he had to rely on his strength and power to bring him through the fight alive.

He always said that if he was smarter he would have become a farmer or cattle man but he loved the law and he loved being a lawman.

The high caliber pistol at his side meant nothing to him it was just a tool to be used if and when he had to, it was the badge pinned to his chest that brought him to life.

He knew the men they were following were nothing like him or his brother, they didn't live for excitement or the law they carried no morals and they carried no honor, to shoot a man in the back was the life they had chosen.

These men thought honest hard working people were nothing but stupid morons and trash beneath their feet, something to be wiped off at the first opportunity! He had dealt with these kinds of men before and knew they were up to something, he just could not figure out what!

"The coffee tasted great, David said, but the little pieces of the crisp bacon are sticking between my teeth and it's leaving a sweet taste in my mouth."

"Quit complaining will you, Perry ordered, it's still better than a cold camp!" David kicked sand over the remains of the fire, "it's been better than an hour since they left," he said picking up his saddle and walking away from what was left of the fire.

Perry threw the last few drops from the bottom of his cup into the hot ambers of the fire then followed that with what little coffee still remained in the pot and stepped back as the smoke rose in a thick cloud covering his face and burning his eyes as it rose towards the sky only to be blown away by a gentle morning breeze.

He then mounted his horse and followed after his brother.

The deep tracks in the soft dirt and sand made it easy to tell which direction the other men had ridden. David had ridden this trail before and knew there was a small town by the name of Lone Oak sitting on the Texas and New Mexico border.

He was certain this was where the men were headed but for the life of him he could not figure out why men like Butch and the others would be riding to the border town or what was so important that it would being these men to the desert town so far from the bright lights and excitement of the larger city they had just left. It seemed the two brothers were thinking along the same lines!

Daryl and his men rode in silence as the miles drifted away each man lost in their own thoughts as the miles drifted away. Carpenter had caught up with them a few miles back and swore no one was following them so Daryl felt more comfortable about his plan. One more day in the saddle and one more night of sleeping on the ground and they would be overlooking the town of Lone Oak.

Daryl knew the false front of the crooked horn restaurant could be seen from the top of the ridge a few miles outside of town along with several of the other building and of course Nita's place. He hadn't been there in a while but he planned on going back as soon as he could. He couldn't remember exactly when the last time was that he was there but that was because he was so drunk he couldn't remember the visit or the woman he had been with. Daryl sat back in his saddle wondering what had happened and whether or not the visit had been worth the cost.

Finally deciding it wasn't worth the cost or he would have remembered what happened.

He was jolted back to reality as a roadrunner sped by kicking up small puffs of dirt in front of the horses
. The small desert bird could run for miles dodging the sharp barbs of the cactus or the lightning fast strike of the desert rattlesnake as it looked to fill its quest for food and water or maybe in its lonely search for a mate the lonely cry of the roadrunner was most often met only with the silence of a vast desert.

"We will camp here," Daryl said still watching the slender bird race across the desert floor. "Why here, Butch asked, there is no water and no shade?"

"We are less than thirty miles from Lone Oak and I don't want anyone from town to see us all together.

If we camp here, we can split up in the morning and there will be less chance of us being seen together." The men watched their new boss giving orders each one of them wondered just who this man was. None of them had been told exactly what they were supposed to do other than drive cattle and John Carpenter was sure there was more to it than that!

Daryl was the undisputed leader and every man there was beginning to realize he was every bit as dangerous as Butch. He might not be as big or as strong but he was vicious and cruel. He might not face anyone of them in a knock down drag out fist fight but he was an expert with a gun or a knife and he had little or no qualms about killing a man with either weapon the fact was they were beginning to realize it didn't make him any difference if the man was wide awake or fast asleep when he killed them as long as he was the one standing in the end!

Daryl pulled the horse into a large box canyon then rode a hundred yards deeper into the ravine where the horses began to pick up speed as they smelled the sweet odor of water. A small pool was all that was needed to bring animals of all kinds along its banks.

Daryl and his men were no different than the rest of the animals needing the precious waters to survive but the difference was that he was willing to share the precious liquid with the rest of the animals as he gathered sticks along the banks to start a fire.

Soon the smell of boiling coffee would fill the camp site along with the smell of frying bacon and biscuits heating by the fire. Daryl had made up his mind, "in this camp there is not going to be any more drinking! If you got any more liquor dump it!" he demanded. Some of the men were not happy about the order but they were less happy about going against Daryl with either a gun or a knife, it was a sure way of dying!

"We'll be riding through Lone Oak tomorrow sometime and when we get there Butch and I will ride into town and I want the rest of you to skirt the town.

The less people know about you the better!" The look in his eyes left no doubt about what would happen if even one of them disobeyed this order.

John Carpenter lowered his head; he didn't want Daryl to see what he was thinking. "Carpenter you and Johnson can skirt the town and pick up the trail again when you are in the clear. When you get five miles on the other side of town the trail opens up even wider and in some places two or more coaches can run side by side letting the drivers talk to one another or even pass a bottle back and forth depending on how smooth the trail is.

After you come to the second fork turn north, the road will take you to the MacCland ranch. When you get close enough to see the roof of the barn turn towards the northeast, once you do that just keep riding you will probably hear the herd before you see it. If you don't someone will find you, just tell them I'm on my way and to get the herd ready to roll.

I want to push it north as soon as I get there!" Carpenter and Johnson nodded at Daryl showing they understood his instructions. "Butch and I are going to ride into town and see if there have been any changes since I left." The small band of men dug into the meal devouring the hot food after a long day in the saddle and then fell asleep almost as soon as their heads hit the sides of their makeshift beds.

There was nothing but dirt and cactus around the area Daryl had picked to camp at and for the first time in four days Daryl and his men were going to sleep in a cold camp. The sound of men snoring brought the lawmen to a stop as they rode along in the shadows of the night

"That was close," David whispered. Perry's answer was just as low, "We passed a draw a half mile back, we can camp in it till morning and with any luck at all they won't know we almost rode head long into their camp."

The sound of the lawman's horses were muffled by the soft dirt and sand as steel shoes cut shallow holes in the trail leaving clean clear marks for the outlaws to follow if they were watching their back trail at all wondering if the lawmen were following them. The brothers rode back to the draw wondering if their little blunder might warn the others that someone was near. "We best keep an eye out, David said, if we don't want someone to sneak up and put a bullet in us while we're sleeping!" "I'll take the first watch," Perry said while pulling his rifle from the saddle boot.

David took his saddle blanket and slapped it on the ground several times trying to drive away any snakes or bugs that might be in the area. "Wake me up around two, he ordered, and I'll take the rest of the watch." Perry set at the edge of the draw with his head barely above the short desert plant life around him watching for any sign of movement from the camp they had just left.

CHAPTER TWENTY EIGHT

Paul sat drinking hot coffee five feet from the heat of the campfire as the wind shifted and now the smoke was being blown directly into his face.

They say smoke follows beauty but this smoke was blind!

It had left Sherlene and Marilyn to breathe in the fresh crisp morning air to follow Paul around the camp like a magnet burning at his eyes and lungs, even the cup of coffee contained the smell of smoke.

Rubbing at the irritation in his eyes had tuned them bright red and tears were flowing down the sides of his face as Bobby sat down across the fire from him well out of the smoke. Steam was rising from the cup of coffee he held in his hand. He looked up as he was blowing into his cup to cool down the hot liquid and he couldn't help but see the tears running down Paul's face.

"You don't have to cry because you're leaving," Bobby teased, after all we will be riding down to Nita's bar to see you every weekend!"

Roy came up in time to catch the last of the conversation and joined in,

"Yeah, and don't forget we'll be seeing you at weddings and funerals, Unck! Why, we will be there so often you won't have time to cry!"

"Shut up," Paul said wiping at the tears with the back of his hand. "The only way I would miss you guys is with a bullet and then it would be an accident!"

Roy and Bobby began to laugh at the remark, they knew despite his act Paul really felt as if the men of the Lazy 'B' ranch were family to him, maybe the closest one he ever had.

"The fire and smoke is just burning my eyes," Paul said still wiping the tears from his cheeks. "What are you crying about?" Mike asked being new to the conversation and not hearing the remarks of the other men. Paul couldn't believe his ears; these men were trying to treat him as they did Marilyn! He may like them and think of them as family but there was no way they were going to treat him like some broken down senile old uncle!

Standing up Paul said "I'm leaving before I give you a whipping you'll cry about for years!"

Paul was leaving as Mike looked at the other men,

"What did I do?" "Nothin, Roy answered, Paul is just getting cranky in his old age." Paul could hear the boys laughing as he walked away. "Where you going," Jim asked seeing the anger in Paul's eyes and face as he walked past the glowing ambers of the fire.

"I'm heading back to town, Paul answered, I'm had enough of these clowns!" It wasn't hard for Jim to figure out what had happened; the men of the Lazy 'B' had gotten under his skin, way under!

"Move over, Paul said pushing the roan aside with the palm of his hand and then threw the saddle blanket over the back of his own horse.

The chestnut shied away as he threw the saddle, "Hold still!" he ordered reaching under the horse's belly and grabbing the cinch.

Bobby and Roy watched the man get ready to leave camp, "maybe we pushed him too far," Roy thought seeing that the anger was still in Paul's face as he pulled the cinch down tight and started to mount his horse.

"Hey Paul, wait up," Roy cried trying to make up for the way they had treated him, "we want to ride with you." Paul was half tempted to tell them to forget it but it was a long lonely ride when you ride by yourself.

"Fine, Paul answered, just hurry up I ain't got all day!" Roy may have felt sorry for the way they had behaved but Mike didn't, "what's the hurry, he asked, you in a rush to find out what Nita has done to your bar or are you in that big of a hurry to see how much of it you still own?

Paul was ready to climb down from his mount and attack the youngster as Roy told him to shut up and mounted his own horse.

"I was just teasing," Mike said seeing that he was once again pushing things too far.

"Just saddle your horse and let's go," Roy ordered. "Bobby, you riding with us or are you sticking around here," Mike asked. "I guess I'll hang around here for a few days," Bobby answered.

"Why, Jim asked, the cattle are close to water and we can keep an eye on them from the bunk house so we don't need the chuck wagon anymore and we can unload that our selves so you might as well ride in with the rest of them at least that way you will have some company."

It was a strong argument, "give me a minute to saddle my horse, Bobby said, and I will be right with you."
The three men stepped down from their saddles as Bobby threw his over the back of his mount. In half a day they would be back in town, "I'll buy the first drink," Paul offered as the men rode out of camp.

"What makes you think you can afford it?" Bobby asked. The vein in Paul's temple began to pulse rapidly and Bobby became silent!
Taking the reins Jim pulled the break handle and released the tension on the break chains then with the crack of the whip the team of horses and the wagon lunged forward almost throwing him backwards and into the bed of the wagon as it took off.

Rick should have been driving the wagon but he was still recovering and the steep ditches and draws between the wagon and the ranch would have been too much.

So it was better if he rode inside the wagon where he could lay down if the beating got too bad. This was another thing Jim wasn't happy about and lately it seemed there were a lot of things he wasn't happy about! Joe and the black circled the herd as the women did the same calming them with their presence as the wagon rolled past with its pots and pans hanging from the hooks they were striking one another with every bump and turn, the loud clatter was enough to start the stampede every cowman feared.

As Jim rode the blister end of the wagon seat he could see the long hair of the women blowing in the breeze as they passed him up. They were headed for the main house, after nine days of living out in the desert, after fighting the dry heat of the Texas sun, the sweat and filth of a cattle camp and spending those days on the back of a sweat drenched horse they were after one thing.

The cast iron bath tub hidden behind the main house with its burned porcelain sides and smooth bottom would be relaxing to the flesh of the women as they lay in the warm clean water. Unlike the snake infested pools they had to sneak around to get into during the middle of the night in order to have touch privacy while on the drive. Later he knew the women would smell of vanilla and lilac as they prepared the evening meal. He could hear Rick muttering as the wagon was pitched from side to side one wheel sank in a chuck hole only to climb out as another wheel fell helplessly into another hole .

Pots and pans, flour and beans were being unloaded as Joe rode up, a fine coat of sweat and dust covered the black giving it a chocolate color in the light of the evening sky.

He slid the saddle off and went looking for something to wash the black down with as he waited for the hot food that he knew would soon come.

Finding some burlap sacks hanging from a hook in the barn Joe walked the black to the drinking trough and began to wipe away the filth.

Jim sat on the steps of the veranda as the women came out, "Ok, it's your turn," Sherlene said as she sat down beside her husband.

"Do I have to?" Jim asked teasing with her and laughing at the look of astonishment on her face.

"You will take a bath tonight or you're going to be sleeping alone!" she threatened. It was a threat with no real power; Jim knew she was never going to leave her sister without a chaperone even for one night. "I'll take a short bath, Jim promised, even if I am going to be sleeping alone!" Sherlene's smile was infatuating, "Thanks," she said as she kissed him on the forehead, "One day she promised, one day."

Paul and the men of the Lazy 'B' ranch made their way slowly up to the ridge overlooking the town of Lone Oak.

The men were as worn dirty and tired as the mounts beneath them, "I'm still buying the first drink," Paul stated as he started the slow descent down the other side. Roy and Mike followed as close as they could while Bobby was bringing up the rear fifty yards behind them.

"I'll meet you at the bar later," Bobby said pulling the reins and heading for the other side of town.

"We know where you're headed, Mike hollered, and you best forget it, she is still mad at you for taking her out in that buggy ride with a corpse in the back!"

"Yeah, Roy yelled after Bobby, you're the only person I ever met that was dumb enough to take a dead man on a buggy ride with you and then ask your girlfriend to marry you with him laying three feet from the both of you!"

Bobby yelled back, "What do you know; neither one of you have even managed to get a girlfriend and if you did you would probably kiss your own butt trying to make her happy!"

Paul put the spurs to the tired horse; it was something he didn't like to do but he was tired of listening to the men bicker.

"Come on boy," he said riding on down the ridge and away from the others they were driving him crazy!

It was easy to see that the town was growing in just the nine days he was away. Several wagons had moved in showing ownership and stability. The people and the families in the wagons were here to stay. Stakes were driven in the ground showing the outline of buildings that were yet to be built. While others had whole foundations framed out and root cellars were being dug showing the determination of the men and women that were moving into the area.

Paul rode past the new buildings looking for his own place; it had not been much when he left town just a Calvary tent thrown over some four by four posts. Carpenters were supposed to be working on it while he was helping Jim with the round up.

The small tent was gone and in its place stood the outline of a huge building

Four by eight posts held up massive beams in spans of twenty feet and each beam was holding up other beams.

The walls were boarded half way up and the tent had been slit open and was serving as a roof over one of the largest buildings he had ever seen!

Nita had gone insane he decided as he walked through the swinging doors.

A long mahogany bar ran half the length of the back wall and the outline of a stage three feet high ran the rest of the distance and hard wood lumber was already being put in place over the joists in the floor.

Roy jabbed him in the ribs with his elbow, "What did we tell you, he stated, you give Nita a rope and she won't hang herself she will hang you!"

Paul sat down at the nearest table wondering if he could afford to buy a drink at his own bar. The waitress that came up was young with a skimpy top and an even shorter skirt!

The smile she wore let the men know she really enjoyed her job, laughing at every joke she heard and watching for the large tips she was expecting.

The waitress looked long and hard at the man when he ordered a bottle of Kentucky bourbon and three glasses.

Paul knew she was trying to decide if they had money to pay for the drinks or not before bringing the drink to their table.

"I've got the money," he said as he took out two dollars from his pocket and placed it on the table.

The waitress was still smiling but the smile had stopped before it reached her eyes,

"The bottle is five dollars," she stated flatly.

Paul would have choked on his drink if he had one.

A slight chuckle reached his ears as he sat fuming; Nita was sitting behind the men watching as the waitress took the order,

"bring them whatever they want, she told the waitress, after all he does own half of the bar." Nita could see Paul's anger rising by the color of his face, if she didn't say something to calm the man down she knew he was going to explode!

The waitress looked as if she still didn't believe the men could afford the drink when Nita said, "And he is making a hundred times the money you are!"

Those words were enough to make a believer out of the waitress and enough to bring a smile to Nita's newest partner!

This time the waitresses smile was real as she started towards the bar stopping just long enough to let the men see she was young but not too young and judging by the short skirt and top she was available.

Paul sat watching her as she made her way to the bar, Paul could see once again the men from the Lazy 'B' had been right, Nita had replaced him.

A young woman dressed like one of the waitresses stood behind the bar mixing drinks.

"What am I going to do, Paul wondered, now that I have been replaced?"

Nita must have been reading his mind as she told him, "We still need a bouncer and a guard." Paul knew his dreams were finally coming true, he was going to be working around beautiful women and making more money than he had ever made in his whole miserable life.

He may have stumbled into a partnership with Nita but he still considered it the smartest thing he had ever done as he sat back with the men of the Lazy 'B' ranch and enjoyed some of the fine Kentucky bourbon he could finally afford!

"Yep, life was gonna be good!" he thought.

CHAPTER TWENTY NINE

The smell of Mexican flat bread filled the camp as K.C. rose from the bite of the saddle blanket. It was not the first time he had heard of bed bugs biting and it was not the first time he had been bitten he couldn't remember a time when he had enjoyed the experience and this was no different.

He shook the blanket as hard as he could trying to drive the little blood suckers out before laying it close to the fire and reaching for a tin cup to put his coffee in.

Manuel had clean plates lying on rocks for the men to use and there were fresh eggs and bacon sitting in an iron skillet along with some sweet onions.

K.C. was surprised that the eggs hadn't broken on the trip but Manuel had packed them with care placing a row of straw in his saddle bags then a row of eggs then more straw then more eggs until he had the bags full of the delicious cargo. The only thing the coffee needed was sugar but that was a luxury few could afford and K.C. knew it was out of his reach as far as money went.

Parker rolled some of the eggs and bacon between the flat bread as K.C. watched, with a little of the onion sprinkled in the eggs it was K.C.'s favorite breakfast.

Don Magel was rising from his own bed, the man was getting older with every hour and the ride was going to kill him if it didn't end soon.

Jose was putting Magel's saddle on his horse as Magel sipped from a cup of the hot coffee that Manuel had handed him.

This was something he would have never allowed just four days ago, he was a man of pride and strength but the aging process was fighting to destroy the older man's aging body.

K.C. watched the men around him, they had been young men when he was a child and he had known most of them for as long as he could remember but he couldn't say they were his friends because in truth he barely knew them but they were risking their lives for him and Nicole and he knew it was all because of Don Magel. These men would follow him to the ends of the world if he asked them to!

He could see the pain in the man's face as he stood looking at the men who followed him and even through the pained look on his face K.C. could tell Don Magel was proud of the men that rode with him.

Magel had picked these men to become vaqueros on the Magel ranch and now they had become more than vaqueros they were family and friends ready to fight and die for the brand and the friendship that bonded them together!

K.C. knew in his heart that he couldn't ask these men to fight or die for a brand or a ranch that they had no part of so he walked over to where Manuel sat at the fire.

If he could talk Manuel into listening to him maybe Don Magel would listen to his longtime friend and foreman.
He began his pitch to a man who he had known for a long time and considered one of his friends, "In two days we will be at the Malloy ranch and if we can surround the place without anyone knowing we are there until the time is right then we can force Mr. Malloy to face me in a gunfight one on one.

In that way no one has to take a chance of getting killed except me and I am pretty sure I can take Malloy, if I win then the rest of his men will have no choice but to leave. We can take the ranch without getting some of your men killed or wounded and Nicole will have her ranch back without a lot of bloodshed and death to remind her of what it cost to get it back!" Manuel thought about what K.C. had said for a few moments before answering,

"Few men or women want to own a piece of land bought and paid for with the blood and lives of the innocent, I will see if Don Magel will go ahead with your plan."

Sixteen men saddled up and rode from the camp, they were strong courageous men known for their courage a valor.

A dozen of them were riding to a hostile foreign land to face an enemy that was as vicious as any they had ever seen. If things kept going the way they were some of these men would wind up in a cold shallow grave more than a hundred miles from their family and loved ones. And they were doing this for a property they could never hope to own!

Daryl and his men sat in the saddle overlooking the town of Lone Oak, from the tracks in the soft ground he could tell others had come this way recently, at least three maybe even four. The tracks were cut clean and sharp while the prints of armadillos and coons were worn and smooth showing signs of age.

Daryl knew the riders had ridden past within the last twenty four hours,

"We'll split up here, he ordered, I don't want anyone to see us together.

You boys pick up the trail on the other side of town; just make sure you pick it up four or five miles past the last building."

Butch and me will ride in and see if anything has changed since the last time I was here."

As the four men split up one set riding towards town and the other riding into Lone Oak.

Perry put the field glasses back into the protection of his saddle bags,

"Their splitting up, he said, do you want to split up or follow them together?"

From the distance and without the aid of the glasses he could barely make out the horse and riders, they looked more like ants as they scurried about.

"Which one is headed where?" David asked trying to decide on which action to take. "It looks like the leaders are headed for Lone Oak while the others are riding around the town." "We'll follow the peons, David said, I don't want to be recognized by someone in town and we don't want to be seen following these guys."

The two lawmen started their horses moving at an easy pace not wanting to kick up dust or draw attention to themselves as they followed the group of outlaws.

Paul sat at the table with a cup of hot coffee in his hand, it had been a quiet night, and cowboys had been coming in and out all night grabbing a few drinks then heading off in search of the girls Nita had hired.

She had brought in some new girls not just to run the bar but others girls to who wore a little less clothing and made a lot more money. Just about every cowboy in the valley and some not from the valley was in a hurry to meet them!

Nita didn't work like the girls did that she hired she was just a very good business woman! There had been a few fights over the attention of the waitresses but they were just knock down drag out fist fights and nothing serious. Paul hadn't been forced to pull the double barreled shot gun known as a greener from under the bar or the long handled nightstick so for him it was a slow dull night!

Nita was setting at the table across from him counting the nights take; it was more money than he had seen at one place in a long time! Paper bills and gold coins were stacked up as smaller change lay in piles adding to the illusion of all the riches he was about to make.

Steam rose from the cup as he placed it near his lips and through the thin light vapor he could see the men that rode from the top of the ridge. From a distance they looked like small dots pressed against the horizon when two of them rode south.

It looked as if they were headed towards Mexico or they were skirting the town for some reason, Paul decided he may not be an outlaw but he had the mind of one and something struck him as odd about their actions!

The others rode straight forward toward the town at first they were nothing more than blurs as the sun reflected on the dust cloud that rode with the winds around them.

Large men were becoming even larger with the misconception of the light and dust swirling around them.

Paul watched with interest as the faces came into focus.

One of the riders was the foreman of the MacCland ranch but Paul wasn't sure who the other one was and didn't really care as he went back to watching Nita count the money.

Daryl's shadow fell across the table darkening the stack of money in front of him.

"Two whiskey glasses and a bottle," Daryl ordered! Paul still hadn't bothered to look up. The men were of no concern to the man or his money and even the slender legs of the waitress failed to draw his attention as he counted the bills one at a time before folding them and putting them in his pocket.

A glance around the bar showed him the faces of the men that had come in from the desert. Daryl's was a face he was familiar with and knew at a glance but the other man's face was a blur coming out from the back of his mind like the hollow scream of a demonic possessed nightmare ! Slowly the memory of a beating his mind had refused to remember came into view.

Paul reached up and touched the scar running down the side of his face with the tip of his finger.

He could see the hand trembling as the memories flooded into his being shaking him to his very soul!

Sitting at the table with his back to the hard wood of the chair Paul remembered what he had kept locked away for a dozen years. He remembered walking down an alley with all the money he possessed tucked in the pocket of his vest. Three months of hard earned wages working drag behind cattle drive fighting half wild cattle and eating trail dust seven days a week for three straight months. It had been his chance at a new life, a home and a ranch!

Then he remembered the board flying around the corner and the stars exploding as it struck him in the face.

He remembered the pitch blackness as darkness tried to engulf him and he could even remember the board breaking as the long splinter dug deep raking a furrow down the side of his face.

In his tormented state he could hear the men running out from the cover of darkness stealing three months of hard earned wages and putting the boots to a man they thought was dying. Two weeks later he had woken up in the bed of a wagon being pitched from side to side as the wheels of the wagon went down into one hole then another.

His face and head was covered with blood soaked rags and his ribs were cracked and bruised. His body had healed but the memories of that night had vanished like the nightmares of a dream leaving only a vague memory of a night long ago.

His legs felt like liquid as he stood and the reflection in the mirror standing behind the bar was that of a dead man.

Pale and white compared to the living while his eyes held a cold hollow look of the dead as he walked behind the bar.

Paul's hands were still shaking as he reached behind the bar and took out a pair of the heavy leather working gloves so many of the younger cowboys used when wrestling the long horn cattle to the ground.

They were the same ones they used when roping or branding, gloves that were as strong and rugged as the land.

Paul could have lived a life time without the memories but now the man behind the board sat quietly at one of his tables sipping from a glass of fine Irish whiskey!

If it cost him his life Paul was going to avenge the most terrifying night of his life!

The tight feel of the leather pulled at his knuckles as he doubled his fist and walked towards the men, his fist was thrown hard, fast and unexpected landing with all the power he possessed and the sound of breaking bones filled the room.

As the first blow landed Butch flew from the chair slamming against the back wall then bouncing forward landing at Paul's feet.

Paul straddled the man with his feet then swung down with all the weight and strength he possessed, the tough leather of the gloves tore the man's skin as the cartilage of the nose broke sticking out in jagged needles where the man's face had once been.

Looking down at the unconscious man Paul's anger flowed as red as the blood that ran slowly to the floor adding fuel to his attack.

His hand drew back one more time as Schon and Rog ran through the bat wing doors. Their pistols drawn and Schon's eyes held the look of terror as he saw Paul draw back his fist to strike one more time as the on lookers gasped in horror and disbelief Schon knew that another solid strike from the crazed bartender would kill the unconscious man laying beneath him.

The cocking of the pistol inches from his ear stopped the mad man in his tracks,

"Back off!" Paul said as he turned to look up into the eyes of the man holding the gun.

Paul had lost his sanity and the lawman knew it, a bead of sweat was forming on the face of the deputy.

He and Paul had been friends for a long time and he didn't like the idea of having to kill him but he was about to have no choice!

Maybe it was the look on Schon's face or the threat of the pistol but Paul began to lower his hands as the onlookers watched knowing full well the hair trigger temper of the bartender was simmering behind the smile that he wore,
"I'm gonna kill him, Paul said facing the deputy and the weapon as if they were nothing more than a wisp of the wind to be pushed out of his way when the moment was right.
Schon had seen the look of rage and insanity before but never like this, hidden behind the eyes was an unveiled mask ready to strike and kill in a moment's notice.
  "Come on Paul let's go," Schon ordered waving towards the door with the barrel of the pistol. Daryl sat at the table stunned by the attack; it had happened so fast and had been so bloody all he could do was sit and watch as his second in command became a mingled mass of flesh and blood destroyed by the fists of a mad man!
  "Your friend can come by the jail later and press charges, Schon said, if he wakes up and if he doesn't then we'll be holding this one for murder!"
Putting the barrel of the pistol in Paul's back and pushing him towards the swinging doors of the saloon.
  Daryl watched as the deputy escorted Paul from the room as his second in command lay bleeding and unconscious, a shell of the man he had been just moments before! A moan escaped his lips as Daryl tried to lift the larger man, "Leave me," Butch whispered as the pain shot through his body and his mind slipped into a black dark void.
Butch awoke to the slow rhythm of the wagon as it bounced from hole to hole adding to his pain, "You gonna live," Daryl asked seeing that the man was once again awake. "I'll live," he said trying to sit up as the movement of the wagon threw him from side to side.
  "What happened," Butch asked still not aware of what had happened to him.

"I guess an old enemy caught up with you!" Daryl said. Butch tried to whisper but his head and face throbbed with every word, "How bad am I hurt," Butch asked. "We will be in camp in a few hours and you can look in the mirror and tell me, but until then if I was you I would just sit back and relax, you were never that pretty anyways!"

Butch lay back in the bed of the wagon watching as a dark cloud blotted out the sun his mind pounding with the same beat as the hooves of the horses pulling the wagon.

"I'm gonna kill whoever did this!" he whispered just barely loud enough for Daryl to hear.

"If I was you I would stay as far away from Lone Oak and Paul as I could.

If he ever gets out of that jail he is going to be coming for you and if anybody is going to be killing anybody my money is on him!

I don't know what you did to him but if he ever gets out of that jail you're gonna be the dead man!

Mark my words, he is insane and you're the one who drove him to it!" Butch sat back against the inside of the wagon trying to remember the man and the reason he would hate him so much that he was willing to die just to get even!

In the end Butch decided he had never seen the man before in his life!

Perry and David saw the dust from the wagon rising up into the dry air putting a haze around the wagon and the men and if it weren't for the high powered field glasses they might not have known it was the men they had been following.

Now at least they knew they were between the two groups of men, "We better pull into a draw or something," David said pulling on the reins and riding out of sight from the approaching men.

Perry rode behind him dodging the cactus and the brush as they navigated through the twisted vegetation looking for a stand of cactus dense enough to hide their location or a draw deep enough to hide them and their horses.

Tall cactus stood with its limbs out stretched giving the impression of soldiers ready for war as its needle sharp thorns searched for blood and flesh to lodge into as the men rode past. The sentry of the desert was an illusion posted to prevent the passage of unauthorized person now it was their cover adding to the illusion of an empty lifeless place, a piece of ground devoid of life.

The rattle of the wagon chains let the hiding men know when the wagon and the men were near, the illusion of a lifeless land broken by the sight and sound of living men and the wagon. The lawmen sat and listened as the wagon went past totally unaware of the life around them. "I wouldn't move if I was you!" the voice was cold, quiet and filled with malice but even worse than that it was behind them.

David started to turn as he realized that Butch and Daryl were not the only ones that had fallen to the illusion of the desert.

He knew their lives depended on knowing his surroundings and now it was too late.

The strong deception of a lifeless baron land was no more than a lie thrown out in anger, too late he realized his mistake, the desert overflowed with a life of its own and for a few seconds he had lived in that lie.

The long barrel of the rifle lay along the rocks the only thing visible was the dark brown eye of a man looking down the narrow sights of the barrel.

David knew one or both of them could die before they got a shot off at the man hidden in the depths of the draw. he didn't know if it was one or a dozen men that lay hidden behind them ready to cut loose at a distance with the use of the long rifles or trigger men hidden up close that used the sawed off barrels of shotguns to cut men in half !

Perry turned slowly dreading the feel of a bullet as it tore through his flesh but he was depending on his strength to carry him through the battle.

A beam of light moved from rock to rock as the reflection of a badge danced across the painted shadows of the desert giving pause to the man hidden in the draw.

"Don't do it!" he said as he saw the man's hand move towards the weapon at his side,

"this time it is not an order it is a request,"   Perry's hand was still as the man came out from the draw, the rifle was held in one hand while the other dangled close to the weapon at his side.

The butt of a forty-four pistol was resting in a cross draw holster on the left.

Maybe he or David could beat the stranger to the draw but it would cost someone their life to find out and Perry knew that was a risk he was not willing to take.

The eyes of the man looked older than his years giving him a twisted tormented look.

They were the eyes of a man that was trying to cover up a life time of violence and death.

He knew they were the eyes of a man seeing the world through a veiled curtain watching others as he hid in the shadows of those curtains always to see and hopping never to be seen. Here was a man with a past that had killed before and hoped he would never have to again. They were cold quiet words spoken low, "Don't do it," was all he said but it was enough to let the men know he would kill if he had to!

His movement was slow as he lifted his hand and pulled the vest back the metal of a badge gleamed against the darkness of the sweat stained shirt.

The shirt dropped back covering the badge as his fingers let go then dropped slowly back down to the pistol at his side,

"Until I saw the badge I didn't know who you boys were and I didn't want to get shot on accident or on purpose by some drunken cowboy trying to settle a grudge."

"Then you saw the wagon, Perry asked, and the man driving it?" "Yes, I saw it, Joe answered, and the men in it.

One of them is busted up bad and riding in the bed of the wagon, it looks as if someone beat him in the face with a poke axe and he ain't stopped bleeding yet!

The other one looked like he ain't too happy about the deal."

"I guess you know we're lawmen, Perry said, and we've been following the men in the wagon."

"Kinda figured that," Joe answered. "We don't know the fellow driving the wagon Parry stated, but he just came out of Dallas and it looks to us like he was their hiring gunmen.

The feller lying In the back of the wagon is a bouncer that was working at a bar called The Pub. His name is Butch and he is as tough as nails and as vicious as they come.

We have both had dealings with him before.

It looks like he quit his job to join up with the driver and some other men but we haven't figured out what their up to yet but we're dying to find out!

They killed a man we were after, the leader said he tried to rob them so they hung him but their story just didn't make sense so we decided to follow them and see what happened next." Joe shook his head at their reference to the injured man," he didn't look all that tough or dangerous to me," he said remembering the caved in butchered look of the man's face as they rode past his vantage point.

"I know what they're up to and why they're here, Joe stated, they're going to steal a herd of cattle from a dead man."

"How do you know that?" David asked. "Don't know for sure, Joe answered, it's Jim's idea. If you want we can ride out to the Malloy ranch and you can talk to him about it."

"Let's go," David said walking his horse out from among the cactus stronghold.

"You ride with him, I'm gonna follow the wagon, Perry said, just in case I can find out something the rest of these guys don't know!"

David rode beside Joe towards the Malloy ranch as his brother rode west closing the distance between himself and the wagon.

Daryl heard the cry of the lost calves looking for their mothers as the pains of hunger gnawed at their empty stomachs. Tomorrow the long trail to Kansas would begin; fifteen men were going to drive three thousand head of stolen cattle close to a thousand miles in their quest for power and riches.

   A lot of cattle would die along the trail and some of the men and most if not all of the calves. Daryl pulled the wagon to a stop next to the campfire and signaled for one of the men to help him unload the injured man.

   "I'm not dead, Butch growled, and I don't need any help sitting up in the back of the wagon and then slid to the back. Just give me a gun and a horse and I'm gonna go back to that town and kill the feller that did this to me!"

   "Not today, Daryl said, I've already lost one man looking for revenge and if you go back you will have the law chasing us before we can start the herd moving! If you want revenge you can have it after the drive until then you stay with the camp!"

CHAPTER THIRTY

The pencil trembled slightly in her hand as the lead moved across the page writing the following

THE LIFE AND TIMES OF A FRONTIER WOMAN
SHERLENE'S DIARY
PAGE ONE
The mighty hand of an unseen angel rested over the top of the covered wagon guarding it and the people inside as the demonic storm of a devils rage tore at the wagons tarp like the raging winds of a ship at sea!

Sherlene put the pencil down as she heard the horses approach and by the sound of it more than one horse was riding into the yard.
  Picking up the rifle she walked to the door. Marilyn was already there and in her hand was a large caliber revolver the hammer was cocked back and ready to fire.
  It was being hidden behind the folds of her dress as Sherlene opened the door. The black strode into the yard with a pride not even the heat of a summer's day could bring down.
  His head was held erect showing the pride and strength of a wild mustang in its element the wide open plains of a savage land.
  Stepping down from the saddle Joe looked like a tired drifter, his movements were slow and precise, almost calculated that was the word Sherlene would have used.
  The man beside him was tall and slender with the build of a gunfighter.
  His movements were almost as fast as his voice, "Howdy, ma'am," David said tipping his hat as he brought his leg over the back of the saddle.
  "Found him out in the desert, Joe said, him and another fellow."

This one's a Texas Ranger from Dallas and the fellow with him is a Deputy U.S. Marshal." "Where is the other one?" Sherlene asked looking for the other man.

The Ranger broke in, "We left him in the desert following a couple of men we've been trailing. Joe here thinks Jim might know what their up to."

"It doesn't take a great mind to know what a thief is up to, Sherlene said, but if you want I'll ride out and see if I can find Jim.

The last I heard he was going to check on the cattle to make sure none of the men you were following rode off with the herd in the middle of the night. Sherlene went to the barn and saddled her horse and rode off looking for her husband.

She was pretty sure where he was and with any luck she should find him within the hour. She absolutely adored her husband with his quiet way and strong presence.

When he was in the room you knew it he stood out from all the others.

There have been times when someone underestimated his strength because he was quiet but that was a mistake they would never make again!

He had black curly hair and a strong chin and to her he meant everything, she knew he would protect her with his life and she hoped and prayed she would never see that day!

But with these outlaws planning something she was going to do everything in her power to protect him even if it meant she had to take another life!

It wasn't long before she spotted him riding along a ridge looking at the cattle below, he looked tired and worn and Sherlene vowed that as soon as this was over she would make it up to him.

Jim saw her at about the same time and headed in her direction and as he pulled up to her he ask, "What do I owe for the pleasure of your company?"

He was glad that at least for a short time they were alone.

"Joe rode in with a lawman and they wanted to talk to you to see if you have any idea of what those men were up to!"

"I'm sure they want the herd and I'm almost as certain they don't care who is in their way and that makes them dangerous."

"Well let's get back, I told Marilyn I wouldn't be gone long and would be back in time to help with supper."

"Do we have to go now, Jim said, it has been so long since we have been alone and I want it to last just a little longer?"

"Come on, she urged, maybe this will be over soon or for that matter maybe nothing is going to happen after all and we can get on with our lives!" They avoided looking into each other's eyes because they knew that there was going to be a showdown and they both were filled with fear for each other. The ride back to the ranch was quiet and strained, each lost in thought about the future. The one thing Sherlene was sure of was that she was not going to tell Jim that he was going to be a father because he had enough to worry about as it was and that would just add to it!

She would wait till a quieter time and she would keep this secret to herself, she wouldn't even tell Marilyn until she could safely tell Jim, she wanted him to be the first to know plus she wasn't sure how he would take the news.

These thoughts stayed with her until they reached the ranch.

Joe and the Ranger were waiting for them and as Sherlene went into the house she could hear the hushed voices of the men she had just left saying they didn't want to scare the women but.......

Scare the women indeed!

Sherlene wasn't afraid of anything except losing her husband and she was not about to start now!

If there was a fight to be had then she would not run and hide nor would Marilyn, they would fight right along with their men or die along with them! Still feeling indignant she went to help with supper.

The bright light of an early morning sun peaked through the bars of the cells turning shadows into rock, brick and steel and it was also bringing the man lying in the small metal cot bolted to the wall into a life of his own.

Paul could hear the coffee perking on the top of the wood burning stove and he could hear its water was boiling from the spout then turning to steam as it flowed down onto the hot cast iron lids.

The voices beyond the cell bars were no more than a whisper and he strained to hear what was said.
It was the voice of a woman used to getting her way and she was talking about releasing him into her custody.

He had never had much use for Nita she was out of his reach and he never thought she had much use for him but she was talking to the deputy on his behalf.

A drunk rolled over in the cell next to his and began to moan.
He was mumbling in his sleep drowning out Nita's softly spoken words.

Schon's voice was louder and stronger "You better ask the judge about that," he was saying as his boots hit the solid wood of the floor filling the room with a slight echo.

The creaking hinges of the heavy wooden door told Paul all he needed to know, Nita was leaving the jail without him.

"How about some coffee before the pot boils out?" Paul asked. He could see Schon from the corner of his eye picking up a cup as he was speaking.

Steam was rising from the cup as Schon passed it through the opening of the bars,

"Nita is trying to get you released, Schon said, but I can't figure out why."

"What's to figure, Paul asked, as long as she is getting me out I don't care!"

"I told her to talk to the judge and if he says your free then I got no say so," Schon said.

Schon was no gambler but Paul was, "What do you think the odds are he'll let me go?"

Schon thought about it for a moment, "If it weren't for the gloves you were wearing it would have been a simple regular knock down drag out fight but those gloves put it in a whole new light!

With the lead weights sown into the palms and you telling everyone that you were gonna to kill the feller it became a case of attempted murder!

By the way you beat him my guess would be that you're looking at six months but the feller left town almost as soon as I had you locked up and if that is the case the judge can't hold you. If he ain't anywhere around to press charges then you might be out of jail before you can finish that coffee."

The drunk in the cell next to Paul's was really beginning to make noise as he wake up, "You really gonna kill that fellow," he asked trying to start a conversation with the man next to him. "If he does he will be spending the rest of his life behind bars or swinging from a stout limb at the bottom of a tall oak tree!" Schon promised.

Paul leaned against the cell bars sipping from the cup, "I don't guess I'm gonna be killing anyone, like you said he left town."

"Yeah, Schon replied, but if I know you it won't be long until you've skipped town yourself!"

"It ain't none of your business if I leave town, Paul said, after all somebody has got to buy booze for the bar and that somebody might as well be me!"

"Just make sure I don't run across any dead bodies, the deputy said, or I will see to it that you swing from the highest limb I can find!"

Paul shrugged his shoulders and turned back to the metal bunk,

"first you have to find a body, he said, and that is something I'm gonna make sure you can't find!"

Nita sat at the table quietly watching the contents of the bottle disappear.

The small shot glass was filled over and over again and every last drop of the golden liquid went into the man sitting in front of her.

It was surprising that one single person could consume so much of the strong whiskey without falling from the narrow stool.

The judge had been here before and at one time he had been considered a loyal customer at the Crooked Horn Restaurant and bar and maybe one day he would be a loyal customer at her bar but for now she had to talk here.

He was not the best friend Paul ever had but he was not his worst enemy either but Nita knew he was no prude and if he hadn't been married with a jealous wife he might have spent some of his hard earned money in the fine house she controlled.

"What makes you think he won't hunt the man down and finish the job he started?" he asked. "It was a mistake, Nita said, Paul didn't know at the time he was attacking the wrong man.

I'll explain to him that Butch could not have been the man he thought he was."

"Well who did he think he was attacking?" the judge asked.

"I don't know who he thought he was attacking, Nita said, but I know Butch was in a Texas prison when he got those scars!"

The judge thought about what she was saying, "Do you think you can convince him of that?" "I know I can, Nita answered, just let him out and you have my word there will be no more trouble!"

"You talk to him first and if you can convince him he was in the wrong I'll let him go free if not I will have the deputy hold him until hell freezes over!

I am not gonna have a man beat to death in my county and get away with it, it wouldn't look good on my record and I won't stand for it!"

"I'll talk to him right now. If he doesn't realize that he attacked the wrong man I'll tell Schon to keep him locked up myself!" Nita promised.

Schon was sitting in the Marshal's chair with his boots dangling over the side of the desk as she entered, the Spanish breaking spurs digging deep furrows in the surface of the polished wood. Schon sat up fast and straight as the heavy wooden door swung open, Nita was breathing hard after the short run leaving her gasping for air.

She had wanted to beat the judge there and talk to Paul before he got there. "I want to talk to Paul," she said.

Schon stood up and reached for the keys hanging from a peg on the wall.

The dark skinned woman with hair as black as the wing of a crow stood defiant in the face of the lawman. "Alone!" she ordered as he turned the key in the lock and opened the cell door. "I'll have to lock you in with him," Schon said not willing to be influenced by the beauty and wealth of the lady in front of him.

"If you want to talk to him you will have to do it while I'm sitting here because that is as close to alone as you're going to get."

Schon sat back down at the Marshal's desk and put his boots back on top of the polished desk. Nita resisted the urge to tell him that the needle sharp points of the star shaped spurs were digging deep gouges into the hardened wood of the desk.

"Don't be too long, Schon said leaning back in the chair, I'm gonna have to make rounds pretty soon or the merchants will think I'm starting to get lazy and with the Marshal gone for a few days it all falls to me and Rog to make sure things run smoothly."

Nita felt that he was an arrogant young man but the town's people liked him and he would probably be the next Marshal if Joe left.

An empty cup sat on the rails of the iron bed as Nita entered she knew that at one time a hundred men might have stayed in the nine by nine cell leaving behind small reminders of their stay.

Scratches in its hard stone walls marked the passing of time carved In with the blunt end of a spoon or fork.

Some of the men had taken the time to carve their full names into the hardened mortar of the bricks to commemorate their stay there.

Nita sat on the metal rails of the bunk watching the man's expression. She could tell him Butch was the wrong man but he would never believe it,

"Shut up and don't say a word," she whispered the order and Paul realized she was about to say something for his ears only.

"If you want another shot at Butch you will agree to whatever I say," the rest of the speech was for Schon's benefit and she was still speaking as the judge walked into the jail, her voice was strong and powerful now and her words were spoken with the authority of a person knowing they were right.

Paul sat on the edge of the bed with his head held low looking for the entire world like a person that had committed a horrible act and was now having to pay a terrible price for a low down cowardly crime done to an innocent person.

The judge cleared his throat drawing Nita's attention to him and the deputy.

Looking into his eyes the judge asked, "You know of course the man you attacked was an innocent bystander and by all rights I should keep you in jail until this matter is resolved but since you are a business man and a property holder I am going to let you lose to appear in court at a later date, that is if the man you assaulted comes back, if not I am sure a fine of some sort will be issued but until that time I strongly urge you to stay out of trouble!

If not, the next time I pass through the town of Lone Oak I will see to it that you personally regret any decisions made in hast that could potentially see you hanged!"

Paul's temper was being held in check by the strength of his will while the judge stood behind the safety of the cell doors and gave him the lecture of a life time.

Little did the judge know even if the cell door was open and Paul held the money and the means to take his life? And to be able to start a new life elsewhere with all the riches he had ever dreamed of and with all the beautiful women he had ever me. He would not have moved from that spot! Not until he could move with freedom to hunt down the man he so desperately needed to kill!

He sat in anger staring at the judge's back as he left the jail. At any other time he would have at least tried to defend himself but not today. Today he didn't want to say a word that might change the man's decision to have him released! Nita was still speaking as Schon turned the tumbler and opened the cell door,

"You heard the man, Schon said, stay out of trouble. The pair of gloves with the lead weights sown into the palms remained in the desk drawer as he showed Paul out. Nita followed a few steps behind him as he left the jail and headed for the bar.

It was in his mind to leave town in search of the man that had brought him so much grief and it was in Nita's mind to stop him until the time was right!

She had her own reasons for wanting the man dead but she wanted to make sure he died this time and no one was going to stop her as they had done Paul's!

This time when the act of murder was committed there would be no one there to witness the crime and no one would hang for an execution that should have taken place a long time ago! The liquor and the metal bars of the cell had given him a false sense of security.

The pale light skin of the judge tuned even lighter as he saw the man walk through the swinging doors of the saloon.

The hand holding the drink began to tremble spilling precious drops of the golden amber as he saw the look of rage on Paul's face.

It was too late to rescind the order; Paul was free by his own hand and the look on the saloon owner's face was every bit as cold and calculating as was the bartenders.

Whatever was going to happen was going to happen fast and quick and now the judge knew he had been tricked by a pretty face and a bottle of fine Irish whiskey .But Paul was not going to waste his time on a man that took his courage from a bottle or hide behind the strength of steel doors to administer justice.

To Paul he was no more than a rat living off the misery of others. He was a man willing to sign a piece of paper to help carpetbaggers run a widow off land that rightfully belonged to her or her family. To Paul the judge was a gutless coward! Everyone had heard about the shady dealings he made but no one could ever prove anything so the scumbag was free to continue his legal stealing and yet this man had the audacity to reprimand him!

It made him sick but he had real men to deal with, true they were the lowest form of human beings, men that would cut your guts out then place bets on how long you would live or shoot a person in the back then drop a dime through the opening just to see if it would come out bloody on the other side!

They were cruel and vicious but they were the kind of men Paul had been dealing with his whole life and the kind of men he understood!

Then there were men like Jim and Joe who would not need the fake courage found in a bottle but men of the frontier that had courage and strength few others would ever know.

Facing the hardships of a wild untamed land had built character into these men and they would never consider bowing down to someone who was threatening them or someone else.

Paul knew good or bad they were men and they were Texas proud and strong!

A bump on the shoulder stirred him towards the vacant table at end of the bar and the pretty waitress from the other night was placing a bottle on the table as he sat down only this time she was not smiling or looking down her nose at him this time a look of terror covered her face, "You're gonna be making butter!" Paul said trying to calm the waitress laughing because her hand was shaking so badly it looked like she was trying to churn butter from the bottle of whiskey before finally placing it on the table in front of him.

His violent temper had scared others before but not like this and until the other day his fights had been harmless, a bruise here or there or a black eye but nothing serious and nothing like the beating he had given Butch

But the waitress looked at him like he was the devil himself ready to kill and destroy at the drop of a hat!

The terror in her face had moved to her body as her tanned skin had turned as white as a sheet.

"I don't bite," Paul said still trying to calm the woman.

"She doesn't want you to bite," Nita said sitting down across from him.

The woman's complexion went even paler if that was possible at Nita's next words,

"She wants you to kill him!"

"If you got me out of jail to kill someone forget it, Paul growled, I've got enough problems of my own!"

"You don't understand, Nita said, she wants you to kill Butch, the man you tried to kill last night!

We know where he is and if you kill him for us then I'll make sure you go free if I have to spend every dime I own!"

Paul sat in silence for a moment wondering why these women would risk everything to see the man dead or were they trying to set him up, trying to frame him and let him swing just so they could take over his business?

Nita already owned half of the bar would she let him die for the other half?

Nita had always been as calm as a kitten but now there was an air of urgency about her that had never come through before. She seemed rattled and that was not at all like Nita so Paul sat and listened.

The judge sat at his table watching as the couple made plans that he knew nothing about but feared would lead to his down fall if he was around when the killing began!

Picking up the half empty bottle of whiskey he proceeded to the buggy out front.

It didn't matter if he was drunk or sober the horses hitched to his buggy had been in the circuit as long as he had and knew the way to the next town.

Even if he was too drunk to drive then he could curl up and let the animals do the work and today he was going to make sure he was drunk as he took a long pull on the bottle. Tomorrow he would wake up to a new day and hopefully this day would be nothing more than a forgotten memory.

CHAPTER THIRTY ONE

The short barreled shotgun cradled in his arms was loaded with nine thirty-two caliber pistol balls in each of its barrels, eighteen all together.

At close range there was enough fire power to cut a full grown man in half but Paul was not thinking of cutting the man in half he was not that cruel.

He didn't want to watch the man squirm or suffer he just wanted to see him dead and he wanted Butch to know who had killed him and why!

The short range of the shotgun was the perfect weapon and his way of making sure Butch was going to be looking deep into his eyes before he pulled the trigger.

The chestnut tried to pull away as he placed the blanket over its back, "that's alright," Paul said patting the horse trapped in the confines of the stall.

"I ain't mad at you." He said talking softly to the animal.

Nita stood beside the saddle with a box of ten gauge shells in one hand and leather saddle bags in the other

, "If you ain't mad at him quit acting like it.

The way you look he probably thinks you're gonna use that thing on him!" Paul picked up the saddle and placed it over the top of the blanket,

"He knows I'd never hurt him," Paul said stroking the back of the horse with his free hand before tightening the cinch.

"You remember what I said? Wait until Butch and the men he is with move the herd off the MacCland ranch before you kill him and then you blow his head off the second he's alone! Don't talk to anyone and don't let anyone see you!"

Paul took the reins and walked his mount from the barn,

"Don't worry, I'll take real good care of both of us, he said, the second he is alone!" The butt of the shotgun hung from the saddle horn as he rode away swinging with the rhythm of the animal from a leather strap.
She sat alone in the corner of the restaurant staring at a small glass of wine as Nita entered;
a single tear ran down her cheek and fell to the table below.
Her pale skin was like the shadow of death crying out to live in a world of light as the fear and guilt she held tried to devour the last of her courage.
Nita was not an emotional person but every bit of her felt sorry for the lady sitting alone in the corner.
The waitress that had laughed and joked with the customers only a few days ago sat terrified and ashamed.
She was so ashamed of what she had done she was not even willing to look up at her accomplice.
Nita was sipping from a glass of whiskey as she sat down, it was not the best whiskey in the place but if you wanted to turn a profit you didn't drink up the good stuff!
"It will be alright," she said patting the out stretched hand.
"How do you know?" she asked. "That's easy, Nita answered, when you want to kill a mad dog you send a mad dog and we sent one of the best! Butch doesn't know it but he is as good as dead already!"
Nita took a sip from the glass and stood up to leave, "Don't worry about it, she said, everything will be fine!"
The waitress broke down sobbing as Nita left.
She was remembering a time that seemed so long ago but in reality had only been a year.
She had moved to Dallas looking for a new life, she was trying to find the life she had dreamed of, a life away from the farm where she had grown up.
Like all girls she dreamed of meeting prince charming and having a fairy tale life but then he changed all that.
In one swift second her life would never be the same!

She had decided to leave work early that night, the stars were out in the millions, and she just meandered through the twists and turns of the city streets not knowing that people in big cities were not always as nice as the people back home on the farm.

As she rounded a corner she came across two men beating another with a board the minute she screamed she knew she had made a deadly mistake.

The larger of the two men grabbed her by the arm and drug her into the alley where they had been beating the man. She saw the man in the dirt unconscious maybe dead beside her as they took turns raping her and beating her.

That night they pleasure in the torment they were inflicting upon her.

She heard the one called Butch say don't hit her in the face it was too pretty to mess up. We want to be able to recognize her later so we could have some more fun with her, beside we don't want to be sleeping with no ugly woman!"

Both men began to laugh then they started kicking her in the middle of her body so many times that all she could do was lay there and pray for death!

Before she finally, passed out from the pain, Butch had lifted her face up to his forcing her to look into his eyes "you tell anybody about this and I will kill you slow!" he warned and after that darkness had followed.

Eventually she was found and taken to the hospital where she recovered physically but the damage had already been done!

When she was told that she could never have children she died mentally her life was over! She knew no one would ever want what was left of her so she moved as far away as she could believing she was safe she never thought in a million years that night would catch up with her in the isolated town of Lone Oak!

Now she wanted him dead but unlike Paul she wanted to know he had suffered, she wanted him to know and feel the torment she had endured. Not just for that one night but for all the pain he had put her through since!

Paul rode towards the southern boundary line of the Malloy ranch wondering if Daryl and his men were going to steal the MacCland cattle like Nita thinks.

They would have to cross Malloy land to get to New Mexico and the trail to Kansas and that is where he would make his play and take care of Daryl's hired muscle and cattle thief.

Paul heard the cry of the cattle before he topped the low ridge.

Twilight was coming and the shadows of the night placed their dark hands across the burning sands of the Texas prairie leading men and animals into thinking they were alone in a vast wide open world. The fire burning low in a camp filled with men broke the deception letting him know one wrong move and death would follow!

Paul rode north into the shadows looking for the perfect place to conceal himself as he waited for Butch and the herd to pass within reach of the deadly pellets from the shotgun at his side. Taking the saddle and blanket from the back of the chestnut Paul slapped it hard with his hand sending it racing back to the stall and the safety of town.

The hand full of food, the saddle and blanket was all he needed until the time was right after that he didn't think it was going to matter!

More than a dozen men sat at the fire or rode night guard around the herd.

Paul knew he was going to be as good as dead when he pulled the trigger of the shotgun but until that time he was going to live second to second basking in the idea that he was about to get even for the years of torment and anguish Butch had brought to him with nothing but the jagged end of a piece of rotted lumber.

The hours left in Butch's life were slowly fading away and his grave was waiting, just the thought of it gave Paul a feeling of satisfaction and comfort!

Perry was lying against the steep embankment of dirt and rock with the blade of the Bowie knife plunged to the hilt as lose gravel and sand rolled down from under his body.

There might have been better places to hide but none close enough to let him hear what the men in camp were saying.

More sand and dirt rolled down as the toe of his boots dug deeper into the side of hill looking to establish a better hold as his body tried to slide further down into the depths of the little draw.

He held fast to the handle of the massive knife listening as the voices carried softly across the dry night air.

Straining to lift his head above the ridge he could see Daryl speaking, "We'll start the herd north as soon as the sun rises and by noon we will be on Malloy property and we will also be close to the herd of cattle they have gathered around the main house.

We can stampede our cattle into theirs and together they will mingle together stampeding across the border and into New Mexico before they stop running!

If they haven't made the border it won't be any problem to get them across before anyone knows what we've done."

Perry pulled the blade from the soft ground and slid into the dry sand filled bottom of the draw. There was nothing he could do now except lead his mount north to the home of the Malloy ranch and prepare the others for the cold hearted death Daryl had planned for them all and in his eyes it was a death sentence.

They were to be trampled under the slashing hooves of the combined herds

. Blood would run into the ground mingling with dirt then become mud as flesh, bone and clothing became rags torn apart and carried on the horns of the bulls and the hooves of the cattle as they ran blinded by the terror that consumed them.

He knew that if Daryl's plan worked later, after the distraction and devastation caused by the stampeding cattle, the victims' bodies would be not be able to be identified and they would all be buried in a common grave and no questions would be asked giving them time to get out of the country with both herds of cattle.

For a while at least everyone would think it was just an unfortunate accident! No one might ever know what really happened to the men and women at the Malloy ranch!

The long dark hours of the night gave way to a blazing sun as the rays of light burned through the shadows of the night.

The tired figure on the lone horse slumped with fatigue brought on by the hours of riding, "just a little ways more," Perry said knowing that his mount was almost as tired as he was.

The outline of a building stood framed against a rugged back ground,

"That should be the Malloy ranch," he said as he patted his horse on the neck. Some of the cowboys thought it was a sign of insanity to talk to yourself but everyone knew it was okay to talk to your horse!

The smell of breakfast being cooked drifted in the wind calling him as he rode closer to the house.

The pangs of an empty stomach were beginning to gnaw at him as he approached his destination.

David set the cup of coffee on the hard wood planks of the porch before starting down the steps to meet his brother.

Perry tied the mount at the watering trough before finding his way to the piping hot cup and helped himself to the dark beverage. It didn't seem strange to any one that even on scorching hot days people liked their coffee hot!

Other people began to emerge from the house upon hearing his arrival. Besides his brother David there were three men and two women.
One of the men showed signs of an injury by the way he walked and carried himself.
At one time he must have been hurt bad Perry decided and later he might find out how and why but there wasn't time for that now.
"We got problems," he said sipping from the hot cup in his hand and watching for the tell tale signs of fear in the men and women around him.
But he should have known these people were Texans and raised in a tough hard land where the sign of fear was a weakness that none could afford.
Fear was equal to the merciless heat of the sun stealing the life sustaining fluids from a dry shriveling body.
"Their planning on stampeding the MacCland cattle as soon as they reach the herd of cattle that you have rounded up here and their counting on the momentum of the stampede to carry them almost to the New Mexico border.
What cattle don't make it will either be left for dead or driven the rest of the way by hand." "What about us?" Joe asked.
"The leader is sending a couple of gunmen with rifles ahead of the cattle.
I guess he figures no one will ever know how you died once your bodies have been trampled over by a couple thousand head of charging cattle.
Joe pulled the short barreled revolver from the holster on his left side pulled the hammer back and spun the cylinder checking the loads.
"You might as well grab something to eat, Jim said, it looks like me and Joe are going to be gone a while!"
Sherlene stepped forward where do you think you're going?" she asked. "I think we're going to stampede a herd of cattle ourselves," Jim answered. The Ranger stepped forward, "When do you plan on doing that," he ask?

"Two seconds after they are all on Malloy land, Jim answered,
That's when it becomes a stolen herd and we won't be dealing with a herd of drifting cattle we will be dealing with rustlers and thieves!"

Within an hour five men and two women rode to meet three thousand head of cattle being pushed north by gunmen who were ready to kill anyone or anything in their way!

CHAPTER THIRTY TWO

K.C. looked around at the men riding beside him; they were strong courageous men living the life they had dreamed of.
They were men of honor bonded together by the hardships of the life they chose to live. These men were vaqueros trained by their fathers and their father's fathers. They had earned the right to be called the pride of Mexico.
He knew there was not a man or cowboy alive that was better than the men he rode with today
. His own men were young but filled with the same courage, strength and honor.
They may be from different countries but they were brought up to believe the same way. He was regretting thinking that Don Magel and his men were anything but honorable and that they would try to take advantage as soon as they could.
These men were risking their lives and their family's lives for them and somehow K.C. would make it up to them.
He felt proud to be riding with them as friends and brothers. They weren't riding in groups but as a whole and it dawned on him that now he too was a man, an honorable man.
He hoped that they all returned unharmed each one to their own lives and their own families. When this was all over he was going to see to it that Eric, Colton and Parker all had a place of their own to settle down in and call home.
In a few hours he knew they would be standing against the gunmen of the Malloy ranch and Nicole's greed driven uncle.
But what K.C. didn't know was that Nicole's uncle was already dead that a greater danger waited for them.

Paul lay on the flat rock listening to the sounds of the cattle as they moved forward. He could have slept with his head pillowed against the saddle and his back comforted by the heavy blanket but he had been awakened by the smell of the snake as it slithered past his face and that smell had been enough to send him climbing to the safety of the tall rock leaving the comfort of the saddle and blanket laying in the dirt.

Paul didn't bother lifting the saddle or the blanket the pungent smell of wet cotton and rotten flesh lingered in the area and he knew the snake was close, too close and he was not going to start hunting that snake when he had something much more important to do!

He checked the loads in the shotgun and sat back to wait while watching in the distance for the cattle to come closer and the man he had learned to hate.

He was almost asleep when the first of the cattle went past. The lead bull was massive with broad shoulders and a twisted horn. The other horn grew straight out then turned forward giving the animal the look of a broken lance being held by a knight fighting from the back of a crippled horse.

Paul wiped off the grease that gave a light shine to the shotgun barrel and peaked around the edge of the rock. Butch was the third man in line riding slumped over and still showing the damages Paul had inflicted on him.

As the buckskin carried his huge bulk Paul slid behind the rock and waited patiently until he knew Butch was close enough for him to carry out his plan before he made his move. The bawling of the calves and the rumbling of the ground muffled the sound of his boots as he ran forward; his breathing was becoming labored as he ran the last few yards gasping for breath. The blood curdling scream was escaping the lips of his mouth,

"Butch, I'm gonna kill you" he screamed as he lifted the twin barrels of the deadly weapon and for the first time Butch got to look deep into the face of the man he had left for dead in a pitch dark alley so many years ago.

For a split second the fear of death showed in the eyes of the man that was about to die. As long streams of flames erupted from the barrels of the weapon and eighteen soft lead balls flew into the air to find their mark inside the terrified look of his face.

Flesh and bone was carried with the speed of the shells as they flew through the back of his head and into the dry desert air far behind the moving herd of stolen cattle.

Pieces of Bone, hair, and flesh tried to follow the pieces of soft heavy lead as they made their exit from the back of the skull but failed to carry the same distance.

Cattle began to scramble as the pieces of human bone and tissue sprayed over the area in a bright red cloud.

Paul stood and stared in disbelief as Butch became nothing more than a memory, a destroyed wasted life that he hoped to forget!

The bolting horse was Paul's last hope as the herd of cattle began to run in a blind rage.

The horns and hooves of a thousand head of Texas cattle pounded what little was left of the body with the weight of their hooves.

Paul could see the line of cattle spreading out and becoming wider as he began to run towards the safety of the rocks. The shotgun was useless and a dead weight, now of little value so he let it fall to the ground as he ran.

The thundering of the cattle drowned out the sound of the shot as the deadly shells flew past him. The sound of thundering hooves and the snapping of brittle bone was the only thing to be heard as he run forward that is until the sound of a waterfall filled his head and the darkness of night took the place of a summers day as the horn of a bull struck him.

It was a glancing blow and drove him head long toward the ground.

He ran stumbling in pain as a line of blood flowed slowly down the back of his neck.

Now he sought the sheltering rocks through blind unseeing eyes as the darkness of death began to take him into a vast damp cavern.

Then the bright warming rays of a nurturing sun began to shine through the darkness and drove back the large void that had covered his eyes leaving him lingering between life and death.

A handful of men and two women rode south towards the southern boundaries of the Malloy ranch enjoying the warming rays of a bright clear sun as the sound of a deadly shotgun blast shattered the silence around them and sent small scavengers around them scurrying for their holes as the echo carried across the glowing landscape.

In a flash the black was running towards the sound of the shot and sand rained down behind the black as the power of his hooves threw more of the small light rocks into the air.

Rifles and hand guns were drawn from oil greased holsters ready for use in a moment's notice as they charge towards a herd of stampeding cattle.

Sherlene watched as mounted men raced towards a running figure weapons drawn and firing as they sought to take his life.

The cattle were forgotten now as she jerked on the reins bringing the running animal to a halt. She leaned forward on her horse and laid the barrel of the rifle across the saddle horn and spoke to her horse, "Hold steady fellow," she said as she tightened her finger on the trigger of the weapon.

The rifle barrel lifted into the air as the recoil slammed the hard wooden stock against her shoulder and almost instantly the rider on the lead horse felt the impact of the lead bullet as it lifted him from the saddle and let him fall helplessly to the ground!

Seconds later gunfire began to open up as the thieves realized they too were under attack. Cattle were forgotten as armed men rode forward to do battle with one another.

Flames flew from the barrels of the attackers and victims alike as men fought to survive and the only trophy won here was the gift of life.

Slipping from the backs of their mounts men and women ran for cover hiding behind whatever they could find to help their chance of survival as each side tried to take the life of the other. Joe was an ex-cavalry officer trained to fight the way the plains Indians did, on horseback and on foot.

He was at home fighting from the saddle or on the ground. He rode forward knowing this was the kind of battles he had been trained for, bloody, fast and violent!

The only winners would be the ones living through the horrors of the day.

The black with its power and strength carried him swiftly into the fight with all the speed and courage of a wild mustang fearing nothing as it fought to protect its herd.

Cattle ran to the sound of a hundred echoes as rifles roared out their massage of death. Barrels coated with oil glistened in the sun as vapors rose from the heat of the burning powder and pieces of hot lead. There in the heat of the desert Sherlene licked the tip of the sight cutting down on the glare of a midday sun before sighting down the length of the barrel waiting for another rider to come into view.

She centered the small dot in the middle of his chest before lightly squeezing the trigger.

The force of a doubled up fist struck her imbedding the rifle stock deep into the flesh of her shoulder as fire erupted from the barrel sending death to the rider in the form of a small lead ball the rider raised the barrel of his own rifle trying to take her life . But Sherlene had been accurate and the man fell from his horse striking the ground even as the barrel of her rifle lined upon the form of another rider.

Paul lay in the shadows of a rock as the black flew past; blood was running from the back of his head turning a light coat of dust into a rust colored stain as the pistols in Joe's hands sprayed out a volley of death to all of those in front of the deadly weapons.

Daryl rode out from the shadows created by a cloud of dust with his own weapons blazing. The long range weapons were forgotten in favor of the short barreled revolvers at their sides as both men sought to take the life of the other.

Flame and lead erupted above the heads of the mounts as their riders fought off the chilling hand of death in an attempt to live through the next few minutes.

A small hole found its way into the front of Daryl's vest as three more followed leaving him gasping for the precious air of life as he rolled from the back of the saddle and fell limp to the ground below.

The desert sand shook beneath their feet as a sea of terrified cattle ran past the bloody battle. Downed riders and horses alike fell helpless to the sheer number of the herd and victims to the power of their hooves as they destroyed everything and everyone in their path.

Horses with their strong bones and tough hides would become small mounds of toughened hide while men became nothing more than scattered remnants of torn flesh carried between the split hooves of the very cattle they had tried to steal!

Joe turned the black and rode back towards the group as the last of the gunfire died away.

Daryl's was dead destroyed by his dream but there would be a few survivors there always were.

A few of the men riding drag would have missed the battle and the cook riding the blister end of a lone chuck wagon would still be alive but they were small men being led by another.

In his eyes there had been enough killing and he was not going to worry about them.

"I think it's over," Joe said as he reached down from the black and took the rifle from Marilyn's trembling hands.
The terrified look on her face told him all he needed to know, she had never fired at another human being and the guilt of taking the life from a living being was already eating at her mind. Sherlene was younger and stronger willed than her sister.
Even though Marilyn had a temper and it showed plenty of times it was Sherlene who was more of a frontier woman and it was going to take more than the death of a thief to bring her to tears.
The smoking barrel of the rifle lay at her feet as Jim rode up.
"Should we run them down?" she asked ready to take on what was left of the disappearing gang.
"Let them go, Jim said, I ain't the law anymore and I don't think we will ever see them again!"
"Have fun digging the graves,"
David said gathering up the reins and swinging into the saddle.
"Me and my brother are headed back to Dallas."
"Heck with that, Joe said, we're gonna load them on a buck board and take them back to town. That way the undertaker can do the burying."
K.C., Eric, Colton and Parker rode towards the valley along with Don Magel and his men when the sounds of gunfire and stampeding cattle echoed off the barren sides of low standing hills. Dodging stands of tall cactus and rugged dry terrain filled with snake pits and jagged rocks they headed towards the sounds.
"We can make it," K.C. urged as his mount struggled to lead the way to the battle field.
Don Magel, K.C. and Manuel rode the fastest horses and each fought for the lead position as the fleeing men rode at them.
Their rifles were spitting lead as they sought to break free of the battle and save their own lives.

It was a mistake they would not live to regret as K.C. and the vaqueros opened up with their own rifles spilling their bodies into the dry sand as easy as if they were target practicing.

The bodies of injured and dead cattle littered the ground as K.C. and his men rode up testifying to the vicious and cruel nature of the men behind the stampede and the need for revenge of a man left for dead so many years ago.

A moan escaped the lips of a man lying in the shade of a rock as Manuel rode past,

"Do we hang this one?" he asked. "Not today, Jim answered shaking his head, that's Paul and he's with us!"